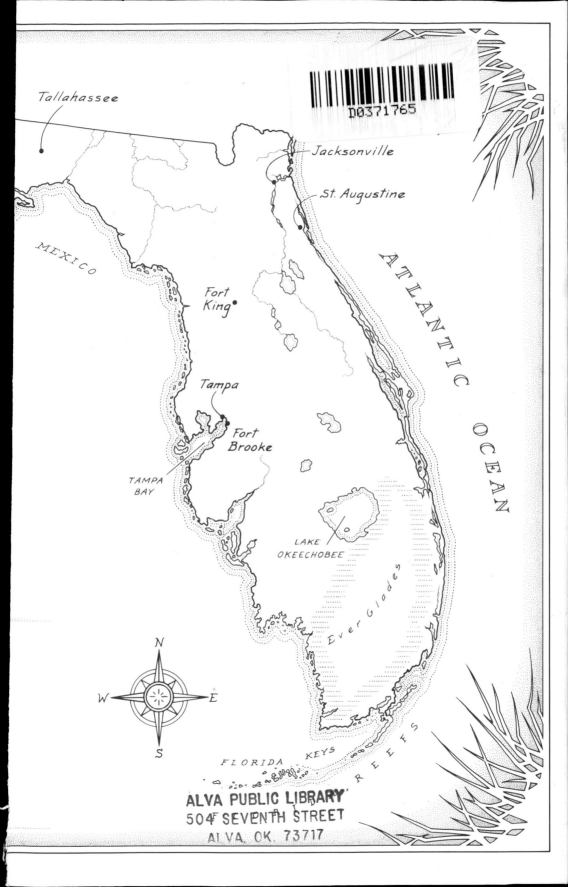

Tallahassee

Jacksonville

St. Augustine

MEXICO

ATLANTIC OCEAN

Fort
King

Tampa

Fort
Brooke

TAMPA
BAY

LAKE
OKEECHOBEE

Ever Glades

N

W   E

S

FLORIDA   KEYS

REEFS

Runaway

HEATHER GRAHAM

Delacorte Press

Published by
Delacorte Press
Bantam Doubleday Dell Publishing Group, Inc.
1540 Broadway
New York, New York 10036

The trademark Delacorte Press® is registered in the U.S. Patent and Trademark Office.

Map illustration by Jackie Aher

Library of Congress Cataloging in Publication Date
Graham, Heather.
    Runaway / Heather Graham.
       p.   cm.
    ISBN 0-385-31264-4
    I. Title.
  PS3557.R198R86   1994
813'.54—dc20   93-48460
                                                                            CIP

Manufactured in the United States of America
Published simultaneously in Canada

September 1994

10 9 8 7 6 5 4 3 2 1

BVG

Dedicated to the Great State of Florida

And with love to five native Floridians
very special to me:

Jason, Shayne, Derek, Bryee-Annon, and Chynna Pozzessere

AUTHOR'S NOTE

I HAVE always wanted to do a series of books about Florida. It is much more than a place to me; it is home. In my own lifetime, I have watched drastic changes come to the state. No matter what those changes, it has always been a land of contrast, from the quiet peace of moss-draped oaks to the violence of 'gator riddled swampland. Some people love it, some people hate it. Some swelter in the heat, and others dream of it during long winters in more northern climates. But to me, home is something like a close relative. I love it for all of the good—and the bad— that it entails, and I am delighted now to be embarking upon a series of books that will bring Florida through decades of change to our present day, the Florida that I know best.

Working on such a series seemed an easy prospect; I had heard so much about the state's history all of my life. The problem there, of course, is half of what we hear is legend, a quarter is truth, another quarter downright lie, and it is amazing to realize that "knowing" about something can also make the research ten times harder. There was no difficulty finding the research books— the difficulty was in deciding which of the various historians' versions about events from a different century were accurate. Also, just as any current movie is different to the eyes of each beholder, history is also different in the hands of those who actually lived it —often the Seminoles, quite naturally, saw events in a different light from the white soldiers, even when both were in exactly the same place at the same time.

Some of the widest differences in historical interpretation center on a man who is a main character in my first two books— the legendary Osceola, or Billy Powell, as he was first known, or Asi Yaholo, Black-Drink-Singer. A number of my research books suggest that the white man Powell was married to Osceola's mother but was not his father, while others strongly argue that Powell was definitely his natural father. A study of his bones suggests a white heritage, though historians bemoan the fact that the war chief's head was removed from his body at the time of his death. Were the skull and certain neck vertebrae only available now, research could be much more complete. Interestingly, study of Osceola's bones has also suggested a percentage of black blood, which seems a fitting amalgam for the chief during the time period in which he was born. For my purposes, though I am well aware of the opposing arguments, I have represented Osceola as the natural son of a white man named Powell. Some historians have suggested that he could not speak English; due to the circumstances of his birth and his many relationships with the white man, I find this hard to believe. It would be more natural, I think, to believe that the chief could speak English—when he chose to do so. Whatever the truth of his birth, he rose to become a powerful force in a bitter war, and then to become legend. He was fierce, courageous, all too human in his failings, and at the very least a remarkable man.

There were many different Native American groups living in Florida at the time of the conflict. Some had moved south during the seventeenth and eighteenth centuries and become absorbed in the remnants of tribes decimated by European diseases and earlier warfare. Even to say that most were Creeks is confusing, since the term *Creek* comes from the very fact that they were peoples living along a creek. Osceola was born a "Creek," but at the time of the conflict all American Indians living in Florida were referred to as Seminoles, and their language group or place of origin did not matter to the white military.

Even the term *Seminole* causes conflict, but again, I have read the many suggested definitions, and chosen that which seem most appropriate to me—*runaway*, from the Spanish term *cimarrón*.

I hope very much that you enjoy the book and feel a sense of the wild, raw, and exotic frontier that existed when fledgling Americans turned their eyes southward to a savage land, a fantastic paradise, a burning hell.

Welcome to my home. I hope you'll stay with me awhile.

Heather Graham
The Great State of Florida
January 5, 1994

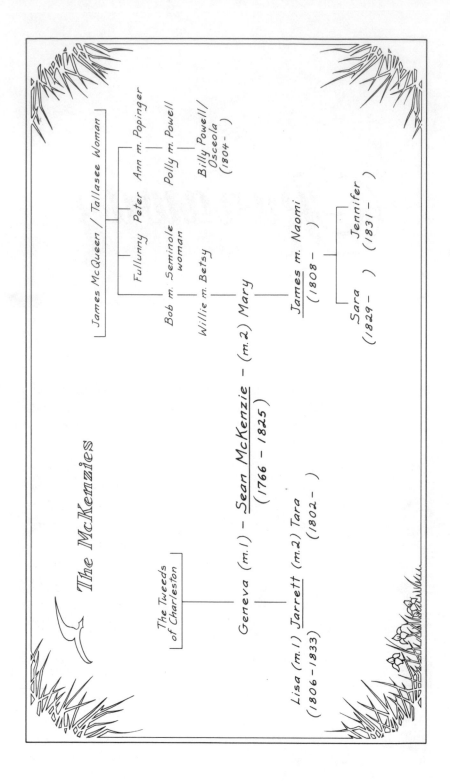

The McKenzies

James McQueen / Tallasee Woman

Fullunny Peter Ann m. Popinger

Polly m. Powell

Billy Powell / Osceola (1804–)

Bob m. Seminole woman

Willie m. Betsy

James m. Naomi (1808–)

Sara (1829–) Jennifer (1831–)

The Tweeds of Charleston

Geneva (m.1) – Sean McKenzie – (m.2) Mary
(1766 – 1825)

Lisa (m.1) Jarrett (m.2) Tara
(1806–1833)   (1802–)

Prologue

Destiny
So It Begins . . .

November 20, 1835

THE DAY was beautiful, crisp and cool. It was, in fact, one of those late fall days in which it might seem that the landscape was an Eden. Nothing but nature's beauty intruded upon the trails. Pines grew in abundance within the hammock, and their needles created a soft green carpet on the ground. Through the trail of trees the water of a clear spring glistened, and even at a distance the reflections of a multitude of wild orchids could be seen wavering just slightly upon the glassy surface of the crystal water. Cypress trees grew along the water, interspersed with strong oaks. Soft lime-green mosses clung to the dipping branches of the oaks, creating another wave of reflection and color upon the water. The air was perfect with its cooling kiss of fall. It was true that in summer the heat could become stifling, but even then the crystal water would be welcoming and cool, the dipping, leaf-laden branches of the trees would offer shade from the merciless heat of the sun.

Beyond the hammock the marshlands, rivers, and swamps swept around rich farmland. Some of it slightly rolling, most of it endlessly flat. Deep in the rivers ringed by the marsh, alligators lived and roamed, hunting the exotic birds that dotted the deep-green and earth-toned landscape. A few wild buffalo still moved within the territory, while deer were in abundance along with rabbits, bears, and squirrels. Wild berries grew in the low brush, and coconut palms were scattered here and there. It was indeed an exotic Eden—with, of course, many a serpent to strike the unwary.

The White Tiger—the name given him when he had left his childhood behind and become a man—reined in his horse, aware of the subtle sounds within the cypress hammock and the marsh-lands and swamp that surrounded it. Though no tigers roamed the land, the powerful panthers here were often referred to as "tigers," and the name had been given him with respect, for which he was grateful. He had ridden deep into Indian country in the Florida territory, a place he knew well, and he sensed he was not alone.

He paused for a moment. He wasn't a man given to flights of fancy, nor was he in the least superstitious. But today he felt a curious sense of destiny, as if he were entering along some path from which there would be no turning back. Forces were being turned into motion, and he had now set his feet upon the trail, the course of action, he was destined to follow.

He held himself very still and listened.

He heard the faint sound of the water rippling beneath the light autumn breeze, the sway of the cypress branches. He heard the call of the bird and then the call that was not a bird. There was a slight rustle in the leaves that was not caused by the air moving so gently through them.

He lifted his hands above his head, showing that his knife was sheathed in the leather at his calf and that his rifle rested securely in the leather loop of his saddle. Hands still high, he threw one leg around and hopped down the distance from the back of his horse.

"I've come alone," he called out.

Three men instantly appeared, all of them exceptionally grand in their choice of clothing for the day. They wore deerskin

breeches and cotton shirts exquisitely designed in a multitude of
colors. Epaulets of brass adorned one, necklaces in silver ran in
shimmering strands from the neck of another. White blood was
obvious in the grave faces of two of the men, the one of medium
height, with dark, intelligent eyes that gazed steadily at him. He
was a striking man, one who had already earned a reputation, not
as a hereditary leader, but as one who had risen among his people,
for in the Muskogee culture a warrior chief did not have to come
from a ruling lineage. When he had left his childhood name behind and taken on his warrior's name, his people had called him
Asi Yaholo, meaning Black-Drink-Singer, but the whites had put
it together and called him Osceola.

The second mixed-blood Indian in the group was very tall,
the White Tiger's own height, and younger. He was an arresting
man of lean muscularity and fluid motion. His face was a handsome one, having taken the best from both cultures. His cheekbones were high and bronzed, his mouth was generous, brow high
and cleanly arched, and against the smooth copper of his sun-
darkened flesh and the ebony sleek darkness of his hair, his eyes
were a rich, startling shade of blue. He had earned the name
Running Bear as a warrior, for as a hunter he could outdistance,
outfight, and outclimb even the most dangerous of bruins. He was
the first to greet the White Tiger, embracing him gravely, then
stepping back in silence. It was he who had arranged the meeting
here today, and though a powerful man himself and the head of
his own family, one confident in himself and his own abilities, he
offered a respectful deference to the two warrior chiefs who had
accompanied him here today.

The third man, of pure Indian blood, was Alligator, brother-
in-law to Chief Micanopy of the old Alachua band, ready to influence this man who had hereditary sway over not only the Mus-
kogee-speaking Seminoles, but the Hitichi-speaking Mikasukis as
well. Alligator was clever, strong, and fierce, and in his dark eyes
the White Tiger saw that the man had little hope for a peaceful
future.

Osceola stretched out a hand to indicate a cove among the trees where the ground had been prepared for them to sit. They did so, in a square, all four facing one another.

"I have come," the White Tiger said—quickly getting down to business as he knew that Osceola would be impatient to do— "because I bring the great sorrow from many good white men who are familiar with the Mico Osceola."

Osceola nodded, waiting. The others remained silent. "Perhaps I am gifted more than most men with my knowledge of the People, and in that, I know that Asi Yaholo does not judge all white men as bad, that he is a clever man who has always taken what he has seen as good from his own world and that of others and put it to his own use. He has made good friends among the whites."

"And enemies," Alligator injected angrily.

The White Tiger sighed softly. This was why he had come. "Osceola, many good men have heard that you struck your knife through the treaty when Wiley Thompson insisted you move west. You know as well that many men are grieved that Thompson had you seized and put in chains."

"No insult is greater to the Seminoles," Running Bear reminded him. The White Tiger met Running Bear's blue eyes, and he nodded, very much aware just what an insult Thompson's actions had been to a warrior of Osceola's wisdom and strength.

"The treaties have all been lies!" Alligator said, gnashing his teeth in a way that reminded the White Tiger of the reptile from which the Indian had drawn his name. "Moultrie Creek promised us lands for twenty years—nine of those remain. Monies promised us have been withheld. We have all but starved on the lands we have been pressed into. When we leave those lands, desperate to fish, to hunt, to find food, we are beaten back."

They had stolen a lot of cattle and drawn a great deal of hatred as well, but the White Tiger knew that most of this had been because the Indians had in truth been starving. So far this year the weather had been mild, but last winter had been so cold and fierce in the north that a frost had killed almost all crops. The Seminoles had grown more and more desperate. Many whites had thought that the Indians' desperate plight would make them more pliable.

It had merely served to toughen them.

The White Tiger stood. "I have brought cattle," he said. "My men follow behind me with them now, ready to turn them over to the Seminoles if Osceola will accept the gift."

"These cattle are from your own herds?" Osceola queried.

"Some. And some from others who respect Osceola and wish to apologize to him. Friends as well. Men you have met through me."

Osceola, with his curiously arresting features, grinned. "This is not an official apology from your government." It was a statement, not a question.

"No," the White Tiger stated honestly.

Osceola, Alligator, and Running Bear rose as well. Osceola offered his hand. It was small and refined, as were his speech and manners. "You are right—I do not judge all your people as evil. And I accept your gift, because many of our people are hungry. It grieves me to tell you that I cannot forgive the traitorous actions of the man Thompson, nor can I be sorry for any action I have taken for the good of the People, nor any that I intend to take."

The last left a feeling of cold doom in the White Tiger's heart.

"You are silent," Osceola said.

"I am silent because I pray that there will be peace among us all. War brings pain and heartbreak, widows and hunger."

"Peace has brought enough hunger!" Alligator said.

"War is still the more bitter course. Peace is life."

"What is life without honor?" Osceola asked softly. "I have not meant to distress you, and I know that you fear for the People when you speak. Remember, we do not forget our friends," Osceola said.

"Our brothers," Running Bear added quietly.

Even Alligator grunted.

"And I will not take up arms against mine," the White Tiger told them. "I will continue to pray for peace and seek it with my heart."

Osceola stared at him with his pensive dark eyes. "We may all pray for peace, but whether it shall be or not is for our gods to decide."

"One God, the same God," the White Tiger said. "Ishtahollo, the Great Spirit of the Seminoles, is the same one God of the Christian whites. He is supreme, no matter what men may call him. I believe he seeks life for your people and for mine."

Osceola smiled but offered no words of agreement. "Where you ride, friend, you will ride in safety. Where you live will be sacred ground. Keep those dear to you upon it, and they will walk in safety too."

"Mico Osceola, I beg of you, don't think hastily upon the action of warfare—"

"You are too proud a man to beg. You are a warrior, a soldier, yourself."

"I am a civilian now. And I dream of this land of ours being an Eden in which we all may live."

"Rest assured, I think hastily on nothing," Osceola said. He smiled. "Once you were a very young man eager for battle. Against the British, against some of my own kin!"

"I was rash. I learned my lessons the hard way."

"You were a good warrior. You learned the courage to know that death is not easy."

"And war is not all honor."

"It is my understanding that you are leaving home for a journey?"

"I had planned on a trip. However, if my staying—"

"No, you must carry on with your business. I have listened to your words. There is nothing you can do here. Go, sail away, for Running Bear tells me that sailing is a great pleasure for you, and that it eases your spirit. The winds sweep away the pain of your loss." He turned, starting to walk away, Alligator following him.

But then he turned back. "Our sorrow remains with you. And we are proud that you have spoken for us, against those who would determine that we caused the death of your good wife. I fear that your words often do little good against the tide of hatred that arises between our two peoples, but we are grateful for them."

"I have spoken nothing but the truth."

"But to some the truth is hard to see. We remain grateful. Go on your trip, my friend. Perhaps, when you return, you will no longer need to run away from your pain."

"I travel for business purposes—"

"Indeed. It is good."

Again, Osceola turned, Alligator close on his heels. Only Running Bear remained behind for a moment, setting a hand upon the White Tiger's shoulder. His fingers squeezed for a moment. "God go with you."

"Which god?" The White Tiger queried, a slight smile twisting his lips.

"Didn't we just agree that the gods were one and the same?"

"We tried to agree. What is going to happen?"

Running Bear shook his head. "I don't know. I have too much white blood in me. I am sometimes part of the councils, sometimes not. I preach the way of peace as well, but Thompson was a fool to have Osceola arrested. He claimed Osceola was abusive and out of control. You know Osceola. It is my belief that Wiley Thompson wanted to prove that no Indian would dictate terms to him. Now the fury festers in Osceola's heart. What exactly is in his mind, I don't know. And there's more, of course, than the incident with Thompson. There is constantly friction between the Indians and settlers. They say we raid; they hunt our land. They want our land. Little changes. It is the American destiny to stretch all across the continent, isn't it?"

"There must be a solution."

"You want a solution. Whether there must be one or not remains to be seen. I must go now, and you must ride on—and then sail away. Perhaps your voyage can bring you happiness. Who knows what you'll find? Time has passed. You still grieve. You should marry again."

"I don't want to marry again," the White Tiger said flatly.

Running Bear nodded in sympathy, then smiled slightly, setting an arm around the White Tiger's shoulder once again. "Then perhaps you should at least consider a mistress. Not that you've been a monk by any means, or so I've been told."

"Dammit, but it is amazing how such news travels!" the White Tiger began angrily, but then he saw the concern in Running Bear's eyes, and he sighed and then even laughed softly. "You'll not leave me be, will you?"

"Surely I will. One day. For now, have a safe voyage."

"You take heed as well," he said.

They embraced quickly. Then Running Bear stepped away, turned, and followed the others down a trail. Fluidly, almost silently. In minutes he had disappeared.

For a moment the White Tiger stood in the cypress maze, feeling the breeze once more and again feeling that wheels were turning into motion.

The sun was falling low in the sky. Colors ripped across it, magentas, mauves, golden, glowing reds and yellows, reflecting upon the water, casting an artist's palette upon the many different trees and brush.

He closed his eyes, felt the breeze on his flesh, smelled the cypress and the hammock, the clean water of the spring, and the musky scent of the marshland that bordered nearby. Listened to the rustle of the leaves. In the far distance he could even hear a swift, smooth plopping sound, one that others might not have heard. But he loved the land, and he had listened to it for a very long time, and he knew that hundreds of feet away an alligator had just slipped from the bank and into the water.

In a far different place the wheels of destiny were also turning.

Forces were being put into motion here as well. They began upon the same day, yet so very differently! There was no forest where she stood. No birds cried, no golden-red sun sat over a cypress wilderness.

Indeed, the young woman stood in one of the elegant homes in one of the most civilized cities of the young American nation. Women were dressed in silks and satins, coffee and tea were poured from silver servers. Persian carpets lay over polished wood floors, damask drapes lay ready to cover the windows from the coming night.

But then the shot rang out. . . .

Loud, reverberating, like a crack of thunder against the silence that had filled the room.

Amazed, she stared at the man who had sat not a hundred feet from her. He had begun to rise, yet couldn't. He seemed startled himself.

Tall, well muscled, his iron-gray hair rich upon his leonine head, he had seemed like such an indomitable man. But a bright red spot was burgeoning out on the snow-white frill of his shirt, and no matter how powerful he had always assumed himself to be, it was evident to anyone that he was watching himself die. The shot had been true to the heart. Time seemed to stand still, or to move in incredibly slow motion. And yet, and yet . . . in split seconds the whole of his shirt turned crimson, and he crashed to the floor, dead.

She looked down at the gun in her hands.

But the bullets in it had been blanks, it had all been fake, it had . . .

She looked past the dead man and saw a set of eyes staring at her from a cruel, clever face. She heard a faint rustling behind her and turned.

The large parlor had been turned into a playhouse for the day. She had stood on the makeshift stage staring downstage to the audience arranged in a semicircle before her.

She now looked to the backdrop behind her.

And she looked just in time to see the folds of the backdrop curtains fall back into place. Someone had been behind her. Someone who had fired a gun with real bullets just in time to coincide perfectly with her coldly playacted firing of the blank. Her amazement at the circumstances caused a momentary numbness within her.

Then she heard the cries from the horrified audience that arose swiftly around her, cutting cruelly through her shield of surprise.

"Seize her!"

"She's killed him!"

"Murder!"

"Oh, my God, seize the murderess!"

More screams and shouts arose. Handsome men and beautiful women leapt to their feet. Eyes narrowed upon her, and it suddenly seemed as if she were staring into a crowd of the most primitive savages. Bloodlust—for her blood—seemed to be abundant.

It had been done to trap her. So heinous, so cruel an act, and all to trap her, dear God!

But she wouldn't be trapped, she wouldn't let it happen, wouldn't pay the price for another's crime. She'd run as far and as fast as she could, she'd run forever. . . .

Time again stood still.

She met those eyes one last time. The hard, glittering eyes of the man who would command a cold-blooded murder in order to entrap her.

No. She could not let it happen.

She turned. She was young, very swift, graceful, agile. It seemed like an eternity had passed. In reality the dead man had barely hit the floor before she fled, racing for the window.

In the distant, savage forest he felt a shudder rip through him, and sighed deeply. He could pray that the tense situation between the whites and Seminoles would simmer back down.

The wind suddenly rose. Fallen leaves suddenly began to swirl and turn, rising into the air. They rustled as if whispering out a warning.

He swore against himself for being fanciful, then gave a whistle for his horse. He mounted and held still again for a moment. Listening.

The wind died just as quickly as it had come. The leaves were still.

For now.

He nudged his horse and started down the trail.

William! she thought as she slipped through the window, leaving the sounds of screams and motion behind her. *Dear God, William!* But William could not be entangled in this, and he was with Marina and therefore safe. He would know, of course, he would know that she'd had no choice but to run. He would be sick with worry. He would be afraid.

But he would understand. She was desperate; timing was crucial. She had only seconds.

To run.

Her feet hit the ground, and she began to race, tearing over the manicured lawn, all but flying for the tangle of trees to the rear.

He left the winding trails of cypress behind and came upon the broader road. His horse sensed his mood and began to gallop. He bent low against the creature's neck and felt the animal begin to move like lightning beneath him. He felt its power, felt its pulse.

Soon he'd be home.

He was anxious to reach it, only so as to be able to leave it. He wanted to feel sea wind sting his cheeks, wanted to escape the mounting tension here, wanted to . . .

Run.

From the pain that lingered, from the loneliness of the nights, the days.

His horse raced on.

She reached the heavy embrace of the trees, far from the house. They were after her, of course, but they had been confused and slow, and she was well in the lead. She made her way quickly through the trees.

William. Oh, God. William.

She had to find new clothing, first. Change her hair. And move. Keep moving.

She burst from the trees. She was alone in the coming night. She saw the path that would lead from the town center. She started to run hard. Her lungs seemed to be bursting. Agony gripped her legs. Run! she commanded herself. Run . . . run . . .

Run away.

Runaway. . . .

PART ONE

Game of Chance

Chapter 1

The Port of New Orleans
Winter of 1835–36

JARRETT MCKENZIE noticed the woman from the moment she first stepped into the entry of the old dockside tavern. Not that he could see much of her at first.

A sweeping, hooded black cape encompassed her from head to toe. He was only certain that it was a woman who had arrived because of the graceful twirl of her body when the master of the establishment, Harold Eastwood, accosted her at the doorway. A new serving maid? Had she joined the ranks of the lovely and available ladies of the New Orleans nights? Was she late reporting for work? Jarrett wondered, and he found himself intrigued, waiting for her to cast off the cloak. If she was working here at Eastwood's fine dining establishment and parlor, then the class of the place was improving.

Not that Eastwood's was a total den of iniquity. For a waterfront tavern it could boast being a respectable one. Most men came here when conducting business in this part of Louisiana, and most of them told their wives about the place. There was always good food to be had, pretty girls to sing tunes at the spinet, liquor from around the world, a woman if you wanted one, and now and then a good fight to choose a side for. The place was situated dead center in the port city of New Orleans, right on the river, and all manner of men and women came here, worked here, traded here, schemed here.

New Orleans was a city Jarrett enjoyed. Established in 1718 by the French, it had grown later in the eighteenth century with the Acadian exodus from the northeast. It had passed to Spanish rule and then back to France before Thomas Jefferson had set forth to find a way to make Napoleon willing to accept his offer on the Louisiana Purchase. Jarrett had come here first as little more than a boy himself when Andrew Jackson had commanded the defense of the city against the British in 1815, and since that time Jarrett had felt a fondness for the city. He liked the narrow streets of the riverfront, the charming architecture, French, Spanish, and American. He liked the wrought-iron balconies, the small gardens, the rolling Mississippi, and the lusty quality of life along the river. He had come to Eastwood's often enough, and though it had a dubious reputation, there were far more debauched places than this along the riverfront. All in all this was quite a respectable place when compared with some of the other establishments it neighbored.

But from his very first sight of the woman enveloped in the black cape, Jarrett was convinced she didn't belong here.

"I fold," Robert Treat, his friend and associate sitting to his left, said with a sigh. Robert threw his cards down on the oak playing table.

Jarrett stared at his own hand. Three queens. Two fours. Full house. He looked at the bills and gold pieces on the table. Smiling Jack, the rich Creole from the bayou country, sat across from him with a broad grin on his face. Hell. The man might be able to bluff Saint Peter if he ever made it to the pearly gates.

Jarrett took the time to drop a five-dollar gold piece on the table, then looked over the top of his cards again, watching the woman in the encompassing cape. She was still trying to explain something to Eastwood, a little potbellied man. She was slim and lithe, at least an inch or so taller than Eastwood. Jarrett wondered with some amusement if the innkeeper, whoremaster—entrepreneur, as he liked to call himself—didn't feel just a little bit intimidated by the woman.

Rupert Furstenburg, the lean blond German down the Mississippi from St. Louis, threw a wad of money down. "I raise you, gentlemen. A hundred dollars."

"Damned good thing I've folded!" Robert muttered.

"A hundred?" Smiling Jack offered the German a broad smile. "Pocket change. I'll see you, sir!"

Jarrett was still watching the woman. Robert Treat gave him a nudge. "A hundred, Jarrett."

"Right," he said absently. He curled his fingers around the stack of coins in front of him, pushing out the correct amount. Robert Treat stared at him with a frown, lowering his voice.

"Are you paying any attention to this game?"

"Ah, is that the question?" Smiling Jack, twirling his dark mustache, taunted lightly. "Is that plantation of yours down in the swamp doing well enough for this game?"

"My swamp plantation is doing just as well as that place of yours out in the bayou," Jarrett said lazily. His cards were good enough. And his plantation was sure as hell doing well enough to support this game.

"Ah, *mais oui!*" Jack murmured. "We've both the swamp, eh? The insects, the gators." He wagged a warning finger at Jarrett. "But you've got the Seminoles. What grows on my land is mine. My house has stood seventy years. And yours, *mon ami?* Poof! Even now the fellows may be sending it up in a cloud of smoke! You were a military man, so I've heard. You must know. They slip in, the Indians, they slip out. They move through the night like wraiths. They can move through the thickest brush and trees. There will be more trouble, you mark my words. Old Andy Jackson fought those savages good back in sixteen and seventeen, but he didn't get them all. There will be trouble again. It's brewing hot and hard right now. Some say those renegades even ride the alligators through the swamp."

Jarrett smiled at the Frenchman's vivid description, even if his smile was somewhat forced. He'd yet to see any man, even a Seminole, riding a gator through the swamp! Jack's attitude was a fairly common one. People had the damned strangest way of looking at the Florida peninsula—and the Florida Indians. Any of the Upper and Lower Creeks who had moved south, speaking varied languages and coming from very different peoples, were grouped together. They were called Seminoles. Some said the name meant *runaway*. Others said that it came from the Spanish word for renegade, *cimarrón*. Runaways, renegades. Jarrett knew that just like him and so many white dreamers, the Indians were just seeking a better life for themselves and their families.

It was a land for dreamers. Despite the summer heat, the abundance of swampland, and the infestation of snakes—and Indians—there were huge land tracts available in the state. Like the western frontiers opening up across the continent, Florida was a raw, new land for Americans. Much of it was exceptionally fine farmland. Crops could sometimes be grown year round. Vicious freezes came upon occasion in the northern part of the territory, and the summer's heat farther south was sometimes nearly as cruel, bringing sickness and disease. But most often the days were warm and balmy. The sun shone overhead. Blankets of snow did not fall, blizzards did not paralyze whole communities. Wild cattle still roamed the center of the territory from the days of the Spaniards; they were there for the taking. The hunting was extremely rich. There were great herds of deer, a few bison still roamed the northern tracks, and there were countless rabbits and wildfowls. In the hammocks and flatlands there were areas of stunning natural beauty. There were crystal springs, incredibly deep, and still a man could see clear through the earth beneath them.

There was beauty, there was danger. It was not a place for the faint of heart.

And the Seminoles added to the savage reputation of the

American territory that Andy Jackson, along with so many others, had been determined to wrest from the Spanish. There had been a time when the Spanish had ceded the territory to the British, and during and after the American Revolution, British sympathizers had flocked south. Then the Floridas—East and West at the time—had gone back to Spain. Americans, being Americans, had kept wandering over the borders, forever reaching for new land. Spain, they claimed, could not control the territory, could not stop the Indians from raiding American farms and plantations, and could not stop them from harboring runaway slaves.

The slave issue was an explosive one. Escaped slaves readily headed south into Spanish territory that actually seemed to be ruled by the savages—but savages with a far gentler attitude where black men were concerned. It wasn't that the Seminoles did not keep slaves themselves upon occasion; they did. And they could be as possessive of their property as white men when they chose. But there was a difference. Slaves might tend a Seminole master while still being free to cultivate their own plots of land. Slaves among the Seminoles were very often granted their freedom after a certain amount of service. Slaves who made it down to Florida very often found freedom, joining with free-black–Seminole bands. Whether blacks remained free or were "owned" by the Indians themselves, the Seminoles did not usually return them to white masters. In the Southern states, where the economy was so solidly based on farms and plantations, slaves were very valuable personal property.

There were many reasons for America to want to wrest the land from Spain, but in the end the most important reason was simply that American settlers wanted the land. They wanted to settle, to farm, to raise cattle, to open salt mines, even to make their fortunes from the sea, with the vast expanses of coastline. Spain ceded the Floridas in exchange for U.S. payment of Spanish debts to citizens and for a more solid grasp upon Texas. Now, over ten years an American holding and solidified into one territory by an act of Congress, Florida still retained much of her reputation for being a haven for alligators, snakes, and fiercely proud Indians. Perhaps the peninsula was just that, a haven for wild creatures and renegades. But it was much more as well. It was that land of gently swaying oaks with moss that drifted from their branches. It was shadowed hammocks where pine needles lay like bedcovers upon the ground. It was crystal-clear lakes, exotic birds with elegant, colorful plumage. It was wildflowers, crimson sunsets, blue skies, balmy rains.

Jacksonville wasn't so far over the border from Georgia and was a fairly civilized place. Some of the north Florida ports were fairly safe, but to most people anything south of St. Augustine on the east coast and the bustling town of Pensacola on the west was too simply and completely raw and savage.

All that those people saw was the wildness of Florida, the danger. But they hadn't seen the things that had become so spectacular and seductive to Jarrett. They'd never seen the sunsets that he watched so often, the amazing palette of colors that stretched out over a lonely horizon, vivid golds and searing blood-reds. Colors that reached out like rippling flames, so vital, then fading to gentle pinks and yellows and incredibly soft oranges, and fading again completely into a blackness that gave a deep velvet backdrop to the stars. They hadn't seen the wildflowers that often grew in profusion, wild orchids in stunning shades of mauve, and they hadn't felt the kiss of the sun to warm their faces in the dead of winter.

The snakes and alligators were there too. And the Indians. It was a wild, savage land with a rare and exotic beauty. But coming now into its own. St. Augustine remained America's oldest European continuing settlement, with the magnificent Castillo de San Marcos to guard its shore and handsome and detailed old Spanish homes and architecture with Moorish influence to add character and charm to its streets. Pensacola was busy, a thriving port, offering goods from everywhere imaginable. A fine naval base had long been established in Key West, and Tallahassee, the territorial capital, was slowly growing into a quiet and dignified center of politics.

The territory had been a gold mine to Jarrett. He'd cleared his lands and built his home, and set to work. His cattle had thrived on the rich grasses in his fields. He'd grown sugar cane in abundance. He'd dabbled in cotton and in grain, and it had seemed that everything he had tried had thrived. His lands were exceptionally fertile, and he'd built right along the river, so he'd had the opportunity to move his goods with exceptional speed. Many settlers now saw what he had seen—some of the land was swamp, but some of it was exceedingly fine farmland. The length of the peninsula stretched out before America now. And much of it was a gold mine of natural resources and fertile fields.

Once it had all been a paradise for him, and he had loved his peninsular Eden deeply. He'd seen a great deal of it, learning about it from his father, from the white military, and from the Indians as well. It had been a place where he had found his own —perhaps peculiar—peace. He'd been in love, and he'd shared his dreams and his small part of the strange Eden with the woman he had loved, who had loved his land and him just as deeply. But Lisa was gone now, and his heart had hardened to the romanticism of his love for the land.

But still, his land remained. Wild, strange, and savage as the pain that sometimes seized him. Caught in tumult. The very challenge and danger of it had become his obsession.

"McKenzie!" Smiling Jack murmured, smiling. "Are you listening to me?"

Listening? He didn't need to listen. Jarrett leaned back. His cards were good, and he was no longer interested in the conversation. His attention was caught by the woman again. He watched her while he replied confidently to both Jack and Furstenburg, "I'd gamble much more than the stakes on the table that my place is still standing," he said. "And will remain standing."

Furstenburg wasn't interested in conversation either. "Are we playing cards here, gentlemen?" he demanded bluntly. He lifted a

hand, summoning one of the little dark-haired Creole girls working in the place. "Whiskey!" he ordered crisply. "Do we play, or
do we argue swampland?"

Jarrett shrugged. "I see your raise also, sir." He took a moment
to offer Jack a dry smile. "I see your raise, and I raise it again." He
pushed out a second stack of coins. Another hundred dollars.

Furstenburg swore something gutteral, staring at his hand. Apparently his cards weren't good enough to afford another raise. He
was a careful player. He threw his hand down. It was between
Jarrett and Jack.

Smiling Jack's smile faded just a bit. Where Furstenburg was
careful, Smiling Jack was a reckless player. He could bluff most of
the men he played with frequently, and he made half his income
off the game. Not tonight, Jarrett thought wryly.

In some things Jarrett was lucky. And tonight he was getting
damned good cards.

Jack fingered his coins. Then he swore in a colorful manner
and pushed out a stack of them.

Smiling Jack wasn't smiling at all now. The glistening pile of
gold that had once sat before him was dwindling.

"You don't care to fold on this one, eh?" Jarrett asked politely.

The Frenchman extracted a thin silver case from the inside
pocket of his elegant beige frock-coat and plucked a cheroot from
it. He leaned against the table, lighting it from the candle that
burned there. He sat back, his eyes level on Jarrett's.

"The gold is on the table, *monsieur.*"

Jarrett shrugged. "As you wish, *monsieur!*"

"You're bluffing, McKenzie! And we will see!"

But at that moment Jarrett didn't really see anything. Just the
figure in the cape.

She turned around, facing him.

When the hood fell back, he saw her hair. It was fascinating
hair, a rich, deep golden blond touched here and there with high-
lights of flame. Even in the muted candlelit gleam of the gaming
parlor, that hair was something like the sun on the most glorious

day, and something like the glow of flame against the deepest darkness of the night.

It was just a headful of blond hair, he tried to tell himself, annoyed for the first time that she had so compelled his attention.

But he was wrong.

It was more than just a beautiful head of hair. He'd never seen hair like it. The skeins of it were rich in color and texture. It was luxurious. He wanted to come closer to it. He wanted to touch it.

Someone ought to warn her that she needed to cover it up. This wasn't the seediest part of town, but it wasn't any church hall here either.

He closed his eyes suddenly, tightly, nearly groaning aloud with the pain that stirred in his heart and the anger he felt against himself. It was one thing to walk the streets here in the heart of town, closed in by the old buildings in their wrought-iron decay and splendor. One thing to lose himself in the tawdry districts of New Orleans. It was something to do, like breathing, like walking along the river, staring at the dark water of the Mississippi as it slugged along. It was one thing to meet a cat in the dark with no real emotion, exchanging words that meant nothing, never seeing, bodies meeting, yet never really, *really*, touching.

He could see this woman. And ever since the hood had fallen away from her face, maybe before it had done so, he had wanted her. Wanted to touch her. Wanted to have her. Not a cat in the dark. Her.

It might have been the way she moved, and it might have been that hair with its extraordinary color. Something both strong and intangible had slipped into his soul from the second he had seen her, even wrapped in the cloak, even in shadow, even before he had really laid eyes on her. . . .

Now, beneath the lantern light in the entryway, he could study her face.

Her eyes were so vivid and dark a blue, he could clearly see their color from across the room. Where her hair was so golden a color, her lashes were rich and dark, sweeping over her eyes. Her brows, too, were a darker shade than her hair, high and delicately arched. Her eyes were wonderful, wide set and shimmering within the frame of an exquisite face. Her coloring was beautiful. The perfect oval structure of her face was enhanced by the clean marble beauty of her skin. Her nose was straight, her mouth was generous, her lips drawn against the porcelain of her flesh as if by some great artist. More than ever he wanted to touch her. Run his thumb over her mouth and explore the pattern and texture of it. Stroke her cheek, discover its softness. Dive into that hair, and become entwined in the silk of it.

Robert cleared his throat. "Jarrett? Poker? You've called the man, Jarrett. Put your cards on the table."

Jarrett did so, barely glancing at the others. Smiling Jack had been sitting on a decent hand, a straight. Not bad. Not enough.

Robert stared at Jarrett, then swept the money into a pile before him.

Jarrett cast a level eye on Jack. He really didn't give a damn about the game anymore. He couldn't even truly appreciate the irritation he was causing the Frenchman. "Do we continue?" he asked Jack. "Are you dealing, *mon ami?*"

"*Oui, mon ami,*" the Frenchman agreed. He started dealing out the cards with a swift expertise. Jarrett sat back, his eyes half closed. He observed everything.

The cards, the Frenchman.

The girl.

That was one good thing about living in the "swamps" with the "savages."

He had learned to watch.

For Tara Brent the evening was already a nightmare. Short, pudgy little Eastwood was going on and on about how late she was, about how he needed her on the floor.

She had made a mistake. Oh, God, she had made a mistake coming here!

But she was desperate for money. Money was her only escape. Money was passage aboard a steamer, somewhere north, anywhere north, far away where she could hide for a lifetime.

Where *they* could never find her.

New Orleans, she had heard, was the city to come to first. It was a place to find work without questions being asked. There were all manner of folk in the city, Creoles, Spanish, English, southerners, and northerners.

It was the gateway to oblivion.

And so she had come, and an old hag-woman in the street had directed her here, and Eastwood had given her work immediately, a job running whiskey and food around to his card-sharking customers. He'd told her that she could make good money taking the gentlemen up to the tiny room he'd given her in the attic, and she'd firmly told him that she didn't take gentlemen anywhere. He laughed and told her that she'd get to it eventually, but he didn't really care, he'd take her on just because she had a classy look about her. Maybe he'd even convince her that he'd make a good "gentleman" for her to take up the stairs eventually himself.

She'd be drawn and quartered first. But she didn't have to say so, because he had hired her, and so far, the few nights she'd been here, he'd left her alone. She shouldn't have spent so long wandering the flower markets and gazing at the Mississippi. She wouldn't have been late coming in for the night, and he'd probably not be yelling at her now. If she wasn't careful, he'd be pressing the issue of her usefulness.

But a number of people had assured her that it was a reputable place. If she had just been either a little less naive—or desperate —she might have realized that these reassuring people weren't all that reputable themselves!

And if this was an establishment of any respectability whatsoever, she shuddered to think of what was not so reputable down by the docks.

She gasped as Eastwood suddenly clutched her by the arms. "Are you listening to me! I run this place, *you* don't! You've already told me in your high-handed way that you won't have men up the stairs. And I went ahead and figured you were so good looking that it didn't matter. But—"

"Get your hands off of me!" she said icily, her words low, but still a dead-set demand.

Eastwood obeyed her. His hands fell from her arms. "Get out there!" he roared. "Get to work if you want wages from me!"

Wages! Slaves probably received more for their efforts!

But she *was* going to work for those wages. She had to get away. Working for Eastwood was better than going back. Anything was better than going back.

Death might be better than going back.

And going back might well mean death, she reminded herself.

She slipped off her cloak and hurried into the kitchen. Eastwood was a tyrant, but his two Creole cooks were wonderfully nice men, and Emma, the plump Irishwoman who ran the kitchen, had a way with her that somehow made working tolerable.

It didn't matter, did it? As soon as she had earned her passage, she was gone!

And all that she had to do was pray that *they* didn't find her first!

"There you are, *ma belle chérie!*" Gaston told her, pulling bread from the oven. Like Emma he was as plump as a pillow. He liked his own cooking. But he was exceedingly kind, and she offered him a shy smile. "I'm sorry I'm late."

He waved a hand in the air with Gallic philosophy. "We are fine on the food. However, there is a table of card players shouting for whiskey. Four men. You will find them."

She nodded, turning about to obey. She crashed into Marie,

one of the pretty little Creole girls who worked the downstairs—
and the upstairs.

"I've men shouting from every direction!" she cried, shaking
her head. *"Mon Dieu alors!* You are here, *chérie. S'il te plaît,* before
that German bites my head off! Whiskey for the card players."

There were always dozens of card players. "I'm going right
now," Tara promised. "Which table?"

"You cannot miss it!" Marie promised her. She took the time
to pause for a minute, looking Tara over from head to toe. "The
German is tall, lean, and very good looking, like a Viking! Then
there is Smiling Jack, as sharp—and dangerous—a Frenchman as
you may hope to see." She had been rushing. Cute, dark, petite—
and very kind—she stopped suddenly to give Tara a word of advice. "Either one of them, *chérie,* would surely pay you your passage in a single night!"

Tara shook her head, blushing slightly, amazed that she could
still do so. Pretty little Marie couldn't begin to understand why
she didn't want to sleep with one man one night and make more
than she could in two weeks slaving away for Eastwood. To Marie
tending to the tables was nothing more than a way to acquire a
good clientele.

"Well, if you could miss the German or the Frenchman,
chérie, I promise you will not miss the Americans. One is very
young, handsome, and light. And the other"—she paused, smiling
—"the other is McKenzie." She said it almost reverently, with no
other description, as if nothing more were needed once the hal-
lowed name was mentioned. It didn't matter. Tara could surely
find the right table from the descriptions Marie had given her
already.

"Well, I'll try not to miss your McKenzie," Tara told her,
amused.

"Oh, you won't miss him!" Marie called, hurrying onward for
a tray filled with steaming crawfish. But she paused, looking back.
"He's black Irish, they say, just so you know."

Tara paused. "Pardon?"

Marie sighed with a wistful little sound. "Black Irish, so they tell me. Sometime, years ago, when the English defeated the Spanish Armada, the Spaniards landed upon Ireland before trying to sail home. So now there are these Irishmen with jet-dark hair and coal-dark eyes! As hot blooded as the Spanish plains and as fierce as those ever-fighting Irish. You'll notice McKenzie, I swear it."

Tara smiled, turning away. Marie noticed any man. All he needed was his hair—well, some of his hair—two legs, decent teeth—and plenty of gold.

She hurried through the bar and found a bottle of whiskey and a number of Eastwood's short, heavy glasses. When she came back into the main room, the smoke from the fire caused her to pause for a moment and look around. A few sailors sat with their doxies, all laughing the night away in a far corner. Another set of river rowdies leaned against the far wall, taunting Lisette, Marie's cousin. Lisette seemed to be doing just fine with the lot of them. There were at least three tables of card players, but Marie had been right.

She could not miss the table of men that had been described to her. There was the German, just as Marie had described. The Frenchmen, and the Americans. One man seemed just a little bit younger. He had an easy smile. He leaned on an elbow, watching the game.

Then there was the fourth man. McKenzie. *Black Irish*, Marie had said. It fit him perfectly. She didn't think that she had ever seen hair so rich or jet in color. In fact, she didn't think that she'd ever seen any man quite like him. From the moment she discovered the table, she discovered that he had been watching her. His eyes were large, sharp, and so dark that they seemed as ebony as his hair. His features were hard, rugged; a stubborn, determined chin, high, broad cheekbones, ebony, high-arched brows, a long, straight nose, deeply bronzed skin. Yet despite the ruggedness of his face it was a strikingly handsome one. The bone structure was excellent. His mouth was full, wide, sensual.

And his eyes were intense. As dark as night. And fixed upon her. He caught her stare. A slow smile curved his lips. She felt a peculiar sensation, as if flames suddenly lapped their way from an intangible place within her soul to roar right through her limbs, searing her from head to toe.

He was well dressed. His shirt was as white as snow, his frock coat an elegant black, his trousers fawn. She noticed his hands, his fingers upon his cards. They were as bronzed as his face. His fingers were very long, the nails blunt cut but clean.

"The whiskey! At last!" The German man said.

Tara quickly put the bottle and the glasses down on the table. She could still feel those dark eyes on her, and she was desperate to get away.

"You're out of your gold coins, Jack. It's time to call it quits," McKenzie was saying. His voice was as rich and deep as his hair. It had a subtle slur of the South to it, though she could not exactly pinpoint the place. He wasn't from New Orleans, but he certainly wasn't from the North.

"Out of coins, but never out of assets, *mon ami!*" the Frenchman said.

Tara was so startled when his fingers wound around her wrist that she nearly shrieked out loud. She fought from doing so, well aware that Eastwood would have her on the streets if she screamed just because a man had taken hold of her wrist.

"The girl!" the Frenchman said. "Yours for the night."

"What?" Tara gasped furiously.

"She's not yours to barter!" the black-eyed American, McKenzie, shot back quickly.

"Eastwood is in debt to me. The girl for a night. Against your three hundred in gold."

"No whore, not even this one, is worth three hundred!" the German said, swallowing down his whiskey, pale eyes assessing her carefully. "Or is she?" he speculated.

Tara wrenched her hand free. "I work for Eastwood!" she

snapped. "I am not his possession, no man's to barter or hold!"
she cried angrily.

She turned to flee. To her amazement her skirt was caught,
and she was hauled back against the table. Dear God, these two
were involved in some wretched challenge in this poker game,
and she had become a part of it! The Frenchman had her by her
skirts, and she'd lose half her clothing trying to rip away from
him. She stared at him incredulously, gripping her skirt. "You let
me go this instant! I'm not an object to be cast upon a table. Let
me go! I told you! I wait tables—"

"Then you will wait on this man's table for a night, *chérie!*"
the Frenchman said.

The German sniggered. "Table, floor, what's the difference,
eh?"

Her eyes flashed to his, blue fire. "You, sir, may go to hell! I'll
get Eastwood—"

The Frenchman's laughter interrupted and terrified her. "You
go get him, *chérie!* He'll set you in the center of the table himself.
You see, I must bet with this blackhearted bastard, but your Eastwood owes me half his inn!"

She tried to control her temper. She really did. But she found
herself lifting the Frenchman's glass and dashing his whiskey into
his face.

He let out a bellow like a whipped puppy and started to rise,
reaching for her.

But McKenzie was up. His gaze was deadly as he stared down
the Frenchman. "Let her go," he said flatly.

"*Sacré bleu—*"

"Let her go!"

The Frenchman started to release her reluctantly. Tara would
have fled then except that she was newly detained.

Now it was he, McKenzie, who had his hand upon her. His
fingers circled her upper arm. She found herself staring up at him.
He was very tall, his shoulders were broad. He appeared lean and
trim but he was solid muscle, she realized. She could feel the force

of his hold and knew that he was a man she would never escape if he chose not to let her go.

"Sit down," he told her, dark eyes enigmatic.

She lifted her chin. "I told you, I don't care who owes who what! I'm not available for a night! For any man, from any man!"

A black brow arched higher. "I didn't say that I wanted you for a night."

"Then—"

"But that all remains to be seen, doesn't it? It's all in a deck of cards." His voice was very soft. Only she heard it. "Three hundred dollars is a lot of money—for any woman. Sit!" he warned her.

"I won't—"

A dry smile curled just the corner of his mouth. "You should be praying it's me, and not the Frenchman!" he warned her.

Why? The Frenchman was the fool making the wager! He'd have to let her go. But if McKenzie won . . .

She was startled to discover herself suddenly in his arms, pulled back against him as he addressed the others. "I want this goddamned game over with!" He lowered his voice again and his words were for her ears alone. "Sit in the chair, or you'll be sitting in my lap!"

Tears stung her eyes. Panic seized her for a moment. No! This was not *her* life!

She grit her teeth down hard. And she sat. She had no choice.

The fourth man at the table, the handsome young man Marie had mentioned with the sandy hair and warm green eyes, set a hand on hers. McKenzie frowned at him in warning, but the man still offered her a wry grin. "It will be all right, miss. It will."

"We're still playing the damned game, Robert!" McKenzie snapped.

He sat, too, those ebony eyes of his on the Frenchman now across the table. "The girl is the wager. Fine. I've been called on my hand. Here it is."

He laid out his cards. Tara felt her heart leap as she stared at them. A three, a four, a five, a six . . .

And a seven.

They didn't look very good to her. Oh, God, this was ridiculous! She wasn't even sure who she wanted to win the hand. What was going to happen if the Frenchman beat McKenzie? At least McKenzie had mentioned that she might not be wanted!

But she had been set down as the wager against a three-hundred-dollar bet.

What if *none* of these men wanted to believe her, that she served tables here and no more? Nothing that she had to say seemed to mean anything to them. Maybe Eastwood had hired her because he knew that there would eventually be an occasion like this.

The Frenchman swore violently, throwing his cards down. Tara's heart leapt again. He had three aces, a king, and a ten.

Who the hell had won this thing? Seconds ticked by in silence. She wanted to scream.

"Mine again," McKenzie said at last, very softly. "I think this time, Jack, the game is over!"

"*Mais, oui!* The game is over!" the Frenchman cried furiously.

Tara screamed, shrieking out in warning as she jumped away from the table. The Frenchman was pulling out a weapon, a pistol. And he was aiming it straight at McKenzie's heart, at a distance of no more than three feet.

But the Frenchman's weapon never fired. McKenzie moved like a cobra, more swiftly than the eye. Even as she blinked, he was on his feet, reaching to a sheath at his ankle and hurtling a blade like a streak of silver across the distance between himself and the Frenchman.

The knife hit the top of the Frenchman's hand. He screamed with pain.

The Frenchman's hand was pinned to the table with the knife. His pistol, freed from his injured hand, went flying across the wood to land with a thud against the wall.

The Frenchman looked furiously from his hand to McKenzie. "You should be arrested!"

"And you should be dead," he said flatly. "You meant to shoot me down in cold blood, and every man here witnessed the attempt."

"You cheated. You should have been shot! And if it weren't for this little whore—"

"How dare you—" Tara began furiously, but neither man was paying her any heed at the moment.

"I'd have *still* been faster than you," McKenzie interrupted him sharply.

"Swamp-loving bastard!" the Frenchman said.

McKenzie stood quickly, wresting his knife from the table and the Frenchman's hand. Smiling Jack screamed out with a cry of pain, then fell silent, nursing his injured hand as McKenzie leaned low against him and spoke softly. "I've never cheated in my life, *mon ami*. And you know that. You should be dead. Be grateful I left you alive."

"You're still the fool, the loser, McKenzie! What woman is worth three hundred dollars?"

"This one!" McKenzie snapped. Tara was stunned to discover his long, powerful fingers winding around her wrist, drawing her to his side. Jesu! She shouldn't have been standing there, gaping! She should have been making a swift disappearance, slipping away while she'd had the chance!

"You make sure your friend Eastwood knows that she's made three hundred dollars for him this evening. And you make damned sure he knows why she's gone," McKenzie continued.

He started walking out with long strides, dragging Tara with him. She tried to hang back, desperate to convince him that she couldn't go anywhere with him. He didn't allow her to stop. He was far too powerful a man for her to break his hold. She couldn't just scream within the tawdry little tavern—Eastwood would come running over to strip her himself for three hundred dollars. No help there. . . .

No help from anywhere.

Everyone in the tavern had gone silent at the outbreak of the fight.

And now everyone was staring at the two of them. Eastwood was watching them, apparently delighted that she'd be paying off part of one of his debts.

"I'd say she's well worth three hundred!" a drunk suddenly bellowed.

She flushed silently, furiously tugging to free her hand. Jarrett didn't release her. He knew her cloak. He lifted it from the peg where she had hung it when she'd come in, barely breaking his stride. At the entryway he finally paused, sweeping it over her shoulders.

"Wait! I can't—"

"Come on. Let's get out of here!"

And for a moment his near ebony gaze touched hers and the curve of a smile just lifted the corners of his mouth. His whisper came close to her lips, sending little shivers of fire to dance down her spine. "You little fool! Run with it. You're mine for the night! Freedom from this hellhole."

But at what price?

Scream! she thought, panic finding a renewed life within her. *Scream and scream. . . .*

But there would be no one to heed her. If a cry of desperation escaped her, no one would give a damn, no one at all.

He was pulling her along once again. McKenzie. The black Irishman with the searing eyes and the touch of steel.

Dragging her with him into the night.

His night.

Chapter 2

In seconds they were outside in the cool New Orleans streets, surrounded by wrought iron and the scent of flowers, with only a faint odor beneath of the river and the wharf rats.

Tara tugged hard upon her hand once again, fighting to remain calm, to reason with the man. "Mr. McKenzie, you've got to understand. I can't really be a payment in a game. I had nothing to do with any of that, I've never seen that horrible man before in my life."

He wasn't responding. He was just walking down the street—still dragging her along.

She jerked back furiously.

"Damn you, I'm not—"

He stopped beneath a streetlamp, swinging around to study her. "What the bloody hell do you think you're doing in a place like that, then?"

She was astounded by the question. He sounded just like her older brother at that moment.

"Trying to make some money," she said irritably.

"Oh, Jesu!" he muttered.

"Not like that!" she defended herself, seeing the way his mind was turning. He didn't believe her! If he had perhaps begun to believe her before, he certainly didn't now.

"I need money! I was trying to make legitimate money!"

He lifted her hand suddenly, running his thumb over her flesh, cocking a brow at the smoothness of it. "I see. You don't come from any, right?"

"Any what?"

"Money!" he snapped.

She tore free, staring at him.

"I was trying to make a few honest dollars and nothing more!"

"At Eastwood's?"

"I heard that it was a respectable place—"

"More respectable than some of the more perverted whore-houses!" he retorted harshly. He continued in a blunt vein. "East-wood, at least, never expects his girls to entertain two or three at a time."

She paled. "But—"

"Jesu, can you really be so naive?"

"Yes! I suppose so!" she cried out. "I was trying to work hon-estly for the money."

"Well," he said softly, black eyes sweeping her, "you'll be making an honest dollar tonight."

She gasped, paling. "I told you—"

"That you serve tables. Fine. You can serve a table elsewhere. Just not here!"

What in God's name did he mean? She remembered the Ger-man card player's comment about serving on a table or a floor. Oh, God!

He turned from her and started walking. He had let her go, she realized with amazement. She thought about turning around to run. It might be very foolish. He would surely report her to Eastwood. Or else he would just catch her. She had no doubts about his ability to do so.

She didn't believe that he'd let her go so easily, and to her own surprise she found herself running after him, catching his arm and causing him to spin around again. She released him immediately and asked nervously, "What do you mean?"

He stared at her. He smiled suddenly, a slow, curious smile. "You're supposed to be worth three hundred dollars. That's quite a sum."

"Where are we going?"

"My rooms."

No, they weren't. She didn't dare wonder about his exact intentions anymore, or spend any more time ruing the fact that he probably had the power to catch her. Foolish or not, she had to take her chances trying to run.

And actually, she was getting good at running. Very good. Maybe she could even escape a man like this one.

She had let him go. He turned and started walking again. She stood dead still and shivered, watching him.

"Come on!" he called to her.

Not on his life! This was it, now or never.

She turned in a flurry of speed and motion and started down an alleyway that led toward the river. She ran like a rabbit, her heart pounding, her feet flying.

To her dismay she burst out on the same street from which she had just come. Eastwood's street. She came to a swift halt, flattening herself against the raw wood of one of the alleyway's shanty buildings. At first she was just irritated with herself, certain that she could slip back into the shadows of the night.

Then she gasped, her heart slamming against her chest.

And then it seemed to stop dead with pure horror. She recognized the two men entering the front door of Eastwood's place.

They'd been sent for her. They must have followed her trail to Eastwood's. And they'd probably offer Eastwood anything to get her.

Oh, God!

An absolute, horrible panic seized her. She turned and ran blindly, trying to double her speed as she became aware that she was being followed. The men had been told at Eastwood's that she was somewhere out in the night! Had she been seen? Heard? She didn't know. But they were in pursuit now. Footsteps fell after her own, echoing, pounding in the darkness and cool of the night. She ran harder.

The night air stung her eyes. She was gasping for breath. Her heart beat cruelly. The darkness seemed to be closing in on her. How long could she run? Oh, God, it was over, over. . . .

She rounded a corner and burst out onto a dock. Tall buildings rose to one side. The dark, muddy Mississippi stretched into oblivion at the end of it.

She could hear the men shouting out to one another in their pursuit of her.

She would never let them catch her. Never. She would die first.

She didn't care where the dock led, if it were into oblivion or not.

She started to run again, blindly, into the darkness.

Suddenly a hand shot out. She started to scream as an arm came around her, sweeping her off her feet. The hand settled over her mouth and she heard a harsh whisper. "Shut up! It's me."

McKenzie. Dear God, it was McKenzie!

Her heart continued to beat like wildfire. He pulled her into the shadowed darkness of the narrow alley she hadn't seen until he swept her there. His hand lifted from her mouth. She could feel his body heat, the rise and fall of his chest, the vital tension of the man. He turned her around. She saw a glistening reflection in his eyes and the flash of his teeth reflected by what dim moonlight combated the darkness. She could scarcely breathe. A trembling raced through her as he held her, staring demandingly into her eyes.

"Who are they?" he barked sharply.

Her eyes widened. McKenzie had been right behind her all along. He'd seen the men—and he'd seen her panic because of them. "I don't know—" she lied.

"The men following you. Who are they?"

"I don't know!"

"The hell you don't, and why the hell did you run from *me?*" he demanded curtly.

"I thought that you would force me."

"I wouldn't think of forcing a whore."

"But I'm not—"

He sighed with aggravation. "I didn't intend to force you into anything—no matter what you are or aren't! I was going to try to give you a decent dinner and some breathing space before letting you go back to that rat hole, if that was your choice."

"You could have just said so—" she began furiously.

"But now you can't go back there, can you?" he interrupted.

She clenched down hard on her teeth. "No," she said flatly. "I can't go back." He was so close. She could feel his warmth and the fine texture of his coat brushing her hands. He smelled good, clean like soap with just a touch of cologne, whiskey and leather mingling in. He was not just the most intriguing man she'd ever seen, he also seemed to be the most powerful. And perhaps the hardest, she thought. He expected answers, he set his hands upon what he wanted, and took it. His black eyes demanded everything. And yet . . .

He could be merciful, she thought.

When mercy was warranted. He was probably also capable of being entirely ruthless when mercy was not warranted. Just how would he see her situation?

It didn't matter. The past was over, and it was hers alone. She would never tell him. . . .

"Why?" he demanded.

She shook her head. In the darkness his head cocked. He was studying her. She was certain that he could see her in the night far better than she could see him. He knew the darkness, he was accustomed to it and comfortable with it.

She closed her eyes briefly. She was certain that she was safe at the moment too. He was very tall, very strong, and quick as a whip, she had seen that. She was certainly blocked from view by his height and the breadth of his shoulders.

But now what? What when he walked away? Would she be seen, chased, caught?

"Why are those men after you?" he demanded again.

She shook her head wildly. She had to run and keep on running. McKenzie was pinning her here and the two men after her were coming closer and closer.

"You tell me the truth about yourself, about what's going on. I'll help you."

"I'm not telling you anything—I can't!" she said quickly. Oh, God, she was running out of choices! He hadn't been going to force her into anything. She wasn't worth three hundred dollars to him, he really hadn't given a damn about the money. So what did she do now? Bargain with him to help her? Offer him what? Herself? He'd already had that opportunity!

One thing was certain. She couldn't tell him the truth.

He leaned back. She could just see the searing light in his eyes, the hard planes of his face. He lifted his hands, palms upward, and shrugged. "Talk to me. Or else you're on your own!" he warned her softly. "I can't protect you when I don't know what the damned danger is!"

Beyond the haven of their slim alley, from along the dock, they could hear the approach of footsteps, the sound of shouts. The men were coming closer and closer.

"Come on!" he urged her in a vehement whisper. "Why do they want you so badly?"

"I can't tell you!" she cried.

He smiled, leaning against the wall behind him. "Think about it. Quickly," he suggested. There was an edge to his tone. A warning. What he wanted, he would take.

And if she failed to talk to him . . .

Jesu! What was it? Jarrett wondered. She was a fighter, that much was certain. She was stubborn and determined. Beautiful and delicate . . . but hard as a rock in her way! She was still staring at him. It seemed—to her, at least—that hounds from hell were after her. But she wasn't going to give in to him under any circumstances.

"Talk to me!" he commanded.

"Go to hell!" she whispered. There was such a desperate note to the words!

To his amazement she shoved him aside, and started to rush past him. She was going to make a dive into the water!

"Hold it!"

He caught her arm, jerking her back and against him. The hood slipped from her head, and once again he found himself staring at her wealth of gold and wheat and flame hair. The hair that had so entangled him from the very beginning.

Then there were her eyes, huge and near violet, staring into his now with a liquid gleam to them.

"What are you, an idiot? Are you trying to drown yourself?"

"I can swim."

"The river here is dark and all but pure mud. Your skirts would drag you down. You've the sense to know that."

"I have nothing to say."

"All right, fine. You've nothing to say. Half of the time I don't have a hell of a lot to say either. So let's leave it at that. You're running. Hard. I don't know from whom or from what, and I'm not even sure I give a damn. I'll still help you."

One of her delicate wheat brows arched upward with wary suspicion. "The only way you can help me is to get me out of here quickly," she told him quietly.

"I can get you out of the city. Tonight, if you wish."

"With no explanations?"

"Yes."

"But there will be a price," she said matter-of-factly. "And I've nothing. Not a stitch of jewelry, not even my wages from the inn. I've nothing but the clothes I'm wearing."

"My dear girl!" he murmured dryly, "Trust me. It wouldn't matter if you came stark naked. I don't need your jewelry or your money." Where did he go from here? She didn't want to tell him anything—he was damned tired of making it so easy for her. "You're the payment. You," he said flatly. There. Let her think on that.

Her color faded from her face, and he was growing ever more curious. She had told him that she waited tables at the inn, nothing more. So what was she running from? An affair turned bad? A cruel father?

A cruel husband?

She swallowed hard. She was still as white as a sheet. "I keep telling you I'm not a—" she began. Then she looked down. *Whore.* It was the unsaid word.

"I'm already supposedly yours for the night," she whispered miserably. "But I can't stay here!" she said flatly. She stared up at him, chin steady, and turned into a businesswoman, pushing aside what emotions had caused her to pale so. "I need to get away, really away. Far from New Orleans, from everything—"

"I can get you away," he said dryly. "Very far away."

"To where?" she demanded desperately.

"Florida."

"Jacksonville?"

"Deeper. I've a plantation down in the middle of the territory."

"The territory has a middle?" she murmured. She was hardly complimentary with her complete lack of enthusiasm! It was painfully evident that she wasn't thrilled about being rescued away to his beloved homeland.

"Top, middle, and a bottom," he informed her wryly. "And I own land down at the bottom of the territory too. I know you'll love it."

"The Indians own your land," she told him.

"They own some, I own some. But what is mine is mine, and it's where I'm going."

She shuddered, then clenched down hard on her jaw, like a woman determined that she might show dislike, but never fear.

"But it's all swamps down there! Swamps and Indians and alligators!"

Hadn't he already heard that once tonight?

It was so different from the way his wife had felt about their private Eden. . . .

This girl wasn't his wife. He didn't even know what he was doing with her, only that she had intrigued him. She had set his blood afire.

But the lady was desperate.

"It's my home," he told her firmly.

"But—but . . . it *is* swamp and there *are* terrible problems with the Seminoles down there—"

"And the Mikasukis," he said pleasantly. She was very pale. "There is one damned good thing about a swamp, though," he told her. "It's hard to look for someone in the middle of one. That's why the Seminoles came south. They're runaways. That's what most folks say the name means."

"What?" she murmured, confused.

"Seminole. Some say it means *runaway*. Kind of fitting, don't you think?" he asked her pointedly. "And if not *runaway*, *renegade*," he added.

He watched her jaw lock and her eyes flash with anger. Something hot streaked through him as he watched her. He felt alive, as he hadn't now in ages. The longer he watched her, the more he wanted her. And the more he damned her. He wasn't so certain that he wanted to feel this alive again.

"You can't just—get me to a swamp and desert me!" she whispered.

"You've got somewhere else to go?"

"No, but—"

"Are you guilty of murder or a like crime?" he demanded.

"I told you—"

"You can't talk to me—or won't. But I'm not asking you what you were accused of doing. I'm asking what you were actually guilty of doing."

"No, no, I'm not guilty of murder!" she cried. Her violet eyes were wild. "I swear it!"

"Then I'll get you out of here. And I won't desert you any-where. How many of them are after you? Just the two?"

"What?"

"How many of them are there?"

She hesitated. "Just the two, I think."

"Can they call out the local law-enforcement people to help them?"

She let her lashes fall. "I don't know," she murmured miser-ably.

"Well, you're not giving me a hell of a lot to work with!" he muttered. "It's damned certain that if they're willing to pay enough, Eastwood will be willing to sell. All right. We buy a little time. Since you won't help me."

"I can't—"

"All right! I'll try not to ask any more questions. But from this moment on you're going to have to trust me."

She didn't say anything. He looked out past the alley, study-ing the shadows with his obsidian stare. Then he took her hand and stepped from their shadowed haven within the alley. "We move, now!" he said, pulling her out, hurrying her along. "They're past the docks for the moment," he muttered.

She was breathless, trying to keep up with him as they walked the tawdry streets of dockside New Orleans. She was dying to ask him questions. At the moment she didn't dare.

They passed the fish markets and vegetable stalls and veered just inland. From the seedier section of the city they moved into an area where the music of the taverns seemed to fade away, where the buildings wore fresh paint and carved shutters. They came into a block of elegant pastel-colored houses with beautiful wrought-iron gates and balconies. Here and there a trellis would crawl the wall, adding to the exotic beauty of the place.

She was staring at one of the homes when the first man accosted them. She hadn't seen him, hadn't heard a sound. But the man at her side had.

He was attacked by a heavyset red-haired man brandishing a knife.

She'd never seen their attacker before in her life.

He started to swing his arm in an upward motion that would have slit McKenzie from his groin to his throat. But McKenzie had been ready before the redhead had begun, and he slammed the full force of his fist down on the man's arm. Tara gasped as she heard bone crack. The knife clattered against a walk leading to an inn. The man swore, clutching his broken arm. McKenzie jerked him back by the collar.

"What are you after?"

"Just your gold!" he cried out. "That pocketful of gold!"

"What has she done?" McKenzie demanded.

The man's eyes widened. "She? I was after the gold, man!"

He shoved the man away, staring at Tara. "Do you know him?"

She shook her head.

He stared at the man again. "You're just a common thief?"

The man nodded, glum and frightened.

"Get the hell away from here!" McKenzie said, shoving him away. The fellow began to nod strenuously. "I'm gone, I swear it. I never saw you, I don't know—"

"Go!"

McKenzie clutched her arm again, hurrying her along. "In the midst of this we have to get hit upon by a common thief?" he said incredulously.

"You asked him about me!" Tara cried. "You said that you wouldn't ask—"

"Here!" he said, suddenly stopping. They had come to another walk. It led to a handsome rooming house under a broad tree. The place was fronted by huge, beautifully crafted porches and balconies, the ironwork all done in pastels that shone lightly in the few streaks of moonlight that touched the ground.

"Around the back!" he urged her. They came around the house. Stone steps led to the second floor. McKenzie quickly rattled a key in the lock, urging her into a shadowed room.

Her heart began to pound ferociously. She backed into the darkened room and fell against a bed. She jumped back up, but he wasn't watching her. He had silently come across the balcony himself and was looking into the night.

"Someone's coming!" he said very softly. He swiftly began to strip his frock coat from his shoulders, then his shirt from his torso. Tara's jaw simply dropped.

"Get your clothes off and get in bed," he said in a low whisper.

Her heart slammed as she watched what she could see of his silhouette. Oh, God, her lip was trembling! Her voice was a squeak of a protest. "But you said that—you promised that you wouldn't force—"

It was too dark to see his eyes. She knew that his glance fell upon her with aggravation. "I'm not even going to touch you!" He slid out of one boot, and then the other. She heard, rather than saw, him peeling his trousers from his thighs. He was naked, and she couldn't see anything but his silhouette, and yet his silhouette was enough to create a tidal wave of shivers within her. Tremors that came hot, and then cold, and then hot again. He was as trim and lithe and tight-muscled as any panther ranging the night. He was as natural and assured as a beast in the wild. The moonlight fell upon the sleek bulge of his forearm and shoulder for just a moment. Oh, God!

"I told you that you had to trust me!" he warned her angrily. "Now, get in there. Trust me!"

He sounded so annoyed—and she was terrified. Courage! "Well, excuse me! It's difficult to trust a naked stranger!" she snapped out.

He paused, his head turning just slightly, his voice both taunting and amused. "The fellows out there are still dressed. Want to trust them instead?" Something outside caught his attention. "Get in there!" he commanded her.

She tried to undo the back laces on her gown. Her fingers were shaking too hard. He strode swiftly across the room, and had them undone in seconds flat. He jerked free the ties on her corset and pulled her gown and petticoats swiftly over her head. He threw the lot of her clothing across the room.

She was startlingly aware of the fire of his flesh brushing against hers. She nearly screamed out at the feel of it, simply because it was so intense. He was smooth, tight, hot as blue flame. And his hands were on her waist, lifting her while their flesh brushed, and she was suddenly flying through the air, landing on the bed.

"Under the covers!" he commanded, and even as she did so, she let out a soft gasp of a protest because he was joining her there, sweeping his arms around her.

"What—" she began.

His hand clamped over her mouth. "Shush!" he warned her. He waited, tense as living steel. In all of her life she didn't think that she had felt anything as acutely as she felt the wired strength of his body at that moment. He waited a heartbeat, waited for the banging to come on the door again. "Now!" he whispered very softly, and right on cue the door burst open.

Chapter 3

TWO MEN stood there, framed by the moonlight.

McKenzie leapt up in a fury in the shadowed room, throwing the covers over her, wrenching a bath sheet from the foot of the bed to wrap around his waist.

"What are you doing?" McKenzie demanded incredulously.

She recognized the men standing there. They weren't the ones who had come to Eastwood's for her—they were Eastwood's servants. One was Rory, a husky farmer from Minnesota, and the other was Geoffrey, a one-eyed, slimmer man who was as swift with a knife as lightning. They both looked after things at Eastwood's. If McKenzie hadn't been so quick to take care of himself tonight, they would probably have entered into the fight.

They had been sent to retrieve her! she thought, her heart pounding.

"What the bloody hell do you want?" McKenzie demanded, his voice ringing with fury.

Rory cleared his throat. "Sorry, McKenzie. But Eastwood needs the girl. Seems that someone willing to pay big is looking for her."

"She's three hundred dollars to me. In gold," McKenzie said flatly.

"But she has to come back—"

"She isn't coming back tonight, and if anyone tries to take her, I'll kill him! Is that understood?"

His words were met with silence. He continued. "She'll come back in the morning," McKenzie said flatly. He lowered his voice. Tara could still hear him, but his words were very soft. "I mean, really, boys, I'm just getting to the good part and the two of you bust in here? Get the hell out! It'll be another gold piece to the both of you, and Eastwood will have her back for the other two in the morning. He can make his money, you can make yours, and I can have the whole damned night that fool Eastwood owes for being stupid enough to borrow money from that gambling Frenchie."

There was some whispering that Tara couldn't hear. She realized that the two men were trying to look over McKenzie's shoulder, assuring themselves that she was in his bed, right where she was supposed to be.

"What's she like?" Geoffrey asked McKenzie suddenly. "I always itched to get my hands on her . . . she claimed she didn't do business with any menfolk, hired help or not. God, I would have spent every cent I ever had—"

He broke off because McKenzie was pushing him out the door. "She's just a little taste of heaven!" McKenzie assured him. "Remember, there's money in it for you both. Just so long as I'm not interrupted again tonight, eh?"

"Right, McKenzie. You won't be interrupted again," Rory promised him. "Excuse us. We're really sorry."

"Just go!"

They did. McKenzie closed the door behind them and leaned against it. Tara could feel his ebony gaze on her. As if he could really see her in the darkness. He laughed suddenly, a bit wickedly. "You're blushing!"

"You can't possibly see that!" Tara cried. What else had he seen? "And you didn't have to say that!"

"Say what?"

"That I was a taste of heaven!"

"I should have said that you were as exciting as a cold piece of driftwood?" he inquired politely. "They would have really wondered why I wanted you for the rest of the night!"

"No!" She wanted to throw something at him, anything! "You shouldn't have said anything at all!"

"No matter what I said, he'd still be licking his chops," McKenzie said flatly.

She was still upset. She'd never felt so horribly cheap in all her life.

Cheap, no. She was supposedly worth three hundred dollars, she reminded herself miserably.

"You didn't have to say anything!" she repeated angrily.

"You wanted me to slug them both unconscious?" he asked her in a soft taunt. "I might have managed it—even though those two are pretty good at brawn. But they don't do so very well when it comes to brain! But it wouldn't have done us a damned bit of good. Eastwood can send out a score of men. And even if I did feel like belting them all for your dubious honor, it wouldn't do us a damned bit of good. What we need to do is buy time."

"Dubious honor!" Tara began angrily.

"All right! I'm sorry. But I did win you in a poker game at Eastwood's!"

Was he serious, or laughing at her? Sometimes he was amused, his smile coming so quickly. And sometimes there seemed to be something almost dark about him, jaded, very hard and cynical.

He strode across the room again, nonchalant in his bath sheet, muscled bronze shoulders gleaming. He retrieved her clothing from around the room, depositing it on the bed at her feet. He let the bath sheet fall, plucking his own clothing from the floor. With no hesitancy or embarrassment he crawled back into his breeches. "Get dressed!" he commanded her. "Now!"

Oh, he could snap out orders like a general! "You just told me to get undressed!" she reminded him.

He paused. Even at their distance she could sense both his amusement and his innate heat. "You want to stay there? We don't have much time, but then again, maybe there's enough—"

"Oh, stop it!" she whispered. "I can't get dressed! You're staring at me—"

She broke off. They were both startled by a light knocking at the door.

"McKenzie, you in there?" came a soft query.

It was dark, but Tara could see the way that the tension eased from his shoulders. He strode toward the door.

"What are you doing?" she called out desperately, instinctively dragging the sheets to her throat.

He didn't reply. Holding on to his bath sheet, he jerked open the door. The handsome young man from the pool table stumbled in. "McKenzie! They're looking for the girl—"

"Well, you're late," McKenzie told him with a touch of amusement. "They were already here."

"You let them take her?"

McKenzie indicated the bed. Tara wanted to shrink beneath it.

"Oh. Oh! Excuse me, I didn't know I was interrupting—"

"You weren't interrupting anything," McKenzie said flatly. "I had to make it look as if we were occupied for hours to come."

"Why are they after her?"

"I don't know. Why don't you try asking her?"

Tara was instantly certain that he didn't have the see-in-the-dark abilities of his friend. He squinted, staring her way. "Why are they after you?"

She didn't answer.

"We don't have time for this. Not now. We've got to get out."

"Right!" Robert said quickly. He stood still.

"Well?" McKenzie said, amused again. "Do you mind? I think that the lady would like to dress."

"Oh. Right! I'll be outside."

McKenzie closed the door behind him. He stared at Tara. "Get dressed!"

She gritted her teeth. "If you're going to stare at me, you might as well invite your friend back in!" she snapped.

"Shall I?"

She threw a pillow at him and he caught it. He laughed. It was a rich, husky sound. Sensual. She felt more naked than ever.

"It's pitch dark in here—and I've already seen you." He was very quick himself. He was already in his shirt and boots and frock coat and coming across the room again. She was forced to swallow down a cry when he lifted her from the sheets, setting her on the floor.

"If it was pitch dark, you haven't seen anything!" she tried to tell him.

But maybe that was wrong. She could see the fiery gleam in his dark eyes and the mocking curl to his lip as he slipped her petticoat over her head and then swirled her around to tie her corset back in place. He was swift and deft with women's cloth-ing, she noted.

"We've got to get going!" he told her.

"And go where?" she whispered desperately. "Down to your swamp?"

"You've a better suggestion?"

"North—"

"I live south."

"But I can't stay there!" she protested in dismay. "It's savage land—"

"And you're afraid? Pity!"

"I'm not afraid," she murmured quickly. "Not any more afraid than I am of going back out tonight!"

"Ah! Since Eastwood's boys will take their time reporting back, you think that your friends will still be after you!"

"They're not my friends."

"Whoever. We'll get past them."

"To the swamp!" she whispered.

"I won't leave you once we're there," he said very softly.

Tara closed her eyes. She tried to remember everything she knew about Florida. It was raw, awful, she had heard. There were horrible, savage battles with the Indians. Most of the state was a wasteland.

She didn't want to be afraid. Ever. But she was.

"How can I be guaranteed that?" she whispered, her eyes pinning his. Damn, but she had a will of steel! Danger lay at the doorstep and she was still negotiating!

A tap came on the door. "Ready?" Robert asked. The door opened. He came through.

"She doesn't like the idea of Florida," McKenzie told him.

"I don't want to be left with a savage in the middle of a swamp!" she whispered.

"Why not? You'll be going there with a savage!" Robert said and laughed. There was silence. "I was joking, you know."

Why the hell *was* he taking her with him? Jarrett wondered. He could just put her on a riverboat and send her north.

And where would she wind up? How long would it be before these people came after her again?

It wasn't his affair.

It was. He had seen her. He had touched her. Oh, yes. He had seen quite a bit of her.

"He won't leave you there," Robert continued. "I know he won't." He swung around, staring at McKenzie in the darkness. His voice was a whisper. "Damn it, it's the answer. Yes, bring her home. You've needed someone. Marry her."

"What!" McKenzie thundered the word. Then he stared at Tara. She backed away into a corner of the room.

"Look—" she began.

"Why not?" McKenzie muttered.

He smiled as a startling chill swept through him. What was he doing? To himself, to her!

What difference did it make? he wondered wearily. He could

never have married any of the women or girls who would have been appropriate wives for him. Not someone he knew, who had known Lisa. Robert had once suggested a mail-order bride because he did need someone. What was a plantation without someone to run the household, without someone—anyone—warm to return to at the end of the day?

Well, she was a hell of a lot better than a mail-order bride!

And he knew that he wanted her. If he should burn any more deeply for her, he would explode like cannon fire.

He stared hard at her, his muscles constricted, the length of him as tight as wire. "I will marry you," he told her. "And then I *can* absolutely guarantee you that you will be safe."

She gasped, stunned. "But I can't—"

"Are you already married?"

"No!"

"Then?"

For once he seemed to have really shaken her. Her lips trembled, the length of her shook. "I don't love you, I don't even know you! I—" she shook her head wildly. "How do *you* know you're willing to do it?" she inquired.

He folded his arms over his chest. "Because I'm a gambler. You must have noticed that by now. And if you were willing to throw yourself into the Mississippi, you have to be one hell of a gambler too."

She was still staring at him, moisture dazzling her eyes, even in the shadowy darkness.

"She's gone! Really gone. I sure as hell can't find her," came an irritated call from the street.

"She can't be gone! Keep looking. We'll find her."

"What's it to be?" he asked her very softly.

What was it to be? What choice did she have?

A shudder seized her, as dark and frightening as the night. Her mouth went dry, her palms dampened. He was a striking man. Even vague thoughts of an intimate relationship with him made her feel very weak.

He was her way out. She was desperate.

But if she accepted his help, she knew that she would be expected to play out her part of the bargain. She might well be leaping straight into the fire. . . .

It was better than turning back!

Dear God! She heard footsteps running along the street. They had moved on.

"Do it!" Robert urged her. He was grinning broadly. Teasing her. Taunting McKenzie. "He's got a temper as bad as the devil's, but he's rich as Midas."

"Well?" McKenzie asked. His words were soft. He sounded angry. He was almost demanding that she do it, and yet he seemed to know that she had no choice, that she would say yes— and that when she did, he would be angry all over again!

"You're the one running out of time!" he reminded her, black eyes still hard upon her.

She tossed back her hair, meeting his stare, and his challenge. "Anything! Anything!" she cried. "Just as long as you get me away."

"Oh, I'll get you away! And then you'll only have to face those savage alligators and Indians—and me!" He turned away from her, staring at the friend who had taunted him into the situation. "Let's move, then. Robert—go ahead, get us ready to leave. Slip out now."

"Right!" Robert saluted. It was an adventure for him. Tara could see his handsome smile flashing brightly against the night.

He slipped out. A second later McKenzie had her arm. "Quickly!" he commanded, leading her from the dark room. In seconds they were rushing down the stairs and hurrying back down the street. The scenery seemed to flash by her. She had never moved so swiftly in all her life.

Suddenly he pulled her into an alleyway.

Someone was coming down the street. Running after them now that it seemed they had disappeared. She could hear the footsteps coming closer and closer. Within seconds she'd be able to touch the man stalking them in the night.

McKenzie knew it too. She could see it in his black eyes. But those eyes never left hers. At just the right moment he threw out his arm.

A man bellowed in the darkness, tripping. He was burly, half bald, and very vicious looking in the shadows as he picked himself up. He caught a glimpse of Tara, smiled, and started for McKenzie.

McKenzie let his fist fly once. It connected with the man's jaw. The big burly fellow went down with a little expulsion of air.

Tara stared down at him. McKenzie reached out a hand to her.

She didn't take it at first. She kept staring down at the man in amazement. "Is he dead?" she asked.

"No," he told her. He paused a moment. "Did you want him to be?"

"No!"

"Good."

She gazed up at him. Those dark eyes were still studying her, as if they could discern everything about her!

He shrugged. "It's good to know that you're not a bloodthirsty little wench. Even if he did deserve killing. Did he?"

"I'm not sure," she said.

"Somehow, I didn't think you would be. He was just a henchman for someone else, right?"

"I can't—"

"Dammit, you know who this one is, right?"

"Yes!"

"One down," he murmured. "For a while, at least."

"Can we go?" she murmured.

"I was just waiting for you to ask."

"*Where* are we going right now?" she whispered.

"To find a minister."

Tara stepped over the unconscious man on the ground. She

looked up at McKenzie, shaking her head. "You—you don't have to marry me!" she whispered. "I'll come with you anyway. You don't owe me. I owe you—"

"Three hundred dollars is much too much for a whore," he told her with a touch of amusement. "Besides which, I don't need one," he said a little harshly. For a moment his ebony gaze touched the stars in the dark sky. "Whores in this town are a dime a dozen," he said softly. "So maybe three hundred is fitting for a wife."

"Wives shouldn't be bought!" she whispered.

"No, they shouldn't," he agreed grimly.

His gaze was on her once again. "But I do need one. And you do need somewhere to go."

It was settled, so it seemed. His hand was around hers again, firm, compelling. She pulled back just a little. "McKenzie," she murmured, calling him by the only name she knew, "you know that the man back there wasn't alone."

"I know."

"Then—"

"I'll be watching."

They kept walking. Tara heard the lap of the Mississippi to their far left, drifting along in a slow motion. A ship's bell clanged somewhere out on the water.

McKenzie walked along easily enough. There were still shadows all around them. Shadows that moved. Shadows that frightened her in the night.

A cry escaped her. One of those shadows came leaping out from behind a trellis.

McKenzie suddenly thrust her behind him, spinning around.

"Let the girl go or you're a dead man!" The shadow demanded. He was no longer a shadow. He was flesh and blood. He wasn't quite as tall as McKenzie, but he was huskier. And he was brandishing a knife.

"No," McKenzie said simply. He hadn't even pulled a weapon.

"This ain't your fight!" the fellow warned him.

"She's with me!" McKenzie insisted. "Anyone will tell you. She's three hundred dollars on the gaming table. And I don't turn that kind of money over to anyone."

"You can damned well give me the girl, or I'll take her!"

McKenzie stood still.

"Do something!" Tara cried, terrified that he would underestimate an opponent.

She never would. She knew better.

But McKenzie hadn't underestimated the man. When the hulk lunged, McKenzie sidestepped him. Quick as a flash he spun, both fists coming down on the big man's neck.

Like his companion before him he fell very quietly and lay there without moving.

He looked up at Tara. "Did I do enough?" he asked wryly.

"Yes, quite enough!" she murmured back.

McKenzie stared at her. "Will there be more?" he asked. He sounded slightly aggravated.

She moistened her lips. "I don't know, I never know!" she cried out. She inhaled, still shaking. He wasn't even breathing hard. Jesu, if he should ever learn the truth about her.

"Let's go, then," he said. That edge of dark, contemptuous anger was in his voice again. She shivered suddenly, remembering the naked man in the darkness, the lithe way that he moved, like a panther in the night.

"I'm sorry, I can't do this," she gasped out. "I can't go with you. Because I never know—"

"Ah, but we're going down to the Seminoles and alligators!" he told her pleasantly, reaching for her hand again. "No one will dare follow you there!"

"But—?"

"We've made a bargain," he reminded her harshly, swinging her around suddenly so that her back was against the brick wall of a warehouse. His hands pinned her there on either side of her head. She could scarcely breathe. He fascinated her. Made her tremble.

And once again, made her afraid. She'd seen evidence of all she had imagined about him from one look in those ebony eyes. He could be merciful.

He could be ruthless.

"Do you wish to renege on our agreement?"

What did she have to lose?

She met his gaze with her chin high and shook her head in a silent no.

"Frightened?" he queried with the amused arch of a brow.

Damn him. She hadn't been beaten yet. And he wasn't going to get the best of her either!

"Bring on your alligators and savages," she said sweetly. "Heaven knows," she murmured, "they can't be worse than some of my relations!"

He laughed. "Some of them will *be* your relations!" he told her.

"What?"

He waved a dismissive hand in the air. "You won't have to worry unduly about either reptiles or Indians," he promised, then added softly, "But you will have to worry about me!"

"What do you mean?" The brick at her back seemed very cold.

"I'm marrying you because I want a wife," he said bluntly.

"So you've said!"

He shifted impatiently, his eyes still impaling hers. "I'd never force a whore," he continued, even more bluntly, "but I don't want a wife I'd need to force."

She tried to keep her eyes level with his. She really tried. They fell anyway.

"I know what wives—do," she said at last.

He lifted her chin. Damn, but his eyes could be like coals that burned, the devil's own!

"I said I know!" she whispered heatedly. "What more do you expect?" she cried.

"Good question. Maybe it's not so much a matter of what I expect, as it is of what I'd like!"

"Meaning?"

"Well, I'm afraid that I'm not just a nice individual—"

"I don't remember accusing you of such a thing!" Tara said, blurting out the words because she was so nervous.

But he still smiled. "I saw you the moment you walked into the room. And I wanted you the moment you walked into the room."

A wealth of color flooded to her cheeks again. Her lashes fell.

"My cards are all on the table," he said politely.

Was he still waiting for an explanation? Well he could wait from now until eternity! He wasn't getting one. "Fine," she said softly. "You want a wife. You'll get one." She looked up at him again and found those eyes impaling her once again. "A good one!" she cried. "I can do many things. I know how to manage a household—"

"I don't give a damn if you know how to manage a household or not," he drawled, smiling with a certain amount of amusement. "I accepted you as payment on a gambling table because you're incredibly beautiful. And I want you for the same reason. Still willing?"

"I'm willing."

"Just don't go back on any of your promises," he warned her.

"If I do?" she inquired, lifting her chin high again.

He really smiled then, brushing her cheek lightly with his knuckle. "I will be forced to see that you keep them!" he assured her.

She pushed his hand away and strode past him. She had to do this thing now and be done with it!

There would be more men to follow the two on the ground.

She swirled around, allowing her gaze to rise up and down his person, from his ebony dark hair to his high black boots.

"You'll do," she said coolly. "Can we get on with this?"

He started to laugh and strode the distance to her, setting an arm around her waist. She nearly leapt away at the searing touch.

"I'll do! What flattery! I won't do particularly well, but I'm better than the man you're running away from, is that it?"

"I never promised explanations!" she retorted. "Only to be—a good wife."

"And that you will be, my love. That you will be." He paused under a lamp for just a moment, searching out her eyes once again, his own a startling coal fire. She shivered fiercely, afraid to be in his arms. . . .

And yet suddenly longing to be there. It would be tempest, it would be flame! she warned herself. And her knees seemed to have turned to water. God, yes! Whatever else, he had already protected her twice. It was a new beginning!

"That I will be!" she repeated. She was marrying a total stranger. She swallowed hard. Yes, just let him get her away from here tonight. She would pay any price.

"Then let's get on with it, shall we?" he said.

"How? We can't just be married tonight—"

"Oh, my sweet innocent! We can do anything in New Orleans tonight. Anything we pay for! Just follow me, my love. Just follow me."

Through it all, she realized, she had never really believed that he was serious.

But he was.

An inquiry to a friend on a tawdry street—the friend was a bit tawdry looking too!—sent them to a nearby house. To her dismay Tara found herself wondering about McKenzie's relationship with the buxom blonde who had sent them on their way.

Whores. They were a dime a dozen. He had told her so.

But the woman had sent them to a duly appointed minister of the church, and the man promised to see to it that they were legally wed once he had a good look at McKenzie's gold pieces.

The minister called to his wife, and she came in, confused at first, but quick to understand that her husband was earning a very nice little stipend for the night's work. She told them they were a beautiful couple, then set her rosy cheeks into a stern pattern to stand and witness the ceremony. It was a strange wedding in their small, dusty parlor. Tara and McKenzie were both standing together in front of the minister before McKenzie turned to her, a very dry smile curving his mouth. "I don't even know your name."

"Tara. Tara Brent."

He studied her for a moment. "The last name doesn't matter anymore. It's McKenzie now. Tara McKenzie."

She opened her mouth to ask him his given name, but the very well paid minister had begun the ceremony.

His name was Jarrett. Jarrett McKenzie. She was married to him. There was a massive ring on her finger, which had come off his, and the magnitude of what she had done suddenly seemed to sweep down on her. Not just her knees, but the whole of her body seemed weak.

"You may now kiss your bride, Mr. McKenzie!" the minister told him.

She had never really known what *weak* could mean. He turned to her with the devil's own smile and swept her into his arms. His lips touched hers with a startling fire that burned and seemed to tear through the length of her, wet, hot, and evocative. She felt it in every limb, spiraling into some intangible center. Her lips parted. His tongue swept into her mouth. She clutched his shoulders as the world seemed to spin.

He set her down, staring at her again. He seemed to know that she would fall if he released her, because he continued to support her. There was hastily dug up champagne, a toast to the newlyweds.

He spoke politely with the minister and his wife. Then he took Tara's glass from her cold fingers and set it down on the buffet table in the hall. He took her hand. "Let's go."

She nodded, closing her eyes, praying for strength.

She had wanted to escape! She was certainly managing to do so.

"Now, Tara! Let's go!"

She was tempted to run again. Run as far as she could go, run forever. But she had made her promises.

And he had vowed that she would keep them.

She could run no longer.

Clive Carter of the Boston Carters, son of the late and illustrious Julian Carter, waited at the inn, seated at the table where the poker players had gambled fate just hours before.

He was immaculately dressed in a crisp white shirt, cobalt breeches, and maroon frock coat with an embroidered waistcoat beneath. He was a handsome man, and a prosperous one. A man to draw respect from those around him. His dark blond hair was neatly queued at his nape, his hazel eyes were steady on those around him. His hands rested upon the curve of a silver-tipped walking stick as he watched those around him.

Seething.

The idiots in this place! And to think that he had missed her by less than an hour. His own men had not returned. Two humanlike apes in the employ of the incredibly stupid proprietor of the place had failed to return as well.

This was preposterous. How many states had he traveled so far, seeking her?

He had to find her before William could come to her aid. He would not let her escape. This afternoon he had learned definitely where to find her. Now he was here—and the wretched woman had escaped him once again! It was not to be borne. And he dealt with such fools. From here on out he would have the law with him. The law, the military—he'd bring his own damned gallows and rope soon!

The babbling proprietor had told him that McKenzie had the girl as payment of a debt, and that they were aggressively searching for the pair, even though it would definitely mean trouble because McKenzie could be a difficult man himself when he chose to be so.

So some bastard McKenzie had the girl!

That had started the pounding and pulsing within his head. The cold, hard fury that gripped his soul and made his fingers tense upon the walking cane while he managed to show no other sign of the extent of the anger that burned through him like the boiling of a cauldron. God, but his very fingers itched to touch her, and she'd been taken by this man named McKenzie!

He'd get her, Clive assured himself. In the end he'd get her. He didn't know if he gave a damn whether it was alive or not anymore. She'd had every opportunity to choose to be with him. He'd managed to take everything that he had wanted from his father.

He would have shared it all with her.

She could have had velvet, lace, and luxury all the days of her life. Velvet, lace, luxury—and him. Now she would have the cold, dank steel of a prison door. She'd be broken, he'd see to that. And it would depend on just how prettily she could beg his pardon, and just how pretty she could stay in such wretched environs, and whether or not he'd see to it she ended her days at the end of a rope.

"Sir!" He stood, a man who had carefully watched politicians and men of means all his life. He kept his voice low, modulated, controlled. He was careful to be the embodiment of a man distressed, rather than one gripped by a deadly fury and obsession. "Who is this McKenzie? I must find Tara. It may mean her life! I have offered you a great reward, and more, sir, the very law is with me! If you refuse to aid me, I can only offer you the most dire consequences!"

Eastwood didn't like the look of this man. Such a man, so evidently from the heart of northern society, meant trouble. Eastwood cursed the night in silence. If this fellow had only appeared moments earlier, or if the Frenchie and McKenzie had only played poker elsewhere . . .

Eastwood was a morose fellow, and it didn't occur to him to blame himself for any of the tumult or drudgery that befell him. Not that it mattered. This fellow didn't want a piece of him. He just wanted Tara. And in Eastwood's mind the girl, with her high and mighty ways, deserved a downfall at this fellow's hands. If that's what the fellow intended. Strange. The man kept talking about the law, but he didn't want the law called in. Didn't matter to Eastwood. This man was offering five hundred dollars for her. She sure was paying her way now. Eastwood couldn't quite tell if this fellow wanted to strangle her or not. It was the girl's fault. She caused trouble, she was trouble. He'd known it the first time he'd seen her, he'd just thought that she was the kind of trouble that might make him a lot of money. Hell, she'd turned down many a good offer from a decent man—including Eastman himself!—but tonight she was getting her comeuppance. She was already making good on three hundred dollars and when she was finally returned, she'd be worth five.

She would come back eventually, Eastwood assured himself. McKenzie had just liked the look of her. And it wasn't that Eastwood was so friendly with McKenzie himself, but McKenzie came to New Orleans often enough, and naturally people talked about such a man. When he'd married a belle out of St. Augustine, he'd been the catch of the season, a rich, well-educated rake with a history of adventure behind him, a man determined on getting richer by settling and working freshly cleared lands just westward of the raw town of Tampa. McKenzie had made good, but the belle had died, and he now had the reputation of being a reckless adventurer once again. His interest in Tara Brent could only be fleeting.

There was no need to be unnerved, to stutter, to worry about this dandy demanding her now. All that he needed to think about was the kind of money—hard, cash money—he was going to make when she was returned. With that kind of money he could even make himself forget the way she made him feel when he tried to touch her, like he was something that crawled. She wouldn't be good once these fellows had all finished with her. Maybe, when his boys brought her back, he'd even find a way to have a few moments with her himself after all. Then she'd be sorry for the way she'd treated him.

And while she was still being sorry, she could go on to this dandy fellow here.

No matter what he wanted her for.

"Mr. Blank, I do assure you, my men are out there searching with the same fervor as your own. I am ready, sir—no eager—to see that she is delivered to you. As to McKenzie, well, sir, he is a planter out of Florida—"

"I will have him ripped to shreds!"

"No, sir, you don't want to tangle with him! He's a bit of a rogue himself, but highly respected by the law, a rich man, and a powerful one."

"No matter how powerful he is—".

"She will return here, sir, I swear it!"

Clive took his seat again, staring at Eastwood. A sardonic smile twisted his lips, his glittering eyes narrowed sharply upon the other man.

"For your sake, Mr. Eastwood, let's hope that she does! Indeed, sir, if you're a praying man, perhaps you should begin right now."

Eastwood felt a shiver seize him. And he wasn't a praying man at all, but suddenly . . .

He damned sure was praying.

Chapter 4

WHEN THE wedding was over, Jarrett McKenzie was determined that they move once again.

"Just where *are* we going now?" Tara asked him breathlessly, trying to keep up with him while he led her along, his hand upon her elbow.

"As far away from New Orleans as we can get," he told her curtly. She watched his dark profile and a hot tremor snaked along her spine. He was striking, rugged, and, at the moment, dead-set determined. Tall and powerful. He knew nothing about her, nothing at all.

But she also knew very little about him.

Those black eyes of his were suddenly staring down into hers once again. She flushed, aware of his scrutiny, and aware that he was aware of it.

"I was just wondering . . ." she murmured.

"What?"

"Where you learned to fight like that," she said softly.

He smiled dryly, arching a brow to her. "Like what?"

"So—fast," she said. "You knew when those men were behind

you. You threw that knife faster than that Frenchman could pull a trigger. I was just wondering—"

"Then you must just wonder away, right?" he interrupted, a challenge flashing in his dark eyes. "I promised you no questions. This is it, watch your step."

This was it—where were they? She hadn't been paying attention, but they had come back to the docks. Yet she couldn't see much of anything, other than darkness.

She nearly cried out with surprise when he suddenly lifted her, for it felt as if he meant to drop her right into the water. But she found herself set down in a small boat, and he was swiftly leaping down beside her. The night seemed to have grown very chill. She hugged her arms about herself while he released the tie rope from a wooden pillar and sent them drifting out into the Mississippi. He picked up the oars and a powerful thrust sent them shooting down the river.

He was quiet. A touch of moonlight fell upon the river, igniting it in a soft glow. Cold, she continued to hug herself, facing him. The moonlight did not touch the dark, craggy contours of his face, and she could not see his eyes, or read his expression.

"You're rowing us to Florida?" she asked at last.

She saw the white flash of his teeth as he smiled. "The *Magda* is just ahead," he assured her.

Tara twisted around and saw the much larger craft upon the water. Lanterns were lit, and the vessel seemed very warm and welcoming. She gazed at her new husband again, trying to grasp the fact that she had actually married a stranger. "Is it safe aboard her?" she asked softly.

"Well, I hope so. I own it."

"Oh."

"Robert told you I was rich," he reminded her, studying her eyes now. She wondered what he was looking for within her.

"What didn't he tell me?" she asked him.

"A lot, I hope. If we're to lead mystery lives, it's only fair that some part of my own past be kept secret, don't you think?"

She shrugged, wishing she hadn't spoken. And then she found herself thinking again about the way he had come to her rescue. He was amazingly quick, almost as if he were invincible. He had knocked out two men without even raising a sweat. And when the Frenchman had pulled that gun . . .

Yes, he was quick, and hard, and could show little pity. What if he discovered the truth about the woman he had married? A second tremor came cascading down her spine, and this time she felt very cold.

"Hello there!" came a friendly voice in the night. The oars lapped against the water once again, and then the dinghy was knocking against the sides of the *Magda*. It wasn't a huge ship, Tara thought, but it did stretch at least seventy feet. She was sleek and new, an elegant ship. As they drew alongside her, Tara saw his handsome young friend Robert with the quick, easy smile staring down at them. A rope ladder was tossed down to them.

"Can you manage?" her husband asked her.

"Yes," she said quickly. Too quickly. When she stood, she was afraid she was going to teeter right over. He caught her, at ease with the little boat rocking dangerously, and set her fingers about one of the rope rungs. "I'll be right behind you."

Within seconds she was aboard the *Magda*, McKenzie at her rear should she falter, and Robert on deck to sweep her over the rail. He was still grinning broadly, apparently very much pleased with what he considered *his* night's work.

"Welcome, Mrs. McKenzie!" Robert said, catching both her hands and drawing her near to kiss her cheeks good-naturedly. She realized that there were four more men on the deck, watching, waiting, and a blush touched her cheeks. But McKenzie was behind her now, his hands on her shoulders. "Gents, this is my wife, Tara. Tara, the first mate there is Leo Hume, and these other riffraff sailors are Ted and Nathan Nailor, and George Adair."

"Hello," she murmured, but the group of them grinned, bowing in return. The oldest of the lot seemed to be the one introduced as Ted Nailor, who she assumed must be Nathan's father, for he seemed to be about forty, while Nathan couldn't have been much more than seventeen. Both were stockily built redheads with freckled noses and quick, flashing grins. Leo Hume was dark and somewhat swarthy, as if there might have been a very dark Spaniard somewhere in his past, too, while George Adair was very tall and lean and dark haired and light eyed.

Ted was the one to address her, sweeping his cap from his head and bending very low. "Mrs. McKenzie, we are all ever-pleased to meet you—surprised, we do admit!—but delighted, and eager to serve you in any way!"

She smiled and was startled by the sudden prick of tears at the back of her eyes. She suddenly felt very much protected and surrounded by warmth. After so long a time of running, and after the people who had filled her life lately. . . .

She closed her eyes. For a moment she could remember the busy streets of the very well-established city she had so recently fled. To her the city had been a dream. She had once thought that her future was there, and all that she needed to do was form it with her own two hands. It was different from the land of her birth, that of the rolling fields she had loved so well, but a place where too many people fought a land that refused to give a yield, where too many little children went hungry. A place where the very future lay in escape, no matter what the beauty.

She had been eager and so ready to love the city. It had been filled with elegant buildings, manicured parks. There had been people everywhere. Clad in fine furs and jackets when the winters came and the temperatures plummeted. The men were concerned with business, the women with the latest fashions. The men talked politics, the women raved over the most recent musician to come to town; they laughed, lowered their voices, talked about one another. Society was tight. If the doors were shut upon one, they stayed closed. The matrons could judge harshly, watch like hawks. She'd been so careful. She'd tried so very hard to be correct. But it hadn't really saved her. She'd nearly won, but *he'd* arranged it to appear that she had killed the one man who had done so much for her.

It would be cold there now. The first snows would have fallen. Everything would be clean and white. Beautiful, but cold. Like him. Like the man she had fled. A man who could spill the blood of his own closest kin to acquire what he wanted.

And he had been close tonight.

She had almost been seized.

When she thought of what the night might have brought, the tremors caught hold of her again. She shivered and felt the tightening of long, powerful fingers on her shoulder. McKenzie. He had brought her here. She had to remember that. With no questions about her past.

"Let's get her under way, shall we, mates?" he asked lightly. "We want to be far gone by morning."

"Aye, aye, sir!" Ted agreed, but he smiled again to Tara. His eyes caught McKenzie's over her head. "We've done the best we could, sir, on such short notice. But I think you'll find your cabin amenable."

He turned around, shouting an order to weigh anchor. The men all scurried to their posts, all flashing her smiles as they did so. The hands on her shoulders suddenly propelled her along the deck.

"Let's see what they've managed to find, shall we?"

He urged her down the deck to a crossways where the mainmast separated two cabins. Double polished doors led to his own, and he pushed them open ahead of her. Once again she blinked, adjusting to the muted light.

A single candle burned upon a large desk in the center of the cabin. Two silver trays were set on either side of the desk, covered and awaiting. It was a very handsome cabin with brass sconces set in the walls and brass accents on the desk and shelving. A large globe was set to the right side of the desk, and portside was a surprisingly large bunk. More surprisingly there was a large wooden bathtub that also sat to the portside of the cabin, and there were streams of steam wafting from it that seemed almost magical in the very dim light.

"They've planned well," McKenzie murmured dryly. Striding by her he found something on the bunk that she had not seen herself. Tara felt a deep coloring flood her cheeks as she saw that it was a very pale blue nightgown.

Well, what had she expected? She had married him, she had agreed that she would be a wife. It was just that he was here now, dominating the cabin with his dark height and subtle masculine scent and power, and she wasn't just trembling, she was shaking.

"Supper and a bath. I imagine the bath looks best to you at the moment. Nice and hot."

Actually the Mississippi looked better at the moment. Nice and cold. She suddenly couldn't move. Thank God for the darkness that at least cast shadows over their eyes.

There was a bottle of wine on the table between the two trays, wedged between two crystal glasses. Someone had already uncorked it. McKenzie poured out a glass and brought it to her. The shadows weren't enough. She felt his eyes while he pressed the wineglass into her fingers, then swirled her around. "Swallow quickly," he suggested. "It might take the edge off the night."

She did so mechanically, not realizing at first that by doing so she was agreeing to the fact that the night definitely had an edge that needed to be taken off.

Once again she discovered that he had a talent and a flair for removing women's clothing. Her laces were all freed by a deft touch from his fingers. Her back remained to him, and she suddenly walked away, eyeing the wine bottle herself. She stood at the table and poured out a second glass and swallowed it quickly. It was tasting better and better. She lifted the bottle again, but discovered that he was behind her, plucking the bottle from her fingers. "I want you to take the edge off, my love. Not go catapulting over it!"

"Does it make a difference?"

"Yes!"

He turned her in his arms again, black eyes meeting hers as he lifted her chin. He stared at her a moment, then his mouth lowered to hers. Warm, sweeping, liquid, his lips formed to hers while his tongue pressed the barrier, filling her. His arms wrapped around her, encompassing her tightly so that she felt him with the length of her body, the steely strength, the hardness of his chest and thighs, the startling bulk of his arousal. She might have stiffened, might have bolted, except for the sheer seduction of his kiss. His lips were mercurial fire, forming to hers, the fullness of his tongue invading and stroking, sweeping the liquid heat into her mouth, and through her body. A sweetness pervaded her system along with a ragged pounding that turned out to be that of her heart. She had played at love before. She had never imagined that it could be like this. Feeling a touch. Feeling it invade her. Feeling the mercury slip and sweep and spiral into her. He played and played at her mouth. Coaxing, ravaging, seducing. She could scarcely stand, yet his arms held her. His mouth lifted from hers at last and his black eyes tore into hers. "Too awful?" he whispered.

She shook her head, swallowing hard, and then she was ashamed of herself that she could so quickly be so taken with a stranger, even if it was a stranger who had married her. It was also incredibly irritating to realize that she was nicely amusing him.

He laughed suddenly, knuckles stroking her cheek. "It's only going to be all right if you suffer somehow, do your duty?"

"Don't make fun of me!" she lashed back quickly, her eyes rising to shoot blue flames into his. But she discovered that he was studying her intently once again, seeking the answers that she could not give him.

"Then again," he murmured, his arms still strong around her, black eyes speculative, "you could know exactly what you're doing. The night may hold no surprises at all."

She inhaled on a gasp, her temper rising swiftly with her nervousness. Her fingers bit back against the arms holding her so tightly. "I told you in the middle of your stupid poker game that I was no man's whore."

"And I didn't accuse you of being so now," he interrupted harshly. "You've quite a temper, madam."

She tossed back her hair, well aware that a good part of her anger was nervousness, and unable to control it anyway. "If you married me for my docility—"

"Not a chance," he promised, unaware that she was setting any pressure against him at all. "I married you for your hair."

"My hair!" She gasped, somehow dismayed. What had she been expecting? *She'd married a stranger, a powerful, handsome stranger who had rescued her from a worse fate!*

She pushed hard against him, freeing herself at last, and spinning around the other side of the desk to accost him. "I could have just chopped off the length of it!" she told him. "Tied it in a ribbon! I—"

"It wouldn't have been the same," he said, still amused, not at all dismayed that she seemed to be running. "It needs to be attached to your head, and then go cascading around the two of us. I married you for your hair and much more. But your hair was the first thing I noticed about you. It attracted my attention. Until I saw more." He grinned suddenly. "In the room," he said very softly.

She flushed furiously, tongue tied for the moment. He walked around the desk to her side of it, arms crossed over his chest. He sat on the edge of the desk, watching her. "Now, my love, as to my earlier statement, there was no accusation there. Unless you're a really fantastic actress? Ah, that's right, no questions. Well, it seems you have come from some gentle life, with some decent income. But you're running away, so you might have been running from a husband."

"And I told you I wasn't married—before," she stated, adding the last a little breathlessly.

"My dear girl, one doesn't have to be married to engage in intimacies."

"Well, I haven't engaged in anything!" she breathed out miserably, wishing that he hadn't pinned her so. Her gaze fell again. She really had no right to be angry—she was the one who didn't want to answer questions, and she supposed that meant he might draw his own conclusions.

He slipped from the edge of the desk. She almost screamed when he caught her arms, pulling her against him again. "The water is growing cold," he said very softly, his whisper warm and evocative as he spoke, his lips just inches from her own. That breath of air suddenly sent a jagged heat shooting through her once again. He was an experienced lover, she realized. Talented, and . . . experienced.

Her eyes fell from his. "So is the food!" she murmured.

"But it will wait. I, alas, will not!" He set her atop the desk suddenly, slipping her shoes from her feet. A sweeping crimson swept over her with the surge of warmth that seared her as his fingers deftly crawled her thighs to find her stockings. Then she was set upon her feet again, heart still pounding, mind still reeling. He turned her swiftly in his arms, and she was aware once more of his incredible ease with women's fashions as ties and hooks were deftly undone. She felt him at her back while her gown, petticoats, pantalettes, and corset fell to the floor. She was painfully, achingly aware of him at her naked back, but the unease did not last for long. A gasp escaped her when she was picked up and set into the tub, her fingers catching hold of the rim as if she would drown within it.

He caught hold of the long cascades of her hair, twisting them in his fingers to keep the mass from falling into the water. The dampness seemed to trickle up her shoulders. Then she felt him, knelt or hunched down behind her, the warmth of his breath at her nape, sweeping her earlobe, touching her throat. His lips pressed against her shoulder. Instinctively she hugged her knees to her chest, shivering despite the steaming heat of the water and that of his light caress. His lips moved, touching her lower on her shoulder, center, against her nape, against her throat. The stroke of his finger moved downward along her arm. In all of her life she'd never known sensations so acute, so intense, touching one place but ripping through the length of her. Sensations so hot, so gripping, so erotic. . . .

She'd never even really imagined *erotic* before, and here it was, this touch.

She had to fight it, she thought vaguely. She might get lost within it.

He lifted her chin, turning her head just slightly. His lips found hers once again. His fingers stroked and held her cheek. His tongue delved into the depths of her mouth once again, provocative, thrusting, discovering. His fingers drew delicate patterns down her throat, and caressed her shoulders. Fell lower and encompassed her breast. Closed over it, the palm of his hand moving in a caressing fashion over the hardening peak.

Some small sound came from her throat and was caught in his kiss. His lips parted from hers. His eyes rose above hers. Her lips were parted and damp, her breath was coming far too swiftly. She closed her eyes against his ebony scrutiny. Fingers wound into her hair, pulling her head gently back. His kiss fell against her throat. His hand continued its bold and evocative caress.

Maybe she didn't have to fight this. She had married him. Married this stranger. He had swept her from the sheer danger and disaster in New Orleans, so just how much more did she need to know?

"Ease up, my love," he whispered, his voice tinged with just a touch of amusement again. Her eyes flew open, and she realized that she was still trying to hug her knees to her chest. Her eyes met his and she felt a rush of embarrassment again, but though his smile was amused, it was also curiously tender. "I've been with you naked before," he reminded her, his tone now definitely wicked, challenging.

She closed her eyes. The steam was very warm. The wine had indeed taken away the edge. She sank farther into the water, her head resting back on the rim. His lips touched her throat.

Skimmed along it, the tip of his tongue slick at the cleft at the center of her collarbone. Her fingers curled around the rim of the tub again. She felt absurdly lethargic in one way while her heart raced in another. His hand was in the tub. He'd found the sponge within it. Water dripped over her knees. The clean scent of soap filled her senses along with his touch, gentle, lulling . . . *erotic.* The sponge moved against her. Along her calf, her thigh. Her belly, her breasts. And once again his lips were against her throat. She couldn't seem to find the strength to move or to protest. . . .

Or to reach out in return.

His kiss moved up her throat now, touched upon her lips once again, tasting, savoring. A light touch, a slow, fluid movement of his tongue. She didn't even notice when he dropped the sponge, yet felt the graze of his fingers upon her once again. Touching her cheek, brushing it so tenderly in that tantalizing kiss. He raised his lips from hers. A sudden coldness descended upon her and she vaguely wondered why.

And then she knew.

He was naked, and she was in his arms, the steaming bathwater dripping down them both. All the things that had fascinated her before were now hers to touch. The gleaming bronze muscles of his chest were taut and slick, the thick mat of hair was coarse, teasing her flesh. She clung to his shoulder, her arms slipping around his neck. Her eyes met his and there were some very different gleams in the ebony depths now, and she knew that it had come full time to be his wife.

She shivered suddenly, violently, not repelled by him, but frightened a little just the same. *What had she imagined this night to be?*

She didn't know. She had been running too long.

Never this intimacy with a stranger.

But she had married the stranger, and oddly enough, he did not seem so terribly strange anymore, indeed, she already knew him better than she had known any man before.

He felt her shivering, and cradled her more tightly against

him. He carried her the few steps to the bunk and held her against his length with one hand while he wrenched the covers free from the bunk to lay her upon the whiteness of the sheets. Her eyes locked with his as he crawled over her. She looked down over the bronzed breadth of his shoulders, the dark matted expanse of his chest. His waist was lean and tight. And below that . . .

Her breath caught and her gaze rose back to his. The shivering that had begun in her became a rampant trembling.

He watched her with an amused expression, yet one that was tender still, setting his fingers into the wealth of her hair to spread the tendrils out upon the pillow.

"You are, my mystery love, extremely beautiful," he told her very softly. His voice was husky and rich still, lulling, yet something more. So seductive. She no longer shivered because of the cold. She trembled now because of the staggering warmth that touched and pervaded her.

She moistened her lips and whispered in turn, "Worth three hundred dollars?" The words carried only a hint of mockery against herself.

His lips curled into a sensuous smile, and he leaned low against her, just brushing her mouth with the breath of a kiss. "Worth a million dollars," he told her.

The warmth of the sun seemed to explode within her. Her lashes fluttered over her eyes.

"I'm afraid not!" she murmured very softly.

"I will judge."

"But I don't—"

"You don't need to."

Those were the last of his words. He fell to her side, sweeping her into his arms. What had begun in the liquid heat of the tub now came to the soft warmth of the bed. His lips touched hers again. Softly, briefly. Then that touch was gone. His mouth closed gently upon the aroused peak of her nipple, his tongue laving the rouge bud again and again. A scorching swept through her, shooting like a falling star to burst in shattering fragments of light throughout her. He continued to arouse and caress her breast with the hunger of his lips while his hand swept down the length of her. Stroked her hip, her thigh. A slow, feather soft touch. She longed to press his hand away.

And she longed to feel it closer. . . .

Her fingers dug into his shoulders; she closed her eyes, trying again to fight the feeling of heat, for it was overwhelming. Then she saw his eyes above hers, so deeply black again. There was no laughter in them now, rather something dark and intense. He studied her briefly, then caught her lips once again. Kissed and kissed her, tasting, exploring with his lips. . . .

And with his demanding caress. The fingers that had feathered so softly over her thighs were feather light no more. His hand kneaded over the soft mound of golden hair at the juncture of her thighs. She felt his kiss still, but her breath caught and she rippled with tension. Yes, farther, parting, stroking, delving. Gently parting petals of flesh and stroking once again. . . .

She dug her nails heedlessly into his flesh, while a wave, as of molten honey, came cascading down upon her. She tried to tighten against him, somewhat amazed, somewhat afraid. His lips broke from hers at last. Breathless, trembling, she met his gaze, tensing again. "No," he commanded very gently. Her lashes fluttered shut against his ebony stare once again, and still she felt his gaze sweeping her. "Worth a million!" he repeated in a soft, husky whisper once again, sending the searing honey to skip down her spine and into her limbs once again. What now?

Oh, God . . .

His lips fell in a series of slow, leisurely kisses. Then she felt the pressure on her thighs. Felt them parted, felt his weight. Felt the searing beat of his sex so briefly against her and then . . .

Now, now . . . no.

His weight suddenly brought lower, his body a bulwark parting her. She nearly shrieked aloud with the first jagged streak of sun that seemed to pervade her as he kissed her anew. This touch parting, delving, stroking, just as his fingers had done before. Her fingers fell upon his shoulders, she swallowed upon her cry, twisting her head into the pillow. His large bronze hands enclasped her hips, holding her steady to his will. She writhed, desperate for a moment to escape anything so sweetly intimate, but writhing only caused a greater sensation and she went still, realizing that she could not free herself from this lover's caress.

Nor did anything cause the sensations to cease. . . .

Wave after liquid wave of searing sweetness began to cascade through her, and she could no longer remain still.

Nor did she twist in protest, for somewhere in his seductive assault he had touched upon a magic she had never known existed. She moved because she had to move. Because his fiery caress demanded 'that she undulate beneath it. He paused, just briefly. She cried out, embarrassed, dismayed, and still yearning. Then his touch came again. The tip of his tongue. So light, she could scarce feel it. Then deeper, deeper . . .

"No!" the anguished cry escaped her lips. He paid no heed. She had not meant that he should.

She flew, she soared, she reached and reached, and did not know for what she was reaching. Her head began to toss, and a whimpering sound filled the air, and she realized dimly that she was the one emitting the cries. . . .

A blistering heat seemed to pervade her, bursting and spilling from that tender bud of desire he had so assuredly awakened, streaking out like the rays of the sun to fill her torso and limbs with shimmering golden warmth. It was staggering, so achingly sweet, sweeping away thought and reason.

It was then, only then, that he rose above her. She lay too stunned to protest, to worry—to fear him at all. This time the fullness of his weight wedged firmly between her legs. And despite the wealth of sensation that still surrounded her, she came quickly to full reality when he first thrust into her. She could not scream, would not scream, when the whole of the boat might hear her! But as careful a lover as he had been, the pain was staggering. Tears leapt to her eyes. She buried her head hard against the muscles of his chest, trying not to let them spill from her eyes.

His hand cupped her cheek. She could not meet his eyes. She was suddenly certain that she could never do so again. "It's all right," he whispered. "It's all right. . . ."

It wasn't all right. She wanted to shake herself from him. It felt as if there were a sword slicing into her!

"Please, God!"

"It will pass, I swear it."

Like it or not, he rose above her, and forced her eyes to his. She blinked furiously, determined that she wasn't going to be a coward now. But she could scarce stand it and he hadn't even begun to move. And she knew that he would. That he would be seeking that shattering splendor he had managed to touch within her. . . .

"It will not be so bad," he whispered softly, watching her eyes. "Remember, I swept you away from some fate worse than death!"

"Death might be just fine right now!" she murmured, and he laughed, but there was something tender in that laughter, and she knew that whatever might come in the black void of a future that loomed before her, she could never fault him for tonight. Just when she thought that she would truly die with the pain, his whisper came against her lips. "Did I say you were worth one million? Make it at least two . . . no, there can be no value set upon you. You are priceless."

Luckily he clasped her to him, for the tears did fall from her eyes. Not from the pain, from the sweet gift of the words. In all of her life no one had spoken so gently to her.

Let it come. Let the pain come . . .

And it did. But oddly enough, as he had promised, it was fleeting. And to her absolute amazement the wonder began to build again. Magical sunrays reached throughout her to touch her. The searing hot pulse of his sex, so alien at first, brought thrusts of silver to shimmer throughout her. Slow at first, so very slow, sliding into her until she thought she would be split in two, until she was filled with it, feeling it from her womb to her heart. Yet she was barely aware when he quickened his pace, when the tension riddled his body so hotly that he could no longer make love with control. All she knew was that she was suddenly swept into it. And it was magic again, the sunrays streaking out, the molten honey coursing through her. She wanted him, wanted something, wanted desperately to taste and touch and feel it all again. . . .

And she did. Raw splendor exploded all around her. Went to blackness. She wasn't sure that she lived, that she breathed. But he was with her still, with her when the black curiously faded to light. She felt the massive, terrible tension of his body, then a thrust that once again seemed to tear her apart. Then the honey again, streaming and racing into her, filling her with something sweet and warm. . . .

He fell to his side beside her, his breathing as ragged as her own, his muscles slick with sweat and glistening. She closed her eyes, biting into her lower lip, both exalted with this wedding night and still embarrassed by it.

She hadn't even known him before this night.

His arm was around her. She curled against his chest, grateful, for the moment, that she didn't have to meet that searching ebony stare of his. His thumb moved over her cheek.

"Tears," he murmured. "I'm sorry to have hurt you."

"I am not hurt," she said. But she was, of course. Now that the shattering magic was gently fading away, she could feel the soreness begin.

He was silent for a long time. "Well, at least you aren't running from a husband—we know that now."

She stiffened, wishing she could withdraw from him and walk away, but she was naked and not at all sure that she could just rise naked before him.

She turned her back on him instead, staring at the candle that was now burning low on the desk between their two dinners.

"I told you that I was not married," she said. He didn't reply. Oddly, tears stung her eyes all over again. He hadn't taken her at her word. He had helped her, but he didn't really trust her or believe in her. "I told you!" she insisted.

"Well," he said, a very light edge to his voice, "you'll have to forgive me." She felt his hand on her arm then. He brooked no opposition when he rolled her around to meet his eyes. "There *is* so very much that you haven't told me."

He had changed. The considerate lover was gone. He was different. Ruthless. Yes, he could be so, she was learning, when he chose. She swallowed hard, assessing the man with his ebony dark eyes, hard-planed face, and sleek-muscled build.

"You chose to marry me with no explanations," she reminded him.

"So I did."

"Then"—she lifted her chin—"are you reneging now?"

"We can't renege on what is done, can we?" he asked her.

Her cheeks colored. She didn't know if he meant the wedding, or the moments that had just passed between them.

"No," she murmured. Her eyes fell down the length of him. He lay so relaxed at her side, his body at ease, but even so, still powerful in its taut build. Just seeing him so created a living warmth within her once again, and to her horror she discovered herself looking at him. Really looking at him. The length of his hair-matted torso. Lower. Down to the ebony nest where . . .

He was at ease. He was still very long and thick. And even as she stared at him, he grew longer. . . .

Her eyes flew to his. She needed to talk. To say something. "No!" she whispered. "We can't undo anything. I'm sorry if you're disappointed—"

It was as far as she got. His husky, sensual laughter rang out and his arms were around her, sweeping her back beneath him.

"Disappointed? My dear little runaway! I have never been so delightfully surprised in all my life!"

"But I—"

His mouth covered hers, sweeping away her words. He was rougher this time. *Hungrier.* More demanding. . . .

And more giving.

Within minutes he had the past swept from her mind.

And she didn't care about the future.

And when the sweet climax seized her this time, it was volatile and shattering, ever more magical. When it was over she lay beside him in silence, her eyes closed, as her breathing slowed and her heart ceased to pound so swiftly.

If he spoke to her then, she didn't hear it. She began to drift to sleep, exhausted by all that had come between them.

Jarrett lay awake a long while, holding her, his own past arising to haunt him, even as he wondered about hers.

The ache of loss had been with him so very long. He had clung to it, clung to the memories. He had needed a wife, that was very true. And now he had one.

He had never expected to feel quite this way about her.

What way? he challenged himself. He barely knew her! She was a runaway, using him to escape.

Well, maybe he was a runaway too.

Using her to escape.

He moved a tendril of deep golden hair from her cheek and stroked the alabaster purity of her skin. He looked down the length of her, feeling a sexual quickening from the mere sight of her. There was a sense of possessiveness about him now. She had been telling the truth about her work—she had served the tables at Eastwood's place and nothing more! The proof was spilled vividly upon the white sheets where she now lay, still entwined with him. She was amazing, he thought. Beautiful, exquisite.

He had demanded no explanations. He had promised not to demand any.

He swallowed hard, clenching down on his teeth. For a moment he felt a tremendous guilt. He remembered his first wedding night, the laughter, the words that had flowed, the hunger that encompassed both of them! And now she was gone, and he had actually forgotten her tonight in the arms of his little runaway.

The past was gone, he told himself. Dead. Buried. His past. Tara's past. She could keep hers. He would keep his own.

She shifted beside him, the softness of her skin brushing his.

He rose carefully and walked across the cabin to the desk. Their dinners remained there, untouched. He should have been starving. He wasn't. His body still remained in a hot tempest.

He lifted the wine bottle and drank straight from it, then set it back on the table. He stared for long moments into the nothingness of the night. Then he came and knelt down beside her, studying the fine lines of her face once again.

Her eyes opened. Dazed, so blue they were near violet. They touched his.

He smiled and touched her lips with the tip of his fingers. She started to rise. He shook his head and swept her into his arms.

"To the future, my love," he murmured softly. "To the future."

And he made love to her again. After all, it was their wedding night.

And he had been right about one thing. She was absolutely priceless.

Clive Carter still waited as the darkness slowly lifted to day, as lamplighters extinguished the flickering flames that had both illuminated and shadowed the sins of the city through the night. Hours had passed. Carter had not betrayed the extent of his impatience or anger even once.

He was the son of a reknowned politician, the only child of a rich, respected man. He had watched as the games of sweet coercion had been played many a time in the politics of state and country, and the greatest lesson he had learned throughout was that a calm demeanor always stood a man well, no matter the events that occurred around him.

Or what events he created himself.

The wretch Eastwood had become something of a blithering

idiot. Clive's two bodyguards were still among the missing. The men Eastwood had sent out had returned, sputtering out some kind of explanations regarding how they had found the girl and saying that McKenzie had refused to return her until his time was up. Sent out again, they had returned with the information that both McKenzie and the girl had disappeared.

"McKenzie must be made to return her," Carter told Eastwood, his voice still a level shield over the twist of emotions seething inside of him.

Eastwood, red in the face, sweat upon his heavy jowls, and a look that combined fear and anguish in his eyes, threw up his hands. "McKenzie is gone. The girl has escaped into the streets again, so it seems. She must be found!"

Clive tapped his cane upon the floor with impatience. "Indeed, sir, she must be found. McKenzie is abetting a murderess, I tell you. Have someone bring him down—"

"It is not a feat so easily done! He is a respected and wealthy man, and more. He—"

"And more?" Clive Carter inquired curiously. "What more can there be?"

"It is rumored he can wrestle alligators!" Eastwood said.

Carter cast back his head and laughed.

"Send your men out again, Eastwood. Find out what has become of Tara Brent. This man who wrestles alligators can be killed with a bullet through the brain, the same as any other."

"Mr. Carter! I fear that you do not understand! The law will no longer be on your side if you tangle with this man!"

"Ah!" Carter said softly. "Find the information for me that I need. You have failed dreadfully so far, sir."

Eastwood sucked in some air and hurried to the door where his men waited, sending them out into the night once again. While he stood there, one of Eastwood's burly fellows, holding his head between his palms, emerged from the foggy pink mist of dawn.

Eastwood nearly jumped to realize that Carter had come behind him.

"Well, what?" he demanded of his own man.

"She had a fellow with her, sir. Fast as an Injun. I went down. I lost track of 'em."

Eastwood snorted and swung on Clive. "Didn't I tell you so? You can't just reach out and take her if McKenzie's got it in his mind to keep her."

"What fine advice," Clive murmured, staring at Eastwood. Eastwood really was a wretched little man. His eyes were beady. He was sweaty, fat. Smelly. A lowlife.

"For the right amount of money I can find McKenzie! It may take some time and expenses—he is sailing back to Florida," Eastwood said. "I know about him," the man boasted. "Where to find him!"

"I imagine I can find him as well," Clive said. Eastwood was actually revolting. His teeth were rotten; absolute greed had replaced the hint of fear in his eyes. Clive shuddered, repulsed, hating the obnoxious little man whose money-hungry ways had already cost him the girl tonight.

Clive smiled and tapped his cane upon the floorboards with a single hard strike. A small, razor-sharp blade suddenly protruded from the tip of it. Without exerting more than a modicum of energy Clive Carter suddenly lifted and swung the cane.

Eastwood threw his hands to his throat. The blood that suddenly spewed from his jugular vein flowed and bubbled between his fingers. Still staring at Clive in amazement, he keeled over, dead almost instantly.

Clive looked to his man. "Drop this refuse in the river. See that a rumor is started that the girl returned and did him in before running away again."

His man did as bidden, collecting the body in an expert manner that didn't allow the blood to run upon the floorboards.

The muddy Mississippi had claimed many another poor soul; it would take Eastwood now, and throw him up elsewhere later.

No one would take much heed, Clive thought dismissively. Men like Eastwood died almost daily along the river docks, the whorehouses, and the gambling establishments. Sometimes, Clive thought, life could be so cheap.

Eastwood had deserved to die.

Oddly enough, so had Julian Carter.

But then, some things had to be planned so much more meticulously than others.

He still felt the burning within him. The fury that she had managed to elude him so far. What ate away inside him was to realize that she'd been willing to sell to anyone rather than accept all that he'd had to offer.

He had to be very careful now. He couldn't talk about the law; he had to have the law. He had to move slowly and carefully this time.

He sat down again, drumming his fingers on one of Eastwood's tables. She'd not have told this man the truth. She'd have seduced him into aiding an escape of some kind. Clive would have to plan carefully to get her back. Very carefully. He would not be coming to persecute her, but to defend her. And he would do so because . . .

He smiled slowly.

Clive knew he would need the proper papers, of course. But then, anything could be bought.

Almost anything at all.

He'd play it on her terms.

But he'd find her. Find her and drag her back. And he didn't care if he had to go to Florida or hell itself to do it.

Actually, from all that he had heard, they were probably one and the same.

Chapter 5

JARRETT DIDN'T awake himself the following morning until an annoying tap upon his door finally entered into his sleep-numbed mind. He arose, discovered his naked body, swept up his sheet—then remembered that he was leaving a naked wife behind him. He scowled, threw the covers quickly upon her, and drew on his breeches. The knocking continued.

He threw open the door to the cabin and found Robert waiting. His friend wasn't at all apologetic but leaned against the door frame, studying his nails. "Sorry to disturb you, *Captain*, but your crew are awaiting a few orders." He tried to look over Jarrett's shoulder into the cabin. "Well?" he whispered.

"Well?" Jarrett responded blandly.

Robert grinned. "How's your bride?"

"Sleeping. When she awakens, you must ask her yourself. And if she's unhappy, remember, it will be your fault."

"My fault?" Robert demanded indignantly.

"This marriage was your idea."

"Right! So you behave like a brute, and it's my fault."

"I behave like a brute?" Jarrett demanded irritably.

Robert shrugged. "Well, the poor thing is passed out in your cabin."

Jarrett gritted his teeth and Robert laughed, quickly stepping out of the way. "My captain, my captain! You're needed. And since I'm fond of my features remaining in the order I was born with, I'll quickly leave you, and say no more! But the men are wondering about your orders for the voyage home, sir!" With a smart salute he turned about to leave. Jarrett closed the door and walked back into his cabin. His wife was out. She slept so very still, barely breathing. He paused, taking a moment to watch her, and realized again that he had not known her just the day before. It seemed amazing. He was married. And whatever truths she was keeping from him, she had held to her part of the bargain last night. Perhaps more than he had even imagined, for he had not thought to feel this morning as if slender golden chains were slipping around him. He had definitely meant to have her—that from the start. Yet he had not expected that he . . .

That he what?

Her lashes were long and thick and luxurious over her cheeks this morning. Her hair still reminded him of skeins of gold. Her flesh was ivory, her shape exquisite. But he had known all that as well. He had just imagined something different.

His ship was sleek and fine, and he loved to sail it, but he could walk away from it, and not miss it. He was deeply fond of his horse as well, rode hard and frequently, and yet could walk away from it too.

And with Lisa gone, once Robert's suggestion had been made, he had, perhaps, thought of a wife in the same light. Something to have, to use, to set aside, to care for and tend, and yet . . .

Walk away from. Forget.

He leaned hard upon the cabin door frame for a second, mocking himself. Wives were living women, not ships. Nor beasts of burden. Yet that was what he had wanted, what he had expected. To have her, aye, use her well, carefully tend her—walk away. And he hadn't even known quite what he had wanted until he had realized it was not what he had gotten. He was entangled in that golden hair. Now that he had awakened after such an evening, he was still convinced that she was, indeed, priceless.

And that he was going to pay the price. He had certainly never expected the emotions she had wrung from him, and he felt oddly defensive and displeased. He was no longer willing to play her game. He wanted more from her. More than what she had given. He wanted what she held away from him, all the truth of who and what she was. He had promised not to demand it.

His shoulders squared and his back stiffened as he strode to the foot of the bunk and studied her anew. He yearned to wake her, to hold her again. To inspect her from head to toe, touch her . . . have her, feel that he could somehow demand in such a way what she remained unwilling to give. But he wouldn't wake her, not now. And he swore beneath his breath, for he had promised not to make demands.

But neither would he give her any of himself, he determined. Any of his past.

Thus determined, he turned his eyes from the tangle of hair that covered her throat and breasts, and swore again as he dressed. He went to the helm and found Robert at the wheel, and discovered, to his surprise, that he might well be needed, for the sun clearly showed him that he had slept through the morning and into the afternoon. Even as he approached the wheel, Leo strode up behind him with a steaming cup of hot coffee.

"We didn't know which way y'had in mind of traveling, Captain!" Leo told him, offering the cup.

"Winds have been low, we're just off the coast of Pensacola now," Robert told him. "Did you want to stop?"

Jarrett hesitated a moment and then shook his head. They'd come into New Orleans for Christmas day, and it was already January second. He realized that he'd taken a wife on the first day of the year. He didn't know if that meant anything or not, but it was certainly one different way to start the year, meeting and marrying a woman all in one on January first.

He might have wanted to stop at Pensacola just to see what news was brewing within the territory, but he was anxious to get home. The situation was often tense down by the plantations just north and south of the Hillsborough River. He didn't like to be gone long. Things could change so quickly.

He hadn't been happy about the state of politics when he had left home. He was worried that men hadn't been paying attention to what was going on.

The territory was beginning to boom, and much of the present trouble dated back many years.

When the fledgling young American country had begun having trouble with the British again and the War of 1812 had broken out, both sides had used the Indians to fight with them as allies. During that war, with those divisions creating some of the havoc, the Creek War of '13–'14 had broken out, and many of the Indian survivors had then moved south to become "Seminoles"— the Upper Creeks, because their lands had been decimated, and the Lower Creeks, because even though they had fought on the side of the Americans, they had returned from their fighting to discover that their lands, too, had been taken over. Trouble had of course arisen again in Florida, still Spanish territory at the time. That hadn't bothered the Americans. They'd come in with their accusations that the Spanish had no control over marauding Indians and British spies. Andrew Jackson had already fought the Creeks, and had given the people a spectacular victory at the Battle of New Orleans—even if the war had been officially over at the time, none of the combatants had known it. Jackson had then come south to settle the problems in Florida provoking a Seminole war. Indians who had fought against one another just years before now became allies. Just as those who had earlier fought side by side now became enemies. But in the end, in the north of the territory, the Seminoles were subdued. Many moved deeper into their hammocks. Some pressed southward into the peninsula. Then events had happened quickly. Spain had finally ceded Florida to America for concessions in return. Jackson had become the first military governor of the new territory, though he had not stayed a full year. And the Indian question had finally led to the Treaty of Moultrie Creek, where the Indians had been granted the right to certain lands, with a twenty-year promise to go with those rights. Nine years were still guaranteed by that treaty. But the Indians and whites had come too close. Despite the fact that the land was wild, much of it marsh, some of it swamp, great vast tracts of it wilderness, some of it was good. Excellent land for raising cattle, for growing sugarcane, for that good southern staple, cotton. Everyone wanted the good land. Men came to make their fortunes; Florida was American now. With a great deal of backbone and a little bit of money, a man could homestead. Poor men could create small heavens. Richer men could create vast estates. That was being done. In the meantime the whites wanted more of the Indian lands. The Indians began to hate their boundaries. The Indians accused the whites of encroaching upon Indian lands, the whites accused the Indians of stealing cattle and raiding their plantations for farm animals and supplies.

Sometimes relations between whites and Seminoles were good. Seminoles traded their furs and pelts for white goods. Earlier on they had traded for liquor, trinkets, and cloth.

They had ceased to trade for liquor recently. Jarrett knew both the Indians and the traders. The Indians had been trading recently for some very particular commodities—bullets, rifles, and gunpowder.

Jarrett knew many of the chiefs, and he knew the Seminole society better, he thought sometimes, than he knew his own. There were not just different language groups in the territory, there were many different bands within those groups. There were dozens of clans. Each clan had its own leaders, just as each band had its own chief. Obedience to a higher power was voluntary. When war was called upon by one chief, the message was sent out to other bands. Sticks were collected from each warrior who was willing to fight a certain battle. The name "Red Sticks" had been given to the hostile Creeks of earlier wars because of the sticks collected from warriors and then used at times to shake at the enemy during battle. Because each chief was virtually free to act on his own, small skirmishes could erupt at any time. But because so many Indians had been trading for so much gunpowder, the situation didn't look good.

Jarrett was still uneasy about his meeting with Osceola as well. The Indian agent, Wiley Thompson, should have known that even among themselves, within their own law, Seminoles did not chain one another. It was the greatest humiliation. Crimes among the Seminoles were settled at the Green Corn Dance each year. Horrible crimes sometimes demanded the death penalty, sometimes banishment. Sometimes men and women were disfigured by ear or nose clipping for such crimes as adultery, but never was a man chained. Wiley Thompson had been angry and frustrated in his dealings with Osceola, and he had claimed that the Seminole had come into his office spouting verbal abuse, and so he'd had him arrested, cuffed, and brought into the stockade. Thompson was still confident that he'd done the right thing. When he'd heard about what had happened, Jarrett had ridden inland to the fort to confront Thompson, but Thompson had told him that the measure had been necessary to break the confidence and arrogance of such a man as Osceola. Jarrett had left him with a stern warning. He'd done his best to make his own peace with Osceola over the incident. He was one man. There were other whites who knew they had wronged the Indians. That didn't matter. Those whites would be caught in the crossfire if there was trouble.

Now Jarrett had a wife to bring home. No matter how secretive he wanted to be about his own life in return, there were things she was going to have to discover. He wanted to have her home when she discovered them.

"We're well enough supplied?" he asked Leo.

"Aye, sir, that we are. If this breeze picks up, I can have us into Tampa Bay by midmorning, day after tomorrow."

Jarrett swallowed down the hot black coffee. It tasted good, sharpening his mind. The fresh salt feel of the air was good too. "I'll take the helm," he told Robert, handing back his empty cup to Leo. "I'll take the best Nathan can round up for a meal as well, Leo, as soon as he's able."

"Aye, aye, sir!" Leo agreed, and turned to do Jarrett's bidding.

But Robert remained several moments at his side.

Jarrett groaned. "What now?"

Robert shook his head. "You're a calm man, Jarrett McKenzie. Had I just acquired such an angel for a wife—"

"You could have acquired her as easily as I," Jarrett told him.

Robert shook his head. "I think not. I'm far more handsome, of course, but . . . let's face it. You're richer. And," Robert said soberly, "much stronger. You're what the lady needed. And, I do believe, she's exactly what you needed."

"Well, it all remains to be seen, doesn't it?" Jarrett said. "She is appalled by the prospects of snakes and alligators—what do you think she'll feel when she discovers the truth of my situation?"

"Want me to find out?"

"I'll slit your throat if you say a word to her."

"Not a breath!" Robert promised him. "But what if . . ."

"Yes?"

"What if she does not handle the truth well? What will you do, send her north?"

Jarrett, his eyes upon the endless waves before them, listening to the splash of the gulf as they knifed through the waters, shook his head stubbornly. "No. She has her secrets, and she made her vows." He was startled by the vehemence he felt himself. "She has made her bed, Robert. She will lie in it."

"Then perhaps you should warn her—"

"When I'm ready," Jarrett said determinedly. "I mean that, Robert. When I'm ready."

"When we reach Tampa, she'll hear things."

"Probably."

"Then—"

"She'll have to ask me what she wants to know," Jarrett persisted firmly.

"Aye, Captain, as you say!" Robert agreed with an exaggerated sigh. He clipped his heels together and bowed slightly. "I shall help Nathan in the galley and see if I cannot hurry a meal along."

He left Jarrett at the helm, and Jarrett discovered that he was glad to be there, alone. The wind felt good, the salt air felt good. The rhythm of the ship beneath his legs felt good. Reliving the events of the night before felt—strange. And reconciling what he had done with his life felt stranger still.

Tara awoke groggily to a tapping sound. She sat up slowly, feeling almost drugged, very tired, strangely stiff. She blinked briefly, stared at her surroundings with confusion first, remembrance, alarm, and then another rush of remembrance that seemed to burn the entirety of her flesh to a rose blush. Dear Lord, things had moved so swiftly and so desperately, and now . . .

The tapping continued. She leapt up, her heart slamming furiously as she dressed with all possible speed. *He* was back, she thought. No, he was not, for he would never knock. He was her husband. Her mind was spinning. She felt as though she were losing it.

No, she had lost it last night. Lost so much, gained so much. A flush of fever seemed to seize her again.

"Tara?" A polite voice queried.

Dressed, her hair still wildly disheveled, she pulled open the door.

Robert Treat had come to the cabin door, bearing a silver tray. He balanced the tray while sweeping her a deep, playful bow.

"Mrs. McKenzie. I am ever your servant on this journey to

your new homeland—well, and then for life, I do imagine!" he said lightly.

She smiled. His manner was charming, infectious. His tawny good looks were appealing, and he had determined, it seemed, that after talking her into marriage with his friend, he was going to make her feel welcome aboard the ship whether his friend intended to or not.

"Thank you," she told him, smiling and sweeping him a deep curtsy in return.

"Will you have this on the desk, Mrs. McKenzie?"

"What is it?"

"The most delicious crawfish stew you will ever taste."

"It sounds wonderful," she said.

He set down the tray and swept the top from the server. He pulled out the captain's chair and seated her with a flourish, then perched upon a corner of the desk himself.

"Don't mind me, I've eaten," he assured her.

The stew smelled enticing. She was starving. She took him at his word and picked up her spoon for a first taste. It was delicious. She ate more hungrily, then remembered she had company and hesitated.

"Are you sure—"

"Mrs. McKenzie, it is late in the day for a weary worker like myself!"

She arched a brow. "You don't look overworked at the moment."

He laughed. "No, I guess not."

"Do you work for Jarrett?"

"Only upon occasion."

"You two are very good friends."

"The best. I'd die for him," Robert said simply.

She arched a brow again, but he hadn't intended to be so deadly serious and he told her, "We share an absolute passion for our land."

She couldn't help a slight shiver. "For the bugs and the alligators?" she said lightly.

"Now, now! Don't tease until you have seen a sunset! Or perhaps, not until you have touched Juan Ponce de León's magnificent Fountain of Youth!"

"It exists?" Tara teased skeptically.

He shrugged. "Perhaps. Who knows? I can promise you this: there are places to be found that offer the greatest enchantment. In fact, marvelous, romantic events took place quite near to where you'll be living."

She arched a brow. "Alligator matings?"

"Mrs. McKenzie! What an indelicate question!" he laughed.

"Well, I imagine I am in a rather indelicate position," she murmured, feeling a telltale rise of heat to her cheeks once again.

But Robert remained the complete gentleman. "Ah, I shall have to see that you do become enchanted with our little corner of Paradise! Now pay me heed. In 1492, as you are well aware, Colombus discovered the New World. Spaniards started to become very wealthy, stripping treasures out of South America. Now, our good friend Ponce wanted to become wealthy as well, and so he came searching for gold and the fantastic treasures that had been found elsewhere. He discovered the West Indies, then heard fantastic tales about another land where there were gold and riches and clear, magical waters. If a man drank from those waters, he would find eternal health and life. He didn't find the magical water, or gold, but he did find Florida. And after his death other enterprising Spaniards continued seeking their fortunes. So now comes the beginning of my story. Hernando Cortés was busy becoming a very wealthy man off the wealth of the Aztecs in Mexico. Velasquez, governor of Cuba, was jealous. He sent a man named Pánfilo de Narváez to explore Florida to find the same kinds of riches. Pánfilo de Narváez landed near Tampa Bay, where we are sailing to now, then sent his ships north along the coast to meet him once he had explored the country. At first he met friendly natives, then the Indians grew more hostile. He found no riches and then, when he came back to the coast, he found none of his ships. He and his men grew desperate. They begged to build ships, which they did. They melted down their helmets and shields, and bolts and bars and nails were made from them. Then they set out on their pathetic little boats."

"This is a wonderful story, Robert," Tara told him, laughing. "I can't wait to get there now."

"Hush. I'm getting to the good part. The boats set out. They were nearly all destroyed, and the sailors were either drowned or killed by the natives, except for four survivors who traveled on through the land to tell the tale."

"That was the good part?"

"Now listen. The wife of Pánfilo de Naváez sent a ship out with supplies for her husband. The sailors saw nothing of Pánfilo, but Indians beckoned them ashore, and two young men came there in a rowboat. They were seized by an Indian chief named Hirrihiqua, who had been very badly treated by Pánfilo de Naváez. The first young man was immediately tortured and killed."

"That must be the good part!" Tara said.

"The second young man," Robert said sternly, "was Juan Ortiz. And Hirrihiqua was about to torture and kill him. He had him bound and placed over a fire."

"Robert—"

"But the chief's daughter would have none of it. She flew to her father's feet, cast herself down before them and wept and pleaded. She begged, sobbed, wept some more. . . ."

"And?"

"Well, he released Juan Ortiz!" Robert said, pleased with the outcome of his story.

"Aren't you perhaps borrowing from stories about Pocahontas and John Smith?"

"No!" Robert said indignantly. "It's a true story, and it happened long before Pocahontas was even born."

"Ah, I see. Did Ortiz then fall in love with the Indian maiden and wed her?"

"No, actually, the Indians kept him as a slave for many years. Hirrihiqua was a tough man, so it seems. But his daughter was a truly valiant young lady, and saw to it that her fiancé, a young leader from another tribe, took in Ortiz so that he would not be so badly treated. Hirrihiqua then refused to give the young fiancé his daughter, but the fiancé had sworn to protect Ortiz and he did so."

"And then?"

"Ortiz was rescued years later by Hernando de Soto. And I'm not sure of the fate of our young Indian lovers. But it's a marvelous story, don't you think?"

Tara smiled and nodded. "A very nice story—I suppose."

"It's history. I love history. And our history is the oldest in the nation, did you realize that?"

She smiled. "Where do you get all this history?"

"Books," he told her, his expression almost grave. "I love books. History books, playbooks—"

"Really?"

He folded his hands over his heart. "I've every last word ever penned by Mr. William Shakespeare. You'll have to come see me sometime. I can't promise eternal life, but I can be a fountain of knowledge."

"Thank you. For everything."

Robert leapt off the desk. "I have to go now. The captain has a bellow about him when he's in a mood." He winked. "See you later. I will be back, I promise."

He strode across the cabin and quickly left her, and she idly twirled a strand of hair with her fingers. He was wonderful. So quick to smile, so very quick to make her feel welcome. He could make her laugh while informing her about awful things.

She felt a strange heat fill her again. Still, he couldn't cause her to tremble the way Jarrett McKenzie did with a simple word, a light touch. By a brush of his ebony-dark eyes.

She clutched her hands together. What had she done? What if McKenzie ever learned the truth?

The truth . . . as Clive Carter had cunningly planned for the world to see it.

～

Jarrett held his course steady for some time, then Robert returned with a bowl of Nathan's crawfish stew, and he ate it hungrily while Robert kept them steady on their way, commenting on the dark clouds that had risen on the horizon. They agreed they were in for rough weather.

They had scarcely spoken the words aloud before the wind picked up in earnest. All hands were summoned on deck to trim the sails as the wind continued to rise, rain lashing down upon them. Again Jarrett took the wheel himself, bracing against the force of the storm. He was standing at the helm, blinking against the drive of the rain when he suddenly felt a presence behind him and turned to discover Tara there, feet planted firmly upon the deck.

"Get below!" he roared to her.

"But I can help—" she began.

"Go below!"

"I'm a good sailor and I do not like being confined—"

"Damn!" He swore, absolutely furious with her. With all his strength he could but hold the wheel.

"Well, do you like being washed overboard?" he demanded angrily.

"I told you, I'm a good sailor."

"Leo! The helm!" he roared above the wind and waves to his first mate, and the second he was relieved, he turned to Tara, sweeping her up, staggering against the wind to return her to his cabin.

Someone had been busy. The bath was gone, the bunk was made. Last night's dinners were gone, and someone had brought

Tara some crawfish stew. Hers had been served on a silver tray with a white linen napkin and a glass of wine.

The tray now slid back and forth on his desk. But he did not stare at the tray long.

There was also a trunk within the room. A familiar one. He forgot the weather, the future—even the woman for a moment— as he stared at the trunk. His *new* wife. The trunk had belonged to his past wife. . . .

He stared from it to Tara. She seemed to move away from him. Almost as if she was afraid of him. He grated down on his jaw, annoyed.

"Robert brought it," she said swiftly. "I—I have nothing, you realize. He said that I should use these things."

She was dressed as she had been when he had met her. "You haven't used them," he said curtly.

"I—I didn't know who they belonged to. I didn't want to use them without asking the woman who owns them."

He didn't quite understand the rush of emotion that swept through him then. The ship was wildly tossing. Tara seemed to weather it well, keeping her balance as she stared at him. Still perfection. And for a moment he hated her. Hated the fact that he had wanted her so desperately from the moment he had seen her. Hated her perfection, her absolute beauty. The very gold of her hair, the softness of her voice.

Hated the fact that she could make him forget the face of a woman he had loved for more than a decade. . . .

"She's dead," he grated out. "And you—you must make use of whatever is here. And don't leave the damned cabin again in this storm, do you understand?"

"I know something about sailing."

"I wish to hell you knew something about obedience!" he snapped. "Don't come out again!"

He left her, slamming the cabin door behind him. Or perhaps the wind took it. He exhaled on a long breath, then remembered that they were in danger of being rent asunder, and hurried back to take the wheel while his men finished struggling with the sails.

It was a fierce storm, made more so by the fact that they were at sea. A Florida storm, he thought, perhaps made wild by that very fact. Warm air and waters met the colder ones coming down from the north. The gales that ensued seemed to rip the very sky. Tonight, as so often in the Tampa area and the center of the territory, lightning slashed across the sky in an almost continual flash of light. Bare seconds passed and thunder rolled, then the sky lit up again. It was beautiful, deadly. The sea churned up beneath it all, and Jarrett clung to the wheel to keep the vessel as steady as possible under the circumstances. His fingers grew numb around the wood but he held on still.

Close to midnight the last streak of lightning flared across the sky. The thunder rumbled and went still. The rain slowed to a drizzle. The sea, which had been a tempest, suddenly became almost dead calm.

Nathan made coffee, which they spiced heavily with whiskey. Jarrett decided that he would keep the wheel through the night with Leo to spell him, and Robert could take the helm at daybreak. The sky was just becoming pink when he went to his cabin, peeled off his damp clothing, and stared at his wife again.

Two days. He had been married nearly two days.

And she had taken her clothing from the trunk. She was not clad in the gown the ship's crew had bought for their wedding night. She had found the longest, thickest white flannel gown imaginable within the trunk. Jarrett couldn't remember ever having seen it on Lisa, and decided that Lisa had never worn it.

Lace from the high neckline rode all the way up her throat. She slept. Demurely.

But she had to be a fool to think that any amount of encompassing cotton could make her less desirable. Naked, he toweled himself briskly, then whipped up the covers to climb in bed beside her. The mere act made him feel incredibly awake and alive. He deftly slipped a hand down to the hem of the gown, dragging it upward as his fingers stroked her bare flesh. He somehow found a bare breadth of skin at her nape and kissed it. His fingers moved lightly up and down her spine, and she slowly awoke.

He was weary and in no mood for the fight he had begun that day. His hands slipped firmly around her hips, positioning her. His fingers slid over her buttocks, caught her thighs. With a swift fluid thrust he entered her, and her soft gasp assured him that she had come fully awake. But no protest rose to her lips, and when his climax seemed to skyrocket from him, he felt her body shudder and then ease, even as the afterwaves of his own fierce passions slowly ebbed and the sweet night air cooled his flesh. She didn't speak, and he felt torn, aware that he should offer some apology for his earlier temper. But the cabin remained dark and shadowed, and his great exhaustion was wearing down on him. He found his eyes closing and sleep claiming him before he could manage to get out his apology.

Again, he slept very late. When he awoke, it was to the sound of her laughter. Puzzled for a while, he lay there listening. The laughter died away. He drifted off to sleep again, then awoke in something of confused panic. He bolted up, pulled on his breeches only, and came hurrying up on deck. The anchor had been cast. Ted and Nathan were fishing, their lines cast over the starboard side. Staring at the two, Jarrett frowned. He heard a splash from the portside and swiftly spun on his heels to reach the bow.

Robert stood on deck, staring down into the water. He seemed to be startled when Jarrett called to him.

"What—"

"Tara is—"

"Overboard?" Jarrett demanded in alarm, rushing to the edge of the ship, ready to plummet over himself. His mind did not really register the sight of the hemp ladder thrown over the hull, as if awaiting a visitor from the sea.

"Swimming!" Robert said quickly. "She said that the water was beautiful and she decided to dive in."

"And you just let her?"

"I didn't quite know how to stop her!" Robert admitted with both humor and exasperation.

Jarrett stared out across the water. They were hugging the western coastline of Florida and were not very far off land. The water here in the Gulf of Mexico was exceptionally beautiful, as if the storm had cleansed even it. The sky was powder-blue without a cloud in sight. The sea was azure, the sun golden, and the colors seemed to stretch out for an eternity.

And there, within the beauty of those fabulous colors, was his wife. He saw only her head for a moment, her hair still golden, even when wet.

He wondered with a renewed surge of temper just what she was wearing for her dive, but when she twisted as easily in the water as a sea nymph and began to swim with luxuriously slow movements on her back, he saw that she was clad in a narrow pair of breeches Lisa had once made for their treks into the interior and one of his shirts, so oversized on her, it seemed incredible that she could move so fluidly within it.

Robert, at his side, shrugged. "She told me that it was a beautiful day and that she loved to swim and had seldom seen such inviting water. Before I quite knew what she was up to, she was diving in like a native spear fisherman. She does seem to be quite at home in the water."

Jarrett grunted at Robert and dived into the water at last.

The whole of his body shuddered fiercely at the contact.

In fact, it seemed that the whole of his body shriveled into nothing!

Granted, winter was warm here, warm and beautiful. Winter was often the best season, with the dead heat that could come in the summer months tempered and the vicious cold of the north never touching down upon them.

Still, it was winter. And the water was chilly, with a true bite to it.

His errant bride did not seem to mind. Indeed, as he surfaced, gasping, still shivering, she was unaware that she had even been followed into the water. Jarrett determined that he would not feel the cold—or that at least he wouldn't let her know that he was freezing from head to toe. With strong strokes he approached her quickly. She floated serenely on her back.

He was glad when she floundered for a moment, jerking with surprise at his touch and swallowing a good mouthful of seawater. She gasped and sputtered, then dived to smooth her hair back and met his eyes across the water again, hers taking on its color.

"You scared the life out of me. I thought you might have been a fish," she said.

"What the hell do you think you did to me? And you should be scared. What do you know about these waters? I might have been a big fish. A shark. And just what the hell did you think you were doing, diving in to begin with?"

He wondered why he couldn't control his temper with her. He—and his men—dived into these waters constantly, even if it was usually in warmer weather.

The glittering sunlight reflected on the water and caught within her eyes. He couldn't read the emotion within them, but she replied evenly enough.

"I told you before that I could swim."

"Ah, yes! Forgive me. That was when I prevented you from pitching into the mud of the Mississippi!"

She inhaled as she treaded the water, taking her time. "I could see no harm in swimming. I am adept in the water."

It was an understatement. Why was he so furious? Because his heart had seemed to catch in his throat when he had heard the splash of water?

"You frightened me and the whole damned crew. Dear Lord, woman, you just don't do such things without asking!"

"But there is only your crew aboard, and you were still sleeping."

"You should have waited until I awoke."

Somehow she managed to move a subtle distance farther from

him in the water. Her eyes were narrowed, brilliant with the sun's reflections.

"I didn't realize that I needed your permission for every move I make."

"When it comes to such things, perhaps you should realize it."

"And perhaps you should be aware, McKenzie, that you do not own me."

"I married you."

"It isn't the same."

"You may see it however you wish. I'll tell you how I view the situation. I found you running, and you promised just about anything in the world to get away. I don't wish to wake up with fear ripping out my chest because I believe you may be drowning."

"But I told you—"

"Damn it, you could have asked, you could have waited."

"Fine!" she snapped after a moment's charged silence. She swirled cleanly within the water, knifing down hard into the depths, her kick catching him squarely in the jaw. For a moment his head rang.

She was fast. Almost like lightning. He lost his view of her in the depths. When she surfaced she was nearly at the ship.

His initial irritation seemed to tear at his insides. She had probably been having a decent morning, and maybe they might have had a chance at civil conversation, if nothing more. But he didn't seem able to control the demon eating at his insides, and he was determined to prove to her that she could get in trouble, that her behavior could put her into danger. Cold no longer, he followed her across the water, swimming hard. She was still ahead of him, cutting cleanly through the surf, nearly to the hemp ladder when he caught up at last. From beneath her he grabbed an ankle, dragging her down, releasing her quickly so that they came to the surface together once again. This time she faced him with her own anger naked in her eyes.

"What?" she demanded. "You ordered me not to swim! I am trying to oblige your command!"

"Don't do that to me, my love," he warned her softly. "I've warned you not to strike."

"I don't know what you mean!" she protested tensely, but the very slight hesitancy in her words assured him that she knew exactly what she had done, and that she had done it on purpose.

"I warn you again, lady. Take care with me." He swam closer to her. She turned, groping for the ladder. Even as she clutched it, his arms came around her.

His heart started beating like thunder. She paused, biting her lip, furious, he knew. Raw emotions flamed within him again. The cotton shirt stuck to her like a second skin, revealing every nuance of her shape. Every man aboard the *Magda* would know every tempting curve on her.

"May I?" she asked tartly, trying to climb the ladder despite the arms that braced her.

"You'd best," he said as pleasantly as he could manage.

She started moving swiftly up the ladder. To Jarrett's relief Robert was awaiting her there with a blanket and was quick to wrap it around her.

By the time Jarrett had crawled aboard ship, she had already disappeared. Run back to the cabin, he imagined.

He didn't follow her. He dripped upon the deck, shivering in the breeze-cooled air.

"Want a blanket too?" Robert asked politely.

"Coffee, scalding!" Jarrett said, and turned to head for the helm, where Nathan was at the wheel. He stared out at the shoreline, at the dense green brush, at the white sands that jutted out here and there.

Leo brought coffee. Jarrett drank it quickly, hot though it was. The chill he had been feeling ebbed away as he drank, his flesh drying in the warm sun, his breeches remaining damp.

"I'll take the helm," he told Nathan. It would be a good place to dry, he thought.

Cool his temper, heat his flesh.

There was little he loved more than sailing, especially with the crew that had been with him for years now. They were fiercely loyal, totally competent, and like a group of chameleons, ready to don whatever colors were needed for the current job. They all made the New Orleans trip about three times a year, and they all also traveled on the annual London trip, for Jarrett's holdings were extensive, and he was managing to grow cotton very well now along with the sugarcane staple. He owned large grazing lands as well, with plenty of cattle. There were chickens on the property as well, hogs for pork and bacon, and he had a stable filled with beautiful horses. Upon occasion they raced, and he had become interested in the breeding of the beautiful creatures, and discovered that there was a great deal of money to be made in their sale as well. To the north and just abutting the land where he had built his house, he owned salt marshes, and they were contributing heavily to the fortune he had been steadily accruing over the years.

Sometimes it seemed strange indeed that he was doing so well. His father had been a man of means who had chosen to lead a life in a wilderness. Like him Jarrett had set out not so much to make a fortune as to wrest a place for himself, and Lisa, from the wilderness. The adventure had beckoned to him, the rawness, the newness. The quality of Eden. Still, there had been some hard times at first, days when they had slept in the woods while building the house, days when they had wondered if they could make a go of the crops. Now those days were long past. But Lisa, who had believed in his dreams even when the heat had sweated them out of him, was gone as well. Without her the land was all that was left, the dream of Florida. One day, he was certain, it would become a state. An important part of America. He wanted to see that day. But he wanted to see the territory at peace as well. He wanted the whites to learn to live with the Seminoles, he wanted the military to learn to live with the civilian population. It was going to be a long haul. His part of it all began at his home.

When he and his men were not at sea, they all had their functions on Jarrett's various land holdings. In their absence the household was run by Jeeves, a tall man of African and Indian ancestry, black as ebony, strong as an ox, a man who had acquired a cultured Brahman accent while working for a senator in Boston. Jeeves was a free man, paid highly for his services, and yet he had been with Jarrett so long that he seemed like a member of the family.

Jeeves himself seemed to be color blind. He directed the household and plantation servants—Indian, African, American, Irish, English, Spanish, Haitian, and Creole—with dignity and authority. Jarrett had a natural curiosity about people, and in his traveling, when he had come across the right person for a certain position at Cimarron, he had hired that man or woman on. He also had a tendency to collect lost souls. Two of his upstairs maids were Irish lasses who had lost their parents to the sea on their journey to the States and wound up orphaned and penniless on the streets of Charleston. Many half-breed Indians, some lost in both worlds, had come to him for work. Sometimes, especially for those men working for him in the fields, the pay was small. But in compensation they all had their little bits of land to till, and they had freedom. Jarrett didn't judge for other men, but in his own mind slavery was wrong. He had learned at an early age that a man couldn't be judged by his color, and he had been privileged to see that men of the greatest integrity might be either full-blooded American Indians or Africans of the deepest ebony hue. The one thing that should never be stripped from any man was his dignity, and no matter how good a master might be, owning a man, taking away his free right to live and breathe and pursue his own dream, surely stripped away his dignity. Cimarron had proven to him that he could survive without slaves, and he meant to do so until his dying day.

Cimarron lacked almost nothing. Except, since Lisa's death, a mistress. Jeeves, Jarrett thought, would be glad to see that his employer was bringing home a new wife. A mistress.

Jarrett swore softly to himself. No matter what pattern his thoughts ran in, they always returned to *her*.

His pants dried, his flesh dried. The sun was already beginning to set in the night sky. He heard laughter and a moment later the sound of Robert's fiddle. Beautiful, plaintive strains of music rose into the soft, crimson and gold splashes of sunset. A moment later he heard *her*.

And of course, her voice was perfect. Crystal clear, true, melodic, lovely. Robert didn't miss a note of the old English ballad, "Greensleeves." A touch of a soft accent—Irish, perhaps?—added a lilt and curved sweetly into her words as she sang the plaintive song.

Alas, my love, you do me wrong,
To cast me off discourteously,
For I have loved you too long,
Delighting in your company. . . .

Robert's pleasant tenor joined in with the beautiful mezzosoprano as she finished the chorus. A moment's silence followed, then a rush of applause, and the sounds of laughter once again.

It was so easy for her to laugh with Robert, Jarrett mused. He realized that he was forever jumping down her throat, but then . . .

There was so much he had to reconcile within himself. And he'd be damned if he'd fall any farther under her spell. Not when she was so determined to keep her secrets.

"Captain?"

Leo was behind him, dark brows furrowed, his features concerned.

"What is it, Leo?"

"You haven't eaten a bite today, sir. Nathan's created a fine gumbo. I swear his stuff is just fine at sea—on land the lad's food is inedible!"

"Anything will be edible at this moment. I am famished," Jarrett said.

"Gumbo's been delivered to the captain's cabin, sir. Robert

thought as how you might like to wash up before you eat, what with the sea salt on you and all."

"Is that what Robert thought?"

"Oh, aye, sir. We're running a bit low on fresh water—Robert thought as well that Mrs. McKenzie would like a hot bath after her swim."

"So Robert thought, eh?"

"Oh, yes—well, your wife was most appreciative, Captain!"

"I do imagine," Jarrett murmured. "But my wife has had her bath, and we're now low on fresh water."

"Aye, but we're almost home, sir!"

"Of course. How forgetful of me," Jarrett said.

His irony was lost on Leo.

"I'll take the helm, sir. Shall we trim the sails in? Does seem the breeze is picking up again, from the northwest."

"Aye, Leo. See to it," Jarrett said. He left the helm, finding that he was not required to speak with any of his men, for Leo was shouting out his orders and the crew—including Robert— were busy with the sails.

Good.

At least they were no longer being musically seduced by his wife!

With a sigh and renewed determination to enjoy the benefits of his new marriage while keeping a careful emotional distance from his mystery bride, he quickened his footsteps. He was suddenly hungry and weary—and annoyingly eager to hear her laughter himself.

Tara heard his footsteps as he neared the cabin. Others had come to the cabin today—in fact, Robert and every man on the crew had come at one time or another to see to her welfare.

But as soon as she heard the tread, remarkably light for such a man, even upon the planks of a ship, she knew that he was coming. She felt her heart quicken, and she was not sure if it was with dread or anticipation.

She had been stretched out on the bunk musing over the strange man she had married. *Yes, he was incredibly, darkly, ruggedly handsome, a man with the lithe but muscled build of a buccaneer. She had never even begun to dream of the fires he could build within her, even if her breath had caught each time those eyes seared her. It seemed he was always demanding the truth, and if he were ever to know it . . .*

She shivered fiercely. She hadn't lied to him. He had demanded to know not if she had been accused of murder, but if she had been guilty of it. And she had not. And he had promised to demand no more of her. As long as she kept to her part of the bargain. Marriage . . . their *bargain.*

There was no hardship in it. Even last night when she had been hurt and angry and he had finally roused her from such a deep sleep. He could caress and arouse . . . seduce, so very easily.

And become so remote and angry again so quickly! She shivered, remembering how his voice could crack like deep thunder, how demanding he could be. Then she gritted down hard on her teeth and squared her shoulders. She had cast her fate with his— and he had swept her away from a fate she had considered much worse than death.

But what now lay ahead?

It didn't matter, she determined. She was going to hold her own. She would keep up her part of this agreement and be whatever he wanted in a wife.

But she'd not let him dictate to her like a tyrant! She'd run too long on her own to surrender her independence and soul to any man. It had been months since she had escaped the disaster set upon her.

The doors opened. Despite all her resolve she found herself tucking her bare feet beneath the white gown she had found in the trunk. She felt that she was looking at him like a guilty child, and she quickly grew angry with herself. She would not be intimidated. She admired him, she was grateful to him. And she had to be very careful, because he did seem to have the ability to steal her soul, bit by bit. She was quite certain he would have the same affect on other women. His power to seduce was as great as his quiet strength, a power that had already wrested her from a few forms of the devil. He had married her; he seemed to want her. He had no regrets, and yet . . .

She was, she thought, like anything else he might have acquired. He would take care of her. Tend to her well-being. And set her upon a shelf when he was busy elsewhere and expect her to behave. He would not want her interfering in his life.

The door closed behind him. He was still shirtless and barefoot, and though his breeches were dry, they still clung to his hips tightly. His shoulders and torso were nearly copper from the sun. The muscles in his calves and thighs were clearly delineated by the hugging fit of his breeches.

His dark eyes lit upon her as he strode the few feet to his desk. A dinner tray sat there, the silver cover still in place. He lifted it and saw one bowl, one round of bread, and one wineglass. He arched a brow at her.

"I've eaten," she said quickly.

He nodded, sat in the chair behind his desk, and lifted the wineglass, black eyes on her while he sipped it. It struck Tara suddenly what an intimate—and awkward—moment this was. For a normal couple it might be a special time. The *Magda* rocked gently, the candle on his desk burned softly. The air was perfect, cool and fresh, and the cabin was both handsome and confining, bringing the two of them quite close together whether they wished it or not.

"So you've eaten—and bathed?" he said softly, finishing the wine, setting the glass down.

She nodded again, feeling a curious heat flood her. "Did I need permission to do either?" she heard herself asking, an edge to her tone.

He folded his hands idly in his lap, a slight curl to his lip as he watched her now. "Maybe. With most women, I could easily say a simple no. But with you, if I say no, you will most likely think of a plunge into the ocean or river as bathing. Or you will tell me that forging into the wilderness on your own is a hunt for dinner meat. You, madam, will thus find a way to have a reason for any course of action you want to take!"

"You needn't fear. I'll not be trudging into any wilderness," she said. A sudden shuddering seized her. She prayed that he did not see the motion. She'd been afraid of spiders and snakes all of her life. She was aware that even Georgians—those living on the Florida border!—often considered the interior of Florida to be the most savage of all wilderness.

"How curious. You're afraid of alligators and the like—yet haven't the least fear of meeting up with a nasty shark!"

She shrugged uneasily. "I'm familiar with the ocean," she murmured.

"Are you?"

She didn't answer. He picked up his gumbo and began to eat. He must have been very hungry, for he finished it quickly, poured himself more wine, and leaned back in his chair, studying its color, his bare flesh gleaming ever more copper in the candlelight, even the dark hair upon it touched by a golden glow. His gaze suddenly riveted itself back on her and she felt as if she had been physically touched.

"It's a good thing you're not afraid of pirates."

"Pirates?"

"Indeed. José Gaspar used to cruise these waters. There's buried treasure everywhere on the barren sand islands. Dead men tell no tales, so they say, and I assure you, many a pirate has left the skeletal remains of his onetime companions to guard his gold and jewels."

"You forget, I was living in New Orleans," she reminded him with a wave of her hand. "Pirates helped defeat the British during the Battle of New Orleans. Jean Lafitte fought with Jackson."

"Indeed he did," Jarrett murmured.

"You say that with authority."

"It's history, is it not? And, alas, we're sailing away from New Orleans."

There was a challenge now in those dark eyes and she determined that she would not allow him to force her to betray herself in any way. She didn't reply, but lowered her eyes, hugging her knees to her chest.

He rose and even before she looked up, she felt the burning ebony of his eyes pierce right into her.

He stood before her where she sat on the bunk, and she looked up slowly, painfully aware of the ridged muscles of his abdomen and the bareness of his coppery flesh. She met his eyes, forcing herself to lift a brow in a regal and silent question. He hunkered slowly down so that he was balancing himself on the balls of his feet, his eyes meeting hers on the same level.

"I'm curious!" he said softly. "When we've reached my one-man's-heaven-another-man's-hell, what then? Will you be seeking to run away again?"

She moistened her lips, meeting his gaze evenly. "I've nowhere to go," she told him.

"Ah! Not a reassuring answer. If you had somewhere to go, would you then be running there, away from me?"

"I've not reneged on any bargain," she whispered.

"You've not been given much chance."

She lowered her eyes again, suddenly unable to meet his. "Why would I wish to run from you? You have rescued me at peril to yourself."

"Ah, but I saw the rage of independence in your eyes today! You seemed to believe that you had shackled yourself to a tyrant."

"You were—extremely rude."

"I can be a tyrant."

"And I, sir, may then have my rages!" she responded, her words suddenly quite heated.

She was surprised when he laughed, rising to take a seat upon the bunk, then leaning against the paneled wall at its head. He pulled her back to lie upon his chest, her hips within the spread of his hard-muscled thighs. His fingers moved gently through the golden threads of her hair as he stretched tendril after tendril out over his own flesh.

"It's really not so terrible!" he told her softly.

"It—"

"Home," he murmured. "Florida. But then, I've watched much of it grow. Imagine, it takes fifteen to twenty-odd days to sail from Pensacola to St. Augustine. So far west, to so far east, and the peninsula so different up and down the length of it! The territorial delegates used to alternate years, meeting in Pensacola, west Florida, one year, then in St. Augustine, east Florida, the next. It was troublesome for the gents to take such long journeys, and once a shipload of lawmakers was wrecked at the tip of the peninsula. They were, needless to say, quite exasperated. That's when they decided they must meet in the middle, and Tallahassee became the capitol."

Tara remained silent, enjoying his musings. She could inhale the rich, masculine scent of his bare flesh, savor the gentleness of his touch.

It had seemed forever since someone had made her feel so secure, touched her so tenderly.

"Tallahassee. It's an—Indian name," she murmured.

She felt him stiffen. "It is."

She shivered.

"What?" he asked softly, the strangest edge to his voice. "Do you so despise Indians?"

"I—fear them," she admitted.

He was silent again. After a moment she felt his hands moving in her hair again. A gentle touch.

The ship moved rhythmically. She closed her eyes, and in time began to drift. Deep, deep in the recesses of sleep she realized that he was touching her still. She lay upon her back, and he was straddling her, naked now, smooth, sleek, the length of him golden and copper.

"Tara?"

"Yes?"

His lips touched hers. She discovered the white gown being quickly slipped over her shoulders. She might have slept again except that his lips and hands moved over her, touched her. Hot mercury followed each caress of his mouth, and each grew more intimate, touching her, here, there, again. . . .

She cried out at the sudden intimacy of his touch, cried out at the searing fever it evoked. Then she found herself within the strength of his arms, within the wild, raw rhythm of his passion. Again the fires created so deep within her seemed to swirl and rise, ignite to greater heights. She didn't think that she could bear any more of the agony-ecstasy, and then it seemed that the sky burst into daylight above her, and the sun radiated a savage but delicious heat throughout her, and she lay again in wonder that anything could feel so wonderful, cause such a hunger, grant such sweet, sweet burning beauty.

She buried her head against him when it was over, embarrassed that she should become so eager at his touch. She felt the pounding of his heart slowly ease and lay very still.

"Tara?" he whispered.

She feigned sleep.

If he knew that she was doing so, he did not force the issue. His fingers moved gently over her hair once again.

In time her sleep was real.

PART TWO

Savage Land

Chapter 6

ALMOST HOME, Jarrett thought, calling out an order to bring in the sails and cut hard to port to bring the ship around to the docks at Tampa Bay. Almost home. He still had to travel along the river to reach his plantation. But tonight he could introduce his wife to these "wilds" in the company of other men and women, friends—military and non—who lived here in this post that was still considered somewhat remote.

What had begun as the military base Fort Brooke at Tampa Bay was now a city as well: in fact, it had become "Tampa" just last year.

The place wasn't exactly what might be termed elegant or even particularly civilized. It was still primarily a military base, and many men sent here felt as if they had been condemned to the bowels of hell.

Others loved it. They loved the clean white beaches, the azure color of the water in the bay, the balmy breezes that swept around them, even in the height of winter. Only a few days each year could actually be considered cold, when even in Jacksonville and Pensacola there could be, upon rare occasion, snow.

It remained a rough town. Where soldiers went, women usually followed. Some of them were the kind who liked to make a good living off the government—through the soldiers. But military men brought sutlers along with them as well; sutlers sometimes had wives, wives had children, and thus towns—rough as they might be—did arise, filled with a little bit of everything and everyone. Tampa was such a place now. The fort, with its high wood walls, was the predominant structure, while all manner of wooden buildings seemed to trail from it, almost as if it were the head of a comet. Docks and wooden sidewalks had been built to accommodate the skirts of the ladies in some areas; in others there was no choice but to walk in the mud after a rainy day. But each year the town grew. There were establishments where ladies might stay, and establishments where a man might want to go when the last thing he wanted was a lady. There were barbers, doctors, dentists, apothecaries, and mercantiles. Chickens squawked, a cow was tended here and there, and along the roads handsome horses moved quickly, most of them now being ridden by members of the military.

"A lot of activity, don't you think?" Robert, standing behind him with a spyglass, asked quietly.

Jarrett nodded, reaching for the glass that Robert offered him. Through it he could see that the base did indeed seem exceptionally busy. Over rough wood fences he could see that the soldiers were moving about quickly, groups of them responding to drills, single soldiers rushing from building to building, as if carrying messages of great importance. Even as Jarrett watched, a company of about twenty men mounted and started out from the enclosure at a brisk trot, men with a mission, so it appeared.

His heart seemed to sink within the cavity of his chest.

"What do you think is happening?" Robert asked.

"We both know what is happening," Jarrett responded tonelessly, feeling ill.

War. War had broken out with the Indians.

Well, he had left with uneasy feelings. He had known the

Indians had been buying powder. He had known that Osceola would never forgive Wiley Thompson.

In truth, perhaps they had imagined what peace there had been between the two factions. Always, always, there had been the raiding. By the Indians against the whites and by the whites against the Indians. The damned Creek War of 1813–1814 had pitted American whites and Indians against English whites—and Indians. Andy Jackson's Seminole War had been downright brutal against the remaining—or newly created—"Red Stick" factions— factions of the Indians who had still been willing to fight Jackson. Though Jackson had all but cleared out many northern towns by the year 1818, he had made those Indians who remained bitter and hard. And those who had remained unbroken often became fierce warriors.

Things had actually come to a head in November of 1835, soon after Jarrett had last seen Alligator, Osceola, and Running Bear. Surely Osceola had known when they had spoken that there was no hope for peace then.

Because Osceola was surely the mastermind behind the murder of the Indian Charley Emathla.

Of course, to Osceola, it had not been murder. Osceola had surely seen it as the proper execution of a man who had betrayed his own people. Many warriors, disheartened by the constant starvation and pressure upon their people, had seen Charley's actions as surrender to the whites. And treachery against those who refused to be pressed farther and farther into the corners of land the whites chose for them.

Emigration west of the Mississippi had long been Andy Jackson's plan for the Indians, and as the whites had become more and more hungry for Florida land to homestead and farm, the issue had been coming more and more to the fore. Finally, Jackson, now President of the U.S., had sent down an order that the Indians were to be compensated for their land and belongings and sent west immediately. The Florida military officers had determined on the spring of 1836 as the time that this must take place. Whether the Indians protested or not.

When he had been asked to take his people and move west, Charley had told the whites that he had no right to speak for the Seminoles. Charley was right in his answer—he had been born a Creek, and as the Florida Indians were really composed of so many displaced and surviving tribes, he couldn't speak for anyone other than himself. He had determined to make his home in Florida rather than go west when many other leaders had done so. Charley had owned a plantation and many cattle in north central Florida, but one day he'd decided that he was weary of fighting the whites—he would go west. He drove his cattle to Fort King to sell them, and on the way home he was ambushed, shot, and killed by militant Indians, among them the rising war chief Osceola. It seemed Osceola had led the party. So Jarrett had heard from friends in the U.S. military at Fort Brooks.

Osceola was quickly becoming one of the fiercest leaders among the Seminoles despite his keen ability to reason. But then, other than what Wiley Thompson had done to Osceola and the numerous injustices done his people, Osceola had another reason to hate the whites.

It had happened long ago. Osceola had, to this day, taken two wives, Morning Dew, his first, and Setting Sun. He had taken both wives as a young man, and many years before the recent trouble had begun, Setting Sun had been kidnapped by white fur trappers. Setting Sun was a Maroon, an Indian with black blood in her veins. At the time of her abduction, she had been very young, exquisitely beautiful. And the fur traders had set her upon the slave block at St. Augustine and made a small fortune on her. She had been rescued before Osceola had managed to kill others or get himself killed. Jarrett had been with the well-dressed and - spoken party of whites and half-breeds, including a very passionate Running Bear, who had carefully negotiated with the planter who had purchased Setting Sun for her freedom. All had seemed well. Many officials in the territory knew nothing about the incident.

Jarrett was certain that Osceola had never forgotten it, even though Jarrett was equally certain that Osceola had gotten his revenge. The fur trappers who had kidnapped Setting Sun had disappeared while hunting one day.

That was in the past. But now, tensions, always at a high, had soared after the murder of Charlie Emathla.

Jarrett should never have left.

What difference could he have made? He didn't even know what had happened yet! Something was going on. Both the fort and the fledgling town were battening down as if they expected an attack.

Jarrett turned around and discovered his crew all but lined up behind him, and all eyes were on the activity at Fort Brooke. "Let's bring her in, men, shall we?" Jarrett said. He was answered by a number of grim nods, and the men turned back to the task of docking their vessel. Tampa Bay was good and deep, with plenty of dockage, and his crew were quickly able to bring her to a crude berth offered by the cruder settlement.

There was excitement onshore. Barricades were going up, windows were being boarded. But beyond the activity he could see that many of the townspeople were milling around the docks to see what he was bringing in—and perhaps to inform him about the military bustle now taking place.

He could see a woman waving. Nancy Reynolds, and beside her, her husband Josh. Old friends, good friends. Others milled around. Naturally, he had brought salt and sugar to New Orleans and had returned with French stockings, soaps and perfumes, crawfish, spices, and news. He was always eagerly awaited.

He had called out the last of his orders and was standing ready to jump ashore when suddenly he heard Tara behind him, softly voicing a strangled question.

"*This*—is where you live?" There was a hint of alarm in her voice. That didn't bother him. If that had been all he heard in the question, he would have tried to reassure her.

But there was much more than alarm in those words. He was certain that he heard contempt. That she was horrified by the very strange Eden that had, since Lisa's death, become all that he had loved. Indeed, the territory was everything to him. All that he wanted to fight for, even die for.

Spinning around, he stared at her. He'd been so eager to touch land that he had planned to do so first and then come back for her.

The tight smile curled into his lips. Her beautiful face was pale as she stared at the shore.

Tara was, at the moment, completely unaware of his anger. She didn't know what she had expected to find when they reached his home, but not . . . this! The buildings were so very crude. So poor. They lacked paint, they lacked architecture, they were little more than boxes. They absolutely lacked beauty.

She clenched her jaws tight, feeling as if her teeth would chatter if she did not. The city she had left had been so refined! The people there had not feared the elements around them. Here, it seemed that men and women were rushing to a squat fort, that they were terribly afraid. This was nothing like the rolling green hills she had once left for a better life. Nothing like the majesty of the well-established city she had fled.

She silently chastised herself. Who was she to judge? She was a runaway, and she should be grateful for this haven, any haven. If she looked around herself, there was beauty. She had seldom seen water seem so beautiful, so aqua, so glittering beneath the sun. The air was balmy, touched by the warmth of the sun, when in the north the day would have been frigid. If she let it, that warmth could caress her, envelop her. The place was new, raw. That's why the buildings seemed so crude. She had to look past them.

The buildings were crude, but not so ugly, she told herself. The land that bordered the town was beautiful as well, touched with green, with traces of wildflowers, even in winter. It was different, so different. But intriguing. It could be beautiful, if only . . .

If only she didn't feel the fear. She told herself that fear wasn't tangible, she couldn't feel it. But she could. She could feel the fear in the little town of Tampa just as surely as she could feel the warmth of the sun as it touched down on her flesh.

Just as she suddenly felt Jarrett's heat as he stood beside her. She tried not to blink, not to speak, not to betray herself more. What a fool. She shouldn't have let him see her dismay in this place. He wouldn't understand, she wouldn't be able to make him understand.

Jarrett didn't understand. Streaks of the anger she so quickly managed to ignite within his soul sizzled through him. She was appalled—and so far she'd only seen Tampa! He'd warned her, damn, but he had warned her! And during the days of their voyage he had come to feel incredibly possessive regarding her—no, damn it, entwined with her. Now he was certain she was regretting her hasty marriage with a vengeance.

And they hadn't even stepped ashore yet.

The intimacy they had shared aboard the ship seemed to melt away. The smoldering jealousy he had felt as well—and tried to deny—added fuel to the tension that was rising within him. It was almost as if he could feel a fire burning within his body. Nothing had changed about her. She was still beautiful. Very regal and elegant this morning. Her hair was swept up off her neck in a neat knot, her eyes were as rich and lustrous a blue, her delicate face seemed still more exquisite, perfect.

She wore one of Lisa's gowns. Blue velvet with a fitted bodice and a chemise and underskirt in white lace. It cinched in tightly at her waist, flared fully at her hips. The bodice just exposed the alabaster rise of her breasts and the ivory length of her throat.

He suddenly wanted to rip it off her, shake the cool blue superiority from her eyes, and remind her that, though innocent in her fashion, she was just a tavern wench who had so seduced his curiosity—and hungers—that he had legally wed her as a way of coming to her aid. She wasn't really his wife. Lisa had been his wife, in all ways that the word could mean. Though Lisa was dead, somehow she was still his *wife*.

No, he thought painfully. Tara was now his wife. He had made the commitment just as she had. And he had found that the heat of his desire for her arose anew each time his passion should have been sated. And still he knew nothing about her. And now, when he saw that trouble was savagely spreading its tentacles out over his precious land, he realized that more tempest than he had ever imagined was awaiting him and must be weathered.

Tara hated his Eden. And she hadn't even stepped foot upon it yet.

"No, this is not where I live," he told her, adding, "it's much more barren where my house lies. This is like—London in comparison!"

If anything she went a shade paler. But her eyes were hard on his, narrowing at his tone. Her stare continued to condemn him, and for a moment he was sorry. Had he, in a matter of seconds, destroyed their chances here? Perhaps, he told himself wearily, he had already done so, admitting as well as demonstrating to her that he did have the ability to be a tyrant.

Then again, perhaps their pasts could not be left behind. Perhaps they had been doomed from the beginning.

She didn't say a word. She continued to stare at the land.

Impatience—and perhaps a bit of shame—brought heated words quickly to his lips once again.

"I told you where I was taking you!" he reminded her harshly.

"Ah, Mrs. McKenzie!" Robert called, stepping cheerfully toward her from around Jarrett's back. "Your first view of our beautiful Tampa Bay! See the water, Tara? The shade is like your eyes. The beaches are magnificent. Ignore the look of the buildings—Mrs. Conolly at the Bay Tavern makes the most wonderful meals, and she has big, clean rooms with beds that don't rock in the waves!"

As Jarrett watched, his wife smiled. Robert, it seemed—most irritatingly—always had the ability to make her happier. Her lips curled into their perfect, full, rose-colored smile and Jarrett felt a tug within his soul once again.

Would she have been happy in this wilderness if Robert had brought her into it?

But what of Robert himself? His charm was quickly going to fail them all, for once they reached shore, there would be no way to hide the truth that Tampa was preparing hard for an attack.

They would soon discover why.

He squared his shoulders, swearing silently at himself. It didn't matter. Tara hadn't said anything, she hadn't done anything. And they were here.

"It sounds—wonderful," Tara murmured in response to Robert.

Truly impatient then, remembering that all his thoughts about his wife had been swept away in his concern about events since his absence, Jarrett stepped forward and took his wife's arm. Robert would be doing so any second if he didn't step in, Jarrett was certain.

He took hold of her more roughly than he had intended. She didn't pull away, but he felt her stiffening beneath his touch.

"Let's move, then, shall we?" he asked. Once again he sounded curt. He didn't seem to be able to help himself.

He escorted her quickly down the plank that brought them to the dock. Even as they reached the shore, Nancy was rushing forward, Josh right behind her. Nancy threw herself into his arms, giving him a sound kiss on the lips, then quickly pulling back, holding him still, heedless of her huge husband lumbering behind her. "Oh, Jarrett, you cannot imagine how good it is that you are home! Perhaps you can do something where no one else can!"

"Nancy," Josh protested, "you're about to push him right back into the bay. Give the man some breathing space. And watch it, you're stepping on the young lady you just shoved from his side."

"Oh! Oh!" Nancy exclaimed. "I'm so dreadfully sorry!" she

told Tara, but then she saw Robert and kissed him too. Jarrett couldn't help but feel a slight tinge of pleasure at the quickly masked look of unease that had swept through Tara's eyes at Nancy's fond embrace.

"Nancy!" Robert said, picking up the slim, dark-haired young woman and spinning her around. "Whoops, there's that bear of a husband of yours," Robert said, and, laughing, put her down to shake Josh's hand.

"Nancy and Josh Reynolds. They own a shop here," Jarrett informed Tara. By then his crew were spilling off the ship behind them, while others of the townspeople were milling closer and closer around them.

Just beyond the crowd Jarrett could see that a military man was awaiting him as well. He recognized the golden locks and wide-brimmed hat of Captain Tyler Argosy, an old friend, and an army man to the core.

"What the hell has happened?" Jarrett demanded, expecting the answer from Josh Reynolds.

The big man inhaled deeply and sighed. "Hell has broken loose," he said simply. "Jarrett, Major Dade was bringing some troops a hundred miles north of here to Fort King. He was ambushed by the Seminoles. There were three survivors. One hasn't made it here, one can't talk, and the third man has put the almighty fear into each and every one of us! We're all getting prepared for an attack, every man armed and ready. Soon's you get a chance, you might want to get to the base and have a few words with that poor battered soldier who crawled his way out of the ambush. The Indians did the killing, then some of their runaway Negroes moved in and scalped and mutilated the bodies. Well, Jarrett, you can imagine. Some of the Negro-Seminoles have been living with the Indians so long, they are Indians. Some of them have been slave to the Indians and earned their freedom. But most of them have been slaves to white men, and some whites are mighty hard on their slaves. I imagine that once the Seminoles had done the killing, some of their black brethren were mighty glad to go in and rip up the bodies of the dead men. Wiley Thompson, the Indian agent, met with his own end as well. They say that Osceola was the leader there—Osceola was good and angry with Wiley Thompson—hell, Jarrett—excuse me, ladies—"

"Go on, Josh!" Nancy urged him. "Jarrett has to know what has happened here."

"Jarrett, most of us knew good and well that Osceola couldn't endure what Wiley did to him. You don't chain a Seminole, you just don't do it, and if Wiley Thompson had used a lick of sense, he would have known it. The Indians caught up with Wiley just outside the fort and murdered him and a few others. It's going to be real war now, Jarrett. No help for it. None at all."

Jarrett was silent, feeling a burning anguish sweep through him.

"Dear God!" Tara whispered.

"Ma'am, I'm so sorry," Josh said. "I didn't mean to be so blunt. Are you here to visit someone? Dear Lordy, I hope not one of those soldiers who was with Major Dade—"

"She's not for any of those poor fellows," Jarrett said wearily, interrupting Josh's fervent spill of concern. "She's my wife."

"Wife!" Nancy gasped. Josh, startled as well, gave Nancy a firm glance. Nancy quickly gathered her wits about her. "Wife! Oh, and we've just scared the girl to death. Jarrett—you—you should have warned us. We could have welcomed her so much more—"

"Humanely!" Josh suggested.

"Oh, move now, you big bear, and let's get her off the dock. Oh, this is terrible, Mrs.—McKenzie," Nancy said, tripping over the name.

"Tara," Jarrett suggested. "Her name is Tara."

"Then let's get her into the tavern before she passes out."

Tara was white. Like a sheet. Her gaze fell upon his with pure rebellion. But she wasn't going to pass out. Indeed, she looked as if she were ready to strangle him.

"You needn't worry. Tara is made of strong stuff. She's very good at eluding enemies. She won't pass out," Jarrett said firmly.

"Come, dear, anyway!" Nancy said, slipping an arm through Tara's. "Such cruel news to hear just as you arrive! The tavern is ahead, down the street a spell, easily walked, if you can make it—"

"She can make it," Jarrett said.

"She can also speak for herself," Tara said, her eyes blue flames as they touched upon him. Her color was returning. He smiled grimly. She did know how to meet a challenge.

Tara started walking along with Nancy. Nancy began saying inane things about the weather. Jarrett turned back to see that their belongings were sent to the tavern for the night, and then he met Robert's eyes. "I'm sorry, Jarrett," he murmured. "We have seen it coming."

Jarrett nodded. The wars, the killing, the hatreds, had been going on for years. The wars didn't begin and end—it seemed that the times of peace did.

"Argosy is waiting for you," Robert said, referring to the soldier in the wide-brimmed hat who stood just outside the crowd at the dock.

Jarrett nodded. "Take Tara on to Mrs. Conolly's. I'll be right along."

He strode up the incline to where Tyler Argosy patiently waited. He offered a hand to Jarrett, and Jarrett took it, clasping it firmly. "You've heard the news already, I imagine. It's bad. There's widespread panic inland. Plantations have been burned. The whites want all-out revenge. Total deportation to the western territories of all Florida Indians. Most people don't want a single red man left behind."

Jarrett paused, shaking his head. "We're in for it, Tyler. You don't know how tenacious the Seminoles are. They've been running a long time. We've lied, we've betrayed them. And they know this territory far better than we. They can fight it well with a third of our military numbers. It will be long, bloody, and fierce, I imagine."

"The local militia is already on the move; we know there will be help from Washington," Tyler told him. "But we need men like you. You know the swamps and the bogs and the hammocks. If you were to accept a commission and take up arms against some of the really bad factions—"

"Can't do it, Tyler. Can't do it. You know that I can't," Jarrett told him.

Tyler inhaled and exhaled, looking out to sea. "Well, I kind of knew that, but our own brand of chiefs wanted me to approach you quietly."

"Ask me again when there is something that I can do. Don't ask me to go to any of the chiefs with lies. But any honest negotiation that needs doing, I'll be your man."

Tyler nodded. "We'll need you in the future. Not to wage war, but to talk." He hesitated a minute. "There are plenty of white men who don't understand your position. A lot of hostility could come your way now."

"A lot of Indians probably hate me, too, Tyler. It doesn't matter. I can only follow my own conscience on this."

"No man can do more."

"But, Jesu, I hate the killing. I'll talk to anyone at any time, that I can promise you."

Tyler nodded again. "You heading inland anyway?"

"I'll be fine inland. My property is neutral territory."

"Let's pray it stays that way."

"Osceola is an important war chief at the moment. If he's calling the shots, I imagine my property will remain neutral. Besides, the men with me—red, black, and white—are all men of their word, and I've never broken any trust with the Indians."

"You fought against the Red Sticks in the Creek War. As a mere lad."

"Different time, different circumstances. The Red Sticks attacked close to my home. There are different alliances now. I've kept my friends and made my peace with my enemies."

"You may be forced into battle again. This is going to be a hard time to straddle a fence."

"It's never easy to straddle a fence."

Tyler shrugged and looked up to the sky. "Well, I guess I knew what you'd say. And I give you my word, I won't be asking you to make any negotiations that aren't honest."

"I'll be there for you," Jarrett said.

"You bringing a wife home?" Tyler asked, indicating the party, which had now disappeared down the street toward Mrs. Conolly's tavern.

"Yes."

Tyler smiled. "Lots of ladies thought they were in line for that position, once time enough had passed. She's a beauty," Tyler told him. "A rare beauty! She might be nervous about the Indians, but then again, she might be in greater danger from a few rivals in these parts! Damn! Where did you find such an elegant creature?"

Jarrett was tempted to admit he had acquired her in a game of chance, but he shrugged instead. "New Orleans," he said simply.

"A southern girl? Impeccable family, I imagine."

"Right out of New Orleans," Jarrett said. He wasn't about to admit that he hadn't the least idea. He reached out, shaking Tyler's hand again. "I'll be home. Call when you need me and I can actually help you."

"Right. And congratulations. On your marriage."

"Thanks!"

Jarrett left him and strode to the tavern, absently returning greetings to those who hailed him, yet moving so quickly that none would stop to detain him. When he entered the tavern, he found that Josh, Nancy, and Robert were seated at a table. Tara was nowhere to be seen.

The beams were low, the room was smoky. A fire burned warmly from a hearth, and despite the somewhat shanty appearance of the place, the aromas within it were pleasant. Jarrett ignored both the slight haze of smoke and the pleasant scents and hurried toward the table. "Where is Tara?" he asked, annoyed at the harshness in his voice. He couldn't help the suspicion that she might have already tried to discover a way to run away. Again.

"Mrs. Conolly has given you two the large room up the stairs to the far rear," Nancy told him. "Tara just wanted to wash up for a moment. She'll be right back."

He didn't sit. He was too tempted to run up the stairs and find out if she was, indeed, within the room they had been given for the night's stay.

But at that moment his wife appeared at the top of the stairs. Swiftly, gracefully, she descended.

Her eyes didn't touch his as she smoothly came around to take the chair at Robert's side.

Jarrett managed to be there in time. The gentlemen rose, but he pulled back her chair and saw her seated. He then took his own chair, hailing plump Mrs. Conolly, wiping her hands on her apron as she hurried to the table behind Tara. "Jarrett McKenzie, but 'tis good to see you back, sir! And with such a fine new wife! Ah, but the lasses will be pining here, and still, such a beauty you've acquired!" Her smile faded. "We're so dreadfully sorry about what you've come home to."

"Thank you, Peggy Conolly," Jarrett said, flashing her a quick smile. "Anything is fine to come home to—as long as you're still cooking your magnificent roasts."

"I've a fine supper coming for you and Robbie Treat and your friends and fine new lady!" She flashed him a smile in return, easily distracted when the flattery was about her good cooking. "Ah, here's Sheila with a spot of tea for the ladies, and good stout ale for you gents. Bread will be right along, and then your roast with plenty of the world's finest mashed potatoes, greens, and yams!"

Mrs. Conolly stepped back as her serving girl, Sheila, stepped forward, her strong slim arms laden down with a heavy tray.

Sheila cast Jarrett a long glance, as she placed the tea things first and then the ale.

She was a curious woman, brown, slim, and exotically pretty. She was an orphan of various races, and the widowed Mrs. Conolly had taken her in years earlier. Mrs. Conolly insisted on Sunday school for her charge. Sheila obligingly went—and seduced all the boys in her classes. She was wild in her ways, but honest and blunt spoken, and she and Jarrett had known one another well for years.

"Welcome home," Sheila told him huskily.

"Thank you."

"You'll not be scared by all the talk!" she said approvingly.

"The talk is bad," he admitted, drinking his ale. Sheila smiled and left the table. Jarrett felt his wife's eyes on him and he smiled. Again, he could not help but be glad that she seemed to be feeling a bit of irritation—if not jealousy. He seemed to be constantly suffering so himself.

He lifted his cup of ale to her. "Welcome home, Mrs. McKenzie," he said softly.

"Aye, welcome to you, Tara!" Nancy said enthusiastically. Her husband echoed the sentiment, and Tara smiled, sipping her tea.

"What a place!" she murmured, her eyes telling Jarrett exactly what she meant, even if her tone did not.

"What did Captain Argosy want?" Nancy asked. As she did so, Mrs. Conolly and a very tall black man arrived, setting down trenchers with roast beef and vegetables and breads. In seconds the sturdy hardwood table was heavy laden. Sheila arrived to serve, even as Jarrett gave his answer.

"He wanted me to take a commission. To lead troops."

"But you—you won't, will you?" Nancy murmured.

Jarrett shook his head. "I can't, Nancy. You know that."

"Will you negotiate if they ask you?" Josh asked him.

Jarrett nodded grimly. "I will do everything in my power to end this with as little bloodshed as possible," Jarrett assured him.

The food had been served. Nancy looked down at her plate.

"The stories were just so horrible!" she breathed. "Half Dade's men went down in the first volley. The Indians ambushed them, hiding in the brush. The wounded screamed and cried out while their fellow soldiers scrambled to bring down the warriors knowing they would soon be mutilated themselves—"

"Nancy!" Josh firmly interrupted his wife.

Jarrett gazed down the table to Tara. She had picked up her fork and set it down again.

"Come, now!" Sheila, standing just at Jarrett's rear, said firmly. "Mrs. Reynolds, don't dwell on it. Eat up, now, all of you. Floridians will need their strength in the days to come."

"Oh, but Jarrett!" Nancy said, staring at him with round, concerned eyes. "As well as I know you and your abilities and connections, I think I might be afraid to be on that plantation of yours now—"

"I wouldn't be," Sheila interrupted, filling Jarrett's ale glass anew. "Jarrett McKenzie is in no danger. None at all. He is needed by both sides, and his plantation is well defended."

"Surely," Tara said, blue eyes sharp on Sheila's exotic dark ones, "Major Dade was well defended as well!"

"Major Dade was taken by surprise. Jarrett would not be," Sheila insisted loyally.

"Do you doubt my ability to defend you, my dear?" Jarrett inquired politely, arching a brow to Tara.

She was silent for a moment. He could almost feel the tension crackling in the air between them. She smiled, answering carefully. "I doubt any one man's ability against countless others, sir."

Sheila sniffed and left the table. Nancy set down her fork. "I'm not feeling well," she said quietly.

Tara was quickly up. "Come upstairs then, Nancy. Lie down for a few moments, and perhaps you'll feel better."

"Perhaps, yes. . . ."

Tara had not wanted to admit that she was not feeling so well herself. She offered Josh and Robert a radiant smile, and ignored Jarrett. "Excuse us, will you, gentlemen?" The men rose—Jarrett, bound by society, standing with the others. Tara felt his ebony gaze upon her, but she refused to look his way.

She led Nancy up the stairs and coaxed her into lying down with her head slightly raised on the downy white pillow. "Oh, this is much better!" Nancy murmured. Then she smiled after a moment, watching Tara. "So he came home with a wife! Who would have imagined!" She laughed softly. "Not that he ever really stopped appreciating women, but . . . well, I had not imagined that he would care enough about one to *marry* her. He and Lisa were both so young when they married, so alike in a way."

"What way?" Tara asked, sitting on the bed at Nancy's side, pouncing on the information.

"Well, they were both in love with the house and the land, the river, and everything around them. It's strange. Josh was with the army until he took a hard fall and hurt his back. I wanted to move back north, but Josh just loves this area. I mean, really, I do not wish to be indelicate, but the place was filled with women of the lowest, the lowest—"

"Whores?" Tara asked softly.

Nancy blushed. "Yes!" she exclaimed. "And the soldiers can be so rowdy . . . but Josh insisted that only by decent folk moving in could we make it a decent place. So, we're trying. And the longer we're here, the more I love it. I love the winters, I love the sun. The beautiful beaches and the sand, and sometimes, some of the lonely places are the most wonderful. I mean, sometimes, you're so far away from society, you can forget all the rules. Why" —she paused, blushing furiously—"we've swum in the warm surf, buck naked, grown-ups! I was so afraid at first, but, oh! what a time to be telling you such things. I just wanted you to see the good . . . except now, of course, I'm a little frightened all over again. Some of the Seminoles are so articulate and polite! I've seen some of them when they've been taken prisoner, half starved, and they tore at my heart! But then again . . ." She broke off, shivering. "Oh, my God! What happened to Major Dade's men was so—so wretchedly savage!"

Tara inhaled very deeply. She bit into her lower lip. Surely, things would be different now. Perhaps it wouldn't be so bad if they could stay here, in Tampa. At least she would be with Nancy and Josh—and the great expanse of the Gulf of Mexico would be at her back. They could sail away when danger approached.

"Poor Jarrett!" Nancy murmured. "He's in such a difficult position. And now, of course, since Lisa's death by Indians in the wilderness . . ."

"By the Indians?" Tara asked faintly.

"Oh! It was nothing like the trouble with Major Dade!" Nancy said quickly, sitting up. "I didn't mean to alarm you. Jarrett hasn't spoken to you about her? He can be so quiet on the subject, and yet you're his wife now, so I simply assumed . . ."

Even as her voice trailed away, there was a sharp rap on the door.

Tara jumped up, staring at it. "Yes?" she demanded. Dear God in His Heaven, what a time for an interruption!

The door opened. Josh and Jarrett stood there. "We've a need to get home, Nancy," Josh told his wife. "You're all right, now, aren't you?"

"Yes, yes, of course!" Nancy murmured, rising quickly. She gave Tara a hug. "We've two little ones at home. I hope you get to see them before . . . well, I hope you get to see them very soon."

Tara hugged her back, wishing she could swear at both the men and send them back downstairs until she had a chance to learn more from Nancy.

What had Nancy really been about to say? She hoped she'd be able to see her children before—what? Before she left? *Before she was massacred?* Like Jarrett's first wife, his beloved Lisa?

"Tara McKenzie, it was our greatest pleasure," Josh assured her, taking her delicate hand in his huge one. "Jarrett, we'll have your supplies ready in the morning," he said, shaking Jarrett's hand as well. Nancy and Josh left. Jarrett closed the door behind them, then turned and leaned against it.

"What are we going to do now?" Tara asked, backing toward the bed to place some distance between them. She knew that the tone of her voice was shrill, but she couldn't seem to help it. The vivid description Nancy had given of the Indian massacre remained very sharp in her mind. She suddenly felt that not even Tampa could be safe, and she wanted to board the ship again and sail out far into the Gulf of Mexico *now*, heading anywhere as long as it was far, far away from the Florida Territory.

It was the wrong question, she realized quickly—no matter how much sense it made for her to be asking it. His eyes narrowed sharply upon her.

"What do you mean, what are we going to do now?" he asked huskily.

She lifted her hands. "Well, we can't go to that plantation of yours."

"Why not?"

"Why not?" Tara breathed in astonishment.

"Why not?" he repeated, his tone growing angry.

"The Indians just massacred an entire troop of men. There's a war on. Didn't you hear all those horrible things—"

"There's trouble, yes. There has been trouble for any Indian in Florida since the Europeans first sailed west."

"The Seminoles weren't the ones who were just slaughtered so horribly."

"Don't kid yourself, Tara. Wars are fought by two sides. Wiley Thompson betrayed his promises and American treaties time and time again. I've seen white troops raid Indian villages and kill women and children. They aren't doing anything new to us."

Her eyes widened on him. Then she felt herself growing angrier. "Well, that's just fine! But I never met a Seminole or Mikasuki in my entire life, and you seem to think that it will be justice for us to be massacred because of promises someone else broke to a bunch of savages—" She broke off with a gasp, stunned and frightened, because for a moment it had seemed that he would strike her. Send his palm cracking across her cheek. He'd stood near the door. Yet even as she had spoken, he had taken a silent step toward her.

He didn't touch her. He seemed more taut than the strings on a fiddle, hard as rock, barely controlled, his arm raised, palm open. But his arm quickly fell. His lips were all but white and the whole of his body still seemed to threaten violence. She swallowed hard, standing still, staring at him.

"You're not going to be massacred," he said flatly at last.

"You're right, McKenzie," Tara said woodenly after a moment. "Because I'm not going with you inland."

"What?" he demanded, the word stingingly sharp.

She stiffened. "I'm not—"

Within seconds he had come even closer to her. She started to back away, but he had moved too quickly. His hands were suddenly on her upper arms, and she was being drawn mercilessly toward him, meeting a tight-leashed and explosive fury in his black eyes.

Her knees felt weak. She should have risked the muddy waters of the Mississippi. She didn't know which might prove more dangerous now, the savages or Jarrett McKenzie. Desperately she lashed out with words. "I'm not going inland to be murdered by savages."

"Stop it! You're not going to be murdered."

"Those men—"

"You married me!" he roared at her with such passion it seemed her head began to spin.

"Yes, you were helping me! And I thank you, truly. But you don't have to be responsible—"

"What, and you think you don't have to oblige?" His fingers bit ever more deeply into her arms. He had shaken her so hard that her hair had come free and tumbled down her back in a tangle of pins. She felt tears stinging her eyes and longed to pummel him with her fists.

"I didn't intend to run off or—"

"What did you intend, then? 'Ah, bring on your alligators and savages!' Do you remember saying those words, my love? You wanted out of New Orleans. Well, you are out now. You are married. So just what did you intend?"

"Let go of me!" she demanded. "You're—hurting me!"

"I'll grip you a hell of a lot harder if you don't start explaining yourself, *Mrs. McKenzie.*"

"Damn it, you don't have to be concerned—" she began, furious with herself for the pleading sound that was slipping into her voice. Dear God! It seemed at this moment that she had hopped from the frying pan right into the fire. "I just meant that you don't have to be obliged, I thank you for what you've done, and I'll really be fine now on my own!" she finished breathlessly. "I'm trying to say that you don't have to be concerned about me, you quite apparently had a life going on here before I intruded on it and . . ."

She wasn't doing well. Her voice trailed away beneath the black anger in his eyes. "You've people you're close to here. You probably have certain . . . relationships already." Dear Lord, she was doing worse and worse. "I'm so very grateful to you, and though I've learned so very little about her, I do know that your heart remains with your wife."

"You are my wife," he said harshly, and it seemed that he could barely form the words from between clenched teeth. She wondered if he was trying to remind her of that fact, or himself.

"Not the one you want!" she cried softly, and realized that she was succeeding only in making him more furious with every word. And nothing seemed to be working. "You're hurting me!" she whispered again.

He suddenly let her go. He strode back to the door. It looked as if he felt he had to escape the room—or throttle her.

But he paused in the doorway, his back to her. His shoulders seemed very broad, his height imposing, even his ebony hair adding to the look of strength and determination in his stance.

He spun around to stare at her again, carefully keeping his distance, and her heart seemed to leap into her throat. She was frightened by his anger. And still, it seemed that flood waters were ripping through her, she wanted to run both away from him and straight to him. She wanted to beat her fists against him and be held by him.

And yet in the end, it seemed, it would make no difference. He was bound on a fool's quest. He didn't want to fight the savages—he had turned down the military man who had offered him an army commission.

He just wanted to go home.

To a plantation that bordered Indian lands.

"If you're interested in your predecessor," he told her, his words heated, electric with emotion, "I can tell you this about her. She wasn't a coward. She wasn't afraid of people who were different, of places she didn't know."

"But I'm not Lisa!" she reminded him.

"As I am well aware. But you married me," he said, and his voice was low, even. Yet it rang with a warning that chilled her to the bone. "And, my love, you are *obliged* to me! Where I go, you will follow! You've spent so damned much time running! But you will not run from me. I will hunt you down. I will find you, wherever you go. You chose to make the commitment. No one forced you. You will honor your vows!"

"And what of you?" she demanded, finding it difficult to give force to her voice but determined that she would fight. She couldn't understand him! He didn't seem at all afraid, even though Nancy Reynolds had told Tara that Lisa had died—with the Indians!

"What!" he demanded.

"What of you?" she cried again. "You vowed to cherish and care for a wife! Would you so easily send another to her death with the savages?"

This time, she thought, he would stride to her and strike her to the floor. Black fire leapt into his eyes, and his features darkened and tightened even as the line of his mouth grew tighter, whiter still. She held her ground, barely able to breathe, suddenly, desperately, wishing that she had never spoken. Tears threatened her eyes, and she blinked them back furiously. She had learned more than that his first wife had somehow perished among the Indians. She had learned that Jarrett McKenzie had loved her deeply, and that he hadn't cared much for anything except his land since.

Tara was simply an acquisition. Men had land, houses, ships, horses—and wives. She had been well worth three hundred dollars. Priceless, he had once whispered. But that had been in the dark. And yet in that same darkness he had touched her, and a tempest had been born within her own heart.

It suddenly didn't matter who was right or wrong. She wanted to back down. She wanted to say something that would ease the tension and anger from his face.

Her words didn't come quickly enough.

"Pity the poor savages!" he said softly.

He spun around sharply, pulling open the door, striding out. The door slammed in his wake.

Her knees gave way at last, and she sank down to the bed, shivering still. She hurt in a way she had never begun to imagine, in a way she didn't fully understand. She was afraid of the future, and yet his disappointment in her created a pain that seemed to outweigh the fear. And yet the fear of the unknown remained pulsing beneath. She wanted to run after him, and she wanted to run away.

Think! she commanded herself. *Think! You've been running so very long, Tara, surely you can run farther.*

But she couldn't think. Or even seem to move. She lay there and wondered and worried.

And prayed that the very man she was fighting had not gone down to spend time with the dark exotic girl below the stairs, who was obviously more than willing to follow him anywhere.

Run! she urged herself again.

But she wasn't going to run. No matter how frightened she was. She was going to meet her damned obligations. She was going to find out the truth about Lisa, and about Jarrett McKenzie, and his strange relationship with the various denizens of Florida. And she was going to fight against—and for!—the searing dark-eyed stranger who had so entangled her within his grasp. The man who had awakened her passions and something even more dangerous within her heart and soul.

The man who loved the courageous Lisa.

Lisa was gone.

And Tara was his wife now. She shivered wildly again, closing her eyes and hugging her arms about her chest. *Had she forgotten that he had plucked her out of New Orleans?* She did owe him, no wonder he was so angry.

But why was she so jealous?

And torn. Even as she listened to herself fight him, tell him that she could not go with him, she had wondered if she could ever willingly walk away from him. He seemed a darker mystery than she could ever be herself, so striking, so haunted, so confident, assured. So compelling in his touch, his words. . . .

The way he held her.

She was emmeshed with him, their lives were interwoven already. It seemed their passions ran so high, their tempers rose so swiftly. And yet, when he touched her, those very passions carried such a wealth of magic.

He was a practiced lover, she told herself.

And she was right! All of the men and women living in Tampa were afraid of Indian attacks, there was a war on. He needed to be afraid. Surely she was right in her arguments!

It didn't help.

She still lay awake. In torment again, wondering about Sheila with the dark eyes and the bold words.

He would come back to her tonight, Tara thought. He had married her.

But the hours passed.

And he did not return.

And the torment haunted her on through the long hours before the dawn.

Chapter 7

Tara awoke with a start, certain that she had just fallen asleep. Then she realized that day had come again, that light was streaming in the windows of Mrs. Conolly's largest, most comfortable room, and that there was motion near her as well. She blinked against the light and realized that she had slept fully clothed, after the hours she had lain awake wondering if Jarrett would come back.

He had come back. She kept her lashes low over her eyes as she watched him. He was clad in hugging breeches and boots and was just donning a clean white shirt. He stared out the window, then his gaze fell upon her. She closed her eyes again and rolled away, still very tired and determined to pretend that she was still asleep. Had he slept in this room? She didn't think so. From the few seconds' view of the room she had allowed herself, she'd seen that his pillow hadn't the hint of an indentation on it. She was appalled by the jealousy and anger that so instantly filled her.

She opened her eyes slightly again and gasped. She was startled to discover he had come around the side of the bed in silence and hunkered down before her by the bed waiting for her to open her eyes once again. There could be no pretense anymore. She sat up quickly, deeply irritated that he had caught her so easily and swiftly in her act. Damn him! How could such a man move so swiftly and without the least bit of noise?

"I see you're awake," he remarked sardonically, standing. "I'm glad. I want to sail again within the next two hours."

Her heart slammed with a thud of hope against her chest. "To a northern port?" she inquired quickly.

"To home," he said flatly. "I'd thought to stay here longer, to give you more time to see the town, meet people—shop for your own things—but under the circumstances I'm very anxious to reach the house."

"If it's standing," Tara said.

"It will be standing," he assured her.

"I imagine that other homeowners will be flocking here for protection. Perhaps we should wait and see what is happening."

"We could wait years," he said curtly, unswayed and growing ever more impatient. "There's wash water on the dresser and coffee on the table by the window. We can't travel half so quickly up the river as we do on the open sea, so I would like to leave as soon as possible."

Tara rose quickly, trying to straighten the wild strands of her hair that were slipping in long tendrils from the pins at her nape. She strode quickly toward the table and poured herself coffee, sipping it as she stared out the window at the beautiful day. The sun was shining brilliantly. The sky was powder-blue.

"Be ready, Tara," he reminded her.

She didn't reply. He turned, opening the bedroom door to exit the room. She heard the door close behind him.

"Be ready!" she muttered angrily. "We want to hurry up and go into the wilderness, where the Indians can slice us to pieces! He's so damned anxious to leave! I'd assumed he'd done so last night!"

She spoke to the window, to the pretty sky. Silence—expected silence—followed her outburst.

But she got a response, the sound of dry laughter.

Stunned, she spun around.

Jarrett remained in the room.

"Ah! Did you miss me, then? And I thought you'd be anxious to be free of my company!"

She was anxious to throttle him at the moment. He'd never left the room. He had started to—but he had come back in and closed the door. Facing him now, she felt her cheeks redden, felt all her frustrations and fears rise high within her.

"I was delighted to be free of your company," she said heatedly.

"You should have thought of that before you married me," he said grimly.

"I'd no idea then that you could be so totally unreasonable."

"Have I failed you yet?" he demanded coolly.

"I don't know."

"Did I abandon you to the cutthroats in New Orleans?" he asked her.

"That's different."

"It's not different. And I gave you every warning about my life. You made the commitment."

"And so did you!" she snapped. "Perhaps whoever shared your evening with you last night is more eager to travel the river than I am!"

An ebony brow hiked over a dark eye and a thick silence followed her words. She was alarmed by them herself.

"You will travel the river with me," he said after a moment.

"But I'm not the one—"

"You are the one who is wed to me, my love. I'll be back for you in an hour."

This time, when the door opened, he did pass through it. Shaking, Tara carried her coffee to the bed and sat at the foot of it. Dear God, what was she doing? She had all but spit in his face when he had once saved her from disaster. She was so afraid again. And jealous as well. And lost, and feeling that she was sinking.

He hadn't failed her in New Orleans, he had fought for her when she had been nothing more to him than an amusing tavern wench. And yet this was very different, and he couldn't deny it! Men had been after her in New Orleans, but this battle was against a whole tribe—or tribes!—of Indians.

And Jarrett didn't want to fight them. The army desperately needed men who knew the interior as Jarrett knew it, and Jarrett was refusing to accept a commission. She didn't want him riding into an ambush like that poor Major Dade, but neither did she want to wait until the Indians came after them.

Her coffee was gone. She leapt up and hurried to pour herself another cup, and drank it down quickly, almost as if it were whiskey or wine. It had no such effect, but it did make her feel more fully awake, and where she had earlier felt numb, she now started to move very fast, washing her face furiously, digging into the trunk for a cooler gown to wear.

She paused suddenly, shivering. She was so good at running. And she had been so wretched when she had lain awake waiting and wondering.

She dropped the clothing she lifted from the trunk as if it had suddenly turned to fire and burned her fingers. These were his wife's things. They had belonged to the woman he had loved. The woman who had somehow lost her life among the Indians. How? She hadn't died like Major Dade and his men, Nancy had said. But then . . . ?

She sat back on the bed again. She didn't want to wear her predecessor's clothing. But she had nothing else. And Jarrett had given these things to her.

No. It was Robert who had brought the trunk to her.

She sighed. There wasn't much choice. She could wear one of these gowns, or nothing, since it seemed the dress and cape she had worn when escaping New Orleans remained aboard the *Magda*.

Don't think about it, she told herself sternly, and she found a cotton dress in a soft flowered pink print. With her mind made up she dressed quickly, and was brushing out the length of her hair to pin it again when Jarrett reappeared in the room. He didn't knock, he just stepped inside. She hadn't even heard him come and hadn't known that he was there until she saw him scowling at her from the mirror's reflection. Her brush wavered. She was still here—she hadn't run—but it seemed she was an errant wife once again. He had come for her, and she was not ready, and the sight of her brushing out her hair and clad in one of Lisa's gowns must have been very irritating.

She whipped the length of her hair quickly into a knot and pinned it securely, then spun around. "Is it time to leave?" she asked icily. As he watched her with his glittering black stare, she felt a swift stab of pain once again. *What had she done? What had they done? Did the dusky-skinned beauty below the stairs care that he had taken a new wife? Would it matter to Sheila in the night what commitments had been made?*

Did it matter to Jarrett?

"Yes. Shall we?" He turned to leave, expecting her to follow.

She remained stubbornly still. "What about our things?" she asked.

"The trunks will be on the *Magda* before we are," he assured her, turning back. "Come on, we must leave."

But she still didn't move. "I want you to know that I am doing this under protest."

"Amazingly, I am aware of that fact," he murmured.

"It's not just the situation," she told him. "The uprising—the danger of being slaughtered in our beds. We should have had— some time. Here. With others. With—with dressmakers. I have only another woman's belongings—"

She broke off as he hiked up an arched brow. "Demanding little runaway, aren't you?" he inquired softly.

She stood tall and straight and silent for a moment, then said softly, "I wouldn't dream of demanding a thing, not when you make the extent of my debt to you so painfully clear. Yet it can't make you happy to see me in your wife's clothing."

"There is little making me happy at this moment," he assured her. "May we please leave?"

Perhaps Tara had wanted him to tell her she was his wife now. He didn't. It seemed he only mentioned the fact to remind her that she was bound to follow his dictates.

She sailed by him, pausing when she was just a step ahead of him. "We're in such a hurry now. It's a pity you didn't know that night when you were playing poker that so much was happening here."

"As it turned out," he said smoothly behind her, "it was rather fortunate, wasn't it? I never would have reached home so quickly had I not been escaping New Orleans with you. Keep walking, Tara."

She clenched her fingers into fists and started walking. He made a derisive sound, and she spun around, finding those black eyes shooting into her like Stygian blades.

"I had not imagined that you would prove to be so—timid."

"I am not, McKenzie. I am simply sensible."

"I ask you again, have I failed you yet?"

"Perhaps you should explain your fantastic confidence in regard to the savages."

"Perhaps you should explain why you are now beholden to live with me among them?" he suggested smoothly.

She swung around again, seething. Trust him—with the truth! —when they were all but bitter enemies.

She kept walking, and this time she didn't stop until she had reached the foot of the stairs, where Mrs. Conolly was waiting to say her farewells and hug Tara and welcome her to the territory once again.

Robert met them at the door to the tavern, winking quickly, lifting her spirits. It seemed that he would be accompanying them as well. Jarrett didn't have anything further to say to her, and he seemed to prefer that she walk ahead of him, idly conversing with

Robert as they made their way back to the *Magda*. But even as she exchanged meaningless pleasantries with Robert, she could feel Jarrett behind her. Feel his eyes, his heat.

His disappointment.

Where had he slept last night?

She was glad to see Josh and Nancy waiting on the dock. Tara had barely gotten to know Nancy the night before, but she had discovered a genuine warmth within the pretty young woman, and she already felt as if she were being torn away from a friend.

"It was so wonderful to meet you!" Nancy assured her, coming forward to give Tara a hug even as Josh called out to Jarrett, "She's well loaded down with the best we could do on such short notice. I think you'll find all that you need for the time coming."

Tara barely heard the two men. She was looking at the tawdry little place called Tampa and thinking that it suddenly seemed like the greatest of cities. She didn't want to leave.

"It was wonderful to meet you," she assured Nancy. She asked herself what would happen if she went hysterical on the dock and started to scream and swear that she simply would not be massacred by Indians.

She would probably be massacred by Jarrett, then and there.

She didn't scream. She tried to smile as Nancy told her that she had filled crates with what fabrics and patterns she'd had in the store and sent new corsets, petticoats, pantalettes, and all that she could find. "Jarrett said that you left New Orleans rather quickly and that your baggage was left behind. I think you'll be pleased. Jarrett's laundress, Cota, is also an exceptional seamstress if you don't sew."

"I do sew," Tara murmured simply. She realized that Nancy must assume she had come from an important, well-to-do family. She didn't want to explain exactly why she was so adept with a needle and thread.

"God bless you, then! I'm delighted for Jarrett's sake that you're with him, and I'll pray for you! Of course, he will keep you safe, he must simply adore you, we are still so very stunned that he actually married—oh, dear, forgive me, I do wander on!"

Not nearly enough! Tara thought with an inward groan, but Nancy was already rushing on again. "When I can, I'll visit. And you'll come back. It's only two days by river and not much longer by horseback or wagon. We're really not so very far!"

"Nancy." Jarrett touched the vivacious brunette on the shoulder. She kissed his cheek, and he held her warmly for a moment.

"God keep you, Jarrett. We love you."

"You too," he told her affectionately. He shook hands with Josh, and Robert said his farewells to Nancy and Josh as well. With Jarrett's hand at her back Tara boarded the *Magda* again, turning to look at the shore and fighting the temptation to flee for what now seemed familiar and warm.

She wasn't going anywhere. He remained at her back while his crew ran about, easing the ship from the dock. She could feel his strong hands set lightly upon her hips.

"My congratulations, my love," he whispered softly at her ear.

"On what?" she murmured dully.

"Your chin was high—and you didn't dive into the river."

"The river's still there."

"Ah, yes, but we are going farther and farther away from civilization."

She didn't reply but heard his soft groan of exasperation as she shivered despite herself.

Angered and defensive, Tara cried and started to lash out at him again. "How can you not see—" she began.

"And how can you give me no faith whatsoever, when I've yet to betray you, despite the fact that you are all too willing to run again?"

"This is entirely different," she tried.

"No, it is not!" he snapped, and suddenly he was gone, calling out an order to Leo, leaving her at the rail and leaping with a seaman's sure agility to the helm.

She could still see Nancy and Josh, waving good-bye.

And just beyond Nancy and Josh and some of the other civilians who lined the shore, she could see the blond man in the crisp military attire and broad-rimmed hat who had stopped Jarrett yesterday: the man who had tried to have him take a commission.

The man saw her. He lifted his hat and bowed gravely. Tara hesitated, then lifted a hand and waved good-bye.

Slowly, those on the shore began to disappear, and as they headed along the river, civilization vanished as well.

Gradually the foliage became more and more dense. And indeed, it seemed that she was sailing into a savage land.

The going was much slower by river than it had been on the open sea, but Tara stood by the ship's rail for hours as the morning passed by, watching the shoreline. Trees grew thickly along much of the river, their boughs dipping over it. Silvery cloaks of moss covered much of the boughs. The river became a darker green, and for a while it seemed that the world itself was all decked in green. The embankment, the water, and even the sky seemed to take on the hue. Yet there were other colors as well, fascinating, intriguing. Here and there, wildflowers grew, their petals creating bursts and riots of color. The river here was wide and deep, and the breeze was with them. The sails filled gently, then began to puff out tightly.

She started at a sudden cawing sound and realized that birds within the tangled foliage were giving off the sometimes shrill, sometimes plaintive calls.

The sky was darkening. They were in for rain again, she thought. The wild foliage on the shoreline began to writhe and undulate, and when she saw a sudden fluttering of color, she was suddenly certain that she was seeing a befeathered Indian stalking them from the concealment of the green bank. The trees began to bow deeper, their cloaks of moss stretching out like webs, their branches like skeletal fingers. She inhaled on a harsh breath, watching.

A bird whistled out a cry and soared out of the bushes. She had seen a feather—but one attached to a living creature. She exhaled on a shaky breath, then nearly screamed aloud when she felt a touch on her shoulder. She spun around. The wind caught her hair and whipped it free. Jarrett held her shoulders. He had stripped down to his breeches only, even his feet were bare, and he seemed as bronze as an Indian himself as he shouted to her, making his voice stronger than the growing moan of the wind.

"Get to the cabin, you'll be soaked in a moment!"

She stared at him with no reply and he frowned, touching her cheek. "You're snow white!"

"I—thought I saw a feather."

"And?" he queried somewhat harshly, a brow arched high.

"It was—a feather."

"You turned white over a feather?"

"I thought it was part of an Indian."

"I don't know what they told you wherever you come from, Tara, but Indians do not *grow* feathers."

"Don't be an idiot, I didn't think that it *grew* on an Indian, I thought that it was part of a headdress. Unless you're going to tell me that Florida Indians do not ever make use of bird feathers?"

"They make use of feathers," he said evenly. "But since you are not screaming and have not plunged into the river I assume that you didn't see an Indian?"

"No."

"You mean that the feather was actually part of a *bird?*" he inquired.

She lifted her chin, swept up her skirts, and shook off his touch as she started by him. "Excuse me," she murmured regally, "I think that I will avoid the rain—and any other nasty and irritating things to be found on deck."

Jarrett clenched his teeth and almost stopped her, but he let her walk by.

The rain started. It was light at first. Hands on his hips, he stared at the shoreline.

He'd had no right to taunt her, and he was damned glad that what she'd seen had turned out to be a bird.

Because the Indians were out there. Watching him. And they would watch him all the way home.

The rain fell throughout the day, light upon occasion, heavy, then nothing more than a drizzle. Tara was able to spend most of the day going through what Nancy had considerately delivered to the captain's cabin. She was pleased to discover that Nancy had indeed done well for her, and she was grateful for the many fabrics and patterns and underthings she found within the boxes. She spent much of the day absorbed in cutting and pinning fabric and adding her own touches. When the afternoon began to wane and she heard footsteps, she hurriedly wrapped up her work and returned everything to a box, but the footsteps went on by her.

Soon, however, Nathan came with a dinner tray for her, and she discovered she was starving. She ate quickly, then paced the cabin. She stepped outside to realize that the rain had stopped. It seemed that they moved at a crawl, and she shivered fiercely as she stood on the deck. Night had fallen. She stared at the shoreline and thought that she had never seen anything so horribly *dark*. Yet the darkness rustled. She wondered if half-naked bodies were moving within the foliage, and after a moment she hurried back inside the cabin. For a while she paced again, certain that she would never sleep. The ship had slowed to a mere crawl, and she could dimly hear the men talking at the helm, their voices low one moment, bursting into husky laughter the next.

The later it grew, the more uncomfortable she felt in her clothing. She had loathed the idea of undressing this night; she was still angry over the night that had passed, still aching with puzzlement about just where her husband had slept.

Where—and with whom.

But at length she undressed and donned a matronly calico nightgown and curled up on the bunk. She laid her head down and began to mentally torture herself all over again, one minute listening for an Indian attack, the next wondering if her husband intended to return to his cabin tonight.

She must have slept. She found herself in a thick, silent green forest. Her feet were bare, and she was running. She was listening and listening. She could hear the pounding of her heart. It was a pulse that blocked out all else. Instinct warned her of sound. The sound of breaking twigs, of footfalls against the hard-packed earth.

William was there, ahead of her. She tried to call out to him: she was desperate to reach him and escape the savage mutilation promised her by the pursuing Indian.

He carried a tomahawk. His head was adorned with a feathered band. His eyes and hair were pitch black; he was bare chested, running after her in a pair of doeskin breeches, nothing more. The expression on his face was determined and grim, and with each passing second he was closer to her. He was an Indian, she thought. One moment, yes . . . then he was Jarrett. She tried to scream, and still there was nothing but silence. She tripped on a root sprawling out from one of the tall, moss-covered trees. Her gown blew behind her as she fell in a slow and terrible motion. She looked up. The tomahawk, adorned with endless little leather dangles that held the blond and brown scalps of white men, began to fall. She tried to scream again. . . .

Chapter 8

SHE MUST have screamed, because the next thing she knew, she was being shaken awake. For a moment she thought she was staring into the eyes of the Indian of her dream, but soon recognized her husband's eyes and taut features, shadowed in the low-burning candlelight. His hair had been tied back in a queue. In a wild panic she fought his grasp, then heard his voice.

"Tara! What in God's name is it?"

She stared at him and wrenched back from his grasp. The dream was still so horribly real!

"Tara, you were dreaming."

"Dreaming the truth!" she cried out, so affected by the dream that she was shaking like the moss-laden tree branches in the storm winds.

"Tara—" He reached out to her again, but she shook her head wildly, avoiding his touch as if he had the plague, curling as far as she could into the corner of the bunk as she hugged her knees to her chest. "Don't touch me! Don't touch me!" she whispered. "You don't know—you don't care! You're just sailing blindly into the midst of them."

He swore, rising. For a moment she hated herself. He had reached out to her. She hadn't been able to let him touch her, not at that moment. Now, as he stood before her, naked torso gleaming in the candlelight, muscles rippling, eyes afire with their ebony fury, she was bleakly sorry.

"The only *blind* thing I have done, madam, is marry you." He spun around with those words, and she was startled to hear herself cry out.

"Where are you going?"

He turned back, a brow arched. "Where I may sit—without touching you," he told her. With an exaggerated movement he drew out his captain's chair from beneath his desk and sat on it, still staring at her as he poured himself a long drink from the rum bottle in his bottom drawer. Taking a swig from it he settled back, propping his legs up on the desk. He suddenly let his feet fall to the floor and stared hard at her. "Unless, of course, you want me entirely out of the cabin?"

She stared at him in silence.

"Ah!" he murmured. "Exactly what I thought. I'm not to leave you alone now that I've so wretchedly dragged you out here, but I am to keep my distance!"

She remained stubbornly silent. In his present mood there was little she could say.

"Go to sleep!" he told her after a moment.

"McKenzie—"

"Damn it, Tara!" His voice was like a low growl. "Go to sleep!"

Stiffly she stretched out, turning away from him. She lay awake, so intensely aware that he was there, his eyes burning into her back. She would not sleep again. She listened to his movements and thought about her dream. The man chasing her had been an Indian, but so like Jarrett.

She listened to him breathe, listened to him drink straight from the rum bottle. He would weary of his vigil sometime soon, she thought. He would come and lie beside her, and even if he was angry, he would touch her again. And he would hold her.

But he didn't come to lie down beside her. In the morning she realized that he must have spent the entire night in his chair. He had said that he would not touch her, and seemingly had meant it.

Wretchedly, she rose. She washed and dressed and came out on deck. She waved to Nathan, who had climbed up the main mast and looked out over the riverbanks.

Looking for savages? Surely.

But he waved back to her cheerfully. She nodded and started for the helm. Jarrett was at the wheel, and he still wore the outfit —or lack of one—that made her think he was part savage himself. His feet remained bare, as did his torso, and all that clothed him were the form-hugging breeches. Strands of black hair fell over his forehead this morning, and when his gaze met hers it seemed both black fire and ice. She winced inwardly, aware that he was not fond of her at the moment.

"Ah, good morning, my love. How did you sleep?"

"Fine. And you?"

"Very well. A rum bottle can be an excellent companion. Surprisingly warm, when bodies that should be are not!"

She might have responded richly to the taunt, but she chose not to.

"Any more Indians in your dreams?"

"Any in real life, McKenzie?"

"Lots of them," he assured her, inclining his head toward the riverbank. His eyes shot to hers again. "But none you need worry about."

"I am immune?" she inquired with polite sarcasm.

"You are."

She strode to the rail. Yesterday's rain had drenched today with beauty. The greens were all the richer. Purple wildflowers twisted from the trees. The sun shone overhead in a dazzling golden brilliance, and the winds had died completely.

"Admit it!" he called to her softly. "It is beautiful; it is paradise."

He was right. It was a strange beauty, savage, different, very far removed from civilization. Its very danger seemed compelling, and still she couldn't bring herself to agree in any way when he was so determined to mock and taunt her.

She spun around. "One man's paradise is another's hell!" she reminded him.

His lips curled into a smile that held little humor, and she lowered her eyes quickly, then hurried past him. She ran back to their cabin and forced herself to once again spend her day sewing.

Jarrett stayed out of the cabin until it was very late. She closed her eyes and feigned sleep, and he took his seat at his desk once again.

And slept with the warmth of his rum bottle.

Tara did not sleep so easily. She lay awake and wretchedly wondered why she couldn't just reach out herself.

But wondering about his activities in Tampa plagued her, cut her heart, wounded her pride. She couldn't reach out.

And so she lay awake.

~~~

She slept very late the following morning. Indeed, she only awoke because she could hear the sounds of so many shouts. The crew called out—voices answered from elsewhere.

She realized that the *Magda* had ceased her constant rolling, and that the ship had docked.

She leapt up and ran to the cabin door, throwing it open, heedless of her nightdress. They had come to a dock, a very large and grand one, stretching into the river for well over two hundred feet along a strip of cleared, rich green grass. Small wooden buildings lay at either end of the dock, one windowless and one with windows. Yet between those two buildings she was given a perfect view of an exceptionally beautiful and grand house, built upon a piece of land nicely elevated above the river. The house was handsomely built in the customary colonial style, with its rear porch to the river, a porch with massive white columns. The house itself seemed huge to her, larger than anything she had seen in the North or the South, with numerous chimneys, a trail of outbuildings, and the most graceful lines she had ever seen. She narrowed her eyes, thinking that the structure itself had been crafted with greatest care, the walls sturdily built of some form of concrete and brick, the columns and porches made of native woods that had been whitewashed and now glistened beneath the sun. There were huge breezeway doors entering into the house from the rear porch, and she was certain, from the house's symmetry, that duplicate doors would open out to the front porch, and that an open hallway would extend between the sets of doors. The function was to catch the breezes from the river and cool the house, and she was certain that this house would function perfectly with the river, the breeze, and the landscape. Above the porch a balcony stretched out across the upper story of the house. Doorways led from the upper rooms out to the balcony. She could imagine the beauty, looking out over that balcony at night, with the stars and the moon casting down soft light upon the river. She could imagine the mystery as well, for the balcony also gave a fine view of the deep, lush forests that began far across the expanse of the rear lawn.

Flowers, even in winter, grew in abundance around the wide porch and the length of the house. Far to the left of it she could see endless fields, and those fields seemed to be in different shades, as if they provided for different crops. It was simply magnificent, and she found herself staring at it, wondering how it could exist in a land that had hitherto appeared to be nothing more than swamp and jungle.

"Cimarron," Jarrett said, suddenly at her side.

"Cimarron?"

"It's what we call it."

"Cimarron," she murmured, repeating the name once again. It

seemed to roll on her tongue, as beautiful as the house. Then she remembered he had once told her the word was Spanish for *renegade* or *runaway*.

And white men had twisted it into the word *Seminole*.

Jarrett McKenzie, she was certain, had never run from anything. But she had. She had come to this house, a startling Eden within the savage land. Perhaps she belonged. She was definitely a runaway herself.

"Making your arrival as mistress of the place in your nightgown?"

She spun around at her husband's question. He was well dressed himself this morning in a white shirt, crimson waistcoat, and ebony frock coat and breeches. His black hair was slicked back—his black eyes appeared almost diabolical as he gazed at her, challenging her once again.

"Surely Lisa would never have done so!" she heard herself say, and she was stunned and horrified by her own words, but it seemed he had mocked her, and though she had not wanted to do so, she had lashed back in return. It happened all too easily. She wished that she had not spoken. She couldn't take back the words that seemed to linger painfully on the air.

"No," he said softly. "She would not have done so."

"If you loved her so much," Tara said, very softly now, ruing her words again even as she spoke, "why did you marry me?"

He swore, a muttering beneath his breath that she didn't quite catch. His eyes seemed darker than ever, obsidian, and as black as stone. "Well, we had barely met, my pet, so I can hardly claim great devotion. We both know why we married."

"But if you loved her so much—"

"For the love of God! What is this foolish argument now? Indeed I loved her. She is gone. And the entire household is about to meet the new mistress of Cimarron clad in a nightgown!"

"No, McKenzie," she said coolly, "they'll not meet me so.

And you'll never have cause to bemoan my appearance or manner, I do assure you."

"Then, madam, I stand assured!"

He'd find no more reason to taunt or mock her, she swore, hurt and seething inwardly.

She swiftly spun on a heel and turned back into the master's cabin, slamming the door. She thought that he would throw the door back open and follow her just to inform her that she was not allowed to do such things, but he did not. She heard his soft, husky laughter as he walked away from the door, and though it stung her, she also thought that there was a sound of bitterness to that laughter, and her heart began to ache.

She dressed quickly, sorry that she had not finished with any of her own creations and that she must come to the house clad in clothing that had belonged to the mistress who had once reigned here. She found that her fingers trembled as she dressed. She had to forget those words, had to cease thinking about Lisa!

That didn't help. She still was trembling. She had realized that Jarrett was affluent, but she had not imagined anything quite as magnificent as her new home.

What a pity it lay so deep in the heartland of so savage a territory!

Her heart suddenly pounded fiercely. And yet, it was a place to run to. And she had done so. And she could only pray that she had run far enough, deep enough, and that the savage land she so feared could protect her.

And the man. The man who loved Lisa. She closed her eyes. The man who had married her. Taken her here.

If he should learn the truth?

Don't think! she warned herself again. She had sworn to be perfect in appearance and manner. She mustn't fall prey to her thoughts.

Dressed, she quickly brushed her hair and swept it into a neat knot, determined that she wouldn't falter a second in coming to Jarrett's household.

When she stepped out of the cabin again, she was elegant in a golden day dress with a mustard underskirt and parasol to match. Her hands were gloved in white, and her feet were covered in the elegant little mustard shoes that matched the dress. They were a touch short and more than a touch tight, but Tara was not going to think about it at the moment.

Jarrett stood upon the dock. As she hurried along the ship's length to the steps and plank, he was in deep conversation with a very tall, slim man with nearly white hair and very blue eyes. Behind him, in stark contrast, was one of the darkest men she had ever seen, equally tall, regal looking. She wondered if he was a slave—if Jarrett owned slaves—and somehow she doubted that this man could be any other man's property.

"Ah, gentlemen! My wife!" Jarrett said, striding back to the plank and steps to help her up onto the dock. "Tara, Jeeves," he said, introducing the black man first. "He runs the house, while Rutger is in charge of many holdings."

"How do you do?" Tara murmured, inclining her head to each man. She gazed up to find them both studying her with curiosity and interest. Neither one, it seemed, meant to pretend that her arrival was anything but a surprise.

"Mrs. McKenzie!" Rutger said, her name slightly accented. He bowed very stiffly, but Jeeves lowered his head and bowed, too, the movement much more fluid.

"Jeeves will take you to the house," Jarrett told her, dismissing her cleanly with his words. Perhaps he realized how curt they sounded, and yet Tara wondered why he should feel obliged to make any pretense concerning her. Still, he added, "I have business with Rutger, and will be along shortly. Jeeves, see that Molly gives Mrs. McKenzie tea or coffee, and I would prefer you wait until I return to show Tara around the house."

"As you say, sir!" Jeeves told him, and, with a brilliant smile, touched Tara's shoulder and led her over the stone path that went down the sloping lawn from the house to the dock.

Tara was silent as she approached the house, gazing up at it. It grew bigger as she approached it, a truly beautiful creation with the elegant length of the balcony stretching across the rear of the house. An abundance of green vines curled up the columns and trailed around the wrought iron of the balcony.

"It's the most magnificent manor in all the territory!" Jeeves said with soft-spoken and very dignified pride.

"I can well imagine," she murmured.

"Mr. McKenzie spent over a decade building it. Indeed, ma'am, he is always at work on the place."

She arched a brow to him and smiled. "Were you here with Mr. McKenzie as the house was built?"

Jeeves smiled. "Indeed, ma'am, I was."

His diction was perfect, as if he had been educated in the finest schools.

"There are twenty-three rooms, Mrs. McKenzie," Jeeves informed her. "Much to manage, and I am delighted that Mr. McKenzie has brought us home a bride to do so."

"Thank you," Tara murmured, and she found herself staring at Jeeves and his fathomless eyes and wondering if he was speaking the truth.

"The house," Jeeves said.

She walked up the back steps to the sweeping porch. Jeeves quickly preceded her to double doors that led to a large breezeway when he opened them. The house had been built in a style that was common to their time, one that easily adapted to the changes in the weather, with massive doors at front and rear to open to the cool breezes that could sweep away summer's heat, or close to keep out winter's chill.

The hallway was beautifully furnished with brocaded chairs, settees, planters, and small cherrywood tables on either side. Six doors opened from it, three on each side. Jeeves explained quickly that they led to the parlor, the main dining room, the breakfast room, the library, the office, and the ladies' sitting room. The kitchen was the first of the outbuildings. The second floor held the master bedroom and sitting room, three children's rooms, a nursery, and three guest rooms. The servants' quarters were on the floor above. Jeeves told her about the house, but showed her nothing except for the breakfast room, bringing her there where she was quickly introduced to Molly, a young Irish girl who was a downstairs maid. Molly brought Tara coffee and soda bread. Once Tara had been served, Molly bobbed her way out, and Jeeves politely bowed and assured her that Mr. McKenzie would be back soon, and if she needed anything before then, she had only to ask.

Tara drank her coffee but found she had little appetite. She prowled the room restlessly, admiring the many beautiful pieces in it. It was a pretty place, filled with light, with windows that opened to the front of the house, showing a great deal of lawn and sunshine.

An hour passed. Tara knew how much time had been going by because she had been staring at the handsome clock on the sideboard as the minutes ticked away.

She fought the rise of her temper. She wasn't angry that he had things to do that he deemed more important than showing her around. She was thoroughly irritated that he had not allowed someone else to do so and had left her to merely sit for so long.

Still, she waited. But when another hour had passed, she leapt up quite suddenly and exited the breakfast room. She hesitated a moment. She didn't want to get Jeeves in trouble, so she determined not to explore the house. She stepped out the front and walked around to the side of the house, noting that a huge stable lay just off toward the fields. She longed to see what kind of horses her husband kept, and she hurried toward it.

She started into the building and then nearly leapt a foot when someone appeared out of its shadows. She heard a confused and strangled "Ma'am?" and shaded her eyes from the sun to study the person. He seemed to be about fifteen, and the sight of him made her heart pound like thunder. She was certain he had Indian blood in him.

"May I help you?" he asked.

"I—" she began, fighting for words. His English was fine; he didn't look as if he was about to hurt her. "I—I'm Mrs. McKenzie," she said rather lamely at last.

It was the boy's turn to look frightened. "Mrs. McKenzie is dead," he told her.

"I'm the new Mrs. McKenzie," she said. And after a moment, "And you are?"

The boy hesitated just a moment. "Peter, ma'am. I feed the horses."

"Well, Peter, may I see them?"

"Of course, of course!" The boy scrambled ahead of her. There were numerous stalls, well tended. The smell of clean fresh hay permeated the place, stronger than the natural animal smells. The hard earth floor was clean-swept as well, and Tara thought that her husband managed to run his plantation very competently —especially for a man who also seemed to sail at whim.

She managed to forget her husband in a few minutes, for Peter knew the horses, loved them, and eagerly told her about each. Inside the house she had been watching the time crawl. Out here she forgot it entirely, as well as her initial fright at Peter's Indian blood.

Indeed, even her fright at the entire concept of her new home.

She didn't know how much time passed, but she should have realized that it was a great deal, for the sun was waning when she heard her name shouted. At a distance first, then closer.

"Mr. McKenzie!" Peter said, his dark eyes growing wide.

Tara instinctively came running out of the stables. It was all but dark she realized with dismay.

And there was Jarrett, his frock coat shed, his hands on his hips, his eyes as black as coal and wild as they fell upon her.

There was no pretense of his being a caring and tender husband as he strode toward her. "Where the damned hell have you been?" he roared. "I've been looking for you for hours!"

"Well, I waited for hours!" she cried back, hands on her hips as well, returning his stare. Her voice, however, wavered slightly.

Suddenly the threat of the Indians seemed to fade a bit, and she wondered if she was to spend her life doing battle with her husband. But she lifted her chin a shade higher—she owed him no apologies. He had accused her of being timid—she would certainly not back down from any arguments with him.

Especially when she was right!

"You had me scared half out of my wits!" he lashed out.

She was painfully aware that anyone within the vicinity could hear them. Still, she couldn't control her reply. "You were frightened? Of what? I am in no danger here, so you have assured me!"

His jaw clenched down hard. "Maybe," he said very softly, "I was afraid you had decided to escape—and then, madam, you would have been in grave danger indeed."

"That's right—I'd have been away from your very strange immunity!" she countered.

"Don't ever think of leaving the immediate grounds!" he warned her.

She started to reply, but she realized that Robert was now standing on the porch, with Jeeves beside him. "Jarrett!" Robert called out. "Jeeves has informed me that Hattie has made her venison stew. And that when the master is ready, it shall be served."

Jarrett kept his eyes on his wife. "Then it shall be served!" he said softly, spun around, and started for the house. Humiliated, Tara lifted her head and followed him with quiet dignity, offering a beautiful smile to both Robert and Jeeves as she approached them.

Robert took her arm when she reached the porch. "You really must be more careful. Jarrett was beside himself as we searched for you."

She glanced at Jarrett, but the dark, forbidding frown on his face seemed to assure her that he had been far more annoyed than concerned.

She decided to ignore him, speaking with Robert. She commented on the house as they went in to dinner. She asked Jeeves if she might meet Hattie, the cook, and she did so. Jeeves served wine in the huge dining room while Hattie and Molly served the meal: fresh greens—in the midst of winter—and Hattie's famous venison stew.

"Robert, do you—stay here when you are all—home?" she asked. She didn't realize how hopeful her words were going to sound until they were out. Surely she had managed to annoy her husband even more. But then, it seemed that since he had come so determinedly to her rescue in New Orleans, she hadn't been able to do much to please him.

No, she admitted miserably. Things had really gone awry when he had realized that she would rather run from him than settle here.

"I'm so sorry, my love," Jarrett replied for Robert. "Mr. Treat owns property just down the river."

"Mine borders this one, so I am not so far!" Robert assured her. Jarrett was silent.

Hattie served a peach pie made from her special recipe, and coffee with rich cream.

"Will you gentlemen be taking brandy in the library, sir?" Jeeves asked, clearing his throat. "I've sherry, Mrs. McKenzie, in the ladies' room."

Sherry would do, but Tara really longed to take a huge swig straight from the whiskey bottle. She kept her hands folded tightly in her lap.

It seemed that her husband didn't intend her to enjoy any libation. He stood, offering her one of his black stares and an outstretched hand. "Robert, if you'll excuse me for just a moment, I'll join you in the library for brandy and cigars. Tara is surely exhausted. I'll show her up."

"But I thought I was to see the house."

"Tomorrow," he said curtly.

"I would really enjoy a sherry."

"Jeeves will bring one up," he told her.

She rose, her teeth gritting furiously. She managed to offer

Robert another brilliant smile and blink back a sudden rush of threatened tears.

"Good night, Tara. You will love it here, in time," Robert promised her.

She couldn't reply. She kissed his cheek and turned quickly, fleeing the room. But her husband was right behind her, catching her arm. He led her to the grand and elegant staircase that curved its way to the shadows above. She walked stiffly, not saying a word, until they reached a door on the second floor and he pushed it open.

A lamp flickered against the darkness to display a huge room with every luxury. The bed was massive, with a cherrywood headboard, side tables, and trunk. Wardrobes, his and hers, sat on either side of the room. A hearth ran half the length of it. Fine carpeting lay in the midst of the hardwood floors, adding warmth to the room.

Still, she hesitated. It was the master's bedroom. There was nothing at all feminine about it at the moment. A ledger lay upon the desk that stood before the windows opening on one of the balconies. The knit covering upon the bed was dark. A razor and cup sat next to the deep washbowl and pitcher.

The room was warm. The man behind her still seemed like fire and ice, ready to throttle her one moment and walk dismissively away the next.

"There are numerous rooms in the house. . . ." she heard herself begin.

"Meaning?" he demanded sharply.

"Perhaps—perhaps I should have my own."

She didn't look at him, but she could still feel him close behind her, and it felt as if his temperature had suddenly soared. She hurried in ahead of him, spinning around quickly to accost him. "You didn't really intend to marry me, and at the moment it does seem that we have a wretched relationship."

"No matter what kind of relationship we have, you are my wife, and you will sleep in this room."

"So you think that you will give me orders!" she charged him, dismally aware that her own temper was rising—and that her wretched jealousy was about to show. "Tell me where to sleep, while you—"

"While I what?"

"I will start doing as I damned well choose!" she assured him.

"You choose to keep running. You will not do it!"

She inhaled sharply. "Me!" She accused him. "Well, you cannot move forward, so it seems. You are living in the past with a dead woman, for all that I can—"

She broke off, a strangled gasp escaping her, for he was suddenly across the room, and she was in his merciless grip, her feet off the floor. A second later she was flung down upon the bed and she struggled up, desperately searching for words as she met his now icy gaze.

"I don't wish—"

"I don't give a damn what you wish! You don't want to be touched, but you do want the security of someone near, a body, flesh and blood, preferably well armed with gun and knife. I don't need to force anything on you, Mrs. McKenzie, nor do I wish to do so. Yet, I hope you'll remember the promises you made, and all the *warnings* I gave you before we married."

"Threats?" she inquired breathlessly.

"Promises! To be a damned good wife."

"I am trying," she whispered.

"Trying to run!" he shot back quickly. "Afraid again, running again."

"You make no effort to reassure me. If you would only explain to me—"

"Why should I explain anything to you when you refuse to tell me anything?"

"I haven't dragged you into my life, forced you to live within my past and with whatever problems—"

"And since I know nothing about your problems, how could I

possibly know if and when your past might catch up with the two of us?" he demanded heatedly.

She'd been about to answer in kind, but instead went dead still. She stared at him, eyes brilliant and wide. Dear God, she could never explain anything to him, not the way that he felt about her. He would never believe her.

"There's a war on now," she said at last.

"Not on these grounds!" he told her angrily. "Not on these grounds!" He walked to the bed. For a moment she expected some violence from him, but he stopped just at her side, staring down at her still.

"Whatever the hell else," he warned her, "don't leave this room. It is my room; you are my wife. And it is where you sleep."

And with that he spun around and left her.

And it wasn't until many hours later that she finally did sleep, miserably aware that though she was to sleep here in his room, he did not return to lie beside her.

Chapter 9

COMING HOME had been a far more tumultuous event than Jarrett had imagined it could be. What he and many others had dreaded for months—years, perhaps—had finally come to pass.

He had never intended to spend their one night in Tampa away from his wife's side. But he'd been compelled to go into the fort, speak with the commanders, and then visit the one wounded, weary, heartsick soldier who had made it back from the Dade massacre, Ransome Clarke.

In bed, scarcely able to lift his head, Ransome had still greeted Jarrett warmly. The territory was as yet a small enough place that most of those who loved it—or were bound to serve it—eventually met, under some circumstance or another. He had entertained most of the military here at his home, and he came and went from port here so often that he was a regular. He'd met young Ransome Clarke several times.

Ransome told him how most of the officers had died in the first volley of fire from the Indians. The men had tried to form something of a line behind their downed horses and the scrub brush around them. The attack lasted several hours, but it had been a losing proposition for the white soldiers after the first shot was fired. When the battle ended Ransome had managed to pull himself into the bushes, out of sight. Then the Indians' Negroes— many of them doubtless bitter against old masters—had come in to finish off the wounded men, mutilate their bodies, and scalp them.

The firsthand account of the attack was gut wrenching to the core, and when Ransome had finished speaking, Jarrett was silent for several minutes.

"You've got to take care," Ransome told him earnestly. "They say that though Osceola was busy killing Wiley Thompson while Dade was being slaughtered, he was the mastermind behind the attack. They've burned down a few plantations already. You never know, Jarrett, you just never know. Those Indians, from what I understand, think more of you than of any other white man alive. But remember—old Charlie Emathla is dead, and he was Creek-Seminole himself."

"My land is neutral ground; Osceola gave me that promise himself."

"What happens if Osceola loses power?" Ransome asked gravely.

Jarrett smiled. "I also have nearly a hundred people living and working at the plantation. And Robert is nearby with another fifty. And I'm damned well armed. I'm respected for my relationship with the tribes, but I think, as well, that it's known Cimarron is well protected. At the moment I've got nothing to fear."

"Pray God it continues that way!" Ransome said, his young face earnest again.

Clutching the young man's hand Jarrett had asked if there was anything he could do for him. He'd left soon after, and made his way back to Mrs. Conolly's, and then he'd found himself spending the rest of the night staring into the dying embers of the fire in the public room.

The world, his world, had really gone right to hell.

And he had brought a wife into the middle of it all.

An unhappy wife at that. One who looked at him as if he had dragged her into the very bowels of hell.

And one who fascinated him more now than ever, one who seemed to have wrapped some strange kind of delicate tendrils around his soul. Robert had been right—Jarrett had needed a wife. Now, he had acquired one. He had never imagined finding himself wedded to a mystery woman who didn't intend to enlighten him in any way. Nor had he imagined how dismayed she would be when they reached his home. The accusation in her eyes after her dream aboard the *Magda*!

The fights that sprang up between them each time they talked now. The way that she fought him. . . .

The way that he fought himself, suffering the pains of the damned when he forced himself away from her.

Perhaps she had every right to her fears—and he hadn't been able to swallow his pride enough to try to explain anything to her. They had come home to pictures of sheer horror, and all described in terrifying and vivid detail.

This morning he had awakened alone once again despite the fact that he had a beautiful and extraordinary new young wife. He had awakened at the crack of dawn, breakfasted quietly with Robert, and felt his friend's silent reproach all the while. When Robert rode out, the roil of emotions in Jarrett's heart and mind had sent him quickly to the stables. He'd called out to Peter that he needed no help and bridled his roan stallion, Charlemagne, himself. He'd eagerly leapt upon the spirited horse, riding bareback, feeling the movement of the animal, as his father had taught him. He'd been so eager to race with the wind, as if the wind could blow the cobwebs from his head and soothe the wildness within his soul.

He'd torn down the long, elegant drive of the plantation, then across his far-reaching fields, into lands that were still his, but nearly virgin, offering nothing more than horse trails through the wilderness. Stately oaks grew tall upon the hammocks here, with pale green moss wafting ethereally from them. Creeks and streams crisscrossed the hammocks, and wildflowers grew here and there in abundance. He'd barely noted the scenery. He'd known exactly where he was heading, to a hammock of pines where the tall branches shaded the earth, where wild orchids grew, where the ground was carpeted in soft needles from the trees, and where a slim bubbling brook of fresh water flowed through the quiet beauty of it all. It had been his favorite place since he had first bought his property. It was a stretch of land adjoining territory that had been ceded to the Seminoles in the treaty of 1821.

Even as they raced, Charlemagne seemed to know where they were riding in such a reckless hurry. The great horse slowed as they reached the hammock, coming to a halt at the water. Jarrett slipped from the animal's back and hunkered down beside the horse to douse his face in the cool water, to sip from it. He watched now as the water rippled and waved from his touch, distorting his image.

He closed his eyes for a minute, squinting them together tightly, wishing he could blink away all of the pain.

Closing his eyes was a mistake.

He heard the *whoosh* of air behind him just a second too late. Arms swept around his hunched shoulders, bringing him and his attacker flying into the water.

It was cold, damned cold. If he hadn't been awake and wary when he had so suddenly been rushed, he was very much awake now. His blood raced through him in a wild fever to offset the cold. He leapt to his feet as quickly as possible, spinning around in the water to meet the combatant who had managed to take him so humiliatingly by surprise.

The man was already up, posed, knees slightly bent, feet wide apart, eyes sharp on Jarrett.

His Indian ancestry was quite obvious in the dead-straight hair that just fell past his shoulders and in the burnt bronze color of his face. His high black boots were European, as were his dark blue breeches. Even his colorful shirt, with full, bouffant sleeves, was of European style, one that had been adopted by many of his people.

Yet there his concession to white ways ended; a band of red cloth was tied around his forehead. Two eagle feathers rose from the band at the back of his head. A deer hide sheath at his calf carried a long knife, the type they were calling a "Bowie" knife in honor of the frontiersman. It was a wicked weapon. He was no youth, but a warrior in his prime, near Jarrett's own height but for perhaps a half inch, and as muscled, taut, and sinewed as a man might be. His features were arresting and intriguing, with broad cheekbones, large wide eyes, clean, well-defined brows.

Startling, striking blue eyes.

Jarrett knew those eyes all too well, eyes that belonged to the Seminole Running Bear.

The warrior smiled suddenly and made a lunge for Jarrett, and Jarrett found himself pitching over again, hitting the ground hard. A grunt escaped him, and every defensive mechanism in him rose to the surface. He made it up again and this time charged the Indian, catching him dead in the belly with his shoulder and throwing them both down to the ground again. This time he was on top, and took advantage of the situation, straddling his attacker, trying to force the man's hands down to the ground above him and pin his wrists. The Indian bucked, Jarrett went flying, but he returned quickly. A minute later they were interlocked tightly with one another in a wild contest of strength, each trying to wrestle the other to the ground, each determined on rising from the action the winner.

But the Indian suddenly slipped from Jarrett's hold, walked five feet away, doubled over, and inhaled deeply, staring at Jarrett, a smile still on his face.

When he spoke today, he spoke in English—slightly accented with a southern drawl—the easy English of one who knew two languages equally well. "Damn, I thought I had you that time," he said.

Jarrett, stretching his back to ease the soreness from it, inhaling on a gasp, arched a brow to him. "You damned near did, little brother," he said. They both grinned, then they were silent for a second. Together they stepped forward, embracing, then pulled away to stare at one another.

"Damn, but it's good to see you!" Jarrett said, his emotion rich in his voice.

"I'm glad you're home. Who the hell would ever have thought it would come to this?" the Indian said, a note of rich sorrow in his voice.

The Indians called Jarrett's half-brother Running Bear. He had been named James McKenzie at birth, and it was a name James retained with pride in addition to his Indian name, for he had loved his father, and he never pretended to anyone that it had been otherwise.

"It was always coming to this," Jarrett said. "We were the blind ones, you and I. We didn't want to see it. Tell me, when we met last, did you know all of Osceola's plans?"

James shook his head. "Those who say that Osceola simply has a grudge against all white men are sadly mistaken. He would not include me in his plans, for he knows all too well that I have white blood—good white blood, in his opinion—and that my ties to you are close."

"He's got white blood himself," Jarrett commented.

"You've known him a long time now," James reminded him. "And as I said, you know that he does not simply despise all white men."

"You've heard of the massacre?"

James shrugged unhappily. "Indeed, I've heard. But you must bear in mind, Wiley Thompson dealt badly with the Indians and you—"

"Major Dade did not."

"Major Dade was a military man, and, brother, you will recall that white military men are quite capable of slaughtering Indian braves—and women and children—without a moment's hesitation."

Yes, he knew that well enough. Too often it was all-out war.

"If the whites would keep just one damned treaty—"

"James, there were so many men massacred! Ambushed. It was a brutal attack. You can't think that the group who did it was right."

"And the whites?" James asked.

Jarrett lifted his hands. "We both know," Jarrett said harshly, "that whites have cruelly attacked Indian villages. We also know that many long to live in peace. You said that Osceola knew that all whites were not bad, and, James, of all men, you can perhaps turn some of the tide of absolute hatred against the whites—"

James interrupted him with a groan. "Of all men, Jarrett, you must know that I pray no harm comes to many a white man. Nowhere was there a greater man than our father, farseeing, giving, eternally granting all men their rights! But, Jarrett, you have to see it yourself. He was a rare man, and though there are surely good white men settling here, we have met so far with mostly the cruel and treacherous!"

A downed log lay near the water. Jarrett dragged his fingers through his hair and sat, staring out at the creek. Yes, there was a great deal that he had to see. He had been seeing it since he had been a very small boy.

Jarrett had been born in Charleston, South Carolina, the son of Irish immigrant parents. His grandfather held the title of Lord McKenzie in Cork, but as Jarrett's father had been the seventh of eight sons born to the lord, life in Ireland on the McKenzie estate had seemed limited. Sean McKenzie had, at the age of fifteen, left the genteel poverty of his family's home and come to America just in time to join in with the Rebels near the close of the American Revolution. When the fighting had ended, he had been on the outskirts of Charleston, and that was where he had stayed. A lot of it had to do with a girl—Geneva Tweed, the daughter of a very prosperous Carolinian merchant. Geneva, an only child with a will of her own and a fascinating beauty, had stood him quite a merry chase, warning Sean that she would have nothing serious to do with a cast-off Irishman. But Sean had been determined, and in time Geneva had been won. But soon after the marriage Geneva caught yellow fever. Sean nursed her through it, somehow evading the fever himself. Geneva's health was never the same. The vivacious beauty became frail and delicate. Sean had always wanted land of his own, and the fur trade fascinated him. But he adored his wife, and due to her health he determined he would remain in Charleston and forget all such vague dreams.

The couple was childless for over a decade. Jarrett was born in 1802 to the great surprise and pleasure of his parents. But Geneva continued in frail health. A few months before Jarrett's fifth birthday his still beautiful mother smiled at him, held him tight, and kissed his father good-bye. With her smile still curving her lip, her hands still upon her son, she breathed her last.

Sean McKenzie was disconsolate, and in such an abyss of pain that he nearly died himself of a broken heart. His father-in-law, bereft himself, made Sean get up and move on with his life. Sean wanted land. Great, endless acres of it. The fur trade with the Georgia Indians was making many men fabulously wealthy. The Americans were just beginning to deal with the "Creeks" there, Creek Indians being those who lived along the creek.

The move was intriguing to young Jarrett.

There were times when he felt very much alone, since few white men lived among the Indians in those days. But Jarrett was a strong boy, both eager to learn and ready to defend himself. And his father, for the first time since his mother's death, seemed to be growing content.

Jarrett discovered what only those close to the Creek Indians knew, and that was just how different the Indians were among themselves. There were many tribes, many peoples, many languages. He learned the Muskogee of the Creek and the Hitichi of the Mikasukis. He learned about their corn dances, about the "black" drink.

He learned to understand that the Creek "Confederation" itself was composed of such a variety of peoples because they'd been pushed to where they were—pushed by the continual encroachment of the whites.

On the day he turned six, Jarrett learned something else. He was to have a brother. His father explained that he had fallen in love with a lady named Mary McQueen, or Moon Shadow, an Indian lady of curious parentage herself. On her mother's side she had white blood, being related to Peter McQueen, a white-Creek leader of the Upper Creeks. Her father had been a Seminole chief from the area around Pensacola in Florida. He had been an old-time Seminole, one of the "runaways" or "renegades" whose family had long claimed the area as home and had interbred with the all-but-obliterated original Indian clans of the peninsula.

Maybe because she was an Indian, part of this very different world, Jarrett had little difficulty in accepting Mary as his step-mother. Maybe it was just that Mary was young and very pretty, kind, and completely loving to Jarrett. Life was much better for Jarrett once he and his father and Mary made a home together in a pleasant log cabin among the People. It seemed that they took the best from both life-styles, enjoying white men's luxuries and the Indian love of the earth and more basic spiritualism. White traders and those pressing ever farther west were constant visitors. The People were their family.

And when James was born, Jarrett was delighted to have a little brother. It seemed strange to many white visitors that Jarrett should have his mother's near coal-black eyes—hers from a maternal Creole ancestry—while James inherited their father's cobalt blue. But in everything else the boys were very similar, both growing very tall, James trailing after Jarrett, Jarrett teaching his little brother what he knew about both white and Indian ways.

In 1812 the United States went to war against Britain once again. A strange war, if one thought about it in retrospect. America's early presidents had tried very hard to maintain a policy of neutrality where other countries were concerned. America had maintained its isolationist stance while Napoleon Bonaparte became emperor of France, and kept its distance while the French and British went to war. But both France and Britain put out embargoes against American ships, and then the British began seizing American ships and impressing American sailors. Finally, war was declared. It was ironic, because at nearly the same time the British had lifted their embargo—since communications across the Atlantic were slow, the Americans could not know the British had relented before they had declared war.

The British, furious that the Americans could go to war against them when they were so strenuously embattled in the war with Napoleon, promised help to a number of Indians if the Indians would side with them. By 1813 the Creek War had exploded, with the Lower Creeks—the civilized Creeks, as the whites liked to call them—mainly at war with the Upper Creeks. Many of these "Creeks" were actually Shawnees and other northern Indians grouped into the "Creek Confederation" simply because of where they had been forced to migrate. The great Shawnee leader Tecumseh, a respected, intelligent man who had learned from the whites and then taught nativism and the power of banding together to other tribes as well as his own, sided with the British, hoping to keep the whites from pressing farther westward into Indian lands. He perished in the war.

Luckily for Jarrett he and his family lived among the "civilized" Creeks—and sided with the Americans. Sean, determined that both his boys would have the best education for mind and soul offered by two very different worlds, had sent his sons to Charleston for schooling, but at the outbreak of hostilities, he called them home. Jarrett and James were glad to be back with their parents, but it was a sad time as well, for Mary was in torment. Her paternal kinsmen were Upper Creeks and Florida Seminoles, and it was a bitter time for her. Through her father's family she was related to James McQueen, one of the most militant of the Upper Creek "Red Stick" warriors. Thankfully they were not destined to find themselves in battle against their own kin.

James was too young to really understand the war, and young

enough to be dragged back by the ears when he mentioned the
very idea of fighting in it. Sean McKenzie, of course, decided to
keep his older son, Jarrett, out of the warfare as well. But that was
difficult, for in the beginning of the war the Red Sticks, as the
Americans then referred to the enemy, attacked Fort Mims,
slaughtering women and children right along with the men, the
majority of victims being civilized or interbred Creeks. When
Andy Jackson came through the embattled territory, Jarrett found
himself intrigued by the general and slipped quietly away from his
father's eagle eye to follow Jackson about and perform small tasks
of navigation and translation when necessary. Jackson was an impressive man. Already past his prime, he was still the most astonishing soldier Jarrett had ever seen, courageous but never fool-
hardy. He was weathered and worn in the face, and in the heart
as well, it seemed, but he was ready for almost anything that came
his way, any deprivation, any surprise attack, any disappointment
—such as reinforcements failing to arrive. He and his Tennesse-
ans were solid, do-or-die men, and Jarrett could not help but find
himself impressed by the man. So impressed that by the time
Jackson had quelled the Red Sticks and was heading on to do
battle in New Orleans, Jarrett decided to run away from home—
leaving his father and Mary a very apologetic note. Jarrett was
already a very tall youth, muscular in his development, and when
he lied about his age to the general, Jackson accepted his age
without question. At the time Jarrett had not yet turned fifteen,
but with Ole Hickory he was given amazing lessons in warfare in
a pitifully scant time. He would never forget his baptism by fire,
never forget the terrible fear of his first battle. Yet it was then that
he learned something about tactical warfare from Jackson himself.
He had learned temperance, patience, and wisdom from his white
father—and courage from his adopted Indian family. Indians did
not run, and they never showed their fear.

Jarrett survived the battle, but barely survived his father's
wrath when he returned from it. And when it was all over—the
fighting and his father's rage—he found that even the Lower

Creeks had lost in the war that they had fought on the side of the Americans. They were paying for their aid with their land. Americans were moving westward and so the Indians must move much farther west themselves.

Sean McKenzie had lived with his wife's family, as was Seminole custom, just as Mary McKenzie's father had moved in with her mother's family. Sean had never staked any type of separate claim for the land. When the Indians' land was threatened, Sean McKenzie's home was threatened as well. Astounded by the turn of events Jarrett decided that there was only one thing to do—confront Jackson about what had happened and demand that his family lands be returned in good order.

Jarrett found Jackson engaged in war with the Seminoles in Florida Territory. The fact that the territory was still Spanish didn't stop Ole Hickory.

Jarrett still liked Jackson, admired him tremendously. He'd come to know a lot about Jackson because sometimes at night, while smoking his pipe in whatever house or cabin they had called headquarters near their battlegrounds, Jackson would talk. He talked about Rachel, his beloved wife. He admitted to having fought a duel over her, for her honor, and he admitted to having killed the man. He admitted to having been a drinker, a swearer, a gambler, in his younger days, but he'd told Jarrett as well that there'd been nothing so fine in life as his love for Rachel and for his country. America was going to be great, it was destiny. It was going to take great Americans to make it so, Americans who would not back down, who would stand their ground. "Whatever that ground is going to be, Jarrett McKenzie, you stand it!" Jackson had told him.

He intended to do so.

In Florida he discovered that he hated Jackson's attitude toward the Indians. Jackson wanted them all removed. There were lands out west. Americans were hungry for Florida—a land that was still supposedly divided into two Spanish territories. The Americans came south to fight the Indians, claiming that the

Spanish couldn't control the ones residing in Florida who were constantly raiding across the Georgia border. By 1818 Jackson was campaigning against Indians, outlaw runaway Negroes, and those who would succor and support them, from Pensacola to the Suwanee. He executed two British citizens, Alexander Arbuthnot and Robert Ambrister, for inciting the Indians to acts of war against the Americans. The British were enraged. Spain was furious. Andy Jackson was there and holding his ground.

He wasn't about to back down.

But these upheavals were nothing new. Florida had been going through many changes since 1513 when Juan Ponce de León had first stepped upon her shores. She was a Spanish acquisition, but ruled by her natives, some of them friendly, some of them warlike. In those early days Spaniards sometimes landed to seek treasure, only to disappear themselves instead. But the natives—friendly and not—began to fall prey to a weapon the Spaniards had unwittingly brought—European disease. In the end Spain enforced her hold upon her possession.

In 1719 the French briefly took possession of Pensacola, but the Spanish very quickly took it back.

In 1740 British General Oglethorpe invaded, yet could not take the Castillo de San Marcos in St. Augustine. Still, the Treaty of Paris in 1763 gave Florida to the British. In 1781 Spain captured Pensacola from the British. In 1783 Florida was returned to Spain by the British in return for the Bahamas.

Florida had been a prize passed back and forth many times. Now the Americans wanted her. There were rich, fertile lands to be farmed, coasts to be fished. Sunny plains to homestead. There might be great treasures somewhere; some still believed in the Fountain of Youth that Juan Ponce de León had sought. More than that, it seemed that Americans could not accept boundary lines. Florida seemed like a natural extension of American land. More and more settlers wanted to come south. With Jackson at the fore America would have her.

But Jarrett could no longer fight beside the commander he so admired. Jackson's war became a war against all Indians living within the Florida borders and Jarrett could not be a party to it. Finding General Jackson at St. Augustine during a lull in the campaign some men called the Seminole War and some men called Andy Jackson's War, Jarrett sought an audience with him late at night. *Stand your ground*, Jackson had taught him, and so he did. He floundered a little bit at first, but he passionately reminded Jackson of how loyally he had followed him to war, how he had fought, never tired, and how he had served the general and therefore his country. He hadn't deserved to go home and discover that he had no home. He also informed him at the time that he'd support him in any endeavor—except for an all-out war with the Indians. Jackson had appeared angry at first, but Jarrett didn't care. And in the end Jarrett was glad to realize he had behaved in exactly the manner the general had taught him—he had stood his ground. While he was still speaking, Jackson had been filling out the papers to assure that the land held by Sean McKenzie and family was properly deeded. "My young sir!" Jackson told him, standing tall to offer him the documents. "I am sorry that we can no longer be comrades-at-arms, but you are a man I would call friend nonetheless, for honesty and courage are virtues I cherish. We shall agree to disagree, but I'd never so dishonor a soldier as I have so unintentionally done you. I owe you better, young man."

"I'm seeking nothing but what is mine."

"If you discover something else should be yours, let me know."

Jarrett gripped his hand and met his steady eyes. He smiled after a moment. They had agreed to disagree. But he would respect Jackson all of his life; fight for him whenever he could.

That night, at a dance in the old city, Jarrett met Lisa. To the tunes of five fiddles they danced in an old coquina-shell mansion built by a Spanish don years before. Lisa spoke about the territory, about the travels into the interior she had taken with her father. She talked about the bays and the crystal springs. About the colorful birds, the exotic plants. The feeling of being alive and alone in an Eden lit only by the stars.

He found himself staying in the town. Walking the streets of the city, staring at the never-breached walls of the Castillo de San Marcos.

He wouldn't fight the Indians, but he would translate. He stayed on.

The old alliances from the Creek War were now gone. Many of the Red Sticks from the earlier war had come to peaceful terms with the whites.

But some Red Sticks had remained hostile. And some of the "civilized" Lower Creeks had come upon their more militant distant kin and become more militant as well, willing to fight the Americans who had cost them their lands once and were ready to do so again. As the Creeks—Lower and Upper—moved into the Floridas, displaced by their previous wars, they joined with those who had come before them and the remnants of tribes native to the peninsula. They were all to become known as *cimarrones*, renegades. Seminoles.

Some Indians managed to hold on to lands in northern Florida, lands deep in hammocks, hidden away, and far enough from white settlements. But for the most part the bands had been pushed south of St. Augustine on the east coast and far south of Pensacola on the west.

Jackson faced tremendous problems before it was all over. He had been sent to fight Indians. He had attacked Spanish positions. The English and the Spaniards were up in arms again. Members of Congress rained down abuse on the general as well. John C. Calhoun, secretary of war, was furious with Jackson. John Quincy Adams, secretary of state, defended Jackson, and was given the task of smoothing over all that had happened by President Monroe.

In 1821 an agreement was ratified between Spain and the United States of America. The U.S. would take on a multitude of Spanish debts to citizens of both countries, and the eastern boundary line of Mexico was also decided, with the U.S. giving up any claim to Texas. Andrew Jackson returned to Florida and received title to the Floridas, East and West, at Pensacola on July 17, 1821, and became the first territorial governor.

Americans began flocking over the border.

Jarrett called on his old friend and commander once again. Like everyone else he wanted land. His own.

Jackson, anxious to see the settlement of the new American territory, was ready to listen to Jarrett's request, and ready to grant him what he could. He would be happy to give Jarrett title to vast acreage in his control, with one catch: It neighbored directly on Indian territory. It lay eastward from the port at Tampa Bay, a savage country bordering rough, wild land that the Indians had been free to take. In 1821 these regions were of little interest to other whites.

Jarrett didn't care how wild or savage other men might consider the place. Sean had spent years teaching him the value of land, and Jarrett had learned his lesson well. He also knew the Florida peninsula better than almost any other man alive, since he had traversed it with both Andrew Jackson and his scouts and surveyors and his own adopted family—which included men without university educations, but the innate common sense and natural ability to blaze trails through any wilderness and discover the means to survive—and prosper—within it.

That seemed a long time ago now, a very long time. Jackson had formally taken hold of Florida, but soon after he had left the state. William P. Duval had become territorial governor, done well with the job, and kept confidence with the Indians, and matters had remained somewhat stable. John Eaton had then been appointed to the office. He had taken his sweet time coming to Florida and had arrived just in time to find the Indian situation exploding. Ole Hickory himself was sitting in the White House, and if Jarrett knew the old warrior at all, he knew that the days— maybe the years—stretching ahead of them were going to be brutal ones. Andy Jackson had always believed in Indian removal.

The Florida Indians didn't want to be removed.

Jarrett stared at his brother. James stood near the water, watching him, hands idly folded at his back, striking, handsome, obviously Indian, obviously white. He could have been part of either world, and he had chosen his place among his mother's people. But he had never broken his bonds with his brother or with other whites he had determined to call friends. Like their father he had the ability to judge a man not by his color, ancestry or creed, but by what he was within his own heart.

"Dear God, but this is bad. There's always been trouble. Always. But now, we're at war," Jarrett muttered hollowly.

"We've been at war before," James said. "And this war will be like other wars. Some men will seek peace. Some Indians will fight *with* the white men. Some will fight against them. Win or lose, we will lose. I didn't attack Dade, and I didn't fight with Osceola. But I understand why they fought."

"I learned in Tampa that General Clinch was out there somewhere. He was on his way to see that the Indians were removed at the same time Dade was being ambushed. There will be more federal troops coming down as well. Militia groups are rising up right and left. The whites are outraged."

"You refused to fight us?" James asked.

"They knew that I'd refuse."

James shrugged and walked to the log, taking a position beside Jarrett.

"You've never broken a treaty with any of your Creek, Seminole, or Mikasuki brothers," James told him, "Hell, you've never even broken your word. And I didn't have anything to do with the massacre of Dade and his troops, nor have I burned any white farmhouses or stolen any goods. We're at war yet you and I have a faith that we keep with each other."

"Yes," Jarrett agreed, "but I have taken up arms against some Red Sticks, I did fight with Andy Jackson, once."

James grinned. "Ah, yes, but even Osceola has forgiven you for that now."

Jarrett shrugged at the comment. "James, though you are capable of seeing that many whites are good men, not so many whites are capable of telling the differences among Indians."

"I'm well aware of that. And though I committed no atrocities, Jarrett, you have to understand—I cannot condemn the warriors who believe that they must fight or else find themselves dead, betrayed, and completely at the white man's mercy. The white military have swept in often enough to decimate entire villages, you know that. I have seen men thrive on the butchery of children."

Jarrett felt a burning sensation in the pit of his stomach and he straightened his shoulders and stared up at the sky. He did know too damned many whites who thought the only good Indian was a dead Indian—and the Indian's age or gender didn't mean a thing. Little Indians grew into big, tomahawk-carrying Indians—or so the philosophy went. Thank God there were enough rational people in the United States to protest senseless slaughter, or else the atrocities committed might be so fierce that no native population could survive.

"What do we do?" James asked Jarrett softly.

"Do?" Jarrett murmured. He stretched out his fingers, then folded them tightly together and looked at his brother. "Do? I'm not in this war."

"They'll make you be in this war," James said.

His brother was right. He still wanted to deny it.

"I have refused to take command of any troops," Jarrett said flatly.

"They will demand that you negotiate and parley with our leaders," James said.

"I will do that—but I will not take up arms."

"What if you find you have to?"

Jarrett cocked his head to his brother. "What of you?" he asked softly. "Men have been murdered by their own kind by not taking up arms against the enemy."

"I haven't taken up arms—but I have never betrayed any of

my people. I have never signed a treaty, or agreed to take my
people to the barren lands west of the Mississippi. Still, it is true.
It seems in this we must take care, for we may both have enemies
among our own people. And by the way, what did your new wife
think about your turning down a military command?"

Jarrett shot him a quick look, wondering that information
could travel so much more swiftly than men. But he knew that he
had been watched all the way home from Tampa, and he'd been
sure the ones watching him were doing so at his brother's command.

Protecting Jarrett from other Indians, perhaps. And keeping
an eye on any white man—his brother included—for the Indians.

James was grinning, pleased to have taken his brother by surprise and pleased especially to taunt him on this issue.

"My new wife has no right to comment on any of my
choices," Jarrett said with a scowl. James's dark brow shot up, his
grin deepened.

"Now, that, brother, is not a chivalrous attitude! Shall I take
that to mean that your so recently arrived bride is not aware that
she is now kin to half the *savages* in the area?"

James was highly amused; Jarrett cast him a deeper frown. No
good. James kept grinning.

"The last thing I imagined you coming home with was a
bride!" James told him.

"I had not imagined to do so either," Jarrett assured him.

"You married her by accident? A man spills food by accident,
brother. It is much more difficult to take a bride by accident."

"I never said I married her by accident." Jarrett groaned.

James sobered suddenly. "It is just that after Lisa . . ."

"Lisa has been gone nearly three years," Jarrett said flatly.

"You said you'd never marry again," James reminded him
softly.

Jarrett shrugged. James was determined to pursue the issue, as
surely no other man would have dared to do. "But you have now
acquired a new wife and brought her into the midst of this powder

keg. And if I am not mistaken, she doesn't know a thing about me or my family."

Jarrett stood, hands on hips, walking to the water, looking across it. The winter sun was clear, yet somehow gentle. The air was cool, the breeze slight; the moss dripping·from the trees to the water was lifted and stirred by it. A crane came into view in graceful flight, sheering above the water, coming to rest just atop it. Light waves rushed out around the creature, causing the water to ripple. The scene was beautiful.

Peaceful.

This was the home he loved, the enchantment he had seen in his mind's eye when Tara had mocked his savage land.

"Jarrett?" James said.

Jarrett didn't turn. "No, she doesn't know about you—or my family. I didn't refrain from telling her because I was afraid of her reaction."

"Then?"

Jarrett turned again. "I married her because she was in some kind of serious trouble."

"What trouble?"

"I don't know. She was . . . running."

"Another runaway?" James inquired musingly. "But how—"

"I won her in a card game."

"You married a woman you won in a card game?" James said incredulously.

"They were strange circumstances. She didn't belong where I found her. Since I did marry her, I can vouch for that."

"If you'd merely bedded her, brother, you could have vouched for the same. This is one time I wish I'd been with you in your wondrous New Orleans."

Jarrett gave a grunt of aggravation and impatience and James immediately sobered again. "All right, big brother. You won her in a card game, then she ran—from whom or what you don't know. So then you married her."

"Something like that," Jarrett agreed, amused himself at last.

"All right, so I'm not so surprised. I've heard that she is exceptionally beautiful. True?" James asked.

Again, Jarrett shrugged. "She . . ." he began, then said flatly, "Yes. She is very beautiful. Nearly perfect."

"Don't resent her for it," James advised him.

"What?" Jarrett said sharply.

"It is almost as if you bear her a grudge for her beauty," James advised him. "A beauty that was enough to bring you to the altar when you didn't intend to be there."

Jarrett shook his head. "I didn't resent bringing her there. Maybe I didn't want a wife, but I do need one. I wasn't coerced, seduced—forced. I married her with full intent to do so. But . . ." He strode back to the log and sat again beside his brother. James was probably the only one he could ever speak completely honestly with regarding the situation. "I noticed her the moment she came into the tavern . . . then I saw the outrage, fear, and determination on her face when she suddenly found herself the stake in the game. At first I meant only to get her out of the situation she was in that night, feed her, give her a reprieve from the place for the night. Then suddenly it seemed we were being followed by half the thugs in the city, and I still didn't know a thing about her."

"And you still don't?" James murmured.

"Right. I couldn't demand or even threaten the truth from her, I couldn't leave her—" He broke off with a lift of his shoulders. "I definitely wanted her," he said very softly. "You're right there. I wanted her badly enough to behave quite rashly, but Robert was the one who suggested that a marriage would be a good idea. She needed to disappear—I had a whole savage wilderness in which she might do so."

"Ah, but you refrained from telling her the whole truth about your savage wilderness—because she refused to tell you the truth about herself even then? Is that it?"

"Yes."

"Ah!" James murmured. "So my new sister-in-law is an elegantly beautiful mystery woman. I can't wait to meet her. Of course, under the current circumstances . . . if I were to ask you both to dinner she'd probably assume that I wanted her to *be* dinner."

"I admit," Jarrett said, "she is . . . not pleased with the situation in which she finds herself."

James laughed. There was a slightly hollow tone to his laughter. "Who is pleased?" he murmured softly.

"She's frightened," Jarrett said. "She refuses to admit to fear, ever. Even when she is running. I've told her that we will be safe, yet she still behaves as if I snatched her from danger only to cast her into the pits of hell."

"We are all savage against one another here," James said with an edge of bitterness. "Why shouldn't she be afraid?"

"I have assured her there is no need."

"But you have neglected to tell her that your house would be spared in any raid. That every major chief, for peace or war, would walk around your property. Because of all white men, you honor your word."

"Because the Indian James McKenzie, Running Bear, is my brother," Jarrett corrected him.

James grinned again. "You lived among my people before I did, Jarrett. You stand among my people as your own man, and upon your own reputation and deeds. Perhaps you should let her know that."

"Perhaps, since I did snatch her from *some* awful fate, she might have some faith in me."

"She arrived to hear about the massacre of Major Dade and his men—I am certain such tales could cause a wavering in the strongest of faiths!" James advised him.

Jarrett stood restlessly again, pacing to the water, staring across it. James was right. Tara had been right. He owed her explanations. It vexed him. He wanted her to have faith in him, and he wanted her to come to him with her own explanations.

"Perhaps she has heard even more," James said behind him.

"There are those who claim that your first wife died at our hands."

Jarrett braced himself, amazed at the pain that could still knife through him.

"And that's a lie," he said roughly. "Who would tell her such a thing?"

"Many men—and women," James said flatly. "Perhaps you should tread gently."

"And perhaps," Jarrett said, spinning around to face his brother, "you remain unaware of just how much she is keeping from me!"

"But you are asking her to live in this world of yours—you are not living in her past."

"Her past may follow us yet, and I will be ill equipped to deal with it!"

James threw up his hands. "I leave you then to your anger, big brother!" he said. "Yet I remain curious to meet this rare new beauty of a sister-in-law, perhaps even the soon-to-be mother of my nephews and nieces."

Jarrett wondered about his brother's words for a moment. He wanted children. He was convinced that his lands would prosper with the years to come, that peace would eventually reign here, and that he had a fine legacy to leave behind him. He wanted a son to hold, to teach, to watch grow. Robert had said that he had *needed* a wife, whether he wanted one or not.

The problem was, he admitted, he wanted the wife he had acquired too much.

He took a deep breath, trying to swallow some of the tense twist of emotions within him.

"I've got to go home," James said. "I was just anxious to see you since all of this exploded on us."

Jarrett nodded, stepping forward, and the two embraced warmly for a moment, then stepped back from each other. "Bring Mother my love," Jarrett said, referring to Mary McKenzie, who lived now with James—Sean had passed away nearly a decade ago. "Give kisses to Sara and Jennifer," he said, referring to his nieces. "And give a really deep, passionate one to Naomi," he added, referring to his sister-in-law, a half-breed like James, and a rare beauty with golden skin, hazel eyes, and ink-dark hair that fell nearly to her knees.

"A passionate one, eh?" James queried.

Jarrett nodded, his lip curling into a grin, his eyes sparkling. "Very passionate."

"Wait till I get my hands on your wife," James warned. "If you want to go around passing out kisses—and watch that passionate one—you'd best come to dinner soon yourself, with or without your new wife. Mother will be anxious to see you, to remind you that you remain her son, no matter what war we may fight."

Jarrett nodded. "I'll come soon," he promised.

James grinned and turned, ready to disappear into the trees.

"James!" Jarrett called to him.

James paused, turning back.

"*You* remember. You're my brother, no matter what war other men fight."

James smiled. "Aye, Jarrett!" he agreed, lightly imitating their father's deep brogue. "We remain the sons of Sean McKenzie!"

"Aye, and that's a fact!" Jarrett returned in kind.

James smiled, turned, and disappeared, his footfalls silent.

Jarrett stared after his brother for several moments, then looked back to the water. The crane had flown away. The surface of the water was serene. The copse seemed encompassed in a sun-dappled silence.

Yet it was all a lie, he thought. It was the beauty he was fighting for, and yet . . .

He didn't even have an enemy to fight.

He inhaled and exhaled. He had been anxious to come back, and all hell had broken loose in his absence. He did have things to attend to.

And a reluctant bride. One who had caused him to lie awake throughout the long night. Agonizing. Wanting to touch her.

Not wanting to want her so badly.

Come what might, it was time to return to her.

And suddenly he was very anxious to do so. He'd been a damned fool. He had been so worried that she meant to run away from him again that he had been, in his strange way, running away from her.

He smiled suddenly. No more.

He whistled sharply. Charlemagne lifted his head from the tuft of grass he had been ripping from the creek bed and trotted obediently to him.

Indian style, Jarrett threw his leg over the stallion's back, flicked the reins, and started back.

Chapter 10

TARA STOOD on the porch, staring out onto the landscape that stretched away from the back of the house. The grass was beautifully green and an abundance of wildflowers grew at the river's edge creating a fantastic splash of color, even in winter. The water drifted by on a swift current this morning. The December air was not cold, but pleasantly cool, with that swift, silent breeze moving it along.

Jarrett was gone. She had stayed awake most of the night, waiting for him, wanting to say something, but he had not appeared in the bedroom where he had so determinedly told her she was to sleep.

She gritted her teeth hard, feeling the breeze, listening. She could hear the men in the fields. Black men, red men, white men, and all kinds of mixtures of the three. All of them hired men. She wasn't sure if it had anything to do with a dislike of slavery on Jarrett's part, or if it was just good business sense. Florida was a place where any runaway could find help. Often the Indians problems were brought about by their refusal to turn runaway slaves back over to white bounty hunters.

She shivered at the soft touch of the breeze, marveling again that a place could appear so serene and so beautiful, truly like an Eden or paradise, and yet offer such an abundance of danger. She didn't understand Jarrett, and perhaps that created half her fear. She didn't want to be afraid, didn't want to be a coward, and that, too, made things so much worse! But there had been so much panic in Tampa. People thinking that perhaps the Indians would attack even there. And yet Jarrett had been determined to come here.

Why hadn't Jarrett been afraid as well? And why had he refused to take a commission with the military? And why did it seem that there had been a strange understanding between her husband and the military man who had approached him and waved to her when she had stood aboard the *Magda*, watching the civilization of Tampa slip surely away? Jarrett, it seemed, wasn't willing to do exactly what they wanted him to do.

They would call on him at another time. And he would oblige them in some other manner.

If they were all to live so long!

She walked to the porch rail, fingers gripping it tightly. He was disappointed in her, of course. She bit into her lower lip, wondering how things had managed to go so badly. Not that they had even begun on terms of the greatest friendship! But nonetheless, she had been fascinated with him from the moment she had first seen him, when she had been warned that the Black Irish one had a certain spell. And it had seemed that passionate emotional ties had wound ever more tightly around her since that time. At first, though perhaps he'd harbored no great love for her, he had been a passionate and considerate lover. And just when she had discovered that she longed for both the passion and the tenderness, life had intruded.

"He is a tyrant!" she whispered softly.

But then she surely hadn't done much for the relationship, screaming that she didn't want him touching her.

And now, despite any debts she might owe him, she was stubbornly determined that she would maintain pride and dignity and surrender nothing of her heart to a man who seemed to sleep wherever he chose while dictating to her.

And all this while she was terrified nearly every minute that a Seminole tomahawk might come crashing into her skull.

She didn't want to be afraid. She simply was.

Not as she had been before. She had known her danger before. And she didn't want to go back. Even if she were to perish here, it would be better than going back.

She just wanted Jarrett to use some sense, to realize what had happened, to see that his wondrous Florida was a savage land, no matter how serene and well run his plantation.

She swung around suddenly, no sound but some instinct warning her that someone had come upon her.

He had.

Jarrett stood at the open doors to the back breezeway, feet apart, arms casually crossed over his chest as he watched her. She wondered what he was thinking, and she didn't like his expression. There was, she thought, a mocking contempt in his hard black eyes, and she had to remind herself just how very disappointed he was in her. She didn't measure up to his *real* wife, Lisa.

She reproached herself quickly for the thought. Lisa was dead. And Jarrett really hadn't said much about her. Perhaps that was it. Jarrett hadn't said anything at all.

"So I see you've survived the night," he said lightly.

"And would it have mattered to you if I hadn't?" she inquired. She wanted to bite her tongue instantly, but it was too late. The childish words were out.

He arched a brow at her without an answer and without further words of recrimination. She felt even worse. As if her back were up against a wall.

But there had been all those whispers in Tampa Bay behind her back. Nancy Reynolds had hinted that Jarrett's first wife had perished at the hands of the Indians.

She stood still for a moment, wishing that she could strike

him in the head with something and make him realize that he should be out . . .

Slaughtering all the Indians? she wondered, the inner question somewhat taunting.

But she didn't know any Indians. And she did know what had happened to Major Dade and other *white* men.

He walked across the porch, smoothly and almost in silence, not a board creaking beneath his feet, and she found herself trembling as he approached. She longed to reach out, to touch him. No, it was something deeper. She wanted to go back to the time before this wall had risen between them. So much had happened so quickly. It seemed that life had become the utmost struggle, and then he had been there. She had been so accustomed to running and fighting on her own. Then he had come. And though the future with such a man had been a challenge all its own, she had to admit that there had been the most wonderful moments when she had felt completely secure. He hadn't married her for love, there had never been such a pretense, but there had been those magical moments in his arms when she had felt cherished. She wanted to be held again. She wanted to feel that the world would be right, because he would shield her from it.

She found herself backing to the porch rail as he came closer and closer. Her hands, behind her, braced against the whitewashed wood, but he didn't touch her, he came to stand beside her. Even then she could feel the heat that seemed to radiate from him like a leashed violence. He wouldn't hurt her, she thought. In very little time she had been able somewhat to take the measure of the man, even if she knew almost nothing about his life before the night he had won her in a Louisiana poker game. Yet she wanted to flee from where she stood. He was angry with her. Worse. He was disappointed. And she thought that he was swifter than any creature that ran in the night, and that he could turn on her with his black eyes an onyx fire at any moment and . . .

"So, my love, how did you sleep?" he inquired, a lazy tone to his voice, yet even that touched by a deeper note with a harsh edge.

"Fine, thank you." The urge to bolt from him remained.

"We must thank the good Lord. You were not snatched from your bed in the middle of the night by naked savages."

"And you were not snatched from . . . wherever," she retorted quickly.

"But I was not afraid of such a thing happening."

"Oh, yes, I know. You are immune to Seminole knives and hatchets, so it would seem. But you do sport a beautiful head of thick rich hair, sir. Perhaps you should be just a bit more wary."

"Is it a beautiful head of hair?" he inquired. "I'm glad there is something about me of which you approve."

"I am rather fond of my own hair. I should like to keep it— along with the scalp to which it is attached."

"It's late to worry, isn't it? You were ready to drown yourself and offer your soul up to the devil—and now you are concerned about a few restless Indians?"

They both knew that the trouble did not concern a few restless Indians.

"It's a war!" she reminded him.

"Yes, and there have been wars before," he muttered. "There will be war again. Men survive war."

"Sometimes. What about women?"

"You, my dear, seem to be a survivor. But then, there is so little I know about you."

"Perhaps more than I know about you," she assured him. "Tell, me, sir, how did *you* sleep last night?" she could not help but inquire.

"This is my home. I always sleep well within it."

At least he had slept in the house somewhere. *With whom?* a plaguing voice taunted.

He hopped on the rail, very close, not touching her, but watching her with his fathomless black gaze.

"Do you find the house lacking in any way?" he asked her politely.

"It would be difficult to know, since I have seen very little of it," she responded swiftly. "I was informed, upon arriving, that I would be given a tour, but, alas, the master of this paradise found himself too concerned with other matters."

"Ah, but the master of the house intended to give you a tour. His heart all but ceased beating when he couldn't find the new mistress."

"Ah, but had he waited much longer to search for her, she might have grown old and gray, and he wouldn't have recognized her anymore anyway."

A slight smile played at his lips. "Would she have grown old and gray waiting?" he asked softly. "Would that I dared think so! It's far more likely she'd have navigated the deepest swamp to find her way out. Yet where would she have gone, I wonder?"

His light tone, she warned herself, could be all too deceptive. Yet she was glad of it. She felt the strangest sense of security with him here on the porch, felt again that he could envelop her in his arms and protect her from any threat, indeed, send his own strength radiating into her like the warmth of the sun.

She had fallen in love with him, she realized at that moment. With everything about him, dangerous dark eyes, the sound of his voice, the splay of his hands, the height and breadth of him, his tone, his touch.

She looked down quickly.

It was not a happy realization to discover she was in love with a man who had married her—to help her, yes—but who in his own heart and mind had seen her as nothing more than an attractive household decoration, a piece of functional flesh and blood.

Yet she didn't want to fight this afternoon. She didn't want to be his enemy.

"You promised me once," she reminded him softly, "that you wouldn't ask me any more questions."

"Did I promise?" he inquired.

"I believe so."

"Ah, well. I cannot help but wonder. If you were to run, where would it be that you'd choose to go? To the North? Your accent is difficult to place, your speech is without regional clue. Sometimes I tell myself that I detect a hint of the South. Then I think, no, perhaps it is Bostonian. Then I think again that I haven't the slightest clue of where you might come from."

"You promised—"

"But I am free to wonder. Of course, you are free to *offer* information anytime," he reminded her, his tone so soft, the words were almost a whisper. He reached out and lifted her chin, meeting her eyes.

"Perhaps," she murmured, "you'll be good enough to explain to me just why you seem to feel that you are encased in steel, that no harm can come to you."

"No answers from you?" he cross-queried.

"You promised not to ask for answers. I didn't."

He cupped her cheek gently. She discovered that she was drawn against him, that she could feel the black heat and fire in his eyes. His fingers moved like a velvet caress against the soft flesh of her face, then his hand was at the nape of her neck and he was drawing her closer still. She stood between his legs where he sat upon the rail, held intimately, close and warm, as his lips touched hers. It was a tender, light, and somehow very seductive kiss. Then his eyes were upon hers again and his voice was very husky.

"I tell you again, if you pay me heed, you will be safe. Stay within the boundaries I have given you, and no harm will befall you."

"How can you be so certain?" Tara demanded.

He was about to answer her, she thought, yet what he had in mind to tell her she would never know, for they were interrupted by a cry from the docks. "Mr. McKenzie! Boat on the river, sir!"

He stood, a deep frown knitting his brow. His hands lay upon her shoulders as he stared down to the river, but then he stepped by her. "Excuse me," he murmured, and she was dismissed.

She followed him as he walked down the steps from the porch to the lawn and made his way to the docks.

The sloop that had come down the river carried eight cannons and soldiers armed with rifles lined the bow. As Tara looked on, she saw the tall man with the golden curls who had nodded to her when she left Tampa. She watched Jarrett's friends greet him, and then saw him speak with her husband himself.

She remained on the lawn, standing back about twenty feet from Jarrett as a plank was lowered and the tall soldier, in full military dress, came hurrying down the plank toward him.

"Tyler!" Jarrett called. "I hadn't thought to see you so soon!"

"I assure you, I hadn't planned on a wild ride down river—the men are complaining blue blazes, we had them rowing away at the slightest sign of a calm. I didn't want to be here so soon, I assure you, but . . ." He shrugged, aware that two of his officers had followed behind him while the others remained on guard at the deck, and that Jarrett's overseer, Rutger, was suspiciously watching the exchange. Even Jarrett's new wife was standing just feet away.

"Perhaps you could spare me some time in your office," Tyler said.

"Of course." Jarrett lifted a hand, turning to direct the man back toward the house. His eyes lit on Tara. "Tara . . . I don't believe you met Captain Argosy. Tyler, my wife, Tara."

The captain stepped forward and lifted her hand, a dashing smile on his face. "Mrs. McKenzie, it's a pleasure and a privilege."

"Thank you, sir, the pleasure is mine," she murmured, her eyes searching out Jarrett's. But the captain had stepped back. "Jarrett, you know Sergeants Culpeper and Rice," he said, indicating the two young men. "Gentlemen, Mrs. McKenzie."

They both saluted her sharply and Tara smiled, nodding. "Welcome to Cimarron," she murmured.

"Tara, my love, I believe the gentlemen will be with us for

dinner," Jarrett said. He wasn't looking at her—he was looking at Captain Argosy. He wanted her out of the way, she was certain, and she wondered what new atrocity had been practiced by the Indians that he would attempt to hide from her now.

But she had promised him that she could be a good wife, and she intended to be one.

"Excuse me," she said to the men, and turned, walking back to the house while they spoke again for several seconds before following at a distance behind her.

Tara found Jeeves in the kitchen, already in a discussion with Hattie, the plantation's head cook, a tall woman with both black and Indian blood who seemed to speak very little but have a magic touch with food. Both of them stared at her as she entered the large kitchen, the first of the plantation's outbuildings. Both of them smiled quickly.

"Good afternoon, Mrs. McKenzie," Jeeves said, inclining his head and offering her his warm smile. Jeeves, Tara thought, would go out of his way to be polite and serve her—unless her desires clashed in any way with her husband's.

And Jeeves was on the lookout to see that her desires didn't clash with the master's.

"G'd afternoon, missus," Hattie added quietly, her almond eyes fixed seriously on Tara.

"We've company for supper," Tara said, "Captain Argosy and two of his men. His crew, I imagine, will remain aboard their ship."

"I'll get the girls on it," Hattie said. "We send those boys pies when they come. We—"

She broke off, for Jeeves was staring at her.

"We have always sent them pies," Hattie amended. "Whatever you wish."

"We must continue to send them pies," Tara said, feeling just a touch of exasperation.

"Miz Lisa always did so," Hattie said. "And Mr. McKenzie carried on with it."

"Tradition," Tara said, forcing a small smile. "We must keep it up."

"I had planned chicken," Hattie said. She glanced at Jeeves. Jeeves stood silent.

"Perhaps," Tara suggested, "we can have a roast? Potatoes, greens? A soup to start the meal, and a fish for the gentlemen as well?"

"She makes the best catfish suppers in the whole of the territory!" Jeeves shot in with pride.

"That would be wonderful," Tara said.

"What about dessert, missus?" Hattie asked.

She smiled. "Have we apples?"

"Bushels, ma'am."

"And her apple pie—"

"Is the best in the territory," Tara said before Jeeves could finish. She smiled. "We're very lucky."

She turned and left the kitchen, wondering just how many comparisons they were making between her and the deceased Lisa. She heard movement behind her and swung around. Jeeves was there.

"Yes?"

"I thought, Mrs. McKenzie, that you might want to give me your preference for tonight's wine," he told her.

"Thank you."

"We've a cellar, next building," he told her.

She nodded and accompanied him. The "cellar" was halfway above ground, and she imagined that in the lowland here it couldn't be much deeper or else it would be a well. But it was well stocked with vintage wines from France, Spain, and Italy and some homegrown specialties Jarrett had acquired on his travels to various places. She selected French wines for the evening, a red and a white, and studied the rest of the selections a few minutes longer before turning to leave. As usual she found that Jeeves was watching her with his somber dark eyes. Judging? Well, she was quite certain she hadn't made any mistakes. She knew the role that she was expected to play here as mistress of the estate.

"Do you approve my choices?" she asked him.

"It's not my place—" he began.

"You've been running the house for quite some time and doing so impeccably well, so I'm quite certain you have an opinion," she told him, but she smiled as she spoke the words, knowing well that she needed him as a friend in this house.

He smiled in return, inclining his head in thanks for the compliment.

"Your menu and your wine choices seem excellent," he assured her.

"What is Captain Argosy doing here?" she asked him.

"Now, Mrs. McKenzie—"

"Jeeves, do I look like a child?" she asked with a certain impatience.

"Please, Mrs. McKenzie, I'm sure that the men are just now meeting in the library—"

"And I'm quite certain that they'd like a whiskey. Would you please arrange a tray with drinks for the officers? I'll bring it myself."

Jeeves chuckled softly. "Mrs. McKenzie, there's a bar in the library. The gentlemen will be helping themselves to drinks as it is."

"Oh," Tara murmured with frustration. Then she smiled and arched a brow to Jeeves. "I'd like a plate of fruit, please. Hattie has just assured me we have plenty of apples, and I'm sure we've a few other light delicacies to tempt the men while they await a heavier meal."

Jeeves let his eyes roll and he shook his head. "Mrs. McKenzie, I don't—"

"Jeeves," she said firmly, "if you will please see to my request?"

He had little choice, but even when she was supplied with her tray of tempting offerings for the men, it did her little good. When she tapped on the door to the library she was greeted first with silence and then a sharp "Come in!" When she entered, she quickly offered them her best and most innocent smile, and the gentlemen were all charming, leaping to their feet, giving her their fervent thanks. But Jarrett, his black eyes sternly upon her, was quickly by her side as well, thanking her for her thoughtfulness and then propelling her back out the door, his hand very firmly upon the small of her back.

She found herself in the hallway again, no wiser as to what was going on.

At length Jeeves found her there. With no comment on the fact that he had tried to warn her about what would happen, he politely suggested that she might want to bathe and dress for supper. He had taken the liberty of sending the hip tub up and it would be available at her leisure.

A hot bath sounded wonderful. She smiled and thanked Jeeves, and she thought that maybe she was acquiring friends in the house.

She soaked in the hot water for a while. When it grew cold, she rose to dress, then decided to finish one of the gowns she had been making. She was determined that she could do so if she hurried. Nancy Reynolds had told her that Jarrett's laundress, Cota, was a skilled dressmaker, and so she asked Jeeves to send for the woman, and she came quickly.

Tara had expected the laundress to be either black, Indian, or of mixed blood, but Cota, it turned out, was a pretty young Italian girl with blue-black hair and bright green eyes and an olive skin. She was still learning English, and she had not been in the household very long. She was very enthusiastic about her new mistress's project, and she could sew both swiftly and beautifully.

The two women were still at work when the door opened and Tara, dressed in corset and pantalettes, looked up to find her husband standing in the doorway. She felt a blush of color rise to her breast and cheeks and her heart skip a beat as she watched him. She waited for him to speak first.

"*Scusi!*" Cota cried, blushing herself and jumping to her feet.

"Cota—" Tara began, but the girl had already slipped past Jarrett and fled.

Tara stood somewhat awkwardly herself, drawing her gown up along with her. It was finished except for the last ten inches of hem.

Jarrett stepped into the room, closing the door behind him.

"I had come to tell you that dinner is about to be served," he said, yet did not move.

She nodded, swallowing. "I'll—be right down."

But still he watched her. And then he took three long strides that brought him to the braided rug before the fire, where she still sat clasping her new gown to her chest. He hunched down himself, picking up the gown.

"Cota made this today?" he queried, his fingers moving over the material, his eyes on her.

She shook her head. "I started it on the ship, but we finished it this afternoon."

His brow rose. "You're an excellent seamstress."

Her lashes fell, but her jaw was tight. "I told you I would make a good, functional wife."

"There's only one *function* that really matters," he murmured.

Her eyes flew to his as a quick wave of fury fluttered in her heart. "And I have failed in that?" she demanded quickly. "I—"

"You've failed in nothing—I have merely allowed you to forget the terms of marriage," he told her, and she realized that he had never been reproaching her, that there was amusement in his voice, and the very curl of his lips was making her feel heated and flushed. Desperately she sought some way to change the subject, and as she hugged the gown more tightly to her chest, she remembered that she had been ready to batter the library door down not so long ago just to discover what was going on.

She inched away from him. "Jarrett, why have they come?" she demanded.

He hesitated. "I'll explain later. There's no time now."

"Just tell me—" she began, but she broke off, because he

gripped her new gown firmly, and she had to release it, or allow it to be ripped. He stared at the style and intricacy of the gown again and then at her. "Paris?" he queried her. "Do you come from abroad? Jeeves is convinced, of course, that you come from the very best of families, that you are running away from some scandal. Right into the heart of the swamp."

She stood, snatching the dress back. "I asked a question first. Why have the soldiers come?"

He didn't answer her. His eyes rested upon her and the gown. "Exceptional," he murmured.

"The gown?"

A subtle smile teased his lip. "Well, that. More so the form it would cover." Again he had the gown in his hands, and she had to let go. But he didn't study it again. He cast it aside. The creation of her hours and hours of labor, so simply cast aside. She started to reach for it, but his arm snaked out and his fingers clasped hard and warm around her shoulders, drawing her back.

"We do need to work on our marriage. I am greatly distressed to hear that you fear you have failed in any way."

She wanted him, wanted his touch, wanted his light, bantering tone. Too much, perhaps. Her heart seemed to be beating like thunder. She was breathless.

"Jarrett, those men are waiting."

"Ah, yes! You did tell me not to touch you. But then, I was truthful from the start about exactly what I wanted from you."

"Jarrett!" she protested, wondering why she felt so desperate. "You tell me you've no time for answers! I demand to know—"

"Ah, yes! You demand!" he murmured. He drew her closer. She moistened her lips, trembling from head to toe.

Then, to her amazement, and perhaps disappointment, he released her. "You'll get your answers tonight," he said, his eyes black and fathomless once again. He swung around, striding to the door, then turned back to her once again. "And, Mrs. McKenzie, be forewarned. This is one night when I'll not sit sentinel at your door. You wonder where I sleep. Tonight, be assured, it will be with you, and it is not a great deal of rest I'll be expecting!"

She had no chance to reply. He was out the door, and it closed decisively in his wake.

Chapter 11

TARA WAS shaking so badly, she had to sit again, her gown of yellow silk and white lace now curled in her hands. She quickly smoothed it. She began to wonder if she dreaded the ending of their evening meal this night, or hated the fact that she must suffer through it before they might be together again.

Then she wondered anew what the men had come to say, and why they had caused such a fierce tension within her husband.

She leapt up and dressed very quickly. She didn't dare think about the rest of the night. She wanted answers to at least the one question now.

The men were assembled in the dining room sipping drinks, politely awaiting her appearance.

There was a shuffle as she entered the room, each man eager to greet her, sergeants Rice and Culpeper deferring to their senior officer, blushing a bit as they took care to step out of her way as Jarrett came forward to seat her at her end of the dining table. The table linen was snow white and impeccable, the silver was shining, the plates were a regal, blue-patterned porcelain, well befitting such a house.

Lisa had probably brought the dinnerware into the house, she thought, and then she again silently chastised herself for resenting the dead woman.

Jeeves cleared his throat, and she realized that he was standing just behind her chair, awaiting her word to serve the wine and the first course. She nodded to him, smiled, and received an encouraging smile in return. Pleasantries were exchanged. Sergeant Rodney Culpeper, sandy blond, freckled, and as friendly as an overgrown hound, told her how much better this winter was than the last. Tyler Argosy talked about the abundance of crops available, about the miracle of growing things throughout the year.

"Ah, yes, and there is the wonder of a bloody Indian war as well!" Tara murmured. She tried not to meet Jarrett's eyes, down the long table. Despite herself she looked at him. Just as she expected, twin orbs of ebony fire were narrowed her way.

"It's true that this is a new territory, a great deal of it wilderness. We haven't the sophistication of such places as New York, Philadelphia, Boston, Richmond, Charleston, or the like, Mrs. McKenzie," Tyler Argosy said.

"Are you from the North, Mrs. McKenzie?" Sergeant Rice asked politely.

"From the North?" she murmured, looking at her plate. She could still feel Jarrett's eyes burning down the length of the table upon her. She raised her eyes to meet his. His brow was arched. Like Tyler he awaited an answer.

"This is surely a southern lady!" Sergeant Rice, who she had learned hailed from Alabama, assured them all.

"We've plenty of exceptionally fine women hailing from the North as well," Sergeant Culpeper argued.

Thank God for the two of them!

"Gentlemen, let it be said that I do not hail from here!" Tara assured them with a laugh. A grateful one, if they only knew!

"But, Mrs. McKenzie, you must—" Sergeant Rice began again, and to her surprise it was her husband who saved her this time.

"My wife is an exceptional lady, and she wouldn't want to

disappoint either of you," Jarrett said smoothly. "We met and married in New Orleans, and of course I was quite anxious to return home, due to circumstances here."

He had saved her, but he had given her an opportunity to learn something as well. She pounced upon it. "Just what are the circumstances?" she asked with soft-spoken innocence.

There was silence for a moment. She met Jarrett's eyes once again. He was the only one who would answer her; she knew that the others would not, not in Jarrett's presence.

His tone was light. "There's a family not far from here that's anxious to reach Tampa Bay. They don't live along the river; they're deeper into the interior. I'm going for them."

Her heart slammed against her chest and missed a beat. "What?" she whispered.

"I'm going to escort them out," Jarrett said impatiently.

"But Captain Argosy has a ship of armed men."

"A company of men, Tara. Not enough to successfully wage battle on land. I can best handle this situation."

The dining room was then uncomfortably, explosively silent.

"Why?" Tara burst out.

"Because we're trying not to provoke an attack, we just want to get the family out and not invite another slaughter. General Clinch is out in the field somewhere, militia units are fighting to hold together, and this way of doing it simply makes more sense," he replied calmly, telling her everything and nothing at all. His eyes were hard as her lips formed another question. "My dear," he said firmly, "I'm afraid that we're making our guests feel quite uncomfortable."

Their guests be damned. She continued to stare at him. "Ah!" she said softly, and set her silver down. She took a sip of her wine, then smiled brilliantly at Captain Argosy, Sergeant Rice, and Sergeant Culpeper.

"I do apologize! Please forgive me. You all must relax and enjoy Cimarron. I shall leave you gentlemen alone for your brandy and cigars," she said politely. Neither dessert nor coffee had been served, but if she was mistress of this house, then dinner was ended.

She wanted to scratch Jarrett's eyes out, and she was sure she couldn't sit calmly at the table while aching with every muscle in her body to leap across it.

She stood; the men leapt up.

"Tara—" Jarrett began, but she was already out of the room.

She left the house, escaping out the back door and flying across the porch and out into the night. She ran across the lawn and incline, not stopping until she had come upon a tall tree. She gripped it, gasping for breath as she stared down to the river where the military ship lay docked so near the *Magda*, both alight with lanterns against the darkness of the night.

He was leaving. Sweet Jesu, he was leaving. He had dragged her all the way out here, and now he was abandoning her as well!

And yet she was not as frightened as she had been before. She simply didn't want him leaving her. She didn't want to lie awake, night after night, wondering if he was alive.

"Dammit!" Suddenly seemed to roar into her ears.

She nearly screamed aloud as a hand fell upon her arm, spinning her around. Jarrett! She hadn't even seen him exit the house, and yet in a matter of minutes he had found her here, amid the trees, where she should have been all but invisible.

"Don't you 'dammit!' to me!" she cried, fighting his hold. She couldn't break it. She went dead still, staring at him. "You're leaving!"

"I hadn't realized that you would miss me."

"I hadn't thought that you would abandon me to the savages!"

"Have you seen a savage on this property yet?" he demanded heatedly.

"Your guests are inside!" she lashed back. "My departure was surely acceptable, for they will assume that I have escaped to absorb the knowledge that my husband is about to offer his head to the scalpers. But you, McKenzie, can hardly walk out on them so easily."

"Alas, my love, but I can!" he said, pulling her close. "I have come to gently console the poor bride who could really care less about my scalp and is furious only because she is certain I have forgotten about hers."

She tried to wrench free from him, but he would not let her go. Furious and ridiculously close to tears, she tried to kick him but he moved too swiftly. He swept her up into his arms despite her wild struggling, heading back to the house with long strides despite the fact that her fists pummeled his chest all the while.

"I'll scream!" she warned him. "Your good friends in the military will really begin to wonder."

"They won't wonder a thing. They've gone back to their ship."

Her threat thus defused, she stared at him with narrowed, totally accusatory eyes. "There is nothing honest or fair about you!" she charged.

"Perfectly fair. I have always given you warning," he told her, his stride now a leap that carried them up the porch steps, then across the flooring, and into the breezeway.

"You *are* a tyrant."

"Indeed?"

She should have been screaming, she thought. She had threatened; she should carry out her threats.

She hadn't the nerve, she realized. And if she were to scream, well, who would interfere with a married couple in their own home?

They were halfway up the long stairway. In seconds a shove of his shoulder was opening the door to her room. His room. Their room.

The windows were open to the cool night breeze, the curtains swaying out into the night. A sweet fragrance of wildflowers swept into the room.

The bed coverings had been pulled down and a single lantern

burned upon the washstand, bathing everything in mercurial shadows.

She was still in his arms as he closed the door with the force of his back and looked down into her eyes. "I'll be damned if I'll leave you tonight," he told her.

She shook her head, wondering again that she should feel so desperate.

"You've no problem leaving me tomorrow!" she charged him.

"Ah! But I will carry tonight with me!"

"What of last night?" she challenged him.

A black brow arched at her. "You were concerned?"

"I say again, you are a tyrant. I am ordered to be here, while you . . ." Her voice trailed. She lowered her lashes, feeling the ebony heat of his eyes on hers. She suddenly found herself on her feet, spun so that her back was to him, feeling the touch of his fingers upon the hooks and eyes she had so carefully fashioned into her gown. She tried to slip away from him but he firmly pulled her back. "Stand still. It is quite evident you worked hard upon this and I would not have you ruin it."

"Me! You're the one—"

"Stand still!"

Trembling, chewing upon her lower lip, she did so. But after he lifted the gown over her head, she scurried away, facing him in corset, pantalettes, and petticoat. He scowled at her, hands on his hips. "I don't recall hurting you, madam!"

"I don't recall saying that you did!" she responded. Then, to her amazement, he leapt atop and across the bed with a startling, swift bound, sweeping her into his arms again and down upon the white, welcoming sheets. She landed upon her stomach, her face in her pillow. He quickly straddled her, and she could feel his fingers deftly moving at the small of her back, at the satin ties of her corset.

"What are you doing?" she cried.

"I like my women to breathe!" he told her.

She was a sudden momentum of strength, as she twisted beneath him, facing him. The impetus, however, finished his task for him, and the stays and lace fell away, baring her breasts. She felt the flood of color rise to her cheeks but kept her eyes steady on his.

"Exactly!" she cried. "Your *women!*"

He paused, easing back on his haunches, as well he might, for with the iron of his thighs straddling her, there was nowhere she was going.

He lifted a hand in the air. "Pray, go on," he said politely.

"If you're so anxious for me to keep breathing, you might consider moving," she suggested.

"Ah, my love! You haven't a prayer of my doing so." His fingers suddenly laced around hers, pinning them to the bed. She started to fight the hold, then went very still, meeting his eyes. He smiled slowly and leaned toward her. His lips touched hers. So gently. Feathering, molding, brushing against hers. His tongue, a streak of liquid fire, drew their form, and then the kiss deepened, coercive, seductive.

He rose above her again, and she dragged air into her lungs.

"I said that I needed a *wife!*" he reminded her softly.

"I never meant to deny you that!" she whispered in turn. Then with honesty and anguish she cried out, "But I cannot be what you want if it is not fair."

"Fair?" he said, truly puzzled, and she found herself struggling for words.

"I cannot be silent and forever grateful."

"Silent?" he echoed, a brow arched very high.

"You saved me once, I am grateful. And you said exactly what you wanted and I—I wanted you with me as well, you—"

"To save you from the Indians."

"You insisted on coming here; you should do so!"

"I am to protect you with life and limb, and at least now I am to enjoy that luscious life for which I would give my own!" he taunted.

"Oh!" she cried out with aggravation, trying to throw him

from her. But he laughed and leaned nearer again, and when she twisted her head from the promise of his lips, his liquid caress fell upon her cheek, then her throat, her collarbone, and downward, his tongue, just the tip of it, circling her breast, teasing the tip of it . . .

"Where were you?" she demanded.

Again, he paused. Ebony eyes met hers, and a slow smile curved his mouth. "When?"

"Last night."

"In one of the guest rooms."

"And the night before?"

He frowned. "On the ship, of course."

"In—in Tampa."

For a moment he hesitated, and she felt her heart begin to sink. Misery crawled over her. He had been with the ever luscious and so very bold young lady, Sheila.

He sighed deeply. "I went to the fort, to speak with one of the men who survived the Dade massacre," he told her quietly, and she knew that he had hesitated because he wondered whether a lie might have stood him better, whether she might have accepted a night with another woman more easily.

"Oh!" she whispered.

"Satisfied?"

"I wish I could make you understand!" she whispered, meeting his eyes again. "If you tell me that I must sleep here—"

His forefinger suddenly pressed against her lip, and she fell silent.

"Then I must sleep here too," he agreed very softly. He watched her eyes for a moment. Waited to see if she would speak again. She did not.

His mouth touched down upon hers again. She could think of no more reason to fight him.

Her lips shaped to his, parted to him. She seemed to sink into a bed of clouds as she felt the fire of his touch, the thirst of it, the sweet heat it elicited within her. Yet it seemed that her sudden, complete surrender surprised him, for despite the wild heat that quickly ignited within the passion of their kiss, he drew back from her, staring down at her. He took hold of her discarded corset and thrust it from the bed, then stood, catching her shoes one by one and swiftly tossing them heedlessly aside. Her petticoats went next, then she felt the hot pleasure of his hands upon her bare hips as he wrenched at the pantalettes, swearing when he ripped a satin tie. He trembled when she lay all but naked except for her stockings, and he paused again, smiling, and wickedly this time, she thought. And she soon knew why, for his hurried touch was somewhat stayed as he began to roll and slide the silk stocking from her leg, fingertips teasing all the way, a pause again here and there as he set his lips against her naked flesh. She held her breath, tried to breathe, tried not to feel the aching sensation that had begun to burn between the limbs he so tormented.

He arched a brow, watching her, as her second stocking fell to the floor. She kept her gaze on his, and he suddenly hurried again, wrenching off his frock coat, waistcoat, heedless of buttons and threads. His steady gaze of ebony fire remained on her while he tugged off his boots and stockings, but she felt her eyes slipping from his, and sliding down the length of his body. For a moment she thought it curious that she could covet him so, admire the taut muscled angles and planes of him, the sleek bronze of his flesh, and know such great anger against him so frequently. Know such jealousy.

Such longing. A fierce, hot trembling set into her as she realized that wanting him was both natural and right. She had married him, she was his wife. And most important, she was falling more and more in love with him.

He cast his breeches to the floor and she discovered herself slipping like a wraith from their bed, anxious to touch him. His back had been to her, and her action took him by surprise, for he swung around with startling speed, his ebony eyes slightly wary as they fell upon her. For a moment she felt awkward, unsure. But haltingly she took a step forward, reaching out to set her fingers and palm upon his chest, near his heart. "I just wanted to—touch you," she whispered.

His hand closed over hers, and he drew her tight against his naked body. "Ah, my dear wife, there is nothing I could want so much as to be touched by you."

She felt a sweet smile of happiness slipping onto her lips, and he lifted her chin, barely brushing her lips with his own, then turned his back to her once more to kick the rest of his clothing out of the way. She stepped closer again, fingers delicately upon the breadth of his shoulders, her body all but brushing his, her lips upon the muscled, bronze flesh of his back. She heard him inhale sharply. He stood very still for a moment, and she came closer still, nuzzling against him, hands now exploring the length of him, her knuckles running down his back, her fingertips riding up again over his length. Bringing them down again she curled her fingers around his hard-muscled buttocks, and it was then that she heard him exhale. He spun around to her, this time all but savagely taking her lips with a heated passion as their bodies pressed close together, as the state of his arousal pulsed hard and insistent against the naked flesh of her belly. She clung to him, savoring the wild hunger of his kiss, the swift, forceful velvet of his tongue, the tempest it all awoke within her. His fever erupted further. She was suddenly off her feet and upon the bed, and his kisses still seared her mouth, her throat, her breasts.

His hand slid down the length of her inner thigh. His palm pressed against her, his fingers caressed her, teased her, entered her. Thrusts of velvet fire seduced her mouth, and stroked against the most erotic and feminine places, swept her into a sweetly drugged splendor, into fierce longing.

Hungry kisses, savage, then light, rained down upon her, bathing her breasts, her throat, the hollow of her abdomen. Where his fingers had trod so boldly, his liquid caress followed. Cries escaped her, protests, gasps. Desire shot into her explosively, ecstasy, anguish, a building inferno.

Cascades of wonder seemed to explode within her. As if in a

half-drugged state she felt the weight of his body, the hard swell of his sex. His kiss came against her earlobe, teased her throat, consumed her lips. And still the shock of his body thrusting hard into hers was a fire that lit into her all anew, and to her amazement she was swiftly swept into the ferocity of his desire once more, undulating to his rhythm, flying again, reaching.

A soft cry ripped from her lips as white stars seemed to burst and soar against the very darkness of the night. She lay on clouds, yet she was so intensely aware of him, of his slick bronze flesh against hers, of the wild constriction of his muscles, of the hard thrust of his sex into her body, again and again.

And then she seemed drenched with him. A deep groan echoed in the golden shadows, and his body shuddered against hers. Then his arms were around her, strong and gentle, as he eased himself to her side, holding her. She curled against him. His arm remained around her, his fingers dangling over her abdomen. She closed her own fingers around them. Her heart still pounded fiercely; her breath came in shallow gasps as she asked softly, "Do you really have to leave?"

He eased up, a brow arched as he looked at her. "Was this wondrous seduction nothing but a ploy to keep me here?"

"I don't remember seducing you," she said, itching to slap him.

"You but breathe, and it is seduction," he said, and she wasn't sure if he was taunting her or not.

"I thought you liked your women to breathe," she retorted.

"I do—see how much?"

She groaned, closing her eyes, only to feel his arms encircling her once again as he lay back down beside her. He was silent for a moment, and though she bit her lip, wishing she dared pull away from him after his comment that she had seduced him to gain her way, she held still as well.

He spoke, and his words were tormented and vehemently sincere, startling in the darkness of the night. "If I didn't have to go, I would not!" he said.

Tears threatened hotly against her lashes, and she blinked them back furiously. He meant what he had said. She didn't reply. She lay there, her back to him, his arm around her. She didn't try to draw away, yet there was nothing for her to say.

"I'll be back as quickly as I can," he told her.

She could still think of nothing to say.

"I have a great deal to come back to now," he added.

Still, she could not tell him that it was fine for him to go, and she closed her eyes very tightly, unaware of just how stiff a body he held.

Perhaps he had nothing else to say, either, for he was silent a long time. Despite her certainty that anxiety alone would keep her awake, she began to drift. Yet even as sleep all but claimed her, she found herself in his arms again, found that she was the one quite well seduced that night, and that she had no protest against his lovemaking.

Still later, she did open her mouth when she felt his touch, the blaze of his eyes again. Ah, he wanted her! Yet he was so set upon leaving her!

"Will you want me so when I am minus my scalp and a great deal of hair?" she challenged him reproachfully.

"You'll keep your hair," he told her, and his next words were whispered against her own lips. "And you will remember me when I am gone."

It was very, very late when she really fell asleep. Perhaps that was why she dreamed and dreamed so vividly and with such terrifying detail.

She was running again. The Indian was at her back, knife in a sheath at his waist, tomahawk raised high to break her skull. She didn't dare look back to see his face, because she was so afraid that it would be the very man she had married, intent himself upon killing her.

She had to stop running, because when she looked before her, she saw William. Someone was holding him up by his hair, and there was a knife at his throat, ready to slash through his flesh.

Words seemed to echo in a strange, savage wilderness, haunting her. "Come back, Tara. Pay the price, pay the price, save him. . . ."

"William!" she screamed his name again and again, certain that she could save him if she could only reach him.

But the Indian was behind her. She had led the Indian right to William, and it was the Indian who threatened him now. Her scalp, or William's.

"Tara!"

A hand clamped suddenly over her mouth, and she awoke with a start. Jarrett was naked, straddling her, smooth and sleek like a great, agile panther in the night. His eyes were black as coal and hard as ice.

"I will have half a regiment of men breaking in here any second now to see if I'm murdering you," he said somewhat harshly, but his hand eased from her mouth.

Her eyes were wide, her heart was pounding viciously. "There's no company of men here. You told me that Captain Argosy and Rice and Culpeper went back to the ship."

"I didn't want you screaming before," he admitted offhandedly, "and I had no idea in hell you'd be screaming as if I were committing some horrific evil in the middle of the night!"

"You lied—" she began to accuse him.

"Who's William?" he demanded.

She couldn't help it; tears sprung to her eyes. She was still shaking.

"Tara, who's William?"

He looked as hard and merciless as tempered steel. Well, she had known that he could be that, even as she had known that he could be strong, protective, passionate—and even tender—at times.

She opened her mouth, wet her lips. But before she could speak she started shaking again and a soft sob escaped her. To her amazement she found herself swept up, cradled in his arms. He asked no more questions. His fingers moved gently through the length of her hair, smoothing its tangled length from around her face.

"It's all right," he told her. "It's all right now. You can sleep, I'm with you."

But you won't be with me tomorrow! she almost cried out.

"You're safe here," he whispered to her. "I swear it—on my land you're safe, Tara. You're safe. . . ."

The words stayed with her. Gradually she ceased to tremble. "Rest, Tara," he commanded her. "Rest, you're safe with me."

His strength, and tenderness surrounded her. The dream faded. She was so very, very tired.

When she finally slept, she did so deeply.

She woke from the depths of that sleep slowly, as if heavy clouds sat over her as she tried to struggle to consciousness. She wanted to remain asleep. But someone was shaking her.

She opened her eyes.

Her reprieve was over.

Jarrett's taut features loomed before her. He sat at her side and leaned over her, arms like bars on either side of her. Despite the fact that the room was barely lightened by the coming of dawn, he had been up for a while it seemed. Perhaps he had never slept. He was fully dressed in form-hugging brown breeches, a white shirt open at the neck, a muted green waistcoat, and a heavier, earth-colored frock coat. He wore high boots, coming almost to his knees. His black hair was queued at his nape, making his handsome features sharp and strong and, at the moment, menacing.

"Who's William?" he demanded.

She shook her head. "No one you need be concerned with."

"Who's William?" he repeated.

"Jarrett—"

"Who the bloody hell is William?" he demanded anew. His

hands fell upon her shoulders, his fingers biting into them. She found herself dragged up to face him, the sheets falling from her naked body, her hair becoming a wild fall that tangled around them both.

"Jarrett!" she protested.

"Who?" he demanded again, and the word thundered out to her.

No questions! He had promised her.

Yet it seemed that this was one question she had to answer, and answer now.

"My brother!" she cried out. "William is my brother!" she repeated, swallowing down the sob that caught at her throat. She wrenched herself from his touch and fell back to the bed, twisting away from him and onto her stomach, closing her eyes tightly, praying that she could fall back into the deep, deep, comforting sleep that had been hers just moments ago.

She still felt him by her.

"Your brother? You swear it?"

She let out a muffled oath of aggravation that must have assured him she was telling the truth.

She felt his hand upon her back, sweeping the fall of her hair from it. She felt the fire of his lips upon her bare flesh, just a touch.

"We'll talk when I get back," he said.

They'd talk, indeed! He'd ply her with questions and refuse to answer any himself!

But his touch had left her. A second later she realized that their bedroom door had opened and closed, and that he was gone.

She bolted up in the bed and started to leap from it. She realized she was naked, wrenched up the sheet, and raced for the door again.

Too late. She could already hear him below, calling out something to Jeeves as he mounted Charlemagne. Even as she hurried to the window, he was riding away. She trailed her sheet back to the bed and sank down to the foot of it, suddenly fighting tears. She hadn't wanted him to go! She had wanted him to stay.

And not just because she was afraid.

But because she had been so glad and warmed to sleep beside him, feel his arms through the night.

Because she did, indeed, love him.

Chapter 12

DURING HER first few weeks of residence in her new home, Tara learned a great deal about Cimarron.

To begin with she quickly realized her husband didn't rely on goodwill alone for his safety.

Armed men guarded the property, almost as if it were a little kingdom unto itself. It wasn't an armed camp, per se, but after a few days she noted that there were always men watching from vantage points atop the buildings at each end of the dock. Rutger rode from docks to fields throughout the day with others at his side, and even along the small stream and woods that bordered the Indian country, men were stationed right in the branches. By the fourth night of Jarrett's departure Tara actually slept well and deeply, finally feeling safe at Cimarron. By then, of course, she was so exhausted that if any dreams did come along to trouble her, she was not aware of them.

She learned about the house itself as well, and the learning was not an unhappy experience. Jeeves showed it to her in its entirety, and it dawned on her slowly just how great an American empire it was that her husband had fashioned out of cypress hammocks, marsh, and swamp. The house had been beautifully designed and elegantly furnished, yet it was exceptionally comfortable as well, a welcoming place. Though his room had seemed exceptionally masculine when she had arrived, little by little it was becoming her room as well. Small things changed it. Her toiletries now sat on the dresser. Jeeves had brought in a long swivel Queen Anne mirror and a dressing table to match.

Throughout the rest of the house, she had discovered, the furnishings had been carefully chosen to complement the home and each sector of it. One guest room was furnished with seventeenth-century French pieces, another was decorated in Tudor style with a large, dark wood canopied and curtained bed. Jarrett's library and office were both more sparsely furnished with cleanly carved pieces straight from New England. The hall, or breezeway, was most elegant with its settees and mahogany tables, but even there the brocade- and velvet-covered chairs and settees seemed to beckon one to sit comfortably.

Only one occurrence during her extensive tours with Jeeves disturbed her, and that was the afternoon he brought her to the small library on the second floor.

There were two windows here, with a broad section of wall between them. It was an area perfect for a large painting and that's exactly what had been placed there. The painting was of a woman. There was no perspective within the painting from which to judge her height, for she stood by a small flower stand, dressed in sunflower-yellow, a gown with a low-scooped bodice and the picturesque sweep of a train. Her neck was long and slender, her stance regal. Her eyes were a deep almond brown with a slight cast to them that gave her an exotic appeal. Her hair was a deep mahogany brown, swept cleanly off her beautiful neck. She had smiled for the artist, and it was a beautiful, whimsical smile that instantly caught the eye of the beholder, compelling, engaging one to smile as well.

Yet Tara felt a hollowness within herself as she studied the painting, for she knew without being told that the lady was the true mistress of Cimarron—Jarrett's "real" wife. Lisa. She had been exceptionally beautiful, and if the painting spoke truly of her, she had been vibrant and sweet as well. She had surely been the perfect social match for Jarrett, the perfect mistress of his home. She had set the standards, here at Cimarron.

But she was dead! Tara reminded herself. She was ashamed to feel such jealousy again, but she was certain that Lisa had shared far more with Jarrett—his thoughts, mind, heart, and soul!—than Tara ever would.

Tara tried to stay away from the painting. Trying made it worse. Sometime during each day she found herself in the library, studying the painting.

When she wasn't studying the painting, she tried to stay occupied, but in attempting to busy herself in any way with the house, she found that, with every task she performed, she wondered if Lisa had done things in the same manner she was doing them. How much soap had Lisa made, how many candles? How much meat was salted, how much smoked? Under Jeeves, of course, the plantation house all but managed itself, and yet he and the others were unerringly courteous to her and anxious to serve her. She quickly discovered, however, that no one would answer the multitude of questions she was always eager to ask. Jeeves, of course, was the one she asked first, asking point blank how Lisa had died. But Jeeves had replied with a long sigh, and then he had told her point blank that Master Jarrett would surely want to explain the situation himself. She tried again with Cota, but Cota knew nothing, and Hattie just rolled her eyes and all but mimicked Jeeves, assuring her that Mr. McKenzie would scalp her sure as a Seminole might if she went talking out of turn.

One night she sent for Rutger, ostensibly to ask him if there'd been any news along the river. He supped with her in the dining room, telling her that one trader had passed by, stopping briefly and assuring him only that Tampa had not been attacked, not as yet. But Rutger either knew nothing about Lisa, or was quite a skilled actor himself, for when Tara tried more subtly to gain information, he slipped from her questions every time.

Great beings might have swept down out of the sky to spirit Lisa away for all the information Tara could gain on her predecessor.

But nothing that elusive had happened, she discovered, for Jeeves did at least have a bit of a heart about her curiosity. One afternoon when he discovered her in the library staring up at the portrait, he suggested that she might like to see Lisa's grave, and —feeling just a little bit morbid—she quickly agreed. He took her out far past the last of the outbuildings and into a copse of trees where a beautifully crafted wrought-iron fence encircled a burial plot. There were several graves toward the rear of the burial plot, but she barely saw them at first, for an exquisitely carved stone sarcophagus with a winged angel above it lay in the center of the graveyard. Tara stepped through the gate to the burial plot as Jeeves opened it for her and stared at the angel as she came close to the grave. She ran her fingers over the engraved words on the stone as she read them. *Here lieth the earthly remains of Lisa Marie McKenzie, born St. Augustine, Florida, 1806, taken by the Angels to Heaven, there to dwell, from her own earthly Paradise, January 18th, 1833. Beloved wife, blessed lady, mourned by all, yet she will live in our hearts forever.*

The words on the stone were not all that helpful. Tara swung around to ask a question of Jeeves, but Jeeves had brought her here and then managed to disappear very quickly. Tara bit her lip and started to leave, but then she observed the rest of the stones in the graveyard and began to read them. She was puzzled when she read one that simply said, *One Who Runs*, and she thought that perhaps Jeeves would answer her about that grave. The one beside it read, *Mary Lyde, born Dublin, Ireland, 1811, died Cimarron Plantation, Florida Territory, 1831, also, her infant son, stillborn. Ashes to ashes, dust to dust, God will bless his children.*

Poor Mary Lyde! Tara thought. And poor Lisa, both so very young.

A chill breeze suddenly seemed to stir as she stood there. There was just one more stone, set back a bit from Lisa's. The large angel on Lisa's grave had overshadowed it, but Tara saw, stepping around the above ground tomb of Lisa's monument, that the memorial was a fantastic piece of art in itself. There was a small but beautiful stone sculpture of the Virgin Mary holding the infant Christ child. Upon the tiny slab of marble that stretched out from it two simple words were etched out in elaborate print.

Baby Daughter.

Puzzled, Tara stared at the stone, then felt as if the cold breeze entered her heart.

Whose baby daughter? Lisa's—and Jarrett's? So it seemed, but there were others buried in this plantation plot.

The breeze picked up again, scattering leaves by her feet. The sun was falling, she realized. She stood and looked to the river. Trees shadowed her vision. In the distance the day was still crimson and gold. Nearer, it seemed to be wrapped in darkness, and she was suddenly, despite herself, afraid. She thought of the beautiful woman in the portrait, sleeping death's sleep, deep in the ground.

Rotting, no matter how beautiful the monument to her.

What had happened to Lisa? she wondered, and she suddenly thought that she was very much alone out here, that darkness was falling, that she couldn't see any of the men she had seen so often before who so subtly patrolled the plantation.

She turned around, eager to flee the tiny cemetery, feeling as if all manner of eyes were staring at her from the encroaching shadows. As she hurried through the gate, her heart skipped a beat as she felt a hard tug upon her skirt. A flash of panic seized hold of her, and she briefly thought that the ghost of Jarrett's first wife had returned to waylay her, to tell her that she was not mistress here, that she was an imposter in all that she had done.

Her skirt was caught on one of the elegantly designed flowers in the wrought iron gate. She wrenched it free, and then, her heart still beating hard, decided that she would not race for the house.

She walked there slowly, almost sedately.

But her teeth chattered all the while.

She hurried into the buffet in the parlor and started to pour herself a sherry. She hesitated and strode into the library, found the whiskey bottle, and poured herself a stiff drink. It scalded her throat as she swallowed down two fingers, but it gave her the desired effect. She felt much calmer, and very foolish, and after a moment's thought she was convinced she could find out the answers to the questions she was continually asking and everyone continually evading.

She told Hattie that she would take a tray in her room that night. When Jeeves delivered it, she took great pleasure in thanking him for having shown her to the graveyard, but she didn't ask him a single question about anyone buried within it. She smiled instead, and told him that she was amazed with the size and efficiency of the plantation.

"Of course, I realize that I've seen very little. Jarrett described many things for me; yet I've not quite got the lay of the place."

"The lay of the place, Mrs. McKenzie?"

"Well," she said innocently, "I have to admit, even the shape of the state is a little confused in my mind." She walked over to her bed, sitting on it, drawing an imaginary peninsula.

"Jeeves, come show me the lay of the land. This stretch of the bed is the length of the territory. What is where?"

Jeeves frowned at her doubtfully for a moment, then shook his head and smiled. "All right," he agreed, walking over to the side of the bed where she had drawn her imaginary map. "There are the Florida Keys down here, and all that swampland! Up here is Jacksonville, and down from there a bit, St. Augustine. Coming all the way around, far on the other side of the panhandle, there's Pensacola. There, inward, toward the middle, is Tallahassee. Know why it's the capital now?" Jeeves asked.

Tara shook her head. "No, why?"

Jeeves answered her, still smiling, involved in his geography lesson now. "Well, the lawmakers used to meet once a year at Pensacola, then the next time all the way around at St. Augustine, but either way it was about a fifty-nine-day journey by water, and once there was a shipwreck off the southern coast and half the men were stranded down there. Tallahassee was right in the middle, a good place to meet. Now, dropping down to the middle of the territory, west side again, there's Tampa. And there's the river. And we've come in here, and all this—this is Indian land."

"All right," Tara said, rubbing a hand over the bed. "Let's start on a smaller scale. There's Tampa, the river, and here we are at Cimarron. Show me all around Cimarron."

"Here," Jeeves said, "is Jarrett's land. Right here—" Jeeves said, pointing, "begins Mr. Treat's property." He kept talking. Tara smiled. Robert was straight down the little stream that wandered down below the lawn from the river. It would be an easy ride.

And she would ride it in the morning!

Jeeves didn't go to bed that night.

He sat up in the master's library, in one of the plush chairs before the bookshelves, and he studied the contents of those shelves.

There were numerous books. Some classics, some fiction. Mostly there were journals on farming, breeding livestock, and building. There were texts on medicinal herbs, on home remedies, on binding and setting broken limbs. There were bound copies of paintings by Audubon, and more journals on flora and fauna, poisonous snakes, and dangerous plants. There were military journals, and one special text had been signed to Jarrett McKenzie from Andy Jackson himself. It was interesting, Jeeves had always thought, to study a man's reading materials. Many a frontiersman —and this was one dangerous frontier at the moment!—disdained reading of any kind. In his day, as a matter of fact, Jeeves had met many a fine planter who couldn't read or write a lick himself. Not so here. Jarrett McKenzie loved books. Not as much as Robert Treat—Treat's library doubled this one, and Treat himself was quite an exceptional scholar on the history of the territory, on the Spanish and British periods, on the pirates—even on the Indians. He knew who'd been here long before the Seminoles, and he knew about trails—which he'd shown Jarrett and James—that had existed long before the encroaching Americans had made the place their own.

Jeeves liked both libraries—and both men. He had been born a free black himself, but not so his parents. His father, Jonah, had been the property of a Georgia cracker, a small-scale farmer so called from the "crack" of the bullwhip many such men carried for use with their cattle. The cracker had just acquired a Spanish land grant to some property just outside of St. Augustine. There, Jonah had met his future wife, Maria, a woman of mixed black and Indian blood, and in the brief time their owner had kept them together, Jeeves had been conceived.

To avoid potential trouble the Georgian had tried selling off his powerful black field hand. But Jonah had joined up with a band of black-Seminoles. The cracker, just a small planter really, had feared Jonah returning for his wife and causing murder or havoc. A decent enough man, and maybe a smart one, the planter had offered Jonah the opportunity to work for his own legal release and that of his wife. Jonah had still been short the money when Jeeves had been nearly due, but the cracker had shown a real heart and given both Jonah and Maria their documents of freedom before Jeeves had been born. They had made good what they had owed him, working hard for the planter and using their spare time at odd jobs for others as well for many years to come.

Jeeves had been lucky. He'd grown up a free black man. But he'd hated a lot of what he had seen. Some men were good to their slaves, almost as good to them as they were to their own children. But other men were cruel, as quick to beat and shackle fellow human beings as they were their farm animals. Jeeves saw

too much of it. The best that a man could be was to be free, even
if a master was a decent enough man.

As a young man Jeeves decided to make his way north. A
French whore in Baton Rouge taught him how to read, and he
used his lessons well. He could imitate accents easily and discovered that an English one could acquire him many interesting jobs.
He'd gained employment in Boston, earned a fair income and
learned a great deal more about human nature, and then realized
he wanted to come home.

In St. Augustine he'd learned his parents had both gone to
work for a young fool soldier who was trying to make a civilization out of a wilderness. He'd met up with Jarrett McKenzie because his folks—both old now and past their prime—had found
easy employment and gentle living with the "fool" young soldier.
Not a soldier anymore, but a planter who'd gotten one big land
grant. They'd known Mrs. McKenzie since she'd been a wee girl,
and through her they'd taken on house work at the place they
were calling Cimarron.

He hadn't been among them a month before his mother had
passed on quietly in her sleep; his father, without her, had willed
himself to die, Jeeves was convinced. Sitting out on a rocking
chair at day's end, he'd simply said that he was tired, and he could
hear his Maria calling softly to him over water. Jesus was comin'
for to carry him home. He'd closed his eyes and died.

Jeeves had taken them both back to a Negro cemetery outside
of St. Augustine to bury them. It wasn't custom to bury white
folks with black, even if the blacks were free. That hadn't mattered to Jarrett McKenzie. It wasn't custom to bury Indian folk
with white folk, either, and Jarrett had already had one of his
stepmother's uncles buried on the property. But Maria and Jonah
had earned their freedom out of St. Augustine, right near the
burying ground, and it had seemed fitting to take them back.

But he'd come back to Jarrett's place. Jarrett already had the
huge German, Rutger, working on the place, clearing land, super-
vising the building of the loading docks, buying up grain and the

like. But for such a fine house Jarrett and his wife needed a butler. Something as good and refined as an English butler—only more serviceable. Jeeves fit the picture perfectly. There was something about Cimarron that was unique and special. Jarrett McKenzie didn't want slaves; he wanted people who worked for him and he didn't seem to care where a man or woman might come from, or what color—or colors—he might be. There were Indians, blacks, half-Indians, quarter-blacks, Irishmen, Frenchies, and all manner of others on the property. Maybe, at first, Jeeves had even thought he owed the McKenzies, who had given his parents such a good home when they'd both been well past their primes. But as time went on, he had simply come to like and respect his employer so much that there could never be a question of his leaving.

Especially after Lisa died.

He hadn't ever seen a man suffer in such silent pain in all his days, except, maybe, his father, and his father had willed himself to die. Jarrett McKenzie had been too young to do that, too vital, too alive—maybe even too needed by too many other people. He'd gone on, gone through all the motions of daily living. He'd put up a damned good front before the world, hardened himself, and kept hurting inside.

Until now.

Jeeves smiled. *She'd* brought new life back to the house. In fact, she'd just about managed to set Mr. Jarrett McKenzie into a tumult now and again. Awfully damned good for him.

Jeeves had heard a lot of accents in his days. He'd learned to do most of them. White folks could be amazing. They were always astounded to hear a black man who could speak with an elocution superior to their own. Speaking and accents had become very important to him at an early age. So he should have known just where this lovely new Mrs. McKenzie came from.

But he couldn't seem to put his finger on a place!

He arched his back, sitting up straighter, staring out into the great hall.

She hadn't come down the stairs.

It seemed he'd been wrong. He'd had the strange feeling she'd been about to take flight from Cimarron. Why, he wasn't exactly sure. He'd seen a certain strange longing in her eyes when she'd watched Jarrett upon occasion—when Jarrett's back had been to her. Jeeves was damned sure without either of them divulging secrets that it was no normal marriage, and yet it was something to watch the two of them. Jeeves liked her. Oh, yes, he liked his new young mistress! She might be afraid, but her determination was far greater than her fear. She liked people, and her curiosity and sensitivity were great. She was as light and beautiful as a golden summer's angel, but she was strong, too, with a wiry, inner strength that would take her far.

Far. Out of the house, he had feared.

But she hadn't moved. He had spent half the night awake, and now he was feeling just a little bit foolish. He'd been wrong, it seemed, thinking she might run away in the night.

Still, he waited.

One A.M.

He'd almost dozed. He jumped as his foot was tapped and looked up to find Rutger towering over him. Oddly enough, the powerful, handsome German and he were now the best of friends. They'd circled one another carefully for months, Jeeves certain the other man was still not convinced that a freed black man was a good idea. Then there had been a Christmas when they'd wound up alone on the porch, the two most important men in the service of the McKenzie main household, and over too much cider and whiskey Rutger had admitted that Jeeves was just the damnedest black man he'd ever seen. Jeeves had told him he couldn't say quite the same—Rutger was the only German he had known. Rutger had determined to teach Jeeves about Germany that night, with an emphasis on Octoberfest.

They'd both worked with killer hangovers the next day, but they'd become very good, if very strange, friends.

"My watch," Rutger said. " 'Ceptin' you may want to make sure Mrs. McKenzie is still sleeping up there. You were snoring."

Jeeves rose to his full height. "I never snore!"

"Then there were buffalo charging through somewhere. Go on, get some sleep. I'll keep an eye on our new mistress."

Jeeves started out of the room, then paused in the doorway, looking back. "Now, you stay awake!" he warned.

Rutger had pulled down a book and was pouring himself a whiskey.

"You're the one who was snoring, Mr. Proper Butler."

Jeeves sniffed and left him. In the great hallway he gave himself a shake. It was almost morning; she hadn't stirred. What had made him think that she was so ready to bolt when he was convinced that she was both intrigued and entranced by her husband —if not in love with him?

He rubbed his neck. Well, it seems he had been mistaken. She wasn't going anywhere. He was glad of it.

He walked on up the stairs, weary, ready for sleep. He'd be damned glad when Jarrett was back. Damned glad.

Although the military still waited in Tampa, no attack by the Indians had come.

Jarrett realized that when he reached town at last with the Pattersons, Jim and Jill, her sister Marianne, his young brother J.P., and their seven children, Paddy, Jane, Anne-Marie, Michael, Seth, and the youngest of the brood, the twins, Caleb and Joshua. He'd ridden Charlemagne through what would have been a few days' ride for the two of them were they not escorting the caravan of two wagons, three cows, four goats, and a pack of boisterous chickens. The roads were poor in the interior and bridges were few and far between, so it had been a long and painful journey. But, as he had always been exceptionally fond of the Pattersons, he did not begrudge them this torturous trip, even if he did wish with all his heart that it would come to a speedy end.

It had not been a good time to leave home. After all the time he had so foolishly wasted, he'd gained himself a wife again.

And though she had kept him awake into the night wondering in a smoldering fury just who William might be, he had, at last, discovered the truth.

Her brother . . . William was her brother.

Not much to go on, he thought. But somehow, that one very simple truth he had ruthlessly dragged from her that morning gave him hope. Eventually the whole of her past might be his, and then . . .

Which would come first, he wondered wearily. The truth about Tara? Or the end of this wretched, accelerating war with the Indians? With his own brother's people?

"Oh, Jarrett! We're all but there!" Jill called out delightedly. She had been walking at the front of the wagon, flicking a whip upon occasion above the heads of the oxen that carried along what earthly possessions they had decided to take.

No one living near Jarrett's Cimarron had yet been attacked, but Indian assaults to the north of them on numerous of the sugarcane plantations had swiftly followed Osceola's well-planned attacks upon Wiley Thompson and Major Dade and his men. Often the owners had escaped, but the plantations had been burned to the ground, and many of those who had lived upon them had disappeared. They had either been taken prisoner by the Indians, were still running through the cypress hammocks to escape them, or lay dead among the ashes of their homes.

Jill left the oxen and came to stand beside Charlemagne. She looked at the homes of the fledgling town of Tampa, the smoke that spewed from numerous chimneys, and the military guard that surrounded the place. "My God, we've made it!" Jill breathed, smiling, looking up at Jarrett. She had a very pretty face. She was nearly forty and thin as a rail. She had been raising her children in all but a wilderness for nearly twenty years, and the cares of her life had drawn deep lines and grooves about her eyes and mouth, but she remained a bright, compelling, and attractive woman, one who seldom gave up a fight. She and Lisa had been dear friends, though they had come from very different worlds. They had been much alike, both ready for adventure, and both deeply in love with their homes, their husbands, and the very wild beauty of the new American territory. Lisa's father had been a very young Revolutionary War hero, a respected politician, a rich man who had raised his daughter with every luxury. Jill had been an orphan, growing up on a plantation in Georgia, picking cotton along with the master's slaves.

She refused to own slaves herself, and like Cimarron, the Patterson property had been worked by free men of many different colors and shades. One by one their people had left them, determined to escape the coming disaster.

Jill had determined it was time for the family to leave their property behind—until the difficulty was over.

"This is it—we're here," Jarrett said, agreeing with her. Jim came up to stand behind his wife. A tall, lanky, almost homely man, worn by hard work, strong and solid in his friendships.

"Thank you, kindly, Jarrett," he said, slipping his arms around his wife's waist and staring at the town they could all but touch. "We wouldn't have made it without you," he said frankly.

Jarrett shrugged. "You don't know that, Jim. I can't see why any of the Indians would have any disagreements with you and Jill."

"Maybe not," Jim said. His pale green eyes lit on Jarrett. "Maybe not, but I sure felt sometimes like we were being watched. I'd hear a rustling in the palms now and then, and I'm certain you heard it, too, though you never let on. Indians were watching us all the while. What might have happened if you weren't with us isn't nice to think about."

"There was no danger out there," Jarrett said. "I'm certain."

"You think it was your brother's men, watching over us?" Jim asked.

Jarrett nodded. "Yes, that's what I think," he said with a smile. "Come on, let's finish this! I'll bet Mrs. Conolly will have something on for dinner far superior to the straggly rabbits I've been catching along the way."

"And her muffins are going to be a heap better than those hard ones Ma packed!" came a cry from one of the wagons. Jarrett eased around, a hand on the back of his saddle. Caleb, five now, a skinny little ragamuffin with his mother's light eyes, straight platinum hair, and never-say-die spirit, leaned out of the wagon, grinning at all of them.

"Don't you go insulting my muffins, young man!" Jill called back to him, but she was smiling too. Jarrett was startled by the sudden stab of envy he felt. Jim and Jill had worked hard, right to the bone, to give their family a good home. They had raised a real nice passel of kids, and every one of the children had been polite and cooperative, working hard along the way as well.

Caleb and Josh, though, with their identical urchin faces, had always been Jarrett's favorites, though he tried not to let on. It was because they were the youngest, maybe. The closest to what his own child might have been, had she lived. He felt his heart beat a little harder. He'd wanted children, but at the time he'd barely felt the loss.

He'd been grieving for Lisa.

"I'm so sorry we took you away from your new bride, Jarrett," Jill said, studying him. "She must be very upset. Oh, not with Cimarron—Cimarron is beautiful. But I'm sure she must not be happy there alone."

"I'll be back soon enough," Jarrett told Jill.

"Come on," Jim told his wife. "Let's get in. Then Jarrett can get some rest and start home."

"Right, let's get the wagons moving again," Jill agreed, and the two turned back, Jim taking the lead wagon this time, Jill heading toward the second.

Jarrett let them both go by and stood still for a minute. They'd come to one of the military log trails, so it would be easier going on the way in.

He listened and didn't hear a thing. They'd left him, he

thought. Jim had been right—there'd been a Seminole escort along with them most of the way.

He was anxious to return home again, but rather than returning immediately he thought he would take the time to go and visit with his stepmother, his brother, and his brother's family. He wondered for a minute if it was his own reputation, James's determination—or Mary's insistence that nothing should ever happen to him—that kept him from the dangers that threatened others.

He might never know.

There was a crowd to greet them as their wagon came into Tampa. Tyler Argosy rode out with other men to help take some of the load off the Pattersons. With the family all offering him their thanks once again, the Pattersons then moved on to such luxuries as baths and good hot meals, and Jarrett found himself in the pub room of Mrs. Conolly's, drinking with Tyler, and learning that they were in for a good hard war with the Seminoles. General Clinch, who had expected to be packing the Seminoles west, had wound up in battle with them, unaware of what had befallen Dade. More men had been wounded and killed. Word had come from Jacksonville that a farm had been attacked just south of the city, the farmer killed, and his wife scalped and left for dead. Minus a patch of hair, however, she had survived and had described in vivid detail all the Indians who had attacked her. Fear, bitterness, and hatred were spreading faster than the plague. It seemed that Tyler could go on and on, telling him about one disastrous occasion after the next.

"You might want to have a few words with James," Tyler warned Jarrett gravely, striking a match against the stone of the fireplace to light his pipe. "Pretty soon there isn't going to be a white man left who won't shoot first and ask questions later."

Despite his own feelings of illness and anger over the bloody Indian attacks, Jarrett felt defensive on his brother's behalf.

"You know James didn't kill anyone, but he's told me right out that he can't condemn the warriors who do, not after the way they've been treated."

Tyler chewed on his pipe. "The white men want the Indians out. It's that simple."

"Some of them will never go. And they've got miles and miles of swamp to retreat into, Tyler, you know that."

"President Andy Jackson is determined to round them all up."

"Then he's going to have a long, long war on his hands."

Tyler nodded for a minute, then said softly, "Give James my warnings, will you?"

Jarrett nodded. Tyler stood. He set a hand on Jarrett's shoulder. "Thanks for bringing in the Pattersons. It must have cost you one hell of a lot to leave home. I know that I'd about have died before managing to do so—under the circumstances."

Jarrett arched a brow at him.

"Your wife."

"She'll be there when I get back," Jarrett said. She'd better be. They had a lot to settle.

Tyler grinned. "It still had to be damned hard to leave."

"It was," Jarrett agreed frankly.

"The boys are still smitten," Tyler said. "Why, they all but think you've gotten yourself a fairy princess. Tell her that if she ever needs—"

"Tyler, go away before I start wondering just what you're getting at, and if I should be trying to flatten you to the wall!"

Tyler laughed, lifting his hands. "I'm going. It's just that if she ever needs anything—"

"Go, Tyler."

Tyler saluted him sharply, grinned again, and left. Jarrett sat sipping on the shot glass of whiskey before him. He closed his eyes. He was tired. He hadn't slept much during the trip; he'd spent his nights listening. When he had managed to sleep, he'd been tormented by dreams. Seeing her face. Almost feeling the long tangle of sun-gold hair around him. Staring into the incredible blue of her eyes, reaching out.

Only, she'd be running again. Running and running. And he'd be trying so hard to catch up with her, reach her, but no matter how fast he ran, he couldn't quite reach her. And yet, the closer he came to her, the greater he knew her danger to be. She was running into it, away from him, and into the darkness and shadows of an unknown danger.

He swallowed down the last of his drink. He was damned anxious to get home. He had to have some sleep, but at the crack of dawn he'd be on his way. She'd be waiting. She'd damned well better be waiting.

He'd taken a small room upstairs, and what with the Pattersons and other folks heading in, he was lucky to have it to himself —much as he loved the kids, he wasn't up to sleeping with a pack of them snoring in his bed. He was so trail worn that he'd also ordered a hot bath, and it was while he was leaning back in it, his eyes closed, that he became aware that he wasn't alone in his room after all. Half opening an eye he saw Sheila standing over him, her lips curved in a pretty smile, the sparkle in her eyes downright lewd. She meant to surprise him with a dive right into the tub, but his eyes shot open wide, and he caught her wrists when she reached for the side of the tub.

"Jarrett!" she protested with a pout.

He sighed. "Sheila—"

"I'm not a child anymore," she protested. He liked Sheila, but even in his wildest days he had kept his distance from her. First because she had been too young, and second because she was as tenacious as a damned octopus with eight tentacles.

"I'm a married man," he told her.

She sniffed. "I never said you had to marry me. I won't marry any man, white, red, or black. I want to make you happy."

"I'm already ecstatic," he told her.

She pouted again, kneeling down by the tub. She was wearing only a thin white shift and her dusky skin was smooth, the peaks of her breasts dark rouge beneath the flimsy fabric, and she was definitely a grown woman now, erotic and seductive. She fluttered her long lashes at him and stared at him with her tilted eyes.

"You never meant to come with a wife; she is trouble. She is something you have somehow acquired, and I don't care at all that you have her."

He arched a brow at her. Sheila wrinkled her nose. "She's white like marble, cold like marble. She doesn't love you. She's your duty—I am trying to be your pleasure."

He had to smile, setting a hand on her head. "Sheila—she is beautiful like marble, but in one matter you are gravely mistaken. She isn't cold. She's hot like fire. And she gives me great pleasure."

Sheila stood with great annoyance. She sniffed again. "Fine, McKenzie. When she betrays you, remember that I am the woman you should want!"

With a wicked toss of her head she left him.

His bath had grown cold. For a moment he wondered if he wasn't half mad. *She doesn't love you,* Sheila had said. And that was damned true. It had been a long ride here; his world was ripping apart with anguishing ease. He'd spent enough nights alone. He should have taken Sheila's "pleasure" for just that.

But he didn't want Sheila. He didn't seem to want anyone else at the moment. He could still remember her eyes in the shadows, hauntingly big, so darkly blue. Almost naked when she had asked him where he had slept. Her voice, just touched with a hint of anguish.

She'd been very accommodating that night. Trying to get him to stay? He still wondered if that might not have had something to do with her passion. But then again, he didn't really care. As long as he could go home, hold her, touch her, touch that passion again.

His bathwater was cold.

He rose from it, toweled dry, and climbed into his bed, alone.

By dawn he and Charlemagne were on the way home. Maybe he would stop by the plantation first. He didn't know quite why—maybe it was his dream—but he was anxious to make sure that she was all right.

That she was there, waiting for him. Right where she'd damned well better be!

Tara was glad she had befriended Peter. She had no difficulty cajoling the boy into saddling her a horse, a pretty gray mare called Celine.

Nor was she any fool. She packed an extra cape for the journey, in case the weather grew cold or rainy. She slipped into the kitchen as she prepared to leave, packing herself a canteen of water, some dried beef, biscuits, and cheese. If it took her longer to get where she wanted to be than she expected, she'd still be all right.

When she started to ride, she pretended not to see the various men who were at their points, guarding the plantation—and surely keeping watch over her. She spent some time riding, working with the mare, keeping her field of travel to the docks, to the trees, near the house, and in the same circle again. She waited until she was certain no one would expect anything from her and then she slipped onto one of the trails through the pines that led from the back of the manicured lawn and deeper into the interior.

She knew exactly where she was going, she was certain. Jeeves had shown her just where Robert's plantation lay. And it couldn't be more than forty-five minutes' ride away.

Maybe an hour.

She had a good sense of direction, and she was an excellent rider. She and the mare did very well, right from the start.

The problem seemed to be with the trail. At first it looked so well traveled! Pine needles lay on the ground, great branches rose high above her. The ground was very dry.

Then the trail seemed to become swallowed up in itself and the terrain began to change. The mare stumbled, and Tara realized that she was leaving the pine trees behind—along with the hard ground. She had been absolutely convinced that it could not be possible to become lost—Robert's property should have been straight through the forest of pines from Cimarron. But she wasn't emerging from a field of pines onto another nearly manicured plantation-house lawn. In fact, she was no longer in a field of pines. The hard ground had given way to marsh. She'd entered into swampland. The mare was wallowing deeper and deeper into the mud.

Tara reined in, trying very hard to get her bearings and to remain calm. She had only to turn around and retrace her own trail. She wouldn't reach Robert's, and she wouldn't discover the answers to any of her questions, but at least she'd be safe back home.

The sudden call of a bird caused her to cry out with surprise. She admonished herself in silence, feeling like a fool. It didn't matter that she had cried out or made a fool of herself—there was no one to see or hear her.

She took a deep breath and looked around. Across the way the ground seemed firmer. She thought that the trees growing there were cypress. The foliage remained dense, and it looked like a green shadow-land, but she was certain that it wasn't so marshy.

She paused in her confusion for a moment, looking around her. She couldn't stay; she needed to move on quickly. And she was growing uneasy with her surroundings. And still, the very surroundings she feared were beautiful. The sun filtered through the green canopy, and its touch was warm, though the day had remained cool. Ahead of her, in a spray of striking color against the dark green and earth tones of the copse, was a patch of wild-flowers, beautiful wild orchids. She narrowed her eyes.

She didn't dare just remain here, staring about! she warned herself. But then again, perhaps she shouldn't do anything. She should just give the mare her head, and the horse would take her home. Surely the mare was well fed and well tended and would know her way back to the stable.

But the mare just stood, apparently confused herself in the muck beneath her hoofs.

So much for beautiful surroundings. They could be deadly. She had heard there was quicksand in Florida marshes. The canopy of trees and beautiful orchids might well be a shield for a deadly patch of sucking mud. A prickling feeling at her nape warned Tara that she was on dangerous ground—the muck, she saw, gave way to a narrow canal. There were downed branches and logs, low-flung branches.

A sudden movement almost caused her to cry out again, but she caught the sound, and for a moment was simply awed by the sight of the huge white bird that stood still in the shallow water, then suddenly took flight. A crane, she thought, magnificent here in the wild. There were more birds. Small white egrets, moving daintily by the water's edge with their stilted little walk.

If there were cranes and egrets, there might very well be things that ate cranes and egrets. Like alligators.

And other awful things.

Indians.

Her heart was racing and she fought for calm. "We've got to turn around, girl," she told the mare. "We've got to start back!"

She turned the mare, nearly being thrown as the horse's rear hoof sank into the mud.

The idea that there might be quicksand returned to her. She couldn't panic, she told herself, but she had to get the horse moving.

"Crawl out of it!" she commanded the horse, and in a minute they were on firmer ground, the canal had disappeared from sight, and she thought that she was on some kind of a trail, moving onto higher ground. She nudged the mare's sides, still reassuring the animal at a walk, but making it a faster one. She was just beginning to congratulate herself on having begun to find her way out when she reined in hard, terror creating a wall of ice around her heart.

She had heard nothing, and she was all but surrounded.

One of them stood dead center in the trail before her. He was copper in color, his hair pitch black. His leggings were as red as blood, and his cotton shirt was adorned with numerous silver ornaments. He wore a fabric headdress adorned with a wide variety of feathers and caught up with a silver ornament as well. Soft-skin boots covered the Indian's feet, perhaps accounting for the fact that he had come upon her so silently.

A sash about his waist created a sheath for his sword. His rifle was in his hands. A long-bladed knife was secured with leather straps to his calf.

He made a motion with his hand, and suddenly several warriors fell from the trees like leaves in a northern winter. Some of them were dressed similarly to the first. Some were naked from the waist up, some were painted, some were not.

Tara screamed instinctively. As the Indians approached her she begin to kick and lash out. To her amazement she caught the first brave right in the chin with her foot. He fell back, rubbing his jaw. She kneed the mare sharply and the horse snorted and neighed and reared high. Tara held her seat. The mare plunged forward, but the Indians were too numerous, all throwing themselves at the mare's neck, bridle, and haunches. Fighting wildly, Tara nevertheless found herself dragged to the ground. Choking, gasping, swearing, flailing, she continued to fight. Someone caught hold of her arms. Someone else straddled her. She started to scream again in wild panic, but then the sound of a shot filled the air and everyone went dead still.

She heard something snapped out in a language she couldn't understand. The Indian atop her rose; the one who held her arms released them.

Stunned, Tara lay still. Then she realized she was free and leapt to her feet.

Another Indian had arrived, this one on a handsome bay horse. He was in navy breeches with doeskin boots that covered his calves to his knees. His shirt was colorful, crafted in horizontal line after horizontal line of different fabrics. It lay open at the throat, one as coppery as any she had seen yet. Her eyes rose to his. An uneasy feeling swept over her, almost as if she knew him, as if she had seen him in some dream or nightmare. He was staring at her, slowly assessing her, looking her up and down. She realized suddenly that he was an Indian with blue eyes, that he must have white blood in him. Which didn't seem to matter. He had raised a hand to beckon her to him.

She was going to die, she thought. Right here, today, in this swamp-rotting jungle.

She could have made things easy for herself. She could have drowned in the Mississippi.

She could have given the hangman her throat!

But, no, she had fought, she had run. And the salvation she had found in Jarrett's arms had been false, for though he had protected her once, he had abandoned her here.

She stared at the Indian on the horse again, then lifted her chin and decided that she was not going to be murdered, scalped, and mutilated without a damned good fight.

She smiled. Then she cried out, "You redskinned, murdering bastard!" And she came at him. Running wildly across the pine-carpeted path that separated them she pitched herself at him with such a frenzy that he was thrown from his horse. She landed atop him, and certain that it would be her last living act, she raised her fists wildly to pummel him again and again.

Shouts rose all around her. The man beneath her let out a furious cry that must have been an Indian oath, but she was heedless of it. She slammed her fists against him again and again.

And she suddenly found him straddling her, those blue eyes piercing into her soul. He swore again, capturing her wrists. The others were laughing now, calling out taunts. She could still feel those eyes.

Something familiar. He had a handsome face. She was becoming hysterical, she told herself. Losing her mind. She was about to be murdered, and she was thinking that he was a proud and striking warrior.

He leapt up suddenly, reaching down a hand to her. "Come!" he snapped out in English.

He leaned down to help her up. She spat in his face. He swore again, in his own language this time, and she screamed when he grabbed her wrists hard, dragging her up, throwing her over his shoulder.

In a bound he was upon the bay horse. They were not treading lightly through the pines and foliage, there was no hesitancy in this wild ride.

They were running deeper and deeper into the savage land.

Chapter 13

JARRETT CAME down the river on old man Johnson's barge. It was a little more than a two-day trip, but it was an easy one, and they were nearing the end of it now.

Johnson, older than any man Jarrett had ever met, toothless, white haired, stooped as a gnarled branch, had been in the area longer than any other living white man, and perhaps because of his age, or perhaps because he had become part of the scenery, the Indians seemed to have no war with him, or Johnson with them. He wasn't frightened of an attack, and when the officers at the fort had suggested he might want to stay in town for a while, Johnson seemed amazed. "As if I'd want to stay in some house with ruffled drapes on the windows—and walled in!" Johnson complained to Jarrett once they had gotten under way. Jarrett, anxious to get home, shrugged. He didn't know where Johnson hung his hat anyway—the only time Jarrett had ever seen him was on his barge. And since Johnson was determined to keep running up and down the river come what may, Jarrett was just as glad to take the barge home. He'd been driving Charlemagne night and day with the Pattersons, anxious to bring them to

Tampa where they would feel safe. Charlemagne didn't mind the river trip one bit, and with bridges and roads being poor, it was still faster than coming home by land.

"They tell me I'm in danger!" Johnson said, offering Jarrett his wide, toothless grin. "Danger! What the hell, danger—they trying to tell me I'm going to die *young?*" Johnson went into gales of laughter, while Jarrett grinned. But then he pulled his wide-brimmed hat over his eyes and leaned back against one of the poles that created a roped-in square around the barge. The day was warm, the river gentle. He relaxed, leaving one eye half open to survey the shore now and then. Once again he was certain that his movements were being watched. The United States government was now at full-scale war with the Seminole Indians of the Florida Territory. Tyler had come out when Jarrett had left Tampa, bringing him the latest news. At General Clinch's request acting governor George Walker had ordered militia general Richard Keith Call to raise Florida volunteers to join the regulars for one big campaign against the Indians. Andy Jackson had ordered General Winfield Scott to take command in Florida, and fourteen companies of regular soldiers were to join Clinch's command.

Some soldiers were already wondering just what they were in for.

And yet Jarrett was aware that the massacre of Major Dade and his men, appalling to the whole of the country, was now fading in importance outside of the Florida Territory because of a tragic event that had just occurred in Texas.

Well over one hundred American heroes had been massacred at a little mission they were calling the Alamo. The men, it seemed, had held out against incredible odds, praying for help. Even when they had known that help wasn't coming, the men hadn't surrendered, because it had been of the utmost military importance to keep the Mexican general Santa Anna from moving onward to fight other battles. Every fighting man within the place had been killed, including the renowned frontiersman Davy Crockett, and the great fighter James Bowie. It was a tragedy of such dimensions that the entire country was up in arms, and so poor Major Dade, whose body still was rotting in the wilderness, had been largely forgotten. Except here in Florida, where Texas heroes might be admired, but where life was still a dangerous game at best.

Jarrett had met both men when he had been but a boy himself, and though he'd known they were both quite human—apt to quarrel, definitely rough at the edges!—he felt the great national sorrow at their passing. They had given everything to their country, and in the end they had died giving their last valiant effort to the battle for their friends and countrymen.

"Seems there's some anxious to see you get home," Johnson said, interrupting his thoughts. Jarrett pushed back his hat, squinting as he stared toward the shore. It seemed that a number of his household had turned out to watch the river. Jeeves stood on the deck; Rutger, mounted, looked as if he were ready to race downstream and shout to him. Even the little Italian laundress, Cota, stood there anxiously.

Jarrett stood, hands on his hips, searching. Tara was not there. What had he expected? That she had suddenly decided to give her all to him because of that last night they had shared together?

She should have been there. If everyone else was on the dock, waiting. . . .

The barge had barely pulled toward shore before Jarrett leapt from it, striding for the place where Rutger and Jeeves unhappily awaited him.

"What's happened? Where is she?"

"Gone, Mr. McKenzie," Rutger said. "We followed her into the woods, but then her trail clean vanished. She meant to elude us, Mr. McKenzie, and that's no excuse, but—"

"What did she take?" Jarrett demanded of Jeeves.

"Food," Jeeves admitted. "Extra clothing, so Cota thinks. She may have just planned a day trip."

"We'll go after her, Mr. McKenzie. The boys and I will go after her, and we'll find her."

"I'll find her myself," Jarrett said flatly. "Rutger, get Charlemagne, give him a good rubdown. Jeeves, give me a roll of clean clothing. As soon as Charlemagne is ready, I'll be riding out again."

"She was my responsibility—" Rutger began.

"No," Jarrett said. "She is mine."

He strode past them. She'd been found, he was certain. On Indian land. He could only pray that it had been by his brother or his brother's people. He didn't think that any of the other chiefs would hurt her—he'd been given Osceola's promise that his land was neutral—but that didn't mean that all the chiefs would obey Osceola.

He didn't take time to bathe. He ran up the stairs two at a time and went to the washbowl to douse his face and chest in cold water, and don a clean shirt and waistcoat.

He turned to leave, but hesitated, his eyes falling upon the bed where they had shared their last night, the one that had haunted him the entire time he'd been gone. He noted that his room—masculine now for so long—was beginning to bear feminine touches. A tuft of lace protruded from a dresser drawer. A silver brush lay on his dresser. Even a soft scent of rose cologne seemed to linger on the air.

His hands clenched tightly into fists at his sides, his face constricted with tension. "Damn you!" he swore aloud. He'd believed in her, he'd trusted that she meant to stay.

And she'd tried to run. She'd married him, entwined herself somehow into his hungers, cravings . . . his soul. And then she'd run.

Well, she was coming back. Damn her. She was coming back, and she'd have some kind of price to pay.

And he would name the price.

And as long as she was facing no real danger.

That thought brought him to instant motion, and he ran down the stairs, out of the house, and back to the stables, where a groomed and watered Charlemagne waited. Jarrett leapt atop the horse. Charlemagne pranced, as if he, too, knew just how important his coming quest would be.

"I'll get word to you as soon as I've found her," he told Rutger and Jeeves. The two nodded anxiously. Jarrett nudged Charlemagne and raced toward the border of the Indian lands.

He prayed to find her quickly.

Tara didn't know what she had been expecting, but certainly not the village they came to. Jolting along so that it seemed her teeth cracked with every movement, they came into the center of a cluster of neatly laid out and well-built, if simple, log cabins.

Tara was so frightened by the time they arrived that she nearly fell when the Indian eased her from his shoulder to let her slide to the ground. He quickly flung his leg over the side of his horse to reach the ground himself and drag her back up. She opened her mouth to denounce him in some way, but he called out a clipped command in his own language that she knew to be a warning to keep silent. For the moment she determined to do so.

She knew that other Indians had followed behind them on foot, and she was dimly aware that some of them were arriving. The half-breed motioned for her to move. She backed away from him, and though she kept her eyes upon him, she also tried to see the layout of the copse where they had come. There was a large fire burning in the circle around which the cabins clustered, and a deer was being tended on a stake over that fire by a number of women. Some of them were dressed in skins, and some wore skirts in European fashion. Like the men they seemed fond of jewelry, many of them adorned with a multitude of necklaces. Off toward the trees children who had been playing with a ball and some netted sticks stopped in their play and watched her arrival.

One young woman broke away from the cooking circle, approaching the half-breed, who was menacingly advancing on Tara. She asked him a question, and he answered curtly. Her eyes widened and she stared at Tara, then began to speak again. Once more the half-breed answered her harshly, and this time, though she still seemed very angry, she fell silent. The half-breed spoke to her again, gesturing, and the young Seminole woman came toward Tara. Tara stepped away, wondering if the women might not be more barbarous than the men, as she had heard was true with some American Indian tribes.

But when she moved away, the Indian woman shook her head impatiently. She lifted a hand to indicate the largest of the log dwellings. When Tara still hesitated, she looked to the half-breed, but he barked out another order, and this time he was obeyed. The girl came forward and took Tara's arm with impatience. Tara resisted, trying to wrench her arm away. But then her eyes widened as she saw the half-breed atop his horse suddenly level his rifle in her direction, and she no longer resisted the young Indian woman's attempt to take her arm. She was led into the large log cabin.

There was just one room to the house. A fire burned to the rear of it, and though it wasn't exactly a chimney that rose above it, there was ventilation at the roof, keeping the dwelling from filling with smoke. There was a circle of stones in the center of the floor, and to the rear and sides were various pallets that seemed to be beds made of skins and furs. There were also rolls, which Tara quickly thought were the homeowner's belongings, neatly tied together.

Just inside the place there was a stack of rifles, leaned one upon the other. Tara gave them a longing gaze, but then looked to the girl who had brought her in, and was stunned to realize that she couldn't just pick up a rifle and shoot this woman. She wasn't sure how, but she knew that the slender young Indian woman meant to offer her no harm.

Even if the half-breed did.

The girl lifted a hand, showing Tara one of the pallets. She indicated that Tara should sit. Tara shook her head nervously, but as she did so, the blue-eyed half-breed entered the log dwelling.

He seemed to assess the situation immediately, and he strode to her, capturing her wrists and bringing her to the pallet, where he forced her to sit. Barely breathing she tried to wrench her hands away. He released her and walked away, talking again to the Indian girl in their own language. Again the girl argued. And again he snapped out an answer. The girl straightened her shoulders, snatched up something from one of the bundles, and came toward Tara, hunching down by her. She had brought a long leather thong, Tara realized. She stared at it, then at the girl, her alarm apparent in her wide eyes.

"No, please!" Tara whispered.

The girl dropped her voice to something lower than a whisper, speaking in English. "Give me your wrists! He will not hurt you."

"Please, please, talk to me—" Tara began, but the girl quickly stood, looking back over her shoulder toward the blue-eyed warrior.

The girl spoke sharply in her own language, her narrowed eyes warning Tara to shut up.

But if Tara was going to be massacred, she wasn't going to submit to it easily. When the Indian girl knelt down to secure Tara's wrists, Tara was quick to take her by surprise, shoving her to the floor and leaping up.

But she never reached the door to the cabin. He was there, standing in the doorway. She found herself grimly dragged back into his embrace. His fingers formed a vise around her wrists as he dragged her back to the pallet, shoved her down, and quickly bound her hands together with the leather, then looped another length around that, creating a leash with it. The far end of that he tied around one of the cabin's support beams, leaving Tara to hope that she could somehow untie it later. But his eyes were very hard on her as he tightened the knot, and she knew with a sinking heart that she would never manage to free herself.

So what now? she wondered. She had read that some Indians saved hostages to torture to death during special celebrations.

Maybe he just wanted her kept in one place while he sliced away her scalp.

To Tara's amazement he walked away from her and the beam, going to the pretty girl with the slender build and deep hazel eyes. Then, to Tara's further surprise and irritation, his voice became gentle, persuasive—tender—as he spoke to the Seminole maiden softly in their own language. The girl looked across the room at Tara, still disagreeing, but then she nodded her head to his will. He reached down a hand to her, and she came to him.

Tara gradually became aware that a frown was searing the half-breed's features, and he wasn't paying her his entire attention. Then she became aware that there was a great deal of commotion outside. There were shouts—greetings, she thought, and the sounds of many hoofbeats.

The half-breed spoke curtly, then spun around. He took the girl's hand, pulling her along, and they were swiftly gone. Tara was alone.

She waited several seconds, but no one came. She could hear voices outside and then the rise of an argument. There were curt laughs, whispers, she thought, more shouting, and then silence.

A second later the first Indian she had encountered on the path, the one with headdress and red leggings, came and stood just inside the cabin for a moment.

She barely dared to breathe as he stared at her. She stood up, backing toward the wall, both terrified and ready to fight again, as he neared her. He grated out a question she didn't understand and she just stared at him, praying that her knees would not give way.

The pretty Indian girl was back in the cabin, the blue-eyed warrior behind her. "He wants to know if you are the wife of the White Tiger," he asked her in guttural English.

"The what?" Tara said, keeping her eye on the man before her. He had an arresting face, small, keen, hazel eyes, and broad, high cheekbones. His stare was level and intelligent, inquisitive—and dangerous, she thought.

The Indian girl sighed. "Are you McKenzie's new woman?" she also asked in English with impatience.

"New woman . . ." Tara murmured. "Yes! I'm McKenzie's wife," she said swiftly. Her heart slammed painfully within her chest.

What had she just done? McKenzie—her husband—was the White Tiger? They even had a name for him? It was amazing that his friends in the military hadn't strung him up, for he surely seemed more on the side of the Indians than of his own people.

Somehow Lisa McKenzie had died among these people. And now here she herself was too.

The Indian leveled a finger at her and said something very sternly. Behind him the blue-eyed warrior spoke up. The red-legged one spoke to her again. She felt like a child being chastised.

She was being chastised. The girl interpreted the scolding for her.

"He says that you should be switched."

"What!" Tara gasped.

"You have disobeyed your husband, you wander where you should not be. You put yourself into grave danger."

"Tell him to go to hell!" Tara said, shaking even as she spat out the words. The girl's eyes widened.

She opened her mouth to speak, and Tara was sure that she had no intention of relaying her words to the red-legged warrior. It didn't matter. The warrior had understood her, and he lifted a hand, stopping the girl from speaking. He grated out another few words himself. The girl didn't offer to translate them to Tara.

"What . . . ?" Tara asked, dreading the answer.

"He says that if your husband does not switch you, he will gladly take up the task."

The warrior stared at her another moment, and though she was certain that he would like to take a switch—or a knife—to her, there was a slight glimmer of admiration in his eyes, and an even slighter curl to his lip. Almost as if he had teased her rather than threatened her.

He turned suddenly to leave. Tara felt her spine stiffen as she realized the blue-eyed warrior was staring at her still, sending rivers of fear cascading down her spine. But then he turned as well, leaving with the other man.

Tara was achingly relieved. Her knees very nearly gave, but the girl was following the two men out. Tara tried to stop her from doing so.

"Wait, please!" she begged softly.

The girl hesitated and saw that the warriors before her were involved in their own conversation now. They were already out the door and not paying any heed to the women.

"What?" she said quickly, nervously.

"Please, what's going to happen to me?" Tara demanded.

"Nothing's going to happen to you."

"Nothing?" Tara whispered.

"Not if you behave. You—you shouldn't have been where you were!"

"I shouldn't have to be in fear, I shouldn't have been attacked! I—"

"Quit talking!" the girl said, and she followed the men out.

The door closed with finality behind her.

This time Tara sprang up quickly. She hurried to the support beam, wildly trying to dislodge the knot tied there.

After several exhausting moments she realized that the leather was not going to give. Frustrated, she walked back to the pallet. She sat down, staring at the circles that now were reddening upon her wrists. Each time she fought the rawhide that constrained her, it tightened.

After a while she stood again. She paced the narrow area of her confinement and tried to see if there wasn't something with which she might try to slice through the leather ties that bound her. Nothing was within her reach. There were cooking utensils neatly set against a far wall, but they were perhaps two feet beyond the area she could reach. She stretched, she swore. She couldn't get where she needed to be. Weary again, she stormed out a few curses, then returned to her pallet, sinking down upon it, resting her head this time on a pillow of furs. She lay still for a second, then thought that she heard a sound at the door and panicked. She started to leap up again, her heart pounding furiously, but if footsteps had sounded near the door, they had hesitated there only a second, and then passed by.

She was thirsty, tired—and terrified. She lay there in torment, wondering if she dared trust in the Indian girl's words—that no harm would come to her. No harm! She was a prisoner here, and she hadn't been scalped so far simply because she was McKenzie's woman. Not his *wife*, to the Indians, but something more like his property! But her husband must know these Indians well. Perhaps he had even taught the young woman to speak English?

Did it matter? she mocked herself. She was keeping all of her hair!

She had almost fallen asleep when the door creaked open. She bolted up, staring in that direction. Shadows were falling now. Late afternoon had come. For a moment all she could see was a dark-haired giant filling the doorway. She bit her lip, fighting the temptation to shriek out loud.

He was back. He moved into the room. Behind him the Indian girl peered at her, then came around the man. She carried a trencher and wooden cup and came to Tara with them. Tara stared blankly at what looked like gruel in the trencher. "*Koonti,*" the girl told her, but the word meant nothing to Tara. "It's a root. We grind it and use it—for everything. Bread—umm —porridge. It will warm you."

The half-breed towering in the doorway snapped out something. The girl with the beautiful hazel eyes seemed slightly aggravated with the situation, but it always seemed that she bowed to his commands. He was waiting for her to exit the one-room dwelling, and she turned to do so.

Tara leapt to her feet, thinking herself a fool, yet still frightened enough to show some reckless bravado. "Wait a minute! You can't just keep me prisoner here! What are you going to do—"

The man interrupted her with a sharp spate of words. The Indian girl answered him, but he cut her off quickly as well. The girl turned back to Tara. "He says that perhaps you should be more worried about McKenzie than you are of him. You will do as you are told while you are with us. You remain in danger here. Yet perhaps there will be greater danger for you later! Elsewhere!"

With that she hastily turned and left. The half-breed spun in the doorway. For a moment his broad shoulders seemed to block out what remained of the fading red light. Then the door closed behind him, and she was cast into shadows and gloom.

In despair she threw herself back upon the pallet, but after a moment she remembered that her thirst was tremendous. She raised the carved wooden cup to her lips, and the water she sipped was sweet and pure. Her stomach growled and she stared at the trencher for a moment, wondering how on earth anyone bound such as she was could manage to eat from it. She had been supplied with no eating utensils, no fork, no spoon. After a moment she realized that they must sip the gruellike stuff from the trencher, and in a few more moments she realized she was hungry enough to try it.

To her surprise it wasn't terrible. It seemed, oddly enough, to be flavored with pumpkin and honey. The texture was stringy, but she tried to ignore that, and she managed to eat most of it before gagging over a swallow and determining that she had had enough. She paced again, very much aware that soon, except for the faint light from the dying fire, she would be in total darkness.

She sat upon her pallet again, staring at the door. She could hear nothing. She inhaled raggedly, on something like a sob, trying to keep from remembering the vivid description she had heard of the Dade massacre. They had said that they would not hurt her. McKenzie might, but they wouldn't. Was it the truth? *But she remained a prisoner here!*

Eventually she lay down. The cabin was surprisingly warm;

the air seemed clean and sweet. The bed of furs was far more comfortable than she might have imagined. She closed her eyes.

Seconds—hours?—later she awoke. She could hear giggling very near her.

In a wild panic she bolted up. She was ready to fight again.

But in the very dim firelight she saw the dark eyes of two children, the younger perhaps three, the older about five. Seeing that she was awake, the little one scurried behind her sister, but then peeked out at Tara again with a big smile. She was a beautiful child, with fine features, almond-colored and -shaped eyes, flashing white teeth, and soft copper skin.

"Hello," Tara said.

They grinned and giggled again.

"Who are you?" Tara asked the children. Then she groaned. "What do I think I'm doing!" she reproached herself aloud, burying her face in her hands the best she could with the tightening rawhide. "They'll not answer me . . . !"

"Hello," came a soft reply.

Stunned, Tara looked up again. "Sweet Lord, you speak English! Or were you mimicking me? Did you understand me?"

The little girl started to answer but the door slammed open. *He* was back again, like a fire-breathing giant, filling the doorway. Tara started to shiver as he chastised the children with a few brief words. They quickly scampered away, the little one following the older one like a shadow.

He came into the room with a menacing step. Tara shrank back against the wall, a scream rising in her throat. A gasp escaped her when he came close and smiled slowly. He lifted his hands, as if showing her that he carried no weapons. Then again he turned and left her.

Again, Tara didn't know how much time had passed. The fire had burned very low, and she knew it was night. Despite her fear she found herself stretching out on the pallet and drifting again. The day had seemed incredibly exhausting, or perhaps it was the very scope of her fear that had so tired her, she could not be sure.

This time when she slept, she was very rudely awakened. The pretty Indian girl had arrived, carrying a large deerskin and a razor-edged seashell.

"He wants this tonight!" she told Tara in English.

"What?" Tara asked blankly.

"I'll show you. Pay attention," the girl said, and she began to work on the skin, rubbing away any little bits of dried flesh that remained adhering to it, smoothing it out to an almost silken consistency.

"Now you. I don't dare do more."

"Me! Oh, no, I am not working for these wretches who are keeping me prisoner and planning on wearing my scalp!"

"No one will wear your scalp," the girl said impatiently, thrusting the shell into her still-bound hands. "But you must work. Everyone works here. In the best of times we all work, or we starve."

"And if I don't?"

"Then you will be sorry, because he will come after you. A woman must have some use."

Tara wasn't exactly sure what those words meant, but neither was she sure she wanted to find out. She lifted her wrists. "Will you untie me?" she demanded.

"You don't need to be untied," the girl said curtly, and left.

For long moments after the door had closed, Tara sat in the dark cabin. She swore out loud that she wasn't going to do it; then, with a sigh, she clamped her lips together and started working on the skin the way the Indian girl had shown her. She wasn't as nimble with her fingers, but neither was she incapable. She wasn't sure when it was that she discovered herself giving the job her complete attention—perhaps when she realized that it would be much easier if she were untied.

She suddenly felt like a complete fool. She had the razor-sharp shell in her hands, all she had to do was slit the thongs that bound her wrists. She began to apply to that task her most earnest efforts, but it was the most difficult thing she had attempted, trying to twist her fingers to work the shell against the rawhide at her wrists. Her fingers cramped; sweat broke out on her brow.

Then, just when she about had it snapped, the door burst open. She tried to turn the shell quickly back to the deerskin, but it was too late. The frayed edge of her leather leash lay dangling from the support beam, and naturally, it was the half-breed who had burst his way back into the cabin. She screamed as she found herself wrenched to her feet, her wrists held tightly together. His eyes met hers in the darkness and he shook his head, greatly aggravated. He called out something and the Indian girl returned. She listened to his harsh words and met his eyes, then quickly scooped up the hide and the scraping shell, departing the cabin. Tara resisted anew, trying to struggle free while the Indian retied her wrists with a fresh strip of leather. She kicked him squarely in the shin, then cowered as he lashed out at her angrily with more words, his hand starting to rise. He seemed to check himself, a twisted smile curved into his lips, and shook his head. He didn't touch her but completed his task, binding her once again to the beam.

A second later the girl was back. This time she had brought a large mortar and pestle and some curious stringy stuff in another bowl.

"*Koonti*," the warrior said. He was going to say more, but he broke off, allowing the girl to give instructions again.

"You will grind it to fine powder for baking," the girl said.

Tara stood very tall and shook her head.

"He said you will do it—he has been ordered that you must work, or pay the price."

"I'm a prisoner here, and I will not be put to work!" she insisted.

The girl looked to the warrior, as if she might have told him what Tara's response would be. He spoke to her quickly, and it seemed the Indian girl gnashed down on her teeth, but she obediently translated his words to English.

"It is not his order. It comes from someone with higher authority over you. And you are warned that you must be cooperative, or else—or else discover that you are asked to do things you find even more . . . difficult."

Once again Tara felt her determination to fight wavering. Grinding *koonti* root just might be better than whatever else they had in mind for her.

She sat down, staring furiously at the both of them.

"May you all rot in a very special heathen's hell!" she spat out. It was even harder to try to use the primitive mortar and pestle with her wrists tied than it had been to use the shell.

Apparently satisfied after a moment, the half-breed left again, the girl following swiftly behind.

Tara's eyes began to burn with tears. She wondered what time it was. Late! Two or three in the morning, she thought. And she was so damned tired. Dead. No! She wasn't dead, dead was what she would be if . . .

They had said they wouldn't hurt her!

But she was hurting. She was exhausted. Her hand suddenly cramped so badly that she cried out with the pain of it, then drew blood biting down upon her lower lip, not wanting the Indians to hear her. She tried to start working again. The fire in the room had all but burned out. She was cold, as well as exhausted and cramped.

The next time a pain struck in the center of her hand, she let her fingers curl around the stone mortar and tossed it hard across the room. Ground *koonti* spewed everywhere. "I won't do it, I just won't do it!" she cried out loud.

She was sorry, for the door opened again. She leapt to her feet, wary, as the Indian girl came upon her. Her eyes fell over the strewn *koonti* and the upturned bowl.

"Now you've done it!" the girl said, and to Tara's surprise she came into the cabin, sweeping up the bowl, trying to gather together the *koonti* root.

But the warrior suddenly burst into the room behind her. He looked from the girl, to the *koonti,* and then to Tara. He snapped out something and turned and left. The girl remained on the floor for a moment, her head bent. She looked up at Tara.

"Now you must come with me."

Tara shook her head. "No."

"You must come with me, or they will simply send others for you."

"I will not come willingly."

The girl stood with a weary, unhappy sigh. She walked to the doorway, stepped out, and started to yell for someone.

"Wait!" Tara said. She lifted her chin. "Where am I going?"

"To the small cabin."

"The small cabin? Why? What small cabin?"

"This is my home," she said softly. "You will not sleep here, not tonight."

"Then . . . ?"

"You are to sleep in the small cabin!" the girl said with just a bit of exasperation.

"Please!" Tara whispered suddenly. "Don't let them—" She broke off. *Don't let them what?* she wondered herself. The children slept here, she would not. Was she just being taken to a different prison?

What did they have planned for her?

Did it matter? Had she any choices here? If she tried to run, others were waiting. Warriors were waiting. A multitude of them. Well-honed men who would drag her wherever they wanted to take her. Who could so very easily overpower her, slice her throat . . .

She had to fight them. If she was going to die, she was not going to do so meekly.

And yet the girl had said that she was just going to a different cabin. Maybe there was a time to fight—and a time for quiet dignity as well.

Tara exhaled slowly, standing still as the Indian girl came to the leather leash and quickly slit it with a long-bladed knife she kept in a pocket of her skirt. She wrapped the end of the leather throng around her wrist. "Come."

Tara followed the girl, her heart barely seeming to beat as they exited the cabin.

A fire was still burning in the center of the yard. Late as it was, there were a number of men seated in council around it. Lances and rifles were stuck in the ground at their sides. They passed a gourd of some drink, swallowing from it.

Watching her.

The Indian girl paid them no heed as she led Tara around the circle, toward a copse of trees and a cabin that stood a ways off. As she walked, Tara could feel the men watching her. They were dressed in a number of fashions, some in white men's trousers, some in breechcloths and heavy leggings. Some wore cotton shirts with lines of distinctly designed colors, while a few were shirtless, their bronze flesh darkened by the dance of the central fire that rose high in the midst of them.

Some wore painted faces and caps or headbands that held brightly colored feathers. Silver jewelry adorned their necks, wrists, and headdresses.

They watched, betraying no emotion. The fire rose to join with the moon and stars and cast down a strange gold glowing light into the night.

Tara squared her shoulders, determined not to look back at the men as the girl walked her by them.

Yet strangely, as they left the warmth of the fire and headed toward the smaller cabin in the copse, she felt increasingly afraid.

A light burned within the cabin; she could see the glow of it filtering out through narrow windows and slits within the log structure. Again, a chimney opening to the night sky toward the rear of the structure. A trail of gray smoke rose above it, disappearing into the velvet of the sky.

She didn't realize that she had stopped, staring at the cabin, until the girl urged her forward again. "Come, move. Else we'll both be in trouble. It is time."

Time? Time for what? Tara wondered. Were the women of the tribe in the cabin? Were they the ones who would slice her into little pieces?

No harm would come to her.

"Now. He has said that you will come now!"

"He?" Tara whispered, but they had reached the cabin door, and the girl had thrust it open—and with a surprisingly powerful shove for one her size, she sent Tara into it.

For a moment Tara blinked. The cabin, smaller though it was, was much like the other. Dried meat hung from some of the beams, as well as drinking gourds and cooking utensils. A large fur pallet took up a quarter of the room, and again there were rolls of belongings about.

But Tara noted little of such things at the moment. Her eyes became focused on the center of the room, right before the place where a small but crackling fire burned in the hearth.

There was a large wooden tub there. A crude but European-looking bathtub filled with steaming water.

And within the tub . . .

She heard a curt command in the Indian language.

"He wants you to serve him," the girl said, and gave her another firm shove.

Tara stood in shock. *He* was within it, she thought. The half-breed who had taken her. His back was to her and all that she could see was a set of copper shoulders covered in the rising steam and a headful of ink-dark hair.

"No!" Tara said the word, but it didn't seem to make any sound. She felt weak again, as if she would fall. She had been so sure that the half-breed had been this girl's husband or lover, she had never imagined . . .

What? She was so frightened now that she still felt paralyzed.

The man in the tub snapped out something that Tara could not understand, and the girl pressed her forward.

"I will not!"

"You must!" The girl's voice dropped to a whisper. "Don't make him come after you!"

Chills swept over Tara. So it had come to this! She wished with all her heart that she could hurry back to grind *koonti* root, yet she was certain suddenly that it wouldn't matter, that this had been planned.

She had been expected here all night.

"Go!" The Indian girl commanded her with another thrust.

"Wait! This is insane! I cannot, don't you see? Untie me!" Tara cried. "I cannot serve—"

The man said something harshly, interrupting her.

"He can see that you will use any trick to escape. And he thinks you are much better behaved when you are tied. You will serve!" the girl said, then Tara nearly fell because the girl abruptly stopped pushing her and turned and exited the cabin.

Tara spun around to follow her, to make any possible mad dash for freedom.

But the cabin door slammed shut, and Tara could hear the sound of a heavy wooden bolt being slid across it. She stood dead still for a moment, then raced toward it, clenching her bound fists together, slamming them against it. A sob choked out of her, and she leaned against the door, fighting hysteria, then wishing that she might become so insane with it that this wretched world she had come upon might disappear.

But a sharp command was snapped out to her, and she went dead still before turning to brace her back against the door. *He* remained. Black head to her, fingers gripped tight around the rim of the tub, muscles rippling in his copper shoulders. He was going to stand any minute and come after her. And she was tied and trapped in the cabin with him.

There was no escape. Not tonight. Not from him.

She didn't know what he was saying, and suddenly she didn't care. She saw that there was a deep pan of water suspended above the fire, boiling away. He wanted to be served; she would serve him.

"God rot you!" she whispered. "I'll not serve you, you will boil in hell!"

She ran to the fire, ready to grab the water and scald him with it. But before she could reach the kettle, bronze arms snaked out and copper fingers closed like bear traps around her wrists. She gasped, choked, fighting wildly, aware of the wet and naked savage who had now leapt out of the tub to wrestle with her, his arms firmly about her in his determination to grip her wrists.

She kicked back wildly and heard a hiss of aggravation. She tried harder to free herself but he wrenched her back, and in so doing brought his own knees back against the crude wooden hip tub. She felt his strength as he fought a moment for balance, but too late. In a second they had both fallen into the water. His arms encircled her as she sat atop him, his fingers grazing her breasts. Beneath her, through the many layers of her clothing, she could feel him. Feel the muscles in his thighs, the heat of them. Feel as well the boldness of his arousal, steel hard and insinuating.

She cried out wildly, thrashing in the water. She twisted and turned, half drowning herself in her reckless efforts.

"Tara!"

The harsh sound of her name brought her still. She had heard it, yes.

Then she felt his arms, tight and restrictive around her again.

She twisted in his arms and this time his hold eased and she stared into his face, her heart beating wildly. She had expected the half-breed with the piercing blue eyes. She had to be losing her mind. She was staring at features that were somehow similar, and somehow not. She was staring into the coal-black and amazingly *merciless* eyes of Jarrett McKenzie.

Her husband.

Chapter 14

"McKenzie!" She gasped.

Those black eyes narrowed sharply on her.

"My God, you!" She gasped again. "You!" She felt her temper rising to a fever pitch. "What—oh, my God! I was terrified! I was afraid for my life. I've been wretchedly worked and all but tortured here."

"Had you been tortured," he snapped, "you would have been well aware of it."

"Let me up!" she commanded, struggling against him as fiercely as if he were one of the savages. At the moment he was more of one than the Seminoles, she decided.

But he wasn't about to let her free. They were both entangled in the sodden mass of her clothing but his fingers threaded through her hair, holding her still and forcing her eyes back to his.

"Let me up!" she insisted again, clenching her teeth against his painful hold. "Oh, my God, I could rip *you* from limb to limb, what have—"

"This is nothing. You should see what punishment sometimes befalls *runaways*, my love."

The tone of his voice was sheer warning, as was the ebony fire in his gaze. Her heart skipped a beat, and she inhaled on a wild gasp as she realized that he had come home.

And not found her there.

"The Seminoles, my love," he continued, drawing a wet trail down her cheek with his forefinger, "like many other Indians, can be harsh. Adultery and betrayal are judged especially brutally. Sometimes the ears and nose of the guilty party are slit and clipped, sometimes—"

"Oh!" she cried, raising her bound wrists and making her hands into a ball to slam against his chest. "How dare you, how dare you! You've been here, you know these people! And you let them—" She broke off, crying out, for he suddenly stood, lifting her with him, his eyes darker and more menacing than ever before. "Don't—!" she cried, but he was standing barefoot, naked and dripping before her, pure gold and copper in the flickering firelight, and she was now drenched and sodden herself. His fingers were like steel clamps around her upper arms.

"Sweet Jesu, lady, don't you think to preach to me!" he threatened, shaking her. "After everything! You still think that you will simply run off as you choose—"

"After everything!" she cried. "You brought me into the wilderness and abandoned me."

"You're my wife!" he snapped heatedly.

No, she thought, she just wanted to be his wife. His wife was the woman who lay dead in the ground, she had felt that from the beginning. She was the stranger he had brought home to fill the void in his life, to sit at the head of his table, to be a warm female form to hold, to take in the darkness of the night.

She tried to fight his grip upon her shoulders and could not. She drew herself up as straight as she could, returning his stare with her own alight with blue fire. She realized that Jarrett had been here for quite some time. He had certainly made himself at home in the small cabin. She saw that one of the rolls against the wall consisted of his saddlebags and belongings. His weapons leaned against the wall, even the luxury of a white man's linen towels lay ready for him upon the furs of the pallet.

She had been set to work scraping skins and grinding stringy roots—*because he had commanded it.* Jarrett! Not the half-breed with the blue eyes, nor even the war chief in the red leggings. No, Jarrett had let her sit there in terror, had forced her hands to cramp, her flesh to blister. Jarrett had held the "higher" authority over her, and he had used it ruthlessly.

"You bastard!" she hissed, and once again her bound fists came up to pound against his naked chest. "I'll rip your heart right out of your chest! I'll never forgive you for this, I swear it. I'll—"

"You'll hush!" he warned her, his voice all but a growl.

"Not in this lifetime, McKenzie—" she began, but she found herself slammed up against his chest, her breath clean knocked from her body.

"They can hear you!" he warned her.

"I don't give a damn!"

"I do!" he warned, and there was a very sharp glitter in his eyes now. "My little runaway wife is not going to put me into any more difficult situations."

"*Your* situation was difficult?" she exploded. She started shaking. She had been so damned terrified. And then she'd all but scraped her fingers to the bone. "Your situation!" she railed again, but she felt a wet hand clamped hard over her mouth. He seemed to tower above her, and she was reminded of the way that the savage half-breed had seemed to tower in the doorway of the other cabin.

"Madam, it would not do well for any Seminoles, no matter how close I am to them at this moment, to become convinced that I cannot even manage my own house. You see, they intended you no harm, but were appalled to find you wandering from lands where *they had guaranteed me you would be safe*. They wanted an explanation, and I must confess, I didn't have a good one!"

She shivered fervently, unable for the moment to offer him an excuse since his hand remained so firmly over her mouth. He suddenly eased it from her, spinning her around. She felt his fingers at the hooks of her gowns and despite her deep longing to shout at him again, she whispered a furious, "What are you doing?"

"Don't worry, there's not a great deal I'm expecting out of my wife for the moment," he taunted. "You're soaking wet."

"I don't care."

"You're not going to make a bigger mess out of this by coming down with pneumonia!" he warned.

He had the gown undone, her corset beneath it, even the ties to her pantalettes and petticoats. She still shivered as her clothing fell from her shoulders, but he could go no farther, for her hands were still bound at her wrists.

"Untie me!" she commanded, still shaking.

He spun her around to face him. He arched a brow high. "Still demanding, eh, *runaway*?"

"Now!" she insisted.

"No."

"No!"

"Maybe if I'd had the sense to leave you bound and tied at home, we wouldn't be here now."

"Maybe if you hadn't abandoned me to the savages, we wouldn't be here now."

"Maybe if you had listened—"

"Untie me! You'll never get these wet things off me if you don't!" she challenged him. Oh, to have her hands free! Just to hit his hard, handsome face once with a stinging slap!

"I won't, won't I?" he asked softly. She was startled as she felt his hands upon the many layers of fabric of her gown. His eyes didn't leave hers as he ripped the dress clear from breast to toes.

"Oh, you bloody, bloody bastard!" she whispered, and pitched herself at him.

He swept her up, and she slammed his chest as he carried her to the fur pallet on the floor. He set her down none too gently, wrenching away her loosened petticoat, pantalettes, and corset. She swore at him all the while, twisting, threatening. "I swear, Jarrett McKenzie, you will pay for this! I shall rip your eyes out—"

"And you call them *savages!*" he taunted.

She was naked and breathless, staring into his black eyes, furious, and yet . . .

Alive. So very alive. He had never seemed more sensual to her, naked, damp, bronzed to a glow, furious himself, and rippling with muscle. Nothing glowed within the room but the fire; she felt as if they might be at the ends of the earth. Perhaps it was cold outside; it was warm in here. She could smell the earth outside, the scent of cypress, of rich grasses, of pine. She felt the air against her own bare flesh, felt a hot coil stirring deep within her. And yet something hurt deep inside as well, and she was determined to fight him—and herself.

He knelt down beside her; she struggled up to her knees. "Damn you, McKenzie! I want to know! How long have you been here? You told her that I was better behaved when I was tied!" He didn't seem to hear her. He was reaching for her, and she tried to inch away, but his arms were on her, holding her still. "Don't you—"

"Idiot!" he grated. "I'm trying to warm you!"

He had set a warm braid blanket around her shoulders. Even as he stared at her, there came a soft tapping at the door. Jarrett stood and started for it. She was about to cry out that he couldn't answer it naked, but he plucked up one of his towels and wrapped it around his waist before opening the door, which had now been unbolted from the outside.

The half-breed had come back. He stared at Jarrett and said something in his language, which Jarrett answered. Tara stayed on the pallet, the blanket wrapped completely around her, staring at them with her chin high, not moving. An unease settled around her. She remembered how she had dreamt of being chased by an Indian.

Jarrett had been the Indian. But Jarrett had no Indian blood in him, or did he?

These two were almost of a height. From the back they might well have been the same person.

The half-breed had brought something with him, a basket, which he offered to Jarrett. "Thank you," Jarrett told him in English.

"You're welcome," the half-breed said. Clearly.

Tara gasped involuntarily. She stood up, hugging her blanket close, staring at the man, her eyes narrowing, her temper rising all over again. "You speak English!" she accused him.

He arched a brow at Jarrett. "You haven't told her yet?" He smiled suddenly, having noticed something about Tara. "You haven't *untied* her yet?"

Tara felt her flesh go crimson.

"I haven't had that much time alone with her yet," Jarrett explained.

"Ah . . ." murmured the half-breed, his lip still curling. When he smiled so, he was a very striking man, Tara thought.

Like Jarrett.

"Is Osceola still here?" Jarrett asked.

The half-breed shook his head.

"Good!" Jarrett murmured softly. His eyes fell upon Tara. "If she carries on till dawn, it won't matter a whit to me now!"

Tara gasped.

The half-breed inclined his head to her. "I think I should leave you two. It was a pleasure meeting you, Tara McKenzie," he said, and while she still stared after him, angry and baffled, he exited the cabin.

"What in God's name is going on here?" she demanded furiously of Jarrett.

He didn't answer her. Instead he walked toward her again,

shedding the towel as he came. Barefoot, silent, a copper wraith with the grace of a panther, he stalked her with determination.

He came before her, set his hands upon her shoulders, and threw the blanket to the floor.

"Jarrett—"

"It's been a long time. Forever. An eternity. All right, so it hasn't been so long, but it feels like *bloody forever!*"

His hands were on her shoulders again, forcing her down. "Jarrett!" she cried out, trying to thrust her bound wrists before her. But he caught her wrists and forced her to the floor, stretching her arms over her head, running his fingertips down their smooth whiteness as he lay atop her. She inhaled sharply, furious, yet feeling the hunger grow as if it were fueled by the very emotion that made her long for the power to scalp him!

"I mean it!" she cried out, her lips trembling. "I'll never forgive you for this. Given half a chance I'll have half of your hair and your scalp and—"

He didn't seem to hear her. "Too damned bloody long!" he whispered, leaning over her. "Jarrett!"—she whispered his name again, trying to twist her head aside. But his lips captured hers. Hot and hungry, giving no quarter. His mouth closed over hers, his tongue forcing her lips and teeth apart. And all the while the lapping fires inside her seemed to grow, heating, igniting, simmering, playing havoc within her flesh and blood. His touch was upon her again, his palm covering her breast, massaging it, sliding down between her legs.

Parting them with a firm thrust.

She gasped as he stretched hard over her for a moment. Then he rose above her on his knees. There was a knife in his hands. She nearly shrieked, but she caught hold of her bottom lip with her teeth and held silent, her heart pounding mercilessly, as he leaned over and slit the leather straps that bound her wrists.

Then he was upon her.

And it had been long, too long, forever. Because she, too, quickly forgot that she had intended to fight him, that she was exhausted, that she had been held prisoner here all day and night, that she had scraped skins, ground roots.

She forgot everything with the wild, searing sensation that came as he lifted her thighs, parted them, thrust himself full within her. Black eyes captured hers. Sleek sweat cast a new sheen over his coppery length as he moved within her, watching her. Her hands fell upon his shoulders. She wanted to push him away. She hadn't the strength, or the desire. She couldn't even close her eyes, twist her face from his. She just held him tight to her, feeling the screwing of the fiery coil within her, the sweet agony of wanting him, of emotions spiraling ever upward with his erotic tempest. It was almost frightening to realize how much she wanted this. Wanted him. Frightening to realize how glad she was of him, of feeling the shudder of his sleek nude body, the force of it, the heat of it. Wild thunder seemed to beat within her ears; it was the pounding echo of her heart. Then she seemed to burst into a field of splendor, of searing light, and she had barely cried out with the violent ecstasy of it when his climax came shuddering through her, creating a new wave of sweet ripples within her as she drifted back to a plane of sanity. She felt the soft furs against her damp back, the slick, hard heat of his flesh against her own. His weight, the still rampant pounding of his heart. His fingers entwined tightly within her hair for a moment, eased from it, and he slid to her side.

She was silent for a minute, catching her own breath, staring up at the shadowed roof. He reached for her again, trying to draw her into his arms, but she protested his hold on her.

"I'm still going to strangle you, given half a chance," she told him stiffly.

"Me?" He demanded, and, rolling onto an elbow, stared down at her. His striking features were tense; a lock of ebony hair fell over one eye. "I wasn't the one who was where I shouldn't have been—running away."

She made an impatient sound, trying to push away from him,

but he was suddenly braced over her again, and maybe it was just as well. They were going to have it out. She stared up at him.

"No, you were the one in the Seminole camp seeing that more and more ridiculous chores were set upon your already terrified wife!"

"They told you they wouldn't hurt you," he said, and perhaps an evasive shadow did cloud his dark stare.

"There are dozens of whites dead across the territory, but I should have felt reassured!"

"You should have felt damned lucky!" he said with a touch of irritation. "Not many whites would have received no more than a tongue lashing from Osceola at this moment."

"Osceola!" she repeated, shuddering. "My God. He was the man with the feathered bonnet and the red leggings!"

"Yes."

She felt a trembling deep inside her. Osceola, possibly the strongest war chief among these heathens now! And he had come upon her in the woods! He might have—

"Oh!" she gasped, suddenly slamming her fists against his chest with a rage born of renewed terror. "You left me in this savage wilderness to be taken by Osceola, a savage who absolutely hates all whites—"

"He doesn't hate all whites."

"That's right—he just thinks the world of you!"

"He's an exceptionally smart fellow who has seen what has happened to his people, yet he does not hate all whites. He is at war with them, yes."

"I do hope you're around to explain the difference the next time he is murdering and scalping your friends and neighbors! Damn you! You left me to—"

"I left you at home, where you had been warned to stay!" he roared in return, catching the fists that had so recently pummeled him. "By the time I found your trail, you had already been taken here."

"And you could have made your presence known hours and hours ago!" she cried.

He didn't deny it.

"You did tell them to make me do all those things!"

His eyes narrowed, hardened. "You were warned not to leave the property. If you hadn't been running away—"

"I wasn't running away!" she protested angrily.

"Then what were you doing?" he demanded.

She opened her mouth, then wondered if it wouldn't be worse to say that she had been trying to reach Robert Treat. Robert was his friend, his best friend, she knew, but she was aware that she had tried upon occasion to make Jarrett jealous where Robert was concerned. Perhaps to soothe her own soul.

"I wasn't running away," she repeated.

He leaned closer to her. "Where were you going?"

"Oh, no!" she protested indignantly. "I'm not answering another question from you. 'White Tiger,' indeed! What is going on here? The blue-eyed one—what's his name?"

"Running Bear," Jarrett said after a moment.

"Running Bear—who is capable of speaking such perfect English!" Tara said bitterly.

"Completely perfect," Jarrett agreed.

She leveled her stare on him, wishing he weren't still straddling her, his hold looser but his fingers still wound around her wrists. The intimacy wasn't painful, but it was distracting. She was very much aware of his hard body, of his sex, at rest, yet still so insinuating against her belly. It was difficult to breathe. She felt as if she were gasping in huge breaths of air, and with each it seemed that her breasts rose and fell a bit more quickly.

"And," she commented, "it seems that your Seminole is just as perfect. Is that what you were speaking?"

"It's a Muskogee language."

"Muskogee?"

He shrugged. "I speak Hitichi almost as well. It isn't a great feat, really, I grew up hearing both of them frequently."

"Growing—up?" she demanded.

He didn't reply.

"I want to know now," she said stubbornly. "What was he talking about? What haven't you told me?"

He released her, rolling to his side once again, staring up at the ceiling. He lifted his hands, then let them fall back to his chest.

"James McKenzie."

"What?"

"Running Bear. He is also known as James McKenzie."

She inhaled a ragged gasp. "But—"

"He's my brother, Tara." He rolled up on an elbow, with the speed and grace of a snake this time, staring at her again. "William is your brother, Tara. James is mine."

She gasped, bolting up. Dear God, yes! But it made sense! She had thought that Jarrett *was* the Indian, from the back, with his head of ebony hair, and the brothers were so close in height and build.

So he had a Seminole for a brother! And he had grown up among the Indians! No wonder he was so damned certain that he'd be safe among them.

And he hadn't told her!

"You bastard!" she breathed. "Oh!" Once again she flung herself at him, and this time with such force that he fell to his back and she straddled him, fists clenched, flailing at his shoulders and chest.

"Tara!"

But she didn't stop.

"Tara!"

Once again she found herself breathless, heaving, and locked beneath him. Her wrists were imprisoned in his grasp. His thighs locked around her hips.

"Oh, I swear I will—shoot you!" she threatened.

"Tara—"

"In both knees! And I'll scalp you and—"

"You'll hush up before your voice carries any farther!" he warned her.

"I'll tell you exactly what I think of you, just as loudly as I—"

"You'll close your mouth, my love."

"I—"

"I'll close it for you."

"How dare you—"

But he did dare, easily, his lips sealing her own, his tongue thrusting to fill her mouth, the force of his kiss robbing her of breath. When his lips parted from hers at last, she couldn't quite grasp why she had been shouting. She inhaled raggedly and told him, "This is no way to carry on a conversation."

A smile curled the left side of his mouth just slightly, and a speck of fire seemed to glimmer in his eyes. "We weren't conversing. We were arguing."

"And I tell you—"

"And I warn you, don't try to make a fool of me here!"

"And what have you done to me?"

"I've tried to show you the dangers that await wandering wives."

"You son of—"

"I don't want to have to teach you more about disobedient ones!"

"Of all the—" she began, but once again she found herself silenced, his lips stealing breath and words this time. Nor when his mouth rose from hers did he intend to allow for further conversation. His hand covered her breast, his mouth clamped down upon it, tongue laving and teasing the tip until she ceased struggling and squirming. Her fingers threaded into his hair, gripping, yet he seemed heedless of their pull, and his hands and lips covered more and more of her with a hungry speed that left her head spinning, her body burning. His kiss burned into the hollow of her abdomen, his hands slid beneath her, cupping her buttocks. She strained against him, crying out even as he nuzzled lower against her belly, against the soft blond triangle between her limbs. Liquid, searing heat seemed to burst within her, shattering in its sensation. She fought both to free herself and to feel more of him, and just when she thought that the world would explode around her, he was with her again, atop her, within her, holding her. Again his rhythm seized her. She eased for just seconds, then seemed to fly ever higher. She trembled when the explosion wracked her this time, amazed at the force of it, of him, the way that it felt to drift downward, held so securely in his arms. She wanted to fight, wanted to protest anew the charade he had played upon her, yet she hadn't the strength, or the real desire to battle further this night.

In a corner of her mind she still wanted to hate him.

In her heart she was only glad of him, and if he was with her, the rest of his secrets did not seem to matter so much.

His arms were around her, and she put her fingers upon his bronze ones where they lay against her belly.

"I'm going to strangle your brother too," she told him softly.

"I'm sure he'll take it like a man."

"Is that bathtub regular Seminole issue?" she inquired lightly.

"No," he admitted after a moment, and though her back was to him, she thought that he was smiling. "The bathtub is mine."

"And this cabin?"

"Mine as well," he said softly.

"And everyone else knows this?" she said.

"Not too many people have been out here, but most of my friends and acquaintances know that I have a brother out here and that I grew up with a band of Creeks-turned-Seminole."

"You should really be strung up by your toes and beaten mercilessly," she said.

"It could still happen. Anything is possible in this wilderness."

She shivered fiercely.

His arms tightened around her. "I didn't mean that we were in any danger here."

"I know!" she whispered. She suddenly turned within his arms, speaking earnestly. "But, Jarrett, don't you see? Anything is possible! Even I understand that. Osceola is not the only war leader."

"No, he's not."

"Then you can be in danger."

"Tara, I can handle myself among Creeks, Seminoles, and Mikasukis, I swear it. And," he added gruffly, "if you'll just learn to listen to me, you'll be safe as well."

"But—"

"Let's not argue anymore tonight," he said.

"But—"

"Tara, please. It has been a long day."

"You don't know how long!" she charged.

"But I have also had endless days before this one trying to get home," he told her, and something in his voice caused her to hold her tongue, even when she was longing to keep on questioning him—and even when she was still longing to berate him for what he had put her through today.

"I will answer anything you want to know in the morning," he told her softly, enclosing her in his arms once again, sweeping her back against his chest. His chin rested atop her head, his fingers entwined around her waist. The fire continued to burn, warm and low and golden.

He had promised to answer all of her questions. She suddenly smiled, burrowing even more closely against him.

It was insane. She was in a savage wilderness, with a people whom her own regarded as savage.

And yet when she closed her eyes, she fell asleep almost instantly.

And slept the most incredibly peaceful sleep. . . .

James McKenzie leaned against the wall of his cabin near the fire, watching the golden rise of the blaze, waiting.

And growing more impatient by the minute.

He sighed and ran his dark fingers through his hair. Naomi had delivered their "guest" to his brother's cabin some time ago but when he had gone out to see to his brother's comforts and needs, he had returned to find Naomi and the children gone. She had said something earlier about the girls staying with his mother. He'd been startled because he knew his wife hadn't been happy about the strange events of the day, and he hadn't imagined that she'd be receptive to intimacy tonight. Well, now he knew. Not only were the children sleeping in his mother's cabin; it seemed his wife planned to do so as well.

His people were Naomi's people; in their society a man joined his wife's family. But since most of his mother's family had been left behind after the Creek Wars, his mother and some of the remnants of her family had come to band together here. Through Mary and her family connections he had the hereditary right to be a *mico*. Death and disease among Naomi's clansmen had left him a natural leader here, and he had led the hundred or so people within his *talwa* for some time now.

He closed his eyes, tired, leaning back. Life had seemed so sweet. Then the war. They had only just begun. He was afraid. He could see the things it seemed so many of the warrior chiefs could not see. But then, he might have lived in the white world almost as easily as he lived in his own; he'd had the education and the resources to do so if he had chosen. But he had fallen in love with Naomi, and their life had evolved here.

Still, they were damned close to the area the whites intended to clean completely of all redmen. It was such a big territory, there was so much land. The whites wanted it all.

He opened his eyes and stared at the flames again, a slight smile curving his mouth. In a moment he'd have to go after Naomi. He was the leader here. He had white blood and a very close association with many whites. He was in a precarious position, since he had straddled two societies since birth, receiving a white education while also being encouraged to learn traditional Indian ways. He had danced in ballrooms with the daughters of white politicians, doctors, merchants, and planters, and he had debated and befriended a number of white soldiers. He had spent his life open and honest in his dealings with both whites and Indians—he had refused to defend his position to either, yet he was well aware of that position himself, and because of it he could not allow anyone to make a fool out of him. Not even his own wife. Not even if he loved her more than anything in the entire world.

But even as he was about to rise to go to his mother's cabin to retrieve Naomi, the door to his cabin opened slowly.

Maybe she had been hoping he was asleep.

He kept his back very straight and hard against the wall as she entered, staring at her, waiting. Naomi closed the door behind her.

She kept her distance from him, her expression showing her displeasure with the day.

"Where have you been?" he asked her softly, though he knew.

"Now you speak English?" she murmured to him, replying in kind.

"Now I speak English. Where were you?" he repeated.

"With your mother and my children."

"Our children," he reminded her politely.

"I had thought you would be asleep."

He smiled, flatly shaking his head. "You knew that I would not. In another few minutes I would have come for you."

"Yes," she said casually. She had known that he would come. He would have had to, to save face. Just as she had felt she must return here before he came for her, to save face.

"I suppose it was good that you brought my brother's wife to him, rather than allowing her to escape."

"Oh, yes!" Naomi said, her eyes flashing. "I brought her to him!" She was still angry over her part in the deception.

He rose, lithe, slow, and walked to her. She held her position against the door, her slender jaw locked in anger.

"It was a mean trick."

"There was no trick intended."

"Indeed? All that she saw while I remained was the back of a head with black wavy hair. She was most probably terrified that she was about to be raped by a vicious half-breed."

He stopped before her, not touching her, hiding a slight smile.

"Ah, but *she* was never in danger of such a wretched fate!"

"Does that mean that I am?" Naomi demanded, chin high.

He no longer hid his smile. "I have never been vicious!" he said in mock indignation. "But other than that—"

Her eyes widened and she turned as if she would bolt out the door. He laughed and swept her up, lifting her into his arms, cradling her tight. He had been in love with her when he married her, enamored of a young girl's grace and beauty. He had learned to love her more with each passing year, for she was many things, kind to all living creatures, gentle and tender, yet fierce as well in her protection of others. She had matured, she had become the mother of their daughters, but she had remained as lithe and graceful as the young girl he had first seduced by the crystal waters of a bubbling spring, her beauty only deepened with the passage of time.

"James McKenzie!" she said firmly, using his English name primly. "Don't you think you can force anything after all that you've forced me to do to that poor girl today. Don't—"

"Force!" he exclaimed, having come to the pallets on the floor. He knelt with his wife in his arms, his bronze muscles glistening in the firelight. "Force! Ah, never my love! Coerce, perhaps, persuade—"

"Seduce!" she accused. And he laughed and laid her down, and stretched out beside her. His mouth found hers while his fingers plied at her clothing. It was quickly gone, along with his own.

Naomi shuddered at the sweet feel of his naked flesh against her own. He loved to be so, close, touching with the length of themselves. She loved it as well, knowing that he wanted her, and knowing, always, he would hold her through the night.

Not even her anger could change that. Mary had told her that anger should not be something to keep a wife from a husband through the night. Naomi had told herself that she had come back because James would have come for her had she not. And he would have come, angry that he had been forced to do so. Even then, though he would appear fierce, though she'd have no choice against his strength, he'd never hurt or force her. He'd have stood in the doorway and stared at her, and told her to come. He'd have stood very tall, stoic, his features so very unusual, handsome, striking, his blue eyes like the cobalt that sometimes arose in a very hot flame. He'd have reached out a hand to her. And she would have come. And if he'd been very angry, they'd have come here and he would have turned his back to her and let her be.

Or else . . .

Seduced her.

Unless, of course, she hadn't been able to stand the silence, and she came to him.

And seduced him.

She closed her eyes. She didn't want to fight. She felt his naked flesh move down the length of her, hot, virile. He was created of muscle, sleek and hard.

He made love as passionately as he chose to live. With fervor, with a strength that swept her breath away. The very earth beneath her seemed to tremble and burn. And when it erupted, she was seized with such a sweet force that it swept away mind and thought and seemed to leave only the soul.

Naomi let her hand fall over her heart, feeling the pounding of it gradually slow. She could breathe again. A smile curved her lips and she curled against him, then remembered that she was rightfully angry.

She pulled away, turning her back on him. He sighed with deep patience, touching her shoulder, drawing her back.

"I'm telling you, she was deeply afraid!" Naomi insisted.

"My brother is not an ogre!"

"She was afraid of you! Of—"

"Of rape?"

"You should have seen her eyes when she saw a head with wavy black hair!"

"Naomi! She wouldn't have been afraid of me. She must have realized that I have a wife."

"She might have been afraid she was about to become a second wife. Most whites are aware a Seminole man may take more than one wife. And she is very beautiful. Pale, a little thin," Naomi said. "But . . ."

He laughed, rolling over to stare into her eyes. "But beautiful in a white-woman way?"

Naomi shrugged. She touched his hair. "You are half white. More white than you know sometimes. Mary carries white blood from her ancestors as well."

He smiled at her. "The color would not matter. I have never wanted two wives. One is definitely enough trouble."

She slammed a tight and surprisingly powerful fist against his shoulder and he laughed.

"I have never wanted two wives, because my one sweet beauty fills my heart with love, and I have no room for another."

Naomi smiled, and met his gaze. As he eased down to lie beside her again, she rested her head against the breadth of his chest.

"I am still angry about today," she told him.

"Today is only the beginning," he said, and she felt him stiffen. Only for the briefest second, and yet she was quite certain that in that breath of time he had suddenly been cold, almost like death, as if seeing some far distant and frightening future. "Only the beginning!" he repeated.

His fingers moved gently over her hair. "If you would be angry about today, there is no help for it. I had to bring her here, and though I am fairly sure Osceola would have done no more than hold her for Jarrett, I could not be certain. I had to take a very hard stance. Naomi, we are at war. Brutal, devastating war. I fear for us, you and me. I fear for our children, and for our people.

Seminoles have killed, plundered, burned, and maimed. Osceola has proven himself furious and incredibly harsh at times. Jarrett's wife had to learn the lesson that it was dangerous to leave Cimarron as she did. Can't you understand that?"

Naomi was silent for a moment. "You didn't have to be so cruel to her."

"I wasn't cruel. I was firm. She is my brother's wife; I am desperate that she survive this war."

Naomi sniffed. "She might want to argue *cruel* and *firm* with you."

"She may argue with Jarrett about all that has happened if she wishes."

"She must have been very frightened just to be here. If she heard just half of the lies that are often spread about Lisa's death—"

"She will learn the truth while she is here," James said firmly. "Naomi," he continued with a note of impatience, "let us not argue anymore."

"She might have been even more afraid of Jarrett," Naomi mused. "He was very angry when he arrived."

"Naomi, that is between the two of them. It's late. Time to sleep."

Time to sleep, because he wished to sleep. His day was done, his hungers were sated. She felt like arguing a little longer for the point of it.

But she smiled instead and silently kept her head nestled upon the warmth of his chest, his fingers resting so gently and casually over her hair.

He could be many things.

Bullheaded, she decided.

But she smiled to herself. Bullheaded—firm. Strong willed, intelligent, tender, confident, sometimes a little too arrogant and sure, sometimes so gentle it was astonishing. She loved him for all the things that he was.

She was very glad she was his wife.

She closed her eyes, secure and confident herself.

From somewhere a wolf howled. But it did not disturb the sleep within the camp.

Chapter 15

JAMES MCKENZIE did speak English quite perfectly, Tara learned in the morning, and he did have a quick and winning smile. She learned that very early, because James was back at the cabin in the morning, knocking before entering, but giving them precious little time to cover up before coming in to greet them with a very regular-looking coffeepot. "Bought right out of Mac-Dougall's trading post, south of Apopka," James told Tara, pouring her and Jarrett earthenware cups of the hot and aromatic brew and bringing it to them where they struggled up from sleep. "She does know who I am now, right?" James asked Jarrett.

"She does," Jarrett assured him with a scowl.

James winked at Tara. It was hard to associate him with the "savage" who had scared her half out of her wits the day before, but she was well aware that both brothers thought that she had needed to learn a lesson about wandering out into the wilderness.

"I hope you'll forgive me my part in this charade, yet you must realize, some of it was very real. Osceola wanted to take you."

"Osceola—take me where?" she demanded.

James shrugged. "To his camp. Out of harm's way. There's a

war on, Tara. You shouldn't have been where you were. The situation is growing ever more precarious, and there may be renegades who, when they see a golden white woman where she should not be, will decide that she is fair game after all."

"You might have told me who you were."

He looked uncomfortable for a moment, then his eyes touched on his brother's.

"I had to negotiate with Osceola, and he is, perhaps, our greatest chief. Then . . ."

"Then there was the matter of your brother!" she said.

"Indeed, there was that matter!" Jarrett said firmly, and she felt the force of his arm where it lay around her waist. "You weren't harmed; you needed to learn a little bit about the danger to be found when you wander where you aren't supposed to be."

He was so casual!

"Perhaps—" she began.

"Perhaps we should discuss this later!" Jarrett said firmly.

She would have argued. But James spoke again quickly. "Come to my home; Mary is eager to meet Tara," he said. "You'll like Mary," James promised her. "Even if she is—an Indian."

Tara almost leapt up, then remembered that she was barely clad.

"I'm not angry with you for being an Indian!" she cried to James, and as she did, a curious feeling poured through her. Yes, she had been afraid because they were Seminoles. She had been certain that they were monsters because they were Indians.

She'd had some right, of course. As James had said, they were at war. But it was strange to realize that she liked him. She liked his quick smile, the blue sizzle in his eyes. Even the way he kept tremendous dignity and deferred to his brother.

"I'm not pleased with the way you deceived me," she added as the men waited, "and I'd be displeased if you were white, red, black—or zebra striped!"

James nodded his head slightly. "Then I add another apology to my earlier words!" he said softly.

When he was gone, Tara, gripping a bear fur to her breasts, held her head very high, and looked at Jarrett with an arched brow. "Mary?"

"My stepmother."

"Oh," she said simply.

"However angry you are with me," he told her, "you had best be courteous to Mary."

She gritted her teeth hard, trying to ease away from the brace of his arm at her back. "She raised you?" Tara inquired.

"For many years."

"Then, McKenzie, if I have any argument with the woman at all, it is with the fact that your manners are gravely lacking!"

His finger fell upon her nose. He was so close again with his musky, masculine scent and intimate nudity. "I'm warning you, my love."

"Warning me! Did you ever think about *asking* me?"

"I asked you not to leave Cimarron."

She lowered her eyes from his. "If you hadn't been so secretive . . ."

"Excuse me. I'm the one who is secretive?"

She had no reply for that.

He leapt up, and in the daylight Tara was startled at how shy she could suddenly feel around his nakedness when they had been so intimate the night before. It didn't seem to bother Jarrett in the least. He stopped by last night's bath to scoop up water with which to douse his face, then swore out something unintelligible. "Cold!" he told her, and she nodded. The fire had burned out completely, and the winter's morning did seem chilly.

"I wouldn't mind a hot bath now," she murmured a little mournfully, staring at the tub.

"Later, or maybe I'll have something actually better a bit later, depending on the sun," he told her. He found his breeches and pulled them on. She stood, carrying her bear fur with her, but she had to drop it to start collecting her clothing, and when she tried to don her corset by herself, she found him at her back, well versed at pulling in the ties. "You will like Mary," he told her, and she suddenly realized that it was important to him that she did, and that as strange as this world was to her, it was one he knew very well.

And loved.

Her back was still to him when he picked up her gown and brought its volume of material over her head and shoulders.

Clearly, he had forgotten the method by which it had been removed, for it fell around her, ripped from bodice to hem. She spun around, staring at him. "Shall I really meet Mary dressed like this?" she inquired sweetly.

He arched a brow at her, arms crossed over his chest, a slight smile playing at the corner of his lip. "Perhaps not." He turned from her, surveying the small cabin and starting toward one of the rolled bundles toward the rear wall. He'd be offering her Lisa's clothing again, she thought. She bit her lip and said quickly, "I can fix this easily if you've got a needle and thread."

He stopped, studying the extent of the tear. "You can fix it— easily?"

"Please, if you don't mind."

With a shrug he turned elsewhere, finding needle and thread in a leather household kit. Tara didn't glance at him as she shimmied from the dress and sat down to mend it, feeling his eyes upon her as her fingers deftly moved.

"You are adept."

"Most women are."

"Not quite so adept as you," he said lightly. "It makes me wonder. But then again, everything about you makes me wonder."

Tara broke the thread and knotted it, looking at him at last. "Please remember, we are sitting in the woods in an Indian cabin belonging to your family."

He came to her, taking the mended dress from her hands, kissing her lightly on the tip of the nose, and spinning her around to set the dress in place once again. "My cabin, my brother's village," he said lightly. "Is it really so wretched a place, then?"

She spun around, staring into his eyes. She hesitated a minute, then softly admitted, "No."

He smiled. She was glad for a moment because she was certain she saw admiration in his eyes, rather than the disappointment she sometimes thought she found there.

But then she caught her breath again, for his smile faded and he demanded, "If you weren't running away, just where were you going, Tara?"

"I was trying to find out about—Lisa," she admitted.

His face seemed to darken instantly.

"And you were going to talk to the trees in the forest?" he asked sarcastically.

A flush rose to her cheeks. "No, I—"

"You were trying to find Robert's."

"Yes."

"You little fool! You did deserve exactly what you got!"

"Really!" she charged back. "Then you cannot begin to imagine just exactly what it is you deserve!"

He was about to answer her when there was a knocking at the cabin door once again. Jarrett kept his eyes on Tara and called out in the Indian language. He must have bade the caller to enter for the door swung open and light entered the cabin in a golden shaft. It was the Indian girl, and she greeted them both in English. "Good morning. Mary has sent me, in case you have forgotten the way." She looked at Tara. "She apologizes for being so eager, but she is anxious to meet you."

Tara smiled, staring straight at Jarrett. "Oh, dear! And just think! I could have met her anytime yesterday!"

"Just think!" Jarrett agreed, and spun her around by the shoulders. "Tara, my sister-in-law, Naomi."

"None of yesterday was my idea!" Naomi assured her.

"But Naomi is a gentle and loving wife and listens to her husband," Jarrett said smoothly. "Shall we?"

It wasn't a question, he was already propelling Tara forward.

Without another word Naomi turned and started out herself, leading the way.

The encampment was already bustling with activity. There were fields surrounding the enclosure of neat cabins, and it seemed that the men had already been out hunting, for there were numerous shafts about with rabbits tied to them, and near the center of the cabins by the large communal fire was a large pole suspended over support posts that held a fair-sized buck.

People greeted Jarrett, and he responded to them. This morning they all smiled at Tara, and though it seemed the entire tribe were sharing a joke at her expense, they seemed to welcome her this morning. Were she not inclined to forgive them simply because she was so intrigued by them, she would have done so in any case out of sheer common sense—white men were at war with the Indians.

They returned to the large cabin, James McKenzie's cabin. When Tara was prodded forward by her husband, she instantly became aware of the very handsome woman who stood in the center of the cabin awaiting her. She was tall and slim, dressed in a patterned skirt, red blouse, and a fall of exquisite silver jewelry. Her hair was peat black, her features barely showed a sign of age, and Tara thought that she couldn't be more than fifteen or sixteen years older than James himself.

She had dark copper skin, almond dark eyes, high cheekbones, and a strikingly handsome and yet gentle face. She arched a brow at Jarrett, greeted him in a low voice, and reached out her hands to Tara.

She would have gone forward even if she hadn't felt Jarrett's trust upon her back.

"Welcome, daughter," she said. Then she lapsed back into her own language, looking over Tara's head and apparently admonishing Jarrett in some way. He shrugged and responded politely, but firmly. He turned and left and Naomi came forward, tapping Tara's shoulder. "Please, sit and have bread with us here."

Mary said something and Naomi flashed Tara a quick smile.

"She says that you're very beautiful, so bright you dazzle and nearly blind."

"Tell her thank you, please."

"She understands you," Naomi said. "She learned English for her husband's sake, yet has not spoken it much since his death."

Tara looked at Mary. "Thank you," she said, and Mary smiled and spoke softly as she laid out pieces of bread and meat and offered up a dish to Tara. Naomi told her that they were eating *koonti* bread, seasoned with pumpkin, and that the meat was dried venison. They kept cattle as well, but had been selling many off lately. "They say that we will be running again soon," Naomi said.

"Running? But this is your land," Tara said.

Naomi smiled and shrugged. "By the Treaty of Moultrie Creek it became our land. There are years left to that treaty, but those years have suddenly faded, so it seems."

"Perhaps this war will end."

"No. It will not end. You see, warriors like Osceola will not surrender. We will not move west."

Mary said something, urging Tara to eat at the same time. Naomi translated. "She says that young whites sometimes cannot understand. Since the whites have come, we have been forced again and again from our homes. We have been driven into marsh and swampland, and perhaps they will drive us farther. But she promises that she will not go west. She is home."

Tara frowned. "I don't understand. If James is Jarrett's brother, then—"

"Oh, well, there is that!" Naomi said with a smile. "And it's true, Jarrett will not make war on his own people, but neither will he forget his brother. Or Mary, me, or the children. We have land that Jarrett has given to us, insisting it is part of our inheritance as James is a son of Sean McKenzie. But it is not an easy road to walk between two warring people. James has cast his fate with his red family, and if the fight forces us to run, then he will run with us, protect us, and in the end fight the whites when he no longer has a choice."

"Perhaps it will not come to that!" Tara whispered miserably.

Mary said something, and Naomi smiled and once again translated.

"She says that you seem to have a great heart, and she is happy you have married Jarrett."

"Tell her—" Tara began, then she looked at Mary and smiled. "Thank you, Mary."

Mary spoke again.

"She prays you will give him many sons," Naomi said.

"Oh," Tara murmured. She felt a hammering in her heart. She looked at Mary. "What—happened to my husband's first wife—to Lisa?"

There was silence for a moment. Mary looked to Naomi, but Tara was certain that Mary had understood her.

Mary nodded, and Naomi turned to Tara again. "She died here, in our camp."

Tara almost cried out as she gasped for breath. Her heart hammered. "But what—"

"Why do the whites say that we killed her," Naomi asked, and she sounded bitter, "seeing that she died among us?"

Tara's mouth was dry.

"Yes. Please, why?"

"She died in childbirth," Naomi said very softly. "Jarrett was gone with James. They were still trying to work things out then without bloodshed. There was a large meeting outside Fort King. Lisa wasn't due for nearly two months, but she woke up one morning and decided that she wanted to wait for Jarrett here, with Mary and me. We hadn't known that she was coming. Jeeves came at night, worried because she had not sent word back to him."

"My God. What—"

"We found her in the forest. She had been thrown from her horse. My mother-in-law is a healer; she knows every root and herb to be found here. She did everything that she could, but Lisa and the baby died. The baby never drew breath. Lisa bled to death."

"Oh, God!" Tara whispered. Her eyes were burning. Such a terrible accident. She could imagine poor Lisa here, perhaps knowing that her child had perished, that her own life was fleeing from her body.

"She was—broken inside," Naomi said very softly. "No white doctor could have saved her, but she did die here, and you can imagine how those who hate us to begin with could twist such a story."

Tara sat in silence, feeling numb and cold. She wondered what it had been like for Jarrett to come back, to find his precious Lisa dead.

And his unborn child.

Mary said something. She spoke long and passionately. Tara couldn't understand her words, but they were earnest and pleading in their tone.

Tara looked at Naomi.

"She says that you must not be afraid of us. That Jarrett is like her son, and she would have gladly died for Lisa." Naomi smiled. "She was absolutely furious yesterday when Jarrett arrived and decided that you must worry about what you had done for a while. She said that you didn't know us, so how could you trust us? But Jarrett"—she paused and shrugged—"Jarrett didn't want you wandering alone into the forest. It is true, these are troubled times. And then there was Lisa. But she wants you to know this is home. It is yours as well, always, and you are welcomed and loved here. She prays that you will see through the boundaries of race and color, and love us as well. If you can."

If she could . . .

Life was so very strange. Not twenty-four hours ago she had been terrified of Seminoles—of Indians, in any shape or form. How quickly lines blurred, things changed. Men were not all red or white or black, or mixed in shades between, and if a man's skin was not pure, it was quite true that his heart could be.

As her own.

Impulsively she set her plate down and stood and knelt by Mary McKenzie. She set her arms around the Seminole woman and felt herself enveloped in a gentle hold as well.

At length she sat back, meeting Mary's wise dark eyes. She smiled. "Tell her," she said to Naomi, "tell her, please, that it has been years and years since I have felt so welcome, as if—as if I have come home."

And when she spoke the words she knew that they were true.

She was glad to have met Mary and glad to discover that Naomi was a friend. She spent much of the day with them. Sara and Jennifer, the two little girls who had come upon her last night, came to be with them, and with some surprise Tara realized that she was their aunt. They were both precocious, and their English was excellent—James had insisted they learn the language and learn it well, since in future they must try to survive in a world where English-speaking whites were continually encroaching upon them. As the afternoon wore on, Tara realized that they were not *Indian* children, but children. It seemed that they were much the same anywhere, so eager to trust, so quick to smile, anxious to play. Sara was the older of the two, and Jennifer the younger. Jennifer had a bit more of the devil in her, and Sara was much more aware of a woman's responsibilities and able to explain to Tara that women were not necessarily the lesser of the two genders in Seminole society. "My grandmother abides with us here, for her family has been greatly torn over the years. But it is really my mother's family we live with, and when I marry, my husband will come live with our family."

Tara nodded at Sara and looked to Naomi, who smiled. "We usually take our clan names from the maternal side, and a husband comes to his wife's family. Usually," she added softly. "Wars change things."

"What happens when a man takes two wives?" Tara asked, smiling and intrigued.

"The second wife joins the first wife's family," Naomi said. "And often she is a younger sister, perhaps a widow, perhaps a relative. And then sometimes, as I have said, things change. Sometimes we just run with whoever we can."

Tara thought about her sister-in-law's words later when she was alone in Jarrett's cabin. She was very tired that afternoon, and when Naomi had brought her back, she had been content enough to lie down on the furs and reflect about the things that she had learned.

She was still angry with Jarrett. But though they were words she would never say to him, she did love him, and she was more intrigued by his life than ever, and more touched by it as well.

She wondered what Lisa had been like, and she thought that she would probably have liked her very much. She was able to put her jealousy of her predecessor to rest at last. She could also imagine how rampantly rumor must have run when word went out that Lisa McKenzie was dead, and that she had died in a Seminole camp.

She thought that Jarrett's ties to his brother and his people must be very strong indeed, and that he would never have doubted the truth himself, only mourned the tragic loss of life. His wife, his child.

She must have dozed on the furs, for when she awoke, she found that a low fire was burning in the hearth, and that she wasn't alone.

Jarrett was at her side, cross-legged on the ground, watching her.

She started up. "What is it?" she murmured groggily.

He smiled, shaking his head. "I was just watching you sleep."

"Do I do it oddly?" she asked.

He shook his head again. "No, you do it rather beautifully," he said softly, but then added a brusque "Tired?"

"I had a rough day yesterday," she informed him flatly, causing him to smile again. He reached out and took her hands. She tried to snatch them away, but he held them firmly. "Ah, yes, I do see a blister or two."

This time, when she snatched her hand away, he freed her. "I've had a blister or two before," she assured him.

A black brow shot up. "Have you? And everyone is convinced that you're such a great lady! How would a lady come up with such blisters? That is, if you are one."

She sat very still and stiff, her head high, her voice cool. "And would it matter to you if I wasn't?" she inquired.

He leapt to his feet. "Not a whit," he told her, reaching both hands down to capture hers and draw her to her feet. "Come on, I said that I had something you might enjoy later. And I do."

"What?" she asked him.

He shook his head. "You'll see. You're not in such poor shape that you cannot take a walk, are you?"

"No. I can walk. Whether you choose to—"

"No choice," he assured. "I'll carry you."

"Even if I were to yell and scream all the way?"

"Then we'd have quite an audience," he told her with a grin.

She freed her hands and started toward the door. He followed behind her and slipped an arm around her back. "Remember, I am your buffer in this land of savages," he told her.

She sniffed. "McKenzie, what would I fear from any other savage when I have married you?"

He laughed softly. "Good! Keep that in mind," he told her.

As they passed through the camp again, she found herself incredibly curious about it. There was something established here, a community, and within it people lived and worked. Again today there was a communal fire. A calf had been killed; it roasted over the blaze. Men were about, cleaning rifles, honing knives. Children ran about and played underfoot. Skins were stretched out on frames, and women and girls worked with the razor-edge shells upon them, preparing them for clothing and blankets.

Farther off, in a circle, another group of women worked hard grinding meal from *koonti* root. Someone tended a patch of pumpkins and other vegetables. They chatted, they talked, they laughed. They greeted Jarrett, and they stared, unabashedly, at Tara. She stared back. Jennifer and Sara were out, kicking a ball made of wound cabbage palms. They rushed to Jarrett and Tara. He plucked up Jennifer, causing her to squeal with delight as he threw her in the air. Tara felt a pull at her skirt. She reached down as well for Sara and smiled at the little girl's joy at being spun around.

Next thing she knew, there was a whole lineup of children, most of the little boys in breechcloths and the very small ones in dresses, while the girls wore clothing amazingly similar to that of the older women. Tara hadn't the strength to spin all the children, but she wound up laughing and directing the crowd of urchins into a line in front of Jarrett. Finally, the last child had been swung and sent back to play or work, and Tara found that Jarrett's hand was on her elbow again, and that he was leading her away from the camp and down a trail through the cypress and palms.

They came to a stream where the water seemed to bubble along at a slow and inviting pace. A huge cypress jutted out over it, letting fall a tangle of vines. The sun was just beginning to set. Its rays remained hot while its color became magical, filling the sky with deep reds, mauves, vibrant yellows, and golds. In the midst of the color various birds strutted through the low march bordering the deeper water, cranes, snow-white egrets, and beautiful, blue herons. Tara gasped at the sight of them, standing very still.

"Blue herons," Jarrett told her.

"I know, I've seen them."

"You've seen them?"

"They had some work on display at a show once, paintings by a Mr. Audubon."

"Ah . . ." Jarrett murmured. "Indeed, he's quite a hunter."

"He hunts these birds?" She gasped.

"He hunts everything," Jarrett told her with a smile. "And when he can't bag a bird he wants himself, he hires other men to do it. He stuffs them, and paints them, giving life back to them."

"You know him?"

Jarrett nodded. "Know him and like him. He's insatiably curious, and though he is a hunter, he loves the creatures as well, and sees the tremendous beauty in them. He's quite an adventurer; he has traveled the wilderness."

"You like him because he loves this savage wilderness of yours!" she accused.

He shrugged. "Maybe. Well, I didn't come just to stare at the birds."

"Then—" she began, frowning, but she broke off quickly and went silent with amazement as she realized that he was stripping. Boots, socks, doublet, shirt, breeches, peeled off.

"Come on," he told her.

She drew her gaze from his naked body, fire and copper against the setting sunlight, and stared into his eyes.

"What?"

"The water is beautiful, trust me. The sun has held all day."

"But—"

"For a woman so quick to dive into the Gulf of Mexico in winter, you are incredibly slow now."

He took a step and she caught her breath, her hand flying to her throat, certain that he meant to strip her himself and throw her into the water.

But he stepped by her, agile as ever as he balanced upon the cypress roots, caught hold of the vine, went flying over the center of the stream, crying out some sound as he released the vine, and went falling into the water.

He disappeared. A few moments later she heard a wild cry,

and a dozen birds suddenly winged their way up in a panic. Jarrett's head appeared, sleek black hair wet and long down his neck.

He was a little more than waist deep in the water. "Coming in?"

She wet her lips, surprised by the smile upon them. "There could be nasty things in there. Like snakes."

"I thought that I was the nastiest thing you had managed to come across."

"You are—but I don't like snakes and alligators, and I warned you about that from the start!"

"There are no gators around."

"How can you be sure?"

"Everyone uses this watering hole. The gators know not to come here. They are hunted and killed here. They stay away."

"What about the snakes?"

"What about God throwing down a bolt of lightning!" he asked with impatience.

"Is the weather going to be bad as well?" she asked.

"Tara . . ."

"I'll just watch," she said, smiling and taking a seat upon the bank, soft with its layers of cabbage palm leaves. "I'd thought for a moment that you were going to strip me and force me in," she said. "But the scenery is beautiful, and I'm glad—" She broke off.

He was up, striding out of the stream, heading toward her with water sluicing from his body.

"What—"

"My way failed. Yours sounds better."

"What way? What are you talking about—"

This time she broke off with a shriek, for damp and dripping, he reached down, catching her hands, pulling her up. Before she knew it she was spun around and his hands were deftly on her hooks.

"What are you—" she began, trying to twist around.

"Stripping you and forcing you in."

"You can't—"

"But I can, and you know it," he told her. "Stand still, will you? I'm trying to preserve what I can of this dress and it's already in a worn state."

"Oh, and I wonder why!"

"Behave. You don't want to walk back naked, do you?"

"Oh!" she cried out in aggravation, just as the gown was drawn over her shoulders. He wasted no time with the ties to her corset and all but tripped her to bring her back to the ground where he could free her from shoes, pantalettes, and stockings.

Naked, she found herself in his arms. She clung for balance as he walked precariously out on the roots. "If there are snakes in here . . ."

"There aren't."

"But if there are . . ."

He paused, arching a brow at her. "Then what? You're already going to slice me up and remove my hair and scalp."

"I'll do it with a great deal more pain and anguish if there's a single snake in here!" she promised.

He smiled. "And to think! I was so very convinced that you were the one who loved a good swim."

"I—"

The water cut her off. He had caught hold of the vine, they had swung out.

And he had let go.

It was beautiful. It was no more than fifteen or twenty feet deep, and amazingly clear. The sun had heated it, and the water was actually warmer than the air.

Freed instantly from his hold, she kicked out and streaked swiftly through the water, delighting in the clean, temperate feel. She shot back to the surface. He was nowhere to be seen.

She felt a tug on her legs. It brought her under, and he was there. His body slid up against hers and the feel was deliciously erotic in the water.

They broke the surface. He treaded water perhaps a foot away.

"Well?" he asked. His black eyes met hers for a moment, diamond bright from the water's reflection.

"Well?" she murmured.

His eyes had fallen. The cool water had hardened her nipples to round red peaks, she noted with a blush, and that was where his gaze had gone.

His eyes met hers again. There was humor in his voice. It was husky as well. "Near—perfection."

"The water is—warm," she agreed.

His smile deepened. "Very. Damned hot, I'd say."

He reached out for her, drawing her with him as his bold strokes and hard kicks brought them to a point where he could stand. He stood still but continued to draw her toward him. Against him. Her breasts brushed hard against his chest. He caught hold of her buttocks, lifting her against him. His hands embraced her thighs, lifting her higher. Pulling her downward upon the shockingly hard shaft of his desire.

She gasped something, her head falling, her face against his neck, her arms around him. He gripped her buttocks tightly, moving her first at his leisure, then to his more frantic pleasure. Arms and limbs locked around him, she felt the heat inside of her grow until she seemed to radiate like the warmth of the sun, searing against the cool of the water. She arched wildly, felt his hands caress her. Her lips pressed against his shoulder, her fingers dug into his back. Then she gasped, stunned by the fiery splendor that erupted within her so very quickly, dizzy with the strength of it. She was still aware of his force, of the molten heat that suddenly seemed to fill her, and of the then gentle power of her hold, as her arms continued to cling to him, as their bodies remained locked together in the cooling water.

"It really can be paradise," he murmured to her softly, a hand upon her wet hair and nape.

"Umm—" she began, but was instantly rocked from her aftermath of pleasure as something touched her from behind. Something that could not be a part of Jarrett's body.

She pushed from him with a wild, fierce force, spinning in the water, trying to find the danger.

"Tara—"

"It's a big snake!"

"What?"

"It's huge! Oh, you're wrong, maybe it wasn't a snake, maybe it is an alligator, a huge one—oh!" She screamed, again, now all but jumping atop him as the massive *thing* went sliding by her feet.

"Tara—"

"Get me out!"

"It's not a snake!"

"Then it's a gator!"

"It's not a gator, I swear it!"

Even as he said the words, he seemed to come thrusting forward, as if he, too, had been shoved by something huge from behind.

"You see! Oh, my God, Jarrett!"

"Tara, it's a sea cow! It won't hurt you."

"What?"

"It's just a sea cow. It's—it's like an ugly river dolphin! It won't hurt you. It's accusomed to the kids playing here, it just wants to be stroked."

"What?"

He released her—left her!—to dive beneath the water. She could see him—and it—swimming out to where it was deeper. Slim and straight, he ran his hands over the creature as he swam alongside it. Tara caught her breath. He was right that it wasn't a snake or an alligator.

And he was right, as well, she thought after a moment, that the creature did look something like an ugly dolphin. Only, bigger. She thought that it was somewhere around ten or twelve feet, round and awkward. Yet it could swim with a strange grace.

She suddenly wanted to touch it too.

She went diving under, stroking hard to catch up with Jarrett and the creature, but they made a half turn that brought them back to her. She reached out. She stroked its somewhat rough hide. It was so much bigger than she, and yet so very gentle.

She suddenly realized that she was about to die for lack of air. She shot back to the surface, gasping. Jarrett shot up next to her, inhaling deeply, black eyes on hers.

"A sea cow, huh?" she said.

"A sea cow. They like those water hyacinths over there," he said, indicating a flower-weed that seemed to grow in the water.

Tara turned and kicked hard, capturing some of the weed. She dived again with her offering. The animal swam straight toward her. It had a face like a walrus, she thought. Whiskers.

It very gently took the weed from her hand and surfaced. It dived again, coming around her legs. Rubbing against her. She stroked it again.

She hadn't realized just how involved she had become with the creature until she saw that she was in the water alone with it. Jarrett had climbed up the bank and sat beneath a cypress on a bed of cabbage palms watching her.

The setting sun now seemed to bathe the entire earth in shades of red. The birds had returned to the edges of the stream. Even the white egrets now seemed shaded with twilight pink.

Tara gave the sea cow one last pat and kicked out, swimming toward the embankment. When her feet touched the muddy bottom, she felt uneasy again, afraid to fully step down, afraid of what might be in that mud.

Her unease must have shown on her face. With a grin Jarrett stood, entirely undisturbed by the mud, and strode the few steps into the shallow water to sweep her up into his arms. She shivered slightly, staring into his dark eyes. His flesh was warm; it had dried in the dying sunlight.

"You—shouldn't have touched me. You were dry. And I'm all wet."

"I'll dry again."

"But I am drenched."

"Then I will dry you as well," he told her, and he laid her down upon the cabbage palms, coming down beside her.

"The creature was not such a monster," she told him. "It was so docile!"

"Ah! Well, you see, all things just like to be . . . stroked," he told her.

"Indeed?" she whispered. She should have been cold; she was afire again. She should have been sated; she was amazed at the hunger that filled her. She cleared her throat, trying very hard to think clearly.

"It will grow so cold soon!" she said.

"No. I will warm you."

"I am doused."

"I will lick you dry."

She trembled, and wondered if there wasn't something in this Eden that whispered of wild, sweet pleasure. And again, perhaps it was not so bad to be so wanted by the rock-hewn stranger who had married her, rescued her from danger, challenged her so fiercely with life.

The breeze passed over her body. She felt deliciously sensitive to its touch. To him.

A smile teased her lips. Her lashes lowered to sweep her cheeks seductively. She met his ebony gaze. "And you . . . do you just want to be stroked?" she whispered.

He groaned, moving over her, burying his face against the sleek wetness of her belly.

"Yes, my love. I just want to be . . . stroked."

She set her fingers upon his ebony hair. She felt his lips, his hands, moving over her flesh. She gasped aloud herself, and she reached out.

Touching him.

Stroking him.

And the sun fell completely, shadows filling the land. The moon rose in the night sky before they dressed and made their way back to the camp.

Chapter 16

THREE DAYS later they were back by the stream. The weather had taken a very sudden and vicious snap, becoming quite cold, so they were not in the water, but seated upon the bank, Jarrett leaning up against a tree, Tara leaning with her back to his chest, their legs stretched out before them. They were quiet, and a multitude of birds had come to the stream. Tara watched them with absolute fascination.

They were heading back in the morning, and to her astonishment she was almost sorry to be doing so. "They seem so peaceful here," she murmured to Jarrett.

"They? The birds?"

"The Indians," she said.

He was silent for a few minutes, then sighed. "It is a different life, Tara. Some things much like the white world, some things not. They are very fair, and the humblest man in the village is welcome to give his opinion on any matter. But murder is punished almost instantly by death; if the murderer escapes, then some member of his family must pay the price. The *mico*—or chief —is usually the eldest son of the chief's sister, but in these days things sometimes change. James is *mico* here because much of Naomi's family is dead. Osceola is no hereditary chief, but has gained his power through his exceptional determination and ability at warfare." He hesitated a minute. "They love their children and are very good to them, but sometimes, when a child might starve to death otherwise, or when the crying of a child might cause an entire tribe to be attacked or killed, infanticide is practiced, and it is accepted."

"Oh, God!" Tara breathed, shivering. How horrible! She could not imagine any parent killing a child, especially some of the little brown-skinned urchins she had met here.

Yet, she thought with a deeper chill, she should know, more than others, that blood ties were not necessarily strong ones, and that perhaps the Seminoles acted with much more compassion than certain white men she had come to know.

"Men and women are punished for adultery. The ears of a woman and her lover are cut off. And if the husband chooses, the lover must take his straying wife off his hands. At a second offense the lips and the nose are cut. When a woman's husband dies, she is bound to mourn for him for four years with wildly disheveled hair. If she dishonors his memory by marrying or sleeping with another man during that time, her dead husband's kin are free to kill her."

"I saw no one in the village with sliced ears!" Tara told him.

"Wives tend to be well behaved," he said lightly.

"Hmm," she murmured.

His arms tightened around her. "They believe in good and evil, in a supreme being. He is the Great Spirit, and he rules both heaven and earth. He is master of all life. They try to do good, and believe when they die there will be a future state of reward in the place of 'heaven,' where the sun rises, or else they will go to where the sun sets and there be punished in a fiery 'hell.'"

"That is not so different," Tara murmured.

"Have you forgiven me?" he asked her suddenly.

"Forgiven you?"

"For your first day here," he said, a twinkling light in his eyes when she twisted to see his face.

She shook her head after a moment. "Ah, there is forgiving, and then there is forgetting. I shall certainly not forget!" she assured him.

"Ah, be honest! What would you have said had I tried to tell you that my brother was among the heathen who so terrified everyone?"

She shrugged. "I still have blisters."

"But think of it this way—you are now growing familiar with our marshes and wilderness. Right?"

"Ah! So I am free to wander where I will now?" she inquired in return.

He leaned back, smiling. "I don't think I could ever clip your ears. But rest assured—I could quite easily redden your backside."

"And you, sir—"

"I know. You are unwilling to let me keep my scalp!"

She was about to respond but he sighed suddenly, slipping his arms around her middle so that they rose together. "I want to be back to spend time with Mary tonight, since I have to get back to Cimarron before the army comes for me again," he added, and there was a touch of bitterness to his voice.

She nodded. She didn't fight him when he took her hand, but she was not uncomfortable when they went back to camp. The people had grown accustomed to her; she had grown accustomed to the people.

He dined with a number of the warriors while Tara ate with Mary, Naomi, and the children. Soon after, the little girls were asleep on their fur pallets, warm and cozy and comfortable. Mary and Naomi conversed softly in the center of the cabin, and from the door, which Tara had left purposely ajar, she watched Jarrett with the warriors. She watched his earnest conversations, the emotional flow of his hands as he spoke. He sat next to his brother. The "black drink" was shared that night between them, and as time passed, Jarrett and James—or White Tiger and Running Bear—were arm in arm.

"They are very close. It is amazing," Naomi told her.

Tara, who had been sitting cross-legged with her elbows on her knees and her chin balanced on her knuckles, looked up. "In all honesty," she admitted, "I know nothing about Jarrett."

Naomi smiled, sitting beside her. "Maybe you know enough."

"He still misses Lisa."

"He finds great pleasure in you."

Tara arched a reproachful brow. "Do you think so? And what of the night when I arrived?"

Naomi merely laughed. "That! Well, he was angry. He thought that you were running again."

"I wasn't running—I was on my way to see Mr. Treat."

"Robert?" Naomi inquired, eyes sparkling.

"So Robert knows everything about Jarrett and everyone here as well!" she said mournfully, and Naomi laughed.

"Of course we know Robert. He is Jarrett's best friend, after his brother, and is frequently a visitor. He brings the children sweets from New Orleans, and they love him very much."

"I like him as well."

"Careful! If you were a Seminole woman, you might be risking your ears."

"Well, I'm not a Seminole woman—and I'm not risking my ears. Robert is a friend to me as well. He's not . . ."

"Not what?" Naomi asked.

"Not Jarrett," Tara said softly, and Naomi smiled. After a minute Tara smiled as well, then told her sister-in-law, "You speak English very well."

She shrugged. "Because I speak it constantly."

Tara shook her head. "But I have been listening to your language for days now."

"Three days. I've been around English all of my life; James does not even have a 'first' language; he learned his Muskogee and his English together as a child, and even now, sometimes, with me, he puts the two together. Jarrett does the same thing. If you wish, in time, you will learn. You already know a few words."

Tara arched a brow.

"*Mico,*" Naomi said.

"Well, I've heard that enough. It means *chief.*"

Naomi picked up an orange.

Tara shook her head. "I don't remember."

"*Yalaha,*" Naomi said.

"*Chief* and *orange!* That will get me far!"

Naomi laughed. "The rest of it will be as easy in time." She motioned out the door. "They are coming," she said, and turned to the center of the cabin where Mary was sewing patiently upon a shirt. She started to repeat her words, but Mary was nodding. "My sons are coming," she said.

The evening was exceptionally pleasant for Tara. Mary was determined to tell Tara tales from Jarrett's past, about his initiation as a warrior, and how he had painted his body blue, drunk the black drink, and taken on his adult name, White Tiger. James, translating, would change a story here and there, making Tara laugh. Naomi would correct him. Jarrett would sigh and correct them all with great patience.

"You should have seen the time he caught the cottonmouth!" James said.

"A poisonous snake?"

James nodded. "I was barely toddling. Jarrett shouldn't have been playing with the snake, but it had crawled up onshore with us, and he was going to be the great warrior, looking out for the rest of us."

Jarrett groaned. "James, this story—"

"Well, he caught the snake. But then he was afraid to let it go. He sat on the bank of the river and waited forever, and finally Father came and rescued him."

"I must have held it for five hours," Jarrett admitted.

"Two," Mary said, smiling shyly, two fingers up.

"Felt like five!"

Soon after, they returned to their own cabin. Tara, very sleepy and contented, lay down on the furs. "I still don't understand rank here. James will not fight the white man. Osceola had Charlie Emathla killed for saying that he would go west, yet he and James—and you?—seem willing enough to leave one another alone."

Jarrett, shrugging out of his shirt, didn't reply at first.

Tara sat up again, frowning. "Jarrett, Osceola was here the day I arrived. I haven't seen him since. Where is he?"

Jarrett shrugged. "This isn't his home. He is distantly related to Mary, and so to James, but he lives with his own family."

Tara hesitated a moment. "He came here for warriors, didn't he? To attack white settlements."

"How do I know, Tara!" he said impatiently.

"But you do know!" she accused him.

"Osceola is at war. He does not share his whereabouts with me under such circumstances."

"But if he needed you, he'd find you."

"And if I needed him, I'd find him!"

Tara lay down again, her back to him, her heart beating. A minute later he was stretched out beside her. She felt the warmth of his bare flesh, but kept her back stiffly to him.

She had been right. Osceola had come for more men to go on his raids with him. James and Jarrett McKenzie were living in a fool's paradise, and they could not go on doing so forever.

She thought that he had forgotten her, or that he was aggravated enough with her to want nothing more to do with her that night. But she was wrong. In a moment she felt his arm pulling her close and tugging on her clothing. "What is this?" he demanded.

"A dress," she said flatly.

"Amazing. But it doesn't belong in bed."

She let out a long, aggravated sigh. "Jarrett, you seem to think that—"

"I think that a dress does not belong in bed where we sleep, and that is all."

She hesitated a moment, chewing on her bottom lip. Then she sat up and shed her clothing, drawing a fur warmly around her. He watched her with his ink-dark eyes, fingers laced behind his head.

"Satisfied?" she asked.

"Wrong question!" he told her, but when she lay at his side again, still stiff, he didn't touch her.

And in the night she grew cold. She inched closer to him and wondered why it hurt that he seemed able to keep his distance so easily when she had discovered all too quickly that she didn't like the distance at all.

Still, when she came close to him, he curved his body to hers, slipping an arm around her. She lay awake for a while, wondering again about the man she had married, and the wife he had buried. Naomi had said that Jarrett seemed pleased enough with her. Yet she couldn't help wondering anew if she was simply filling a physical void.

Or if he felt the difference in the woman he held through the night.

Since her mare had run home days ago, Tara seated herself on Charlemagne in front of Jarrett, and the huge horse did not seem to notice the added weight. She had hugged the children, Naomi, Mary—and even James—but it had surprised her to see the way that the others in the village had smiled and waved to her as well as to Jarrett. She had smiled and waved in return, and felt a strange surge within her heart. For a moment she wondered how Jarrett could stand the crossfire in which he stood. She prayed that he would stand fast through the bitter bloodshed.

They didn't speak much as they headed out. Tara remained weary from the night before, and leaning against her husband's chest, she found that she kept dozing. But late in the morning she awoke as he eased her up. Puzzled, she realized that they had stopped by a stream for water.

She bathed her face and drank deeply, shivering slightly, for the day had remained chill. She heard the noisy gulping of Charlemagne close by and rose, then noted that Jarrett had walked off a short distance and was staring into a copse. She came behind him quietly and looked past him.

A covered, hollowed-out tree lay there with a pole arranged above it like a spit. Clothing lay upon it, furs rested by it. Gourds and plates of rotting food were set by it; flies buzzed all around.

It was a burial ground, she realized. The hollowed-out tree looked exactly like a casket.

Jarrett didn't take a step closer. "Little Wild One," he said after a moment.

"A friend?" she inquired.

"Someone I knew. Once."

"Perhaps he died of illness."

"There lie his rifle and his spear, both ready for the spirit world," he told her, pointing out the weapons that lay over the coffin itself. "He was killed in battle."

She hesitated. "A warrior would rather die in battle than suffer through illness, wouldn't he?"

Jarrett shrugged. "Perhaps." He looked at her. "He was only about fifteen. A hard time to die. Come on. Let's get on home."

He lifted her back on Charlemagne. It wasn't too much later that they came to the cypress forest where she had first found herself lost—and accosted by Osceola. In no time they were riding onto the lawn of Cimarron, and Tara was amazed to realize how happy she was to see the house again. When she had left, it had still seemed like Lisa's house.

Lisa was no longer her enemy. It remained Lisa's house, yet was hers now as well.

"There's Jeeves. Anxious to have us home," Jarrett commented. "He'll be eager for a dinner meal."

"I'm eager for a very hot bath," Tara murmured.

"Then you shall have it," Jarrett said, slipping from Charlemagne's back first and reaching up his arms to her as members of the household quickly appeared, Peter running out to take care of Charlemagne, Jeeves hurrying forward with a snow-white smile cutting a clean swath across his handsome black face. "Welcome home, Mrs. McKenzie, welcome home! We missed you sorely."

"Thank you, Jeeves," Tara told him.

"She'd like a hot bath," Jarrett said, shrugging with a smile to his main servant.

"Well, sir, I did imagine that she might, and since you had sent word when you'd be coming, I did take the liberty of arranging the tub. It rests in your room, sir, half filled with steaming water, while more hot water awaits in the kettles above the hearth."

"Thank you, Jeeves," Tara said, surprising him with a hug as she walked by him. Was such a thing done here? She didn't really care. "Thank you." She left them all behind, running up the back porch steps, bursting into the house.

She paused for a moment, swirling around the elegant breezeway, glad to have reached it again.

Home.

She took the steps two at a time, marveling at how the world had changed since she had been here last. Upstairs she burst into Jarrett's room—their room—and found that the tub was indeed waiting, that extra water was simmering above the fire.

Yet, for a moment, she paused. She trembled, thinking that she was suddenly absurdly happy to be here. Perhaps Jarrett didn't really love her, but perhaps, as Naomi said, he was pleased enough with her. Cimarron was beautiful. This room, even with its masculine feel, was warm and inviting. She had been so comfortable on the bed.

She had lain awake so many nights in it, thinking about him. Tormenting herself.

Perhaps in time . . .

Yet she clenched her hands into fists at her sides, wishing suddenly that there were no more secrets in her own life. If only the truth were out.

But had the truth been told, she might never have come here. And no matter how it burned within her heart, she still couldn't chance any confessions to Jarrett.

She closed her eyes tightly for a moment. She had to pray that she could eventually find out about William. And she had to believe that he was safe, much safer with her far, far away!

Her bath waited, a cloud of steam rising above it.

She stripped quickly, poured in the rest of the water, and sank into the tub. It had been scented with roses. A sweet-smelling soap awaited her and a lush fluffy towel lay across the rocker that sat by the tub. She swept up her hair and plunged in. Pure bliss. She sat there, feeling the delicious heat sink into her body. She laid her head back on the rim of the tub and closed her eyes. She had to forget her own past, put it behind her.

Far behind her.

She opened her eyes, frowning slightly. Then she saw that Jarrett had entered the room with his silent tread and now sat in the rocker by the tub, hands folded idly before him, watching her. A swift shaft of trembling danced its way through her spine. She knew that brooding, curious look in his eyes. Knew the tension in his bronzed, handsome features. Knew the sun-darkened hands and fingers that folded and unfolded now as he watched. Knew so much of him so well.

Loved so very much about him.

And now she also knew how he had learned to move so silently!

"You might have knocked," she remonstrated softly.

He lifted his hands. "But I live here. It's my room. And you're my wife."

It was quite an opening for an argument, but she wasn't ready to give him one. She smiled slightly, her lashes falling over her eyes. "I didn't really expect you to knock," she admitted. "I know you too well."

Too well, and too little still!

Yet it didn't surprise her when he knelt by the side of the tub, leaning his arms upon it as his fingers played in her water. "You know all my deep, dark secrets now," he said, his tone casual.

"All of them?" she murmured.

"All of them. So I thought, perhaps, you might want to share a few of yours."

The water seemed to cool. She felt as if clouds were falling over her eyes.

"I—I can't!" she whispered.

"Tara . . ."

"Jarrett, I swear to you—"

"Why do you dream about William?"

"He is safe!" she murmured.

"Where?"

She shook her head vehemently. "He is safe while I'm far away."

"Tara . . ."

"Please, I have sworn to you that I am innocent!"

"But of what?" he demanded, frustrated. "I still know nothing about you. In hours you can stitch together amazing creations; you tell me that you've had blisters before. I found you in a tavern that was all but a whorehouse, and yet you were as innocent as a newborn. Your manners are impeccable, and your speech is perfect. No one seems to be able to glean the slightest accent from it. I don't know if you were born the greatest lady or a street urchin."

"You said that it didn't matter!" she whispered fervently.

"It doesn't," he said passionately. "We can't forget that this is a new world, that we've fought a revolution to be free, and in that new world this is surely one of the wildest of wildernesses. What counts here is not birth, but spirit and courage, and those virtues are yours in abundance. But, Tara—"

She felt her lip trembling, felt herself grow colder and colder.

"Jarrett, you have promised me that you would ask no more questions!"

His eyes were ebony, yet tonight she could read the emotion in them, the fire. Once again he wanted answers.

"Tara, I need the damned truth!"

"You have promised!"

He locked his teeth together, sighing. In this it seemed that he must admit defeat—he could not deny his promise.

"Jarrett, please . . ."

"Yes, yes! I have made idiotic promises! Never mind!" he said, a finger beneath her chin as he lifted it so that she met his eyes again. "Never mind! I hate to see you tremble so, hate that look in your eyes. I'll not plague you with questions. Not now."

"Thank you!" she said softly.

"But I do ask something of you."

"What?"

"That we try."

"We try?"

He nodded gravely. "I want—my wife."

She shook her head, not understanding exactly what he meant. "I don't know what—"

"I want a promise from you. That you'll never try to run again."

"I wasn't trying to run. I told you that."

"Ah, yes! You were only trying to reach Robert!"

"For answers!"

"Oh," he murmured, his forefinger stroking her chin. "I want —my wife," he repeated.

She felt the start of a very different trembling, deep inside her. Warm. Molten. "But," she breathed, "you have . . . everything that you want."

"Indeed, I have what I can take. I want what you are willing to give."

Her brow knit in perplexity. "But . . . I have given you everything that I know to give!"

"That could be argued," he said with a half smile.

"Jarrett . . ."

"In some ways you have given me everything. I simply hope that nothing of it was . . . begrudged, or in payment?"

She felt a flush cover her cheeks. "There's nothing I have begrudged you!" she assured him. "I am glad to be here."

"Here? In this wild territory? With the alligators and snakes— and savages?"

She smiled and nodded. "In this savage wilderness. With the alligators and snakes. And all the savages. Including you."

He was silent and a moment's panic seized her. Had she given too much, too quickly? She mustn't forget that he still loved Lisa in his heart, that she . . .

She filled a void. Perhaps she even filled it well.

"Jarrett . . ."

But he was off his knees. And she suddenly found herself lifted, sweet-scented water sluicing down her breasts, between her thighs. She was swept up, brought to the bed.

His kiss never touched her lips. Never set down upon any spot of her body than that which was most achingly intimate. He laved her mercilessly. Seduced and aroused her until she was all but frantic, crying out. Crying his name. Gasping, pleading . . .

He didn't take time to disrobe. Still clad except for the most essential area, he was suddenly within her. She soared and shrieked into a wild, convulsive climax, then lay shivering and benumbed by the force of it. Moments later she was most tenderly held in his arms.

"Your bath has probably grown cold," he told her. "And it was what you wanted most."

"It's—all right."

"We'll heat more water."

She curled against him, her face rubbing the cotton fabric of his shirt.

"We will manage this!" he said suddenly, intensely. She didn't know quite what it was that they were going to manage, be it the tempestuous state of their lives in this wilderness, or that of their marriage.

She didn't want to know, not at that moment. She lay curled at his side, just glad to feel his warmth and strength.

And his tenderness.

Yet suddenly, even as she lay there, longing for nothing more than that tenderness to continue, she found herself whispering a soft question.

"Jarrett?"

"Umm?"

"What was she like?"

She felt him stiffen. "Who?"

"Lisa."

"For God's sake, Tara . . ."

"Please, Jarrett, I'd just like to know something about her."

He was silent so long, she was afraid he wasn't going to reply. And she bit her lower lip, wishing she had never asked the question.

"Confident," he said after a moment. "I met her when I was very young, and she was even younger. She was born in St. Augustine. Her father had grown very wealthy in the fur trade with the Indians and she had traveled with him frequently through the peninsula. She was adventurous, soft spoken, very sweet. She loved Florida, she was an avid historian about the territory, just like Robert. She envisioned the future, certain that Florida would become a state. She always had faith that the Indian problems could be solved." He hesitated a moment. "She could also be very stubborn," he said softly. "We had waited forever for children, and we both wanted the baby very badly. She should never have risked the ride to my brother's home."

He fell silent and remained silent. She'd had something of him, something from him, an intimacy Tara thought, something that she could almost really hold close and cherish—she had it for a few moments. But she'd lost it. Because she couldn't keep silent. She couldn't let poor Lisa stay buried.

"I'm sorry," she said softly after a moment.

He rose suddenly and she was afraid that she had lost him more thoroughly than she had realized. She closed her eyes, once again wishing she had kept silent.

She was startled when he suddenly lay down beside her again, his clothing now shed. He pulled her closely against him, his hold intimate and secure. "It's late," he said. And that was all.

But it didn't really matter. His touch was tender. A sense of peace seemed to settle over her. She was content because he was beside her again. Holding her through the darkness of the night.

It was a good start on the future.

PART THREE

Destiny
So It Comes Full Circle

Chapter 17

I N LATER days Tara would think of the time when they first came back to Cimarron as pure magic. The nights they dined together, and the days she rode with him, learning more about the plantation.

She had taken to bringing flowers down to the graveyard, and though Jarrett was aware of her activity, he said nothing about it.

Sometimes she caught him watching her, and she knew that he was brooding about the questions that remained unanswered between them. Yet she also thought that he was biding his time, and that when he thought the right moment had come, he would demand answers. She was certain that he hoped she would volunteer to tell him the truth.

The whole truth.

The longer they were together, the more she did want to talk to him. But equally strong was her desire not to let anything touch this sweet time of peace between them, and she remained afraid to speak.

He was pleased with her, pleased with their marriage. He was quick to say that he wanted her, quick to be passionate, even quick to be tender. But he had never whispered a word of love, and so she held to her own reserve as well.

Yet the days maintained their elusive magic.

One day she learned how to take the trail to Robert's house. Jarrett mentioned that he had business with Robert and asked her if she wanted to come with him for the ride.

Wild Oak, as Robert called his home, was smaller than Cimarron. It had no front porch, but a sweeping wide verandah in back, fewer columns, but lots of handsome red brick decoration. Like Cimarron the house had been planned around a central hall or breezeway. The kitchen was attached to the house by a covered walk as well, and the downstairs of the house had four main rooms, a solar, as Robert called it, with large windows that opened to the east and caught the rising sun, the dining room, a drawing room, and last, in Robert's tour of the downstairs, a room that took Tara's breath away as he threw open the door for her. It was one of the largest libraries she had ever seen.

"Oh!" she cried with delight, leaving Jarrett and Robert behind to walk into the center of the room and just spin slowly around, looking at the three walls, with their floor-to-ceiling shelves of books. Robert had everything. French plays, Italian works. Operas. Defoe, Bacon, Shakespeare, Molière. He had a section of political works by American authors, Jefferson, Adams, Madison, Franklin. He had a section on New England, with volumes on the unhappy persecution of the so-called witches at Salem, works on the subject by current scholars, by Cotton Mather and Increase Mather. He had shelves of fiction, and shelves of nonfiction and all sizes and shapes and manner of pamphlets and documents.

She turned to the doorway where Robert and Jarrett waited. Jarrett watched her with an arched brow; Robert smiled broadly, as if he had anticipated her appreciation and was glad of it.

"You've nearly everything," she marveled to Robert.

He followed her into the room, pointing to the rows of fiction. "There are some wonderful books in there, stories of adventure and romance. Pirates' glory and days of yore!" he told her. He turned back to Jarrett. "I think we can leave her here happily exploring while we talk about produce, orders, and shipment schedules."

But Jarrett walked on into the room, approaching one of the shelves and drawing out a log bound in leather. He brought it to a large oak desk in the center of the room, beckoning to Tara as he opened it. On one side of the first sheet was a beautiful water-color, a river scene, with moss-draped oaks falling over the water. She could see just such a picture almost daily by looking out to the river from the house. On the reverse side, fastidiously hand-printed, was an enumeration of the landscape features in the picture.

Tara looked at Jarrett, and he turned to another page. This one was a watercolor of scrub country.

"These are beautiful," she murmured.

"Tell her about them, Robert," Jarrett said.

"I'm sure she'd like to browse the shelves," Robert told him.

Tara stared at him. "Did you do these?" she asked him.

He shrugged and came forward, pointing to the painting she had in front of her. "They show the countryside," he told her. "Our countryside. This is scrub and high pine country, we've much of it around us. There are high pine trees, sand pines, ever-green oaks, or Florida rosemary. The soil is fairly poor for growing, but even in our wilds some of the flora and fauna are very rare. There's plenty of wildlife, the gopher tortoise, raccoon, spotted skunk, gray fox, white-tailed deer, Florida black bear, bobwhite quail, red-cockaded woodpecker, and more." He turned a page. Another beautiful painting appeared, as clearly and neatly docu-mented. "Swampland again, there is plenty near us. Cypress often dominates the swampland, with a multitude of fish, birds, small mammals. And the gator, of course." He turned another page. "This shows the marshland, and this"—another page—"the flatwoods and dry prairies." He became enthusiastic as he spoke.

"Freshwater springs and some of the rockland down in the tip of the peninsula."

"These are beautiful, fascinating," Tara murmured. She began turning pages herself, and now came upon sketches, pen-and-ink drawings, and more paintings of birds and animals in their habitats. She looked at Robert.

"I did some traveling with Jarrett and Mr. Audubon when he was here, and I learned a great deal from him."

"These must be published."

"Oh, yes, I imagine. One day."

She turned a page again. There was a picture of one of the old Spanish missions, and the text beside it described the Spanish efforts to Christianize the Indians in the early days after their initial discovery of Florida.

"Things were difficult even then," Robert murmured. "The Spanish soldiers never did really well with the natives, as you might recall from our discussion about Juan Ortiz." He smiled at her. "The first missionary to come to Florida was Cancer de Barbastro, and he brought others with him. The king of Spain was glad, for he said that the early explorers had been four tyrants, they had done mischief, and now it was time to send priests! Cancer sent some men in and they were captured by the Indians. He raised a cross above his head and tried to go in himself."

"And?" Tara inquired.

Robert shrugged. "The Indians struck him down as well."

"Robert, you are being extremely helpful in convincing Tara that this is a beautiful paradise, a wonderful place in which to live," Jarrett commented dryly.

Robert shrugged to Tara. "Well, they were different Indians, you know. Only the remnants of the old tribes remain. The Spaniards kept sending their missionaries."

"Yes," Jarrett agreed dryly. "The priests in Havana learned Indian languages from captives taken in Florida. A priest named Father Corpa taught at a mission in northern Florida and one day made the mistake of scolding a son of the local chief. While at prayer poor Father Corpa was slain, and the chief's son and his friends then went from mission to mission, killing the priests."

"She's going to really love living here now!" Robert informed Jarrett, his eyes rolling.

"Didn't the missionaries ever think it might be a good idea just to give up?" Tara asked.

"The king suggested they leave," Robert said, "but the missionaries were men of God—on a mission. They stayed. Then Spain demanded a 'corn tax' be put on the Indians, and the chief of each band was to carry the Spanish government's payment in corn to the collection sites. Now, the priests knew that the chiefs did not do such work, so they tried to sail to Havana to have the order repealed. But their ship sank, they didn't reach Havana, and the Indians and whites went to war."

"So that ended the missions?" Tara said.

"No. Governor Moore of South Carolina came to Florida in 1702 to make war against Spain, and the missions were all razed. But you must bear in mind that they did serve a purpose. The priests taught the natives, the natives learned from them. They brought horses and cattle. They made their mark. But when Florida came under a British flag, what remained of the missions naturally began to die out. By the time Florida was returned to the Spanish, Spain hadn't the money left to reorganize them. You have to remember, Havana was always the most important port for the Spanish in the New World. Florida became a burden, and of course, our government certainly helped that along! Our government, and of course, Jarrett's good friend Andy Jackson."

Tara glanced up at her husband, who had moved away from the book, leaving her and Robert to peruse it alone. He stood before the fire, his back to them. He turned to face Robert with a brow arched.

"I have never pretended to approve all of Jackson's deeds," he said.

"I realize that," Robert murmured. "Tara, I doubt if you're old enough to remember, but there was a huge furor when Jackson came here and actually attacked Spanish positions. You see, according to our government at the time, Jackson was simply leading troops against Indians who had crossed the border into Alabama and Georgia and threatened American lives and properties. But you have to realize, all this happened just after the War of 1812. If the English had won the war, the Indians in the North Florida area might have taken back lands that were now American soil. But the Americans won, and there were a few Englishmen around who were ready to urge them to attack Americans. When Jackson came in, he was brutal."

Tara stared at Jarrett. "You fought under Jackson here?" she asked.

He shook his head, annoyed. "I fought under Jackson at New Orleans. He was an extraordinary commander, an extraordinary man. But he was at times less than humane. He had two British men executed by a military court when he'd no right to do so; he took Spanish property when he'd probably no right to do so. And God knows, he has always been eager enough to take all Indian lands. If you two will excuse me, I think I'll find some fresh air." With a slight inclination of his head he left them.

Puzzled, Tara looked at Robert. "I shouldn't have brought up the old days," Robert murmured.

"Why?"

Robert turned a page in the book. She gasped slightly, for his next picture was another watercolor, and an exceptionally excellent one. It was of Jarrett and James in the midst of a green hammock, their backs to one another, their expressions grave. Jarrett was dressed in a dark frock coat, high boots, tight breeches, frilled white shirt. James was in doeskin breeches and boots. A single silver crescent hung around his neck, a red turban was wound around his ink-dark hair.

"It's so strange, they are both so very passionate about the territory," Robert murmured. "And so caught up in the tumult of it. Jarrett has always seen great things to come for the territory. He has tried to wear blinders regarding the Indian question. He has fought for schools and roads, and in his heart he is eager for statehood. But he'll not become involved with politics, he can't. Especially now. Because we are at war."

"But he is always trying to use his influence."

"Yes, and there are other men who are temperate as well, and there are very many who think that the Indians here—as well as elsewhere—have been wronged. But their voices are like the lonely cries of wolves at night howling to the moon. Roads are being built, the territory is growing. And with the growth come more and more people demanding that the Indians be removed, and so those who fight for their rights are like those trying to fight the surge of the tide. So Jarrett throws himself into the activities of his own land and tries to do what he can."

Tara listened to him, nodded, then kissed his cheek. "You're a wonderful friend."

"Thanks. I think I'll go find him and get down to business. Prowl where you will."

Tara nodded. He left her, and she turned another page. Robert had done a pen-and-ink drawing of an Indian girl by a stream, dipping her hands into the cool water to bathe her face. The girl was beautiful. Expression and nuance had been caught in the drawing. The girl must be someone he knew and knew well, she thought, but when she turned to see if she could catch him and ask him, he was gone.

She closed the book and wondered if she should ask him about the girl, or just let it be. There had been something unique and special about the drawing. To ask him about it might well be prying.

She set the book back on the shelf. One day, she hoped, he would offer more information.

She became engrossed in a pirate novel and hadn't even realized that it had grown dark when she started, aware that she was being watched.

Jarrett stood in the doorway. She wondered how long he had stood there.

"Enjoying the library?" he asked her.

She nodded. "It's very nice. But then, so is yours."

"Ours," he said.

"Ours," she repeated, flushing softly.

"Still, I imagine I could lose you here for days," he told her.

She shook her head. "No."

He came to her chair, kissed her on the top of the head, then reached for her hands, drawing her to her feet. "Dinner is about to be served," he told her.

It was late when they returned to Cimarron that night. Jarrett did not come straight up to bed with her when they arrived, but stayed below with Rutger, going over some of the business he had discussed with Robert.

When he did come up, Tara was half asleep. Yet she became aware again that he was watching her from their bedroom door-way.

He doused the last of the candles. She heard him stripping off his clothing and he came to their bed naked, his flesh feeling as if it were afire.

He quickly woke her, making love to her passionately, roughly. He lay awake after, staring up at the ceiling.

She wanted to talk to him, to reach out, to say something. But she knew if she were to question him, she would open the way for him to question her again. And she was afraid. Something had developed between them that was infinitely sweet, yet so very fragile. She couldn't tell him the truth about herself as yet. She wanted to. She just didn't seem to be able to.

So she lay silent, curled within his arms.

The tempest of the times would not let them be.

~~~~~

By the following morning they had been back from his brother's village less than two weeks. Tara paused in gathering flowers, hearing a commotion down by the dock. She walked around the lawn, biting her lip with worry as she saw that another military ship had arrived from downriver.

"Damn them!" she swore. "Oh, damn them all!" She seemed to freeze for a moment, yet she knew there was no way to make the military ship disappear. She hurried to tell Jeeves that it seemed they would be having company again.

Jeeves was in the breezeway, instructing one of the young maids on just how he wanted the silver polished.

"Tyler Argosy is back, I believe. I don't know how many men he is with, but I'm certain we'll have at least three extra for supper."

Jeeves nodded. "I'll tell the cook, Mrs. McKenzie."

Tara handed him her bundle of flowers. "Please—see that these go on the hall table. And—enlarge the wild-turkey menu we had planned . . . choose any wine. Jeeves, I've got to know what they're doing here this time!"

Without waiting for an answer from him she spun around and hurried out of the house once again, almost running for the dock. Jarrett wasn't about, she realized—he had ridden to the far side of his fields, and though he would have been quickly informed that the ship was arriving, he had not made it back himself. Neither was Rutger there. Leo Hume stood on the dock, ready to greet the men who would soon spill from the ship.

"Morning, Mrs. McKenzie," he said.

"Good morning," she returned, smiling pleasantly and waiting very determinedly at his side.

He looked at her with unease, but as the ship came in and docking orders were shouted out, she held her ground. Tyler Argosy was the first man to stride off the ship, and he was immediately pleased to see her. "Tara McKenzie!" he said, saluting first, then stretching out his hands to take hers. "Hello, Leo."

"Hello, Captain. Men have been sent; Mr. McKenzie will be on his way right soon."

"Thank you, Leo," Tyler said, and gave his full attention to Tara. "That's fine. Mrs. McKenzie is really much prettier."

"Ah, Captain Argosy! What a flatterer!" She lowered her voice to a soft modulation. "All to ease the blow! To what do we owe this great pleasure?" she demanded.

"Oh, Tara! How lovely you are today," he said softly, coming closer to add, "You're not thinking that my appearance is a pleasure at all, are you, my dear? You're wondering why this wretched soldier has come to take your husband away again."

"You are taking him away again?" she asked.

"Not for long, I hope. Yet, I swear to you, Tara, there is no help for it."

She didn't get a chance to say more because Jarrett came riding up hard on Charlemagne, slipping down from the stallion, his brow knit in a frown as he greeted their visitor, pulling off a riding glove to offer his hand in a firm shake. "Hello, Tyler. What is it?"

Tyler gazed at Tara. "Perhaps we could talk in your library."

"Perhaps we could all talk in the library," Tara said softly.

"Tara . . ." Jarrett said.

"Are you alone today, Captain?" Tara asked. "Where are your young sergeants?"

Tyler looked at Jarrett. Jarrett took firm hold of her shoulders, turning her about to propel her toward the house. "My love, please go tell Jeeves that Captain Tyler will be joining us alone."

"*My love,*" she responded swiftly, turning back. "I've already spoken with Jeeves."

"But he won't know that Tyler is alone. Tyler, have you a preference for wine?" Jarrett asked.

"Definitely! That same fine Bordeaux."

"Tara, if you will, please?"

The words were firm. The men wanted her gone.

She stared at them both. "You'll have to tell me what's going on eventually!" she said, her tone level and hard. She turned regally and strode back toward the house.

When she reached the porch and looked back, she thought that Tyler had brought very grave news. He and Jarrett were deep in conversation and Jarrett's features were more taut and drawn than she had ever seen them. Leo and a number of the other men on the dock had gathered around, all of them listening gravely.

Tara found Jeeves, then paced the hallway. She waited for the men to make their way to the library.

But it seemed they had determined to do their talking on the lawn—now that she was off it!

Jeeves came to the breezeway where she was pacing. He watched her unhappily. She paused in front of him at last. "It's madness!" she told him. "They're always trying to protect women from words, but words don't bring about evil—they can only warn against it! I'm sure the husbands of wives killed in their homes were very careful not to let them know the danger before they lost their scalps!"

"Mrs. McKenzie, you know you're in no danger."

She closed her eyes for a moment. Poor Jeeves! He couldn't begin to know what danger might be out there—waiting in the world—for her.

"I'm sorry, Jeeves," she murmured to him. "Did you want something?"

"Mr. McKenzie sent word that they wouldn't be returning to the house until dinner; he'll see you at the table at six."

She went very still. "Fine!" she said softly. What did they think they could hide from her? The newspapers still arrived, even if very late. Eventually she would know what was going on.

"Thank you, Jeeves. I will see the gentlemen then."

She went upstairs, shaking with both worry and anger as she dressed for dinner, going very much out of her way to be as perfect as possible, coiling her skeins of hair atop her head, finding a low-cut emerald gown and then a tiny pearl drop necklace to draw attention to the graceful bodice. She was spraying a dab of perfume at her earlobe when there was a knock at her door.

Not Jarrett. He never knocked.

She walked to it, throwing it open, expecting at first that

Jeeves had returned to tell her the men had decided to dine aboard the military ship—and thus avoid her all night.

But it wasn't Jeeves standing there—it was Robert. She cried out in delight and threw herself into his arms, hugging him fiercely.

He hugged her in return, but then quickly pulled away, holding her at arm's length. "Now, that, Mrs. McKenzie, is the kind of greeting that's going to make me go away just so that I can return once again. Unfortunately, I think it might also get me shot!"

She smiled. "Well, not until later, at any rate. Jarrett is avoiding me. He's with that Tyler Argosy."

"Oh," Robert said, and she was certain that some instinctive desire to hide things from her as well came instantly over his eyes.

"Robert, if you know something . . ."

"You do want to get me shot, don't you?" he accused her.

"Robert . . ."

"There's really nothing I know that you don't," he said, "But if you'll come downstairs and offer me a whiskey like a good hostess, I'll be delighted to share what I know."

"Come," she told him, heading for the stairs. "I'll absolutely douse you in whiskey if it will enlighten me at all!"

In the library she poured whiskey for Robert, a brandy for herself, and sank into the comfortable sofa in the center of the room, watching her husband's best friend as he paced to the long window, looking out on the lawn. Waiting.

But he wasn't going to give away his secrets so easily.

He turned and smiled at her. "How have you been? I heard about your outing into the wilderness. But you've been home some time now too. How are you faring here now?"

"Very well," she replied, then lowered a finger at him. "You should have told me about Jarrett's family. And how do you know about my excursion into the wilderness?"

"It wasn't my place to tell you about his family—Jarrett would have gotten to it."

"Perhaps—when we were old and gray and on our deathbeds."

Robert grinned. "He is too close to his brother to have let it go that far! I know about your excursion because I've just come from the village. I'll tell you more about it, but you finish first."

She shook her head. "I'm fine."

"You look it. In fact you look wonderful. More beautiful than ever."

"Thank you. Well, perhaps I am fitting in," she said softly, then looked at him and admitted, "I'm scarcely jealous of Lisa at all anymore! Oh, Robert! I went to her grave, and then Mary and Naomi told me what happened to her. I was so sorry! For everyone."

Robert looked down at his glass, a curious smile curving his lips. "Yes, it was a tragedy. But you never should have been jealous of her. You would have liked her."

"It's just that . . ."

"What?"

"Jarrett still loves her."

He was silent for a minute. "Tara, he can still hold love in his heart for her and love you as well, you know."

She shrugged. "Ah, but there's little I can hide from you! You know exactly how I came to be here."

"How you came to be here doesn't matter. That you are here does."

"Thank you," she said again softly. "And now, no more procrastinating, sir! What is it that you know that I don't?" she demanded.

He shrugged after a moment, then looked at her. "Things are getting very serious in this war, you know," he told her softly.

"But what can it be that I haven't heard?" she asked him. "Not much could sound more terrible than what befell Major Dade!"

Robert took a big sip of his whiskey, rolled it in his mouth for a moment, then swallowed hard. He looked at her. "James Mc-Kenzie is moving his people," he told her, setting his empty glass down on Jarrett's desk.

"What?" Tara gasped. "But I thought that his land—"

"His land is being overrun by the military. The Treaty of Moultrie Creek is no more than a worthless piece of paper with politicians playing games with every point."

"But Jarrett owns so much of this land."

"Tara! Tara!" Robert walked over, kneeling down in front of her. He took her brandy glass from her fingers and set it on the side table, then took both of her hands. "James was born with white blood, and he reveres his father's memory. But his mother is Seminole, his wife is Seminole, his children are Seminole, and his life is Seminole. This war has come too far, and too close. He must begin to move out of the way of the soldiers crawling the woods for battle and searching for Indians to ship west. Don't you see, James has no choice."

"But Jarrett will—"

"No, Tara. Jarrett won't stop him. It would be wrong; he could endanger his brother. You have to understand."

"This is so insane!" she told him. "Jarrett and James are brothers. You have made good friends with these people. I don't see—"

"Tara, that's exactly it!" he said with a sigh. "We have brought it down to people. To flesh and blood. Little children we love. Men we admire, women we like." He smiled. "Even you've done that now, Tara. Yet remember how frightened you once were of the very idea of the Seminoles?"

"I still have the good sense to be afraid of vengeful warriors."

"But Osceola is the fiercest of the warriors—are you afraid of him?"

"I'm Jarrett's wife," she said flatly.

Robert smiled. "You simply have to try very hard to understand what no man can really explain."

She didn't know if she understood anything or not, but when she looked up, she felt a sharp stab of unease sweep through her.

Jarrett was in the doorway.

Robert remained on his knees before her, his hands clasped warmly around hers. It was certainly a disturbing picture.

She wanted to snatch her hands away, but she didn't dare. She had no intention of looking guilty when she and Robert both were perfectly innocent. She rose slowly, indicating the doorway. "Jarrett has come back, Robert. And Captain Argosy is with him. Perhaps they will be willing to share their decisions respecting Jarrett's whereabouts in the next few weeks, if not the cause and reason for them!"

"Jarrett, Tyler." Robert was smoothly off the floor, shaking hands with both men. If Jarrett's enthusiasm for a greeting in return was lacking, Robert didn't seem to realize it. Only Tara felt the fiery force of those ebony dark eyes on her, and the heat that seemed to radiate from him with each smooth and catlike move.

"There's no cause or reason of which you are not aware, my love," Jarrett told her, standing behind her, his hands upon her shoulders, his lips just brushing her nape. "There is a war on. But supper is served. Shall we?"

He escorted her into the dining room. Robert and Tyler followed. Jarrett kept the talk conversational as the meal was served, urging Tyler to tell Tara about social events in Tampa, sparse now, admittedly, but no matter what great events were taking place in the world, gossip remained.

Halfway through the meal Robert told Jarrett what he had already told Tara. Robert had been right: though a deeply pained expression appeared on his face, Jarrett did not intend to oppose his brother's decision.

"Of course, James intends to see you himself, but under the circumstances . . ." Robert's voice trailed away.

"Just what exactly are the circumstances?" she demanded.

Tyler remained uncomfortably silent. Jarrett picked up his wineglass and spun it around. "Dozens of homes have been destroyed. Farmers killed. Rich men, poor men. But you are aware of that."

Tara felt a chill.

Jarrett continued. "The military has suffered deeply as well, despite the federal troops sent. Some fine men have been sent here, but local militia drop out, the men are desperate to return to their homes to see to their own families. The federals know little or nothing about this terrain, they are bogged down in marsh and swamp, the Indians fight and strike and slip into the foliage, down the streams and rivers of grass in their cypress canoes."

"So you are leaving again?" Tara said coolly.

"Tara, I am in a good position to help," Jarrett informed her. His voice was as sharply edged as her own, and she saw his black gaze fall upon Robert. Was he worried again about leaving her? Had these days meant so little?

Yet hadn't she worried herself? Fear that some other woman out of his past who had offered him comfort or entertainment or simple forgetfulness after Lisa's death might offer again something that she did not?

Like trust and honesty? she taunted herself.

"Jarrett, you cannot be the only living human being who can solve this thing!" she protested.

Tyler leaned forward suddenly. "Sergeant Culpeper was killed last week, Tara. In a skirmish with one of Osceola's subchiefs, Coacoochee, or Wildcat."

She swallowed hard. The knowledge hurt. She could remember Sergeant Culpeper, sitting here, in this room, right in front of her. So very polite, so very young. With so much life left to live!

She glared at Jarrett.

Tyler continued. "Osceola sent word to General Clinch after escaping one of his traps. He told the general that the whites had guns—so did he. The whites have powder and lead—and so does he. The whites will fight—so will he, until the last drop of Seminole blood moistens the soil of this, his hunting ground."

"What has Jarrett to do with this?" she demanded.

"Jarrett can reach Osceola. Few white men can."

Osceola! She wanted to hang him herself! She wanted to lay her head down on the table and cry for poor Sergeant Culpeper.

And so many others. She could almost feel her heart hardening against Naomi and Mary, James and the girls. But Robert had been right—the relationship was between people, and none of them was happy to be on opposite sides of a devastating and painful war.

The meal had ended. Plates remained half full. Jeeves would come into the room any minute and offer the men cigars and brandy in the library. They'd talk again—without her.

She stood abruptly, determined that she wouldn't wait tonight to be left, she'd do the leaving herself.

"Well, if you are determined to do the army's work, Jarrett, I can only assume you will leave in the morning. Tyler"—she hesitated, ready to tell him she was already sick to death of seeing him, but she held her tongue and managed to say other words just as true—"take care of yourself, Tyler. Keep your head down under fire."

The men stood up. Tyler nodded gravely to her, knowing there was little he could say now that she would want to hear. Robert caught her hands and kissed her cheek.

She smoothly eluded Jarrett when he would have stopped her, slipping gracefully from the room, then speeding away from it.

She didn't go upstairs right away, but rather wandered out to the porch. The night was cool, but mild enough. She thought of the chanting and songs that filled the fields, of the laughter the servants shared within the house. She thought of the nights when she had held both her husband and happiness, and she was suddenly afraid that it was all slipping away, that when Jarrett left this time . . .

"Ah, if I could but read your mind! Smooth that troubled brow!"

She spun around. Robert had come outside.

"It would not be difficult to read my mind. I am in a tempest! I am sorry for James, I am furious with Jarrett. He cannot end this war! He cannot control Osceola—"

"And he cannot turn down Tyler when Tyler has terms for him to bring to Osceola."

"Tyler could spend the next decade sending Osceola terms. And I hate him now. I hate him because so many people are dead, and I hate him for Sergeant Culpeper—" She broke off. "Lisa would probably have managed all this so much better!"

Robert shrugged. "She'd have been upset."

"Oh, how can you know?" Tara cried out passionately.

"Well, I knew her all my life," Robert said defensively.

"What?" Tara demanded.

He was very still for a moment, then he cocked his head slightly, staring at her. "You mean that Jarrett has never mentioned our relationship. You still don't . . . know?"

"Oh, my God! What don't I know now?"

He smiled, shaking his head. "Nothing like the fact that you're related to a tribe of Indians, although I suppose it is a similiar situation. Lisa was my sister."

"What?"

"Lisa was my sister. I came with her when Jarrett bought this land, we were friends from the start. We—" He broke off, worried as he stared at Tara.

The world was spinning. Not blackening, just spinning in a white whir. *Sister!* Oh, what a fool she had been making of herself all this time. What had she said to Robert? Had she ever said anything hurtful in her jealousy, had she said or done anything foolish that might have been hard on Robert? She had imposed on him, when he must still have been in pain for a woman he had loved himself. She desperately hoped not. Robert had been so kind to her.

Damn Jarrett, damn him, damn him.

And she was still so dizzy. It was ridiculous, but she was afraid that she was going to mimic southern belle behavior and faint there on the porch. She was starting to fall. Robert rushed forward.

It was just when he caught her in his arms that Jarrett came walking out onto the porch.

Tara fought to still her spinning head. She blinked, gritted down hard on her teeth, and willed herself to gain strength to stand alone. Robert tried to right her. Jarrett stood just outside the doorway as tall and still as a cast-bronze figure. He walked over to Tara and Robert and for once, seemed not at all in a mood to mince words with either of them.

He wrenched Tara from Robert's hold, his fingers biting around her upper arm. "Well, my love, I'm not so sure that you'll be at all unhappy or lonely with my departure this time."

"Jarrett—" Robert began.

But Tara meant to have none of it. She found all the strength she could possibly want and let fly with fury, her hand striking with a determined violence against Jarrett's cheek. He was so startled that his hold eased, and she wrenched free from him, tearing into the house and up the steps.

In her room she paused by the window, inhaling great gulps of air. After a moment she could breathe. She still couldn't think.

She stood gazing out at the darkened lawn, her back very stiff.

She heard Jarrett when he entered the room, and she knew that he was staring at her long and hard.

"How dare you!" she said after a moment, shaking. "How dare you! To accuse us, when you were hiding the truth again!"

"What truth?"

"He's your brother-in-law!" she cried.

"And what the hell difference does that make?" Jarrett demanded furiously.

"Oh, my God!" she breathed. "You didn't tell me, you didn't warn me! And I said so many things to him!"

"Whatever indiscretions you shared with him were by your own choice."

"I wouldn't have hurt him!" she cried raggedly. "I wouldn't have spoken about Lisa to him. If you hadn't kept this particular secret—"

"I didn't mean to keep it a secret!" he snapped in interruption. "But then again, why not? Your life is one huge, continual secret!" he reminded her.

"And your life is one compromise after another!" she charged him.

"We aren't talking about me at the moment."

"I'm talking about you. And the fact that you're leaving again."

"Damn you, Tara, I have to go."

"Yes, you have to go! Always you! You can't fight for them, and you can't fight against them. You'll just have to go and convince that murdering bastard Osceola that he must stop his war!"

"Yes, I have to try, Tara. For the Seminoles and the whites—I have to try!"

"And you think that you will have the power to tell Osceola he must cease his violence and make an entire people surrender and go west to live on barren lands?"

"Tara . . ." he warned, his voice becoming a growl, but she couldn't seem to stop herself.

"Well, McKenzie, if you can't stop Osceola, then you have to quit befriending him!" she said heatedly. She spun around at last. "You have to stop trying to negotiate with him! Let others go. You can't take up arms against your brother, but Osceola has no problem making war on the whites. The insane thing is to send you in. Someone else should go—let someone get close enough to kill him."

"If someone were to kill Osceola like that," Jarrett spat out angrily, "we'd have a martyr on our hands!"

"*You* can stay out of it! You can refuse to see him, to talk to him! Jarrett, all those plantations burned, so many people killed!"

"Indian villages have been razed as well."

"You're white! You're white!" She wasn't even sure why she was feeling so hysterical. Perhaps it was Sergeant Culpeper's death. Perhaps it was all the fear and anger bottled up in her heart.

"I will not go to war against my brother!" he thundered out.

"But you are very quick to doubt your brother-in-law! And me!"

"I have never really doubted Robert."

"Then it was only me you were doubting on the porch when your manners were so lacking!"

"My manners?" His brow suddenly arched up very high. "You're forgetting where I found you."

"I don't forget. You don't let me."

"And I can't change who and what I am!" he roared. "And if I do appear disturbed, it may only be because you are running to him at every available opportunity!"

"He's far more pleasant to be around!"

Jarrett was dead still for a moment. She could see the pulse ticking furiously at his throat.

"Well, he just may be accompanying me out tomorrow," he said very softly. "So alas! You will be minus his company as well."

"You're still going? No matter what I say?"

"You're my wife. You will please see my point of view in this and honor it!"

She inhaled, drawing herself up stiffly. "I'm not allowed a point of view?"

"Damn it, Tara, you've seen—"

"Then perhaps you've no longer got a wife!"

What was the matter with her? She was just so sick at heart, and most of all she didn't want him leaving again. He'd wanted to stay at peace with his family. But the war was escalating; it was horrible. He wasn't going to be allowed to remain at peace, and he didn't see it. The military had come to him; he would go. If Osceola had sent for him, he would have gone. And when he left, her heart would go with him, and she would pray that one of his own people, angered by his stand, didn't kill him, and pray that some renegade Indian, hating all whites, didn't decide to chop him up into little pieces.

"I don't have a wife?" he demanded. The words were deep,

husky, and each shook with anger and emotion. From head to toe he seemed composed of sinew, muscle—and tension. Silence followed his words. His hands clenched and unclenched at his sides.

"Maybe not!" she cried, wishing with all her heart that she hadn't started this argument, yet very much aware now that she had taken it too far and frightened, suddenly, by the intensity of his anger. *Courage!* she warned herself. She couldn't back down, not now, not when she had come so far. "Maybe not!" she repeated, and she squared her shoulders, striding back across the room, determined to walk by him and escape downstairs until he had cooled off.

She brushed past, yet got no farther. His hands clamped down on her arm, pulling her back.

"No wife, eh?"

She'd never seen his eyes so black, yet so touched by glittering fire. She could feel the biting pressure of his hands upon her, the searing anger that seemed to create an inferno within him, between them.

"You don't care to treat me as one!" she cried, head thrown back, eyes blazing as well. Dear God, she was losing her mind, pressing him so! "A real *wife* is allowed an opinion. If Lisa were here to tell you not to go—"

"Lisa would never dictate to me!" he snapped in interruption. "Lisa knew the situation, she was familiar with it, we shared—" He broke off suddenly, throwing a hand into the air. "Lisa knew the situation!" he repeated angrily.

"And she wasn't a coward, and she understood!" Tara said, enunciating the words as crisply and evenly as she could manage.

"And she's dead!"

"But you would have treated her as a *wife*. You would have listened—"

He never heard the last because he was already interrupting her. "You are sadly mistaken! My greatest pleasure in life is treating you as my wife!"

"Memories of a ghost are your greatest pleasure!"

She shouldn't have spoken. His eyes narrowed. His teeth clenched. "You needn't fear. There are no ghosts here tonight."

"She is always in your thoughts."

"She is always in yours! Leave it be, Tara! I am telling you, leave it be!"

"I—"

"Stop!"

She gasped, the breath knocked from her, for she was suddenly up in his arms and all but flying through the room, for his strides were fast and furious as he carried her to their bed, all but throwing her upon it.

"You cannot plan to leave me and have me in the one breath! You—"

"I could not bear to leave you without having you!"

"Damn you, Jarrett! If you think you're going to ride out, don't you dare think that you're going to—"

He was down beside her, his fingers entwined with hers, his lips a fire upon her own, the force of his body upon hers overwhelming. Oh! She longed to fight him into eternity, defy him, beat him with a response that was pure ice.

But God help her, it seemed that the very flames of his being took flight within her. Sweet simmering honey poured through her veins. She throbbed; she ached. She longed for the weight of him, the feel of him, the heat of him, and she even understood completely his words to her, for she really couldn't bear his going away if he didn't touch her, if she didn't try to hold on to him one last time, cherish and remember the scent of him, the feel of his flesh, the ripple of muscle and sinew, the thunderous rise and fall of his breath, the feel of his kiss.

His lips raised a breath from her. She twisted away. "I hate you!" she sobbed out. "I hate you for leaving, I hate you for it!"

"Damn you!" he whispered hoarsely. "Damn you!" But he swept her into his arms again. His lips found hers. Blue flames seemed to burn around her. She tried to slam her fists against him again.

But then her arms wound around him. Her hunger and passion soared to frightening, dizzying heights, a tempest that raged
both wild and sweet.

She had barely exploded with the cataclysm of it when it
began again. His hands, his kiss, upon the length of her. Touching
her, lightly, slowly. Stroking. Brushing, teasing. Her throat, her
belly. Thighs, the small of her back. Her breasts, her lips, the very
heart of her desire. And again she burned, more deeply, more
hungrily, and yet, when the sweet explosion seized her, she drifted
down in misery.

None of it meant anything. He was leaving. And he was furious with her.

"Tara!" he demanded, his hand upon her shoulder as she lay
with her back to him.

"I hate you!" she whispered again.

He was silent. "Indeed, Tara! Perhaps you are not the wife I
needed here!" he murmured after a moment. His tone was flat.
Laced with disappointment.

She would have turned then—should have turned to him. But
his warmth was suddenly gone, for he had turned away from her.

This wasn't what she had wanted, to part in bitterness. She'd
wanted him to understand that she was afraid. Not for herself. For
him. And she didn't want to be away from him. The words never
came out right. She was afraid to speak the truth.

She suddenly thought of what he had said to her. *She* was the
one who always brought up Lisa. Perhaps she was. Well, he had
loved her. But maybe he was the one living in the present while
she was the one dwelling with fears of the past.

She tried to moisten her lips. Tried to speak. She couldn't find
the words she wanted to say. She lay there, awake, miserable.

Finally, she turned to him. His back was to her. "Jarrett?" she
whispered softly. She tried to practice the words she would say to
him in her mind. *I simply don't want you to leave. I am afraid that
you will not be able to be neutral forever, that white soldiers will turn
against you, that a renegade Indian will pierce your heart with shot or*

arrow. I'm afraid that you won't come back, and now I'm afraid that you won't even want to come back.

"Jarrett?" she whispered again softly. He didn't respond. She bit her lip. She lay again in misery. He had turned his back on her—washed his hands of her. He had been disappointed in her once, and he was doubly so now. She had said that she hated him. She wanted to take the words back.

She wanted to say . . .

"Jarrett! I love you!" she whispered aloud.

But she was still speaking to his bronzed back. She bit into her lower lip, catching her breath, listening for his. It came, deeply, evenly.

He hadn't heard her. She had found the right words to say, but had said them too late.

Or perhaps he had heard her. Perhaps he was feigning sleep now because he had heard her and just didn't care.

She caught a sob in her throat and turned her back to him again. A weight of agony lay with her in the night.

Yet finally she slept. For when she opened her eyes again, the room was filled with bright yellow daylight. Candles and fire had burned out. The sun lit upon tiny dust motes in the air, making them dazzle.

Her bed was cold.

She turned swiftly. It was empty as well.

Once again Jarrett was gone.

And she realized that she, like the bed, was empty.

And cold.

Dear God. So very, very cold.

Chapter 18

TARA DID little but move about Cimarron in a mechanical way the first few days after Jarrett left, but on the fourth morning, as she sat at the dressing table brushing her hair, she suddenly remembered what Robert had come to tell them.

James, Naomi, Mary, the children, and all those within their village would be leaving very soon, and she didn't know how far away they would go, or how often she would be able to see them once they had gone. Without Jarrett at Cimarron she not only felt laden down by the wretched way that they had parted, but she was lonely and anxious as well, and she longed to be with people.

Well aware now that the trails she might travel could grow dangerous, Tara went to Rutger first, hoping that now an excursion to the village would not be something Jarrett's men would deny her. She tried to tell him casually that she wanted to spend some time with her sister-in-law, yet she could barely breathe with nervousness while awaiting his answer.

She might have asked him to escort her on nothing more

difficult than a stroll in the garden, he was so quick to try to help her.

"I don't know exactly where the camp is, Mrs. McKenzie, but I'll send young Peter ahead, and he'll find one of the village sentries. Leo and I will take you in the hammock, and an escort will find us there. But if you don't mind, ma'am, I'd ask you for a day or two here for me to catch up."

She agreed that would be fine.

Rutger and Leo acted as her escort two days later. They left Cimarron early in the morning and arrived near the village just in the afternoon. Long before they could actually see the encampment, painted warriors stepped from the cypress trees, crying out a greeting. They were guarding the camp, Tara realized, and she was pained to see the danger they considered themselves to be in.

"White soldiers ride the land now," one of the men, the warrior Oklawaha, or Twisted River, told her. His English was stilted; he was not comfortable with it, but he made himself clear. "Not so close as yet . . . but . . . ?" He lifted his arms in a shrug. "I will see that the White Tiger's woman reaches her family," he assured Rutger solemnly.

"Thank you," Tara said.

"I'll come back in two days' time," Rutger told her. She thanked him as well and smiled and waved to Leo, then watched with her Indian guide as the men turned to head back to Cimarron.

"Come, I'll take you in," Oklawaha told her. Running ahead of Tara he let out a cry that warned the others in the camp that he was coming with a rider, but a friend, not a soldier.

Tara was instantly dismayed to see the camp—it was so painfully evident that its inhabitants were planning on leaving. All manner of household goods were packed up, pots and pans, guns, powder bags, kegs. A huge travois lay in front of the large cabin where Naomi and James lived with their daughters, and it was piled high with their belongings and covered with skins.

She leapt down from her horse as they entered the clearing.

Naomi, having heard the warrior's cry, came out of the cabin. She smiled broadly and ran to hug Tara. Tara hugged her fervently in return. "I'd hoped you'd come! I thought you might after Jarrett came through."

"Jarrett came here?"

Naomi nodded. "James went with him to find Osceola."

"Oh!"

"I knew then that you'd be at Cimarron alone, and I didn't want to press you, but I was so anxious for you to come! I've never had a sister, and now that I've found a sister-in-law again, I'm to lose her almost instantly!"

Tara shook her head. "You won't lose me."

Naomi smiled sadly. "Well, it will be difficult. We have to go south and east—into swampland. Where we can live, but where the soldiers will have difficulty following."

"Naomi, this can't last forever."

She sighed deeply. "We have to fight forever—or let them send us west."

"But they can't force James to do anything, they can't! His father—"

"Tara! You know that James will not call himself white to gain a foothold when his people cannot surrender!"

She did know it. And she was outraged for these people, just as she had been horrified about the settlers who had been burned out and killed.

And she had tormented Jarrett on this very point, when she felt the tearing anguish of it herself! She wanted to sit down in the center of the cabin and cry. If she could only go back and unsay so many things!

She couldn't. She could only pray that he wasn't too disappointed with her. That he wouldn't decide he was weary of battling her, that he no longer wanted a wife.

"Let's not think of the future for the moment. Come inside and visit with Mary. Then, if you wish, you can help me pack."

"Can someone start me a fire in Jarrett's cabin? I would do so myself, but I'm afraid of burning it down," she told Naomi.

"Anyone would be glad to help you. You're welcome to sleep with us. No, I think you'd rather be in his cabin."

Tara smiled, slightly startled by Naomi's intuition. "Yes, I guess I would."

"He will be safe, you know."

"I hope."

"Osceola will never hurt him. I know you think that Osceola is a vicious murderer, but he is a man of great convictions, and he keeps his word. He would not fight Jarrett."

"Thank you for the reassurance. But there are other warriors out there, men who may not agree with Osceola."

"More so than the whites, the Indians cherish a man they can trust. Even if he is, by the color of his flesh, the enemy. But come now; Mary will be delighted to see you."

Tara shared *koonti* bread and fresh cow's milk with Mary—who greeted her as warmly as if she were, indeed, a daughter—Naomi, and the children. Two of the village boys came to assure them that they would light her fire for the night. Mary then returned to her own cabin to rest, the girls went out to play, and Naomi looked about the cabin, sighing as she saw what she still had to pack.

"How will you live?" Tara asked Naomi unhappily.

Naomi shrugged. "We have run before. And we will not manage so badly. We will sleep in our *hooties*—"

"What?"

Naomi laughed. "A '*hootie*' is like a lean-to, quickly thrown up, roofed by cabbage palms. Easy to leave again."

"Oh, Naomi!" Tara said unhappily.

"I'm just grateful that you came to say good-bye. We'll break this camp just as soon as James returns. It won't be so hard again, because we'll stay ready to run."

"I just wish—I wish there were something I could do."

"There isn't."

"Then I wish that I could help."

Naomi smiled. "Then perhaps you'll take a walk with the girls. They're underfoot when I'm trying to pack up the things we will take."

Tara smiled. "Children are like that everywhere," she said softly.

"They do their share of the work, little as they are. They weave cabbage palms, they even do well with cleaning skins. We learn young here. But you're right, children remain children, and they are very much aware of the move, and they are more hindrance now when they try to help."

"Little white ones are much the same!"

"I imagine, though I really know little about white children. I was so anxious to hold Lisa's white baby—oh, I'm sorry, Tara."

Tara shook her head and Naomi set a hand on her arm. "You mustn't be afraid of having children because of Lisa. The circumstances were tragic but accidental!"

Tara shook her head again. She didn't want to tell Naomi that she wasn't afraid of having children, she was simply afraid that her husband might not want them very much anymore—not with her.

"You have white blood in you," Tara reminded Naomi with a smile.

"Diluted!" Naomi said with a laugh. "In fact, I could just imagine trying to tell one of the white soldiers that I was part white!"

"Naomi . . ."

"I know!" she whispered. "I know that Osceola and Wildcat and other warriors attack plantations and kill your people. I wish that—I just wish that the war would end. And that we might all be allowed peace. But—I don't think it can ever end. I think we'll be running forever.

"Oh, Naomi."

"Go with the children, please. They love you, and they'll be distracted for a while. For now, we are only moving deeper into the marshland, and we will still see each other now and then!"

Tara embraced Naomi. Naomi called out for the children, and Jennifer and Sara hurried into the cabin. They cried out with delight when they heard that Tara was going to play with them. "I guess we'll start with a walk!" Tara told the two, glad of the complete love and trust in the huge, beautiful eyes that turned up to hers.

"Don't get lost," Naomi warned.

"We'll head west," Tara said, thinking that she would follow the trails that went just beyond the stream she knew so well. Indian country. She'd be safe with the girls there.

"Don't wander too far," Naomi warned.

"I'll stay close."

Tara started away from the village with the children, telling them that they shouldn't be worried, their parents would be taking them on a big adventure.

"We're running away from the white soldiers!" Sara told her gravely.

"You are going to where it's safer," Tara agreed. "But perhaps it won't be for very long. Or perhaps you'll like your new village better."

Jennifer sniffed. "It will be away from you."

"Not so far. You've got me now; you won't lose me so easily!" she teased.

Jennifer, holding Tara's hand, set it next to her cheek and rubbed against it. Tara bit into her lip, wishing there were something else she could say to the children.

"Hey! Let's play a game. It's called hide-and-go-seek. You two go forward a bit into the trees, then I'll come running after you and find you."

"All right," Sara agreed, eyes alight. "Come, Jennifer, take my hand!"

Jennifer let go of Tara and went running after her sister. Tara didn't want them really getting ahead, so she gave them only a ten-second head start. She caught up with them, spun them, hugged them.

They ran off again. She caught them the same way. Delighted, the girls demanded that they get to play one last time.

"All right, then, run along!" she said. She gasped for a few minutes, catching her breath. Then she started after them for the third time.

But just as she slipped onto the trail, she paused with a frown. She could feel something, a beat, a rhythm of the earth. Then she realized that horses were coming, a number of them.

She didn't think that there should have been so many horses. Many of the Indians had mounts, but James was away with several of his warriors.

Some inner sense suddenly warned her that a terrible danger was approaching.

"Jennifer, Sara, come here! Now. We aren't playing!" she called out. She heard a giggle. The threat of tears seemed to tighten her voice. "I am not playing, you must come to me, now!"

They sensed the danger. Both little girls streaked out of the trees, huge eyes on Tara.

Her first instinct was to run for the village. But through the trees she could see blue uniforms. Soldiers.

She didn't want to lead them to the village.

Instead she swooped up the children and started running as fast as she could in the direction of Cimarron. Foolish! she thought. She could never make it. With a horse, yes, but her mount was in the village. She was simply determined now to get as far from here as she could.

She ran down the trail, gasping for breath. With a child clasped in either arm, she was wearing down quickly. Yet still, she thought that she could reach one of the marshy copses she was coming to know, perhaps hide until the soldiers had passed by.

She wished that she had headed east—that she were on her own property. She would have some rights that way. But this was

Indian land—or, at least, according to the Treaty of Moultrie Creek—it had been Indian land.

That would make the soldiers feel they had every right to be here.

Just when she thought she might have escaped, a blue-clad soldier on a handsome army horse suddenly came down the trail straight toward her.

She was trapped.

She came to a dead standstill in the center of the trail, clutching the children to her.

The man was regular army, Tara thought, one of those sent here with the thousands from the federal government. On his horse he seemed tall. He was slender with a sharp face, a goatee, and a slick-curled mustache.

"Well, well, well!" he called out. "What have we here!"

He drew his horse to a halt, dismounting. Tara could hear other soldiers draw up behind her. She didn't turn. She kept her eyes on the man who had accosted her first.

"What do you want?" Tara demanded, trying very hard not to show how she was shaking.

The man pointed to her arms. "The Seminole brats!" he snapped out.

"Why?" she asked imperiously.

"Why?" he repeated, stripping off yellow gloves as he took another few steps toward her. He looked behind her to the mounted men in his company. Tara turned slightly. That's what it was. One company, she thought. Scouting? Perhaps just looking for small villages, eager to slay everyone within them and burn them to the ground.

They would know that most of the warriors were out, following the war chiefs. It would be a good military tactic to many to sweep down and kill old men, women, and children.

James had been right. The war was coming after him whether he wanted it or not.

"*Why?*" the soldier began again, directing his men. "Why on earth!" he said, laughing, and came nearer Tara, thrusting his face toward her. "Because little brats grow up to be big Indians. With rifles and knives. Because I don't want to see a white scalp on one of these little heathens' shirt sash in another twelve years, that's why!"

"These are little girls!" Tara said angrily.

"Little girls—little Injuns, lady. They'll grow up to make more redskins. Hell, ain't you realized it yet? There is no good Indian but a dead one, and it don't matter what its age! Who the hell are you and what are you doing out here anyway?"

"Tara McKenzie, and we are bordering my land!" she snapped back.

"McKenzie?" The name took him aback. One of the other soldiers rode forward.

"Captain, sir, can I speak with you?" he said anxiously. The captain followed him a few feet away.

"He's going to kill us!" Sara said, trying to sound wise and unafraid. "He's going to swing us around and around, and bash our heads in against a tree!" she said in a hush. No matter how brave a little Seminole girl should be, she was trembling with fear and tears filled her eyes.

"Sweetheart, he will have to kill Aunt Tara first, I swear it," she promised, planting a quick kiss on each little forehead. How things changed! It had not been so very long ago that the very idea of a Seminole had sent her into terror. She had almost believed it herself that the only good Indian was a dead one! The white soldiers didn't know; they hadn't seen that people were people, with desires, hopes, dreams, fears. Born to love, to hurt, to age, to die.

"Aunt Tara—" Jennifer began.

"Shush!" Tara said quickly, because she had to hear what the men were saying.

"He's an important man in the territory, owns all kinds of land, no title, but he sometimes works for the army, for Zach Taylor, straight through Andrew Jackson! If she's his wife . . ."

The mustached captain gave an impatient wave. "They told us to clean out the Indians, didn't they?"

"Mrs. McKenzie, with all due respect," he said to her, yet his eyes flashed, and there was no respect intended at all, "hand over those children."

She clutched the little girls tighter against her and stared at the blue-clad soldier on his horse. "These children are staying with me."

"We don't want to hurt you, ma'am."

"Then you had best not."

"I'm an officer with the United States Army."

"Then perhaps you should behave like one. I don't recall the murder of children being among the duties of army officers!"

The captain sighed, truly aggravated. "Sergeant Dicks, get down, and take these little vermin from the lady." His eyes narrowed. "And if she isn't careful, she'll find that she is pleading for herself!"

She felt a shiver race up her spine. He wouldn't dare touch her! But he had that look about him, she thought. He was a cruel man, and his uniform allowed him to vent that cruelty.

Thank God it seemed that Dicks was no fool. "Captain, I cannot wrestle with a lady!" he said.

The captain swung around. "You're disobeying my orders?" he demanded of Dicks.

"No, Captain!" Dicks said with dismay.

"Move on!" he suddenly told the company. "Move on. I've a few more words to share with Mrs. McKenzie, then I'll be with you."

Dicks looked to Tara unhappily. He was a young man, barely shaving, she thought.

"Move on!" the captain roared.

"Sir—"

"That's a direct order."

Dicks and the other mounted men began to move past them.

Tara was tempted to run, yet she thought that perhaps against this man alone, she might have a chance.

Besides, she couldn't run with the children. She could barely hold their weight any longer.

In a matter of seconds the cypress forest was silent.

"Now!" the captain said. "Hand them over, lady."

She shook her head slowly. "These children are my husband's blood."

The captain seemed surprised, then he sneered at Tara. "He's got you, and he likes a bit of red as well—he keeps a Seminole mistress?"

Tara fought her fury. "They are his nieces."

"Give them to me. Perhaps if you do so swiftly enough, I won't be tempted to hurt you to get them. Nor to hurt you in getting what I want *after* I get them!"

"You have to be insane!"

"Lady, one way or another . . ."

She drew herself up as tall as she could, thinking desperately now. She was stunned. He meant to kill the children—and rape her!

She forced her voice to stay level. "Perhaps I cannot stop you from hurting me to harm them, but Jarrett McKenzie will tear you limb from limb if you do!" she threatened.

"Well, he'd have to know what happened here to do that, wouldn't he?" the man demanded.

He was still a good ten feet away. She had one chance, at least to save the girls.

She dropped instantly to her knees, whispering as quickly as she could. "Into the cypress, run! As deep into the trees as you can get."

"But Aunt Tara—" Sara began.

"Go!"

When their little legs touched the dirt, they were off. The captain swore, drawing his gun, but Sara and Jennifer had long traveled the cypress trails and could swiftly disappear down them.

Before the captain could shoot and possibly hit a running child, Tara ran and threw herself at the captain and his weapon.

His shot went into the earth.

He swore, shaking off Tara's hold. He raised the butt of his gun, ready to strike her head. Now, instead of plunging at him, she was desperate to escape him. She ducked low, avoiding his blow. Then she sprang into a reckless run, heading down a trail opposite that which the girls had taken.

He was in swift pursuit.

She was fast; she was beginning to know the trails. And she might have escaped him, except that her shoe caught in a root, and before she knew it, she was flipping into the air and then falling, landing flat on her back. She tried to scramble up. He was behind her, slamming into her back so that she fell again. Her arm was wrenched. She was thrown over. Her head slammed against the root, and she saw stars.

She felt the army captain with the sharp face and cruel eyes crawling on top of her. His hands were on her face, on her cheeks. "You cost me the brats, witch! So let's see just what you're worth yourself. . . ."

She fought the blackness that filled her head; she tried to kick and lash out. She heard the sudden rending of the fabric at her bodice, felt his fingers on her flesh. She started to scream, certain that no one could hear her, yet so very desperate.

"You'll pay!" she cried out, wrenching wildly beneath him. Sweet God, his hand was on her thigh as he thrust her skirt higher and higher. She was flailing, scratching! He swore at her. His hands were on her throat, squeezing. She slammed her fists against his chest, and she thought that she was going to die. Either he was going to kill her and rape her, or rape her and kill her, and it didn't seem to matter very much to him which came first.

She couldn't even scream anymore. She hadn't the breath with which to do it.

Suddenly her throat was freed. The world was spinning in

black whirls, but she could gasp for air, and she did so, gulping in huge breaths. She blinked furiously.

The captain was being wrenched off her. He was all but flying through the air. He landed on the ground with a *whoosh*, and Tara became aware at last she wasn't alone in the cypress forest.

Some dark-haired figure, clad in doeskin breeches and cape, was now reaching down in a fury for the captain. Tara tried to stagger up. The captain had drawn a knife. He was thrusting it at the man. A roar echoed chillingly from the newcomer's lips. As Tara watched, the knife the captain was trying to direct into the other man's chest was deflected with a furious blow.

"Go!" she heard shouted at her. She couldn't go. She couldn't stand; she couldn't walk.

Then he spun around. Her heart skipped a beat, and she thought that she'd pass out again.

It was Jarrett, black eyes blazing. He wasn't really clad like an Indian, he just had on the doeskin breeches, one of his own white cotton shirts, and the fur cape against the cold. Yet even as he turned to her, the captain was up—with another knife.

"Jarrett!" she couldn't scream; she choked out the warning. He turned in time to deflect the second blade.

Tara heard the distinctive sound of the captain's arm breaking. She heard his anguished cry, and the fall of the knife with which he had meant to kill her husband.

She choked out a cry of horror, yet the captain's agony didn't tear at her heart or soul. The fury in Jarrett's eyes frightened her more than anything, and she was terrified for him and for their lives, and their future together.

He had turned on the man, his hands now going for his throat, his attack filled with lethal intent.

"Dear God, Jarrett, don't kill him! You'll go to trial for murder, he's white!" she gasped out. She didn't think that he had heard her. She ran forward. "Jarrett!" she cried, trying to pull him away. She tugged on his arm. He came up, turned, and stared at her through a black cloud of fury.

"Jarrett!" she gasped. "Don't kill him! He's a white army man. They could hang you for murder, the army—"

She broke off as she heard the sound of a gun being cocked. Jarrett instantly thrust her behind him, turning to stare at the incensed captain with his one dangling arm—and the good one that held an army-issue pistol on them both.

"Right in the heart, you Indian-loving bastard!"

Tara screamed, falling to her knees as she heard a shot. But Jarrett hadn't been hit—the captain let out with another shriek of agony.

Then went still.

He'd been shot by someone behind Tara. She twisted around and saw a party of five Indian warriors, Osceola at the head.

Osceola, silent and dead still upon his mount now, had shot the captain. His rifle still smoked.

She stared at the Indian, and continued to stare as he urged his horse closer and closer to her. She felt Jarrett's hands on her, lifting her.

She didn't even protest when she found that her husband was handing her over to the Indian. She was too shocked, too numb.

But her thoughts were her greatest anguish. Jarrett might have been killed, and it would have been her fault. Once again he had bested her enemy for her. And an army captain now lay dead.

"Take her to Mary, please," Jarrett said.

"Jarrett . . ." she managed to whisper.

"I'll be along. As soon as I've—done something with him."

Osceola's pony began to move. She could smell bear grease, feel the warrior's taut strength. Her teeth were chattering.

"You saved us both," she murmured, looking into his dark eyes. "But you don't speak English, do you? You don't know what I'm saying, but I thank you, even if you have murdered other people horribly . . . oh, God!"

He smiled suddenly, staring down at her. "I understand much," he said, "and then there are those whom I do not wish to know that I understand their language."

"Oh . . ."

What had she said? She'd called him a murderer!

"You are safe from me," he told her.

"Because I am McKenzie's wife?"

"Because you wished to trade your own life for that of the children. *Seminole* children."

"My nieces," she reminded him. "And besides—I never thought that he'd dare kill me!" she admitted huskily. Her throat still hurt. Lots of her still hurt. She was badly bruised, she realized. And her neck seemed to hurt more and more every minute.

He smiled down at her, and she knew that he had killed white men and women, that he had burned plantations.

That he was at war with her kind.

But there was a deep, almost anguished wisdom in his eyes. When he smiled, his face became an intriguing and very likable one.

She was finally losing her mind, she thought. Swamp fever, perhaps.

"You're very brave," he told her. "You're the *White Tigress*. A fitting wife for such a man as McKenzie."

"Thank you," she whispered. She remained in pain. She allowed herself to close her eyes, and she either dozed or passed out because when she opened them again, she had come to the village, and Osceola was letting her down into Mary's arms. James suddenly rode in hard behind Osceola, leapt from his own mount, and came forward to take Tara.

"The children?" she asked, clinging to him.

"They are here, and fine. Hush, let Mother care for you; your throat is nearly purple."

"Jarrett—"

"Jarrett will come soon."

"You don't understand. There's a dead soldier—"

"Jarrett will manage."

Tender, caring hands were upon her. She was sinking down

into the softness of furs. Cool water bathed her forehead, her throat.

She sipped from a bowl, some bitter brew that nearly choked her anew, but Mary made her drink it.

Then blackness descended again, but it was gentle, and good.

Chapter 19

T HE PROBLEM with sleep was that sleep brought dreams.

At first it was night. Darkness and shadows lay all around, and the fog was thick and chill. The black muddy water of the Mississippi surrounded her on a dark New Orleans night. She was running. She could hear the sharp click of her shoes against the street. The sound seemed to echo and to grow, like the sound of her breath, gasping and dragging as she ran. There was a beat to go with it all, and that was the desperate pounding of her heart.

Footsteps followed her. She heard the staccato clack of her own feet. Yet after each footfall came another. And another. And the sounds were coming closer and closer. . . .

Murderess . . . murderess . . . murderess . . .

She was no longer running. The world was dark around her, and she had gone back to the house in Boston. She was standing there, with the gun in her hand, staring at it. . . .

She saw the blood on Julian's shirt. Saw the shock in his face. Saw him fall. Saw the spread of crimson. Saw him die.

And then she looked up. She saw Clive staring at her. She felt the noise, the rustle behind her, and she turned to see the curtain just closing. She looked at Clive again and saw in the eternally pleased gold glitter of his eyes that he had planned the murder, orchestrated every step, and that she was to appear guilty. And then, of course, if she agreed to his lewd proposals—ah, surely much worse ones now!—he would somehow save her from the hangman's noose. He would prove her innocent somehow. But if she defied him, she would hang.

Oh, God! She was there again. She could hear the cries of horror going up in the room. She could see Clive's cold, cruel eyes, the hint of a smile that curved his lip.

His father lay dead in a pool of blood. He would have it all now. Money—and freedom.

But he wouldn't have her! She would hang first; but not if she could escape.

She could see the window, feel the cool breeze touch her fire-heated cheeks. She promised herself that she was quick and young and more agile than any of them, except the other players from the show, of course, and none of them would come for her. Each one of them knew her innocence.

William! her heart cried out. But no one could tie William to this, and William would have Marina by his side. When Tara could, she would write, and let him know that he mustn't grieve, that she was safe.

But to be safe she had to run. Run. . . .

She could feel the ground beneath her feet again. She'd run so very hard.

Ah, but no matter where she went, it seemed that she was running again. The neatly manicured lawns were gone, the New England row houses had disappeared. She was running through streets with wrought-iron gates and fences. She could feel the chill of the Mississippi, the dampness of the night. The very darkness of it surrounded her.

Someone was screaming at her again. *Murderess, murderess, murderess.*

No! No! She wanted to shout out. She wanted to scream with fury that she had been manipulated and used!

Suddenly she could see him.

Someone tall and dark was at the end of the street. Calling to her. Towering there, an ebony silhouette. She strained to see, tried so very hard to pierce the fog and the shadows. She needed to keep running, reach that voice.

Yet it seemed that shadows and fog stretched between them forever. No matter how fast she ran, it seemed he was still so far away . . .

Run . . . run . . . runaway . . .

The fog swirled. The street was encompassed in blackness. She could hear her name being called over and over.

Jarrett!

He was there. Seemingly at the end of an ungodly long trail. He reached out to her. She could see him almost clearly now in form-hugging doeskin breeches, high black boots, snow-white shirt, ebony hair queued at his nape, jet eyes upon her, handsome bronze features tense.

"Tara!"

She could see his large hand, the fingers so long and strong, reaching out. She just needed to touch him. She just needed to come close enough to touch him, and it wouldn't matter who was behind her, the danger of the past would not matter!

"Tara!"

Arms were around her. Strong arms, warm arms. Jarrett was calling out to her. It was a dream.

It was not a dream. She opened her eyes. She lay in their cabin in the village. She was held against his chest, rocked within his arms, as he whispered soothingly to her. She saw his eyes, his hard, handsome, well-beloved face, and she cried out softly, throwing her arms around him.

"Jarrett!"

"You were dreaming."

"Yes."

"A nightmare?"

"I couldn't reach you. You were very far away," she told him. "Oh!" she whispered softly, for her throat remained sore. "Such dreams . . ."

"That bastard all but strangled you to death," Jarrett said heatedly. "Mary gave you one of her special drinks. Warriors have been known to dream of fighting entire battles under the spells of such concoctions!"

She might have smiled, and she would have been deeply glad of the tenderness in his words, except that she had been harshly drawn from the fading images of her dream to the grim reality of their present situation.

"Jarrett, he's dead."

"You can't fault Osceola for that killing, Tara."

"Oh, God! I don't! He saved your life! But they'll be trying to hang one of us for it, Jarrett! His entire company knew that he was with me."

"Hush, Tara."

"But, Jarrett—"

"Tara, I caught up with his company, and a young man named Dicks. I happen to know him rather well, and I told him only that you had escaped with the children and that I had come upon the body of his captain in the woods."

"But won't there be an inquiry? Were you so easily trusted and believed?"

He smiled, and she felt a stirring inside. She loved the way his teeth seemed to flash so whitely against the bronze of his flesh. She loved the naturally sensual curve of his lip, the ebony fire in his eyes.

"His entire company was appalled by his behavior. Don't get me wrong, Tara. A lot of military men—men you might consider decent—wouldn't think much of shooting down Indian women or children. But Dicks and his fellows had had a bellyful of their captain, and they were worried about you. They consider you a valiant and courageous woman, a very great lady. They won't have the least difficulty when they bring in his body, and there won't be an inquiry. There is a war on here," he said a little wearily, a little bitterly, "and the wretched captain will just be another fatality."

"Thank God," she breathed.

He held her for a moment, stroking her hair. She opened her eyes again and found him studying her intently.

"You need to rest again, without battling your nightmare demons," he told her. "We'll stay here tonight and head home in the morning."

"So soon?" she murmured softly.

"Tara, you've slept nearly around the clock. James will not go while you are here, and his people are in danger now."

"Oh!" she said, trying to struggle up. "Then we should leave right away—"

"Tara, we are all set to leave in the morning," he told her firmly. "They will be running often enough in the future," he added. "They are glad of this last night in their home."

He left her, going to the fire, then coming back with a cypress cup of cool water. She tried to drink from it quickly, but he warned her just to sip at it. She did so. She felt him watching her all the while. When he brought her a bowl of some kind of warmed gruel a moment later, she found his eyes on her again.

"Something *koonti?*" she asked.

He shrugged and laughed. "It's a staple."

"So is venison."

He shook his head. "No meat right now. You couldn't swallow it. Come on, eat up!"

"Aren't you joining me?"

He shrugged, returning to the fire and the pot there and dishing himself out a bowl. They ate with wooden spoons, and she found herself surprisingly hungry. Either she was acquiring a taste for the stringy *koonti* root or was just so hungry that she could have eaten dirt.

When they were done, Jarrett took the plates and put them by the low-burning fire. He stretched out behind her on their soft bed of skins and fur, his arm around her waist.

"Jarrett . . ."

"We rise early and ride early," he told her softly.

She lay still for another few minutes, very glad he was beside her, of the warm strength of his body seeming to give strength to her own. Her lashes fluttered. She had just been told she had slept nearly a day, and yet she did remain very tired. But she wasn't quite ready to go to sleep.

"Jarrett, you should really know," she whispered after a moment. "I'm not—a great lady."

He was silent for a moment. She wondered if he had already fallen asleep. But then she felt his arms tightening around her and felt the husky warmth of his whisper against her ear.

"You are to me."

"Oh, Jarrett . . . !" she whispered, turning within his arms.

"Tara, you risked your life for the children. It was incredibly courageous."

"It wasn't so courageous. Anyone who has held little ones like that would try to keep them from a monster!"

"No, Tara, not anyone," he assured her. He eased up and leaned upon an elbow to look down at her. "Once upon a time you were convinced that the Indians here were scarcely a cut above the snakes and alligators."

She flushed. "Jarrett, I'm so sorry! I didn't know any Seminoles—"

"Tara! You owe me no apologies. I can't tell you how grateful I am that you can see my family as *people*. I am incredibly proud of you, and you are quite mistaken if you think that anything about your own birth or family could mean anything bad to me. You are, as I said, a great lady. My lady!" he added gently, tenderly, his palm cupping her chin, fingers stroking her cheek.

She cried out softly, catching his hand, placing her lips against his palm. She eased down again to lie at his side, and he came back against her, holding her close once again.

He meant her to rest. It still terrified Jarrett to realize just how close to death she had come. Tara couldn't see them, but the bruises from the captain's hands remained blue about her neck. Each time he saw them, he felt raw rage build within him anew. Yet she had tried to stop him from killing the man.

Shaking anew as he held his wife, Jarrett was glad that Osceola had done the deed.

He wanted her to rest, to lie still, to do nothing more strenuous than heal.

But tonight, though they lay still for some time, she knew that he wasn't sleeping, and as the fire burned lower and lower, she turned against him again. Her fingers played against the buttons on his shirt, slid within it, stroking him, slowly, sensually.

"Tara," he protested. "You need rest."

"I need you," she told him. She rose against the glow of the fire and shed her clothing as she stared into the low, whispering flames. The shadowed glow of the fire bathed her from head to toe, emphasized the beauty of the fall of her hair, the sweet perfection of her high, rounded breasts, her long, graceful limbs. She turned from the fire, and it seemed there was a glaze of tears in her eyes, but he saw it only briefly, for she was quickly down on her knees by his side, draping the velvet fall of her golden hair around him as she leaned down to capture his lips in a kiss, to cover the hardness in his breeches with the cup of her hand.

Then her lips were on his throat, on his bare chest where she had loosened his shirt, and for a few moments the blood rushed wildly in his head and the pure physical pleasure of her touch banished thoughts and sense. But even as his hunger flamed, he managed to reach out for her, pulling her beneath him, pinning her so that she didn't stroke or tease him to madness. He stared into her eyes again, holding her still.

"What's wrong?" he demanded.

She shook her head defiantly. "Don't you want me?" she whispered.

"Hell, yes, but . . . damn, Tara, not when you're in tears over it!"

"I'm not in tears."

"You're eyes are damp."

She tried to twist from him. "If you don't . . ."

"But I do! I just want to know what's going on in that head of yours!"

"Would that it were my head!" she whispered.

He pulled her around, straddling her. "What?"

She struggled against his hold and then cried out softly. "You dolt! It's just that I—I love you! I love you very much, and I'm still sometimes very scared because I do!"

The words were so startling and so incredibly sweet. He let them wash over him for a moment; he savored them, cherished them. Then he realized that he had cherished them just a bit too long, that she was alarmed by his response, that she was struggling against him once again and would be doing so in earnest any second.

She loved him. It seemed a miracle he had dared not hope for, a craving he had harbored but dared not see, since he had touched her that very first night. He had needed so badly to be healed, yet he had thought himself the confident one rescuing her.

He had been wrong. She had rescued him.

"I shouldn't have said anything!" she cried, and indeed, she was trying to twist away from him. Strenuously so. "Jarrett Mc-Kenzie, if you've nothing to say, I beg that you let me go."

Let her go? Never. Not in this lifetime.

He held her hands firm, leaned close to her. "I've plenty to say!" he told her.

She lay dead still then, staring at him. Her eyes seemed cobalt. Her hair, in the firelight, was spun gold. She trembled slightly, but her chin was high again, and she was wary.

His runaway.

"What?" she whispered.

"Dolt!" he said.

"What?"

"You just called me a dolt!"

"I what?—oh, McKenzie, I knew I was a fool, I knew that you—" she began, but broke off awkwardly.

"That I what?" he demanded, smiling.

The fire went out of her for a moment. She was very still.

"I know that you are still in love with Lisa," she said very softly. "I should be grateful for that fact. Had you not felt such grief for her, you might have wanted to marry again for all the right reasons, and you might not have been willing to take on an unknown, runaway bride. Indeed, the fact that you loved her, love her still, is probably the only reason you were willing to marry me."

"Wait, Tara, just a moment!" he challenged her, and he eased his hold from her wrists to touch and stroke her cheek with his palm, softly, tenderly. "I did love Lisa, and I beg you to understand—there is a part of my heart that will love her always. But I was enmeshed in self-pity, and you brought me from that. And marrying you had nothing to do with my feelings for anyone else —dead or alive."

"Robert forced you into it!" she whispered.

"No man on earth forces me into anything. Or woman, for that matter. I married you because I wanted you above reason or sanity, I wanted you from the moment you walked into that tavern. I wanted you for the way that you walked and moved, then I wanted to touch your hair, see your eyes. I had never hungered so for anyone in all of my life, and now, I'm aware that I've never loved anyone with such a passion as I have for you, Tara. Even Lisa. It was a different love. Good, gentle, sweet. And that part of me will always love her, but even that pales beside the emotion that entangles my heart with you."

She stared at him, wide, unblinking eyes fringed by rich dark lashes. She seemed so still. She scarcely breathed.

"Did I say enough?" he asked softly after a moment.

He must have, for she suddenly cried out and threw her arms around him. Her lips were sweet fire against his, her breasts pure seduction as they crushed against the wall of his chest. He swiftly forgot that he had worried about her well-being, for she was like a wildcat in the cypress forest, vibrant, vital, graceful, hungry. She was a tempest of seduction against him, lips against his bare flesh, touching him, holding him, making her cry out in the shadows and glow. He was amazed at how quickly she swept him into a violent climax, then he determined that she, also, would find so merciless a lover. Soon, in the gold and shadows, she was crying out, too, and he was deeply glad of the shattering pleasure they both found; yet, that night, the words she whispered as she drifted down were far more dear.

"I love you, Jarrett. Oh, dear God, but I love you so much!"

"I love you!" he responded fiercely.

"Love—"

"You . . ."

And their words blended together as their lips did once again.

The embers of the fire burned very low, and in one another's arms, they slept.

It was difficult for Tara to say good-bye to her new family again in the morning—she would be riding back to Cimarron.

Naomi, Mary, James, the girls, and their tribe would be riding into an unknown future, fraught with danger and uncertainty.

Naomi was strong, Mary was stoic, the little girls wouldn't let themselves cry, and Tara watched them start out with their horses, sheep, cattle, and belongings tied to the travois without losing her encouraging smile either. Yet James, atop a long-maned pony, came back to them as the exodus of his people began, stretching out a hand to his brother first. The two sat still atop their mounts, gripping each other hard for several moments.

"You'll always be able to find me," James told Jarrett.

"And I will always be there for you," Jarrett swore.

James nodded, smiling. He released Jarrett's hand, and came around to where Tara sat atop her horse. He grinned at Jarrett, then reached up and plucked her down, kissed her on both cheeks, and hugged her hard.

"We are eternally in your debt, sister!" he whispered to her.

"James! I did nothing—"

He leaned back, holding her shoulders, meeting her eyes. "We love you, little sister. *White Tigress.*"

She flushed. "So Osceola has given me a name!"

James grinned. He hugged her to him again, whispering—ignoring Jarrett's scowls. "Just know, as wretched as this war might be, we do not forget our debts, nor do we hesitate in our love for our friends and family. If you ever, *ever* need us, we will be there!"

"I love you and your family, too, you know!" she told him. He grinned, caught her by the waist, and hefted her back up to her mount. He leapt up in a flash on his own horse, whirled it to wave at them once again, and was off, racing around his people to take the lead on their journey deeper into the wilderness.

The camp was empty. The fires within it were all dead. Tara didn't want to see it this way. She turned her own horse quickly and Jarrett followed.

She felt like crying, and he rode silently behind her. He nudged his horse and came up by her side, reached out for her hand and squeezed it. "We will all survive this!" he promised her.

She shook her head. "It could last forever."

"However long. We will survive it."

She smiled, glad of his rock-hard determination and faith. But it was still going to be a hard road to tread. She had encountered both sides, and she knew that the whites were often fighting from fear and that the Seminoles were doing the same. The whites were hungry for land and progress; the Indians were just desperate for homes and survival.

"Tara," Jarrett said after a moment, "terrible things are still going on, you know. I own land in the south—swampland, some say, but along the Miami River. It's never been highly populated down there, but there are some folks settled along the river. Most of them have deserted their homes. The lighthouse on Key Biscayne was attacked and burned to the ground. A negro helper was killed; the lighthouse keeper was left for dead, yet somehow he survived. It was a vicious attack."

Tara looked down at her hands and nodded. "I know that there is a war on!" she said.

"Perhaps you should go north. . . ." he began.

"No!"

He inhaled sharply. "Tara, there may be times when I have to leave again. You were right; I managed to settle nothing with Osceola this time. Yet the effort was there. And when I can do something, I will have to leave you again."

She didn't look at him. "I hate it!" she exclaimed after a minute.

"I know. So do I."

She rode in silence.

"Tara, I can take you to Atlanta—"

"No!"

"Charleston—"

"No!"

"Boston, perhaps—"

"Dear God, no!" she said with a fierce shudder.

He arched a brow at her.

"I take it you've been to Boston?" he inquired dryly.

"Jarrett, I promise, I will handle myself much better. I will not like it if they call you away, but I will not fight you on it again. Please, I don't want to go anywhere else!"

He smiled. "Thank God! I couldn't stand sending you anywhere else!"

"Then—"

"I just wanted you to promise to be on good behavior," he told her with a grin.

She lifted her chin. "You had best be glad I haven't a flower vase around!" she warned. "I should crack it right over your head!"

"Would you, then?" He laughed.

"Indeed."

"Ah, but then I'd have to do something back, wouldn't you think?"

"You'd not have the chance."

"Ah, but I'm quick as lightning when I choose!"

"And I can be faster than a sunray, McKenzie, when the occasion demands!"

He laughed. "Let's see, shall we?"

His ebony eyes were blazing. Tara realized that she had challenged him to a race along the cypress trail. She inhaled sharply, then flicked her reins over her mare's neck at the same time she clicked her heels against the horse's haunches.

The mare took off.

Charlemagne was in hot pursuit.

She raced down the trail. The leaves fell around her head and neck, the shadows closed around her, the sunlight dappled through. She burst into a clearing of thick, rich grass, and there Jarrett caught up with her, sweeping her from her own horse, leaping down from Charlemagne so that she and Jarrett rolled and rolled in the grass.

She found herself laughing, then tasting his kiss, then meeting his dark eyes, then feeling the wondrous burst of emotion within herself once again.

She trembled.

She had never known that life could be this good, this sweet. She loved him so much.

And he loved her!

The happiness was so dear that it was almost agony.

She gasped in a breath, still afraid to let him know just how desperately she loved and needed him. "Wretch!" she cried out to him.

"Umm," he teased. "An absolute savage!"

His lips found hers. They made love in the grass, and they laughed again as they both itched and scratched from the grass irritation for the rest of the ride.

Then Cimarron rose before them again.

She was home, Tara thought. Oh, God, really truly home!

Yet once again, she had barely reached out for her happiness before it was to be cruelly snatched away.

For even as they approached the estate, a ship was also coming down the river.

Destiny was almost upon her.

Chapter 20

I<small>T WAS</small> good to come home, better than ever. Peter was ready to take their horses, Jeeves was quick to tell her that her bath was waiting. There were fresh flowers on the side table in the breezeway, the afternoon was beautiful with a clear blue sky and strong sun that came sweeping through the windows.

Upstairs, she quickly shed her bedraggled clothing, glad to step into the water. She was fully immersed when Cota knocked on her door, announced who it was, and at Tara's bidding, came on in to tell her excitedly that she had finished a number of their sewing projects while Tara had been gone, and that the dresses Tara had designed and cut had come out beautifully.

Tara thanked her, smiling as she sank back into the tub. Dear God, she did love this place so much! Just as she loved Jarrett. And she loved the sun, and the warm waters, the cabbage palms and cypress trees, and the flowers that bloomed forever. She loved her Indian relations—and at the moment she was so sweetly content that she could be convinced that she loved the snakes and alligators in the swamps and marshes as well!

Cota showed Tara where her clothing was neatly stacked into

her trunk at the foot of the bed, or hung in the wardrobe. Again, Tara smiled lazily, realizing that her possessions were slowly encroaching upon her husband's domain. It was a room they shared.

Cota, near the window to the sloping back lawn, paused suddenly, frowning.

"What is it?" Tara asked her.

"Another ship," Cota said with a shrug.

Tara closed her eyes, stricken with pain. *They had just returned!* What could Tyler Argosy want with Jarrett now?

Perhaps just a report on what had happened with Osceola, she thought. She could not believe that he would want Jarrett to be riding out again!

She reached for the large linen towel that lay over the edge of the tub, rising and wrapping it around her. She stepped from the tub and came to stand beside Cota at the window.

The ship had docked, and it was indeed one of the military vessels from Tampa. Tara watched as the plank was secured against the dock. Tyler Argosy was first to walk off.

Tara didn't realize that she had ceased breathing until instinct caused her to inhale on a ragged gasp.

No! He couldn't have come here, oh, God, no, he couldn't have come here, followed her.

But he had.

What a fool she had been to think that she might be safe! All because she hadn't seen Clive in New Orleans. That hadn't meant that he hadn't been there. He must have been. He must have followed her himself.

And when he had discovered her gone he had tracked her. It probably hadn't even been that hard for him to do. Indeed, it had taken him longer than she might have imagined.

But he would have been careful. He would have found out about Jarrett McKenzie. He would have made certain that he knew what he was dealing with, and he would have discovered that Jarrett was powerful and wealthy.

He would have waited until he could come with all the right weapons to use against them both.

And he was here now.

Clive Carter, tall, elegantly blond, clad in a crimson frock coat, always the perfect-looking gentleman, walked behind Tyler. His much-shorter henchmen, the pockmarked Jenson Jones, was at his side.

Of course he had come with Jenson! she thought. Clive had never been a fool. He had come south, to the home of a southern gentleman, to try to drag her back to justice. He would have to have his witness, a magistrate from the Commonwealth of Massachusetts, to drag her back with him.

To make her beg for his mercy, accept his demands.

Or meet with the hangman.

Her fingers trembled—the whole of her body was shaken like a palm beneath the wind. But he wouldn't touch her now. Ever. Not since she had known Jarrett, loved Jarrett. She would cast herself into a river or ocean to avoid him, she would gladly die.

Except that she didn't want to die. She wanted to live. And wanted to believe that somehow she could cling to the love that she had found, find it shimmering again somewhere in the days to come.

They were coming to the lawn. Rutger had already greeted them. Jarrett, who had been with Jeeves since they had come back, was walking across the lawn. Tara briefly compared the two men. Clive, born and bred to Boston society. Vain, determined. The greediest wretch she had met in the whole of her life, yet he was artful and talented, oh, yes, he was talented, much more so than many a man with whom she had shared a stage. He was a good-looking man, a wealthy man, and yet, even if she hadn't despised him with all of her heart, he would have come up short beside Jarrett. Her husband remained dressed in nothing but his white shirt, skin breeches, high simple black waistcoat. Clive, with all the color in his dress, the brocade of his waistcoat, the velvet of the frock coat above it, seemed like a peacock next to an eagle. Even as Tara knew that she dared not stand there any longer, she felt the sudden flip of her heart as she thought of how very much she loved Jarrett, of how strong and wonderful he seemed out on the lawn, ebony hair queued back, skin so bronze he might have had Indian blood himself, straight as an oak, standing his ground, master of his world.

She dared stay no longer. She turned around, heedless of Cota, and threw open her trunk, where her newly fashioned clothing awaited. A dusty-rose riding habit lay within the finished pieces and she dragged it out, grabbing only pantalettes and stockings and a soft chemise to wear beneath the coarser, warmer top fabric. She was growing so nervous now that she was all but willing to race out of the house naked, but the long spell of running she had already done had taught her that nights could grow cold and damp, and that she desperately needed something warm.

Cota stared at her, baffled, as she stumbled into her clothing. Tara came to the pretty Italian girl and set her hands on her shoulders. "Cota, I need help badly. Please, go to Peter, tell him I need a horse, a fresh horse, and that he mustn't let anyone know, not anyone at all. Neither you nor he can even go near Master Jarrett now, else I might be in serious jeopardy. Please . . ."

"Signora McKenzie! I will help you, *sì*. But—"

"I can't explain, Cota, I haven't time. There's a man who has come on that ship who wants to see me taken away. For something I didn't do, I swear it. Whatever you hear, Cota, please believe that I was innocent. But I don't dare take more time now. Go to Peter. Please tell him to have a horse for me where the lawn meets the cypress forest. Go now, I beg you!"

Cota's eyes were filled with distress. She looked as if she would like to protest anew.

"Go!" Tara begged again.

Miserably, Cota shook her head. Tara gave her a little shove, and the girl then seemed to whir into action, all but flying out of the room. Tara dared not think anymore herself; she dragged on a pair of boots and sped out of the room, pausing to make sure that their demon visitor had not yet come to the house. She could hear no voices, and so she sped down the stairs and out the front door of the house.

She was certain, as she closed it, that she had done so just as the men had entered the house by the rear breezeway door.

It didn't matter. She was out; she had made it. She paused for a moment, dragging in a deep and ragged breath. Oh, God, it had never hurt like this before! What if Jarrett believed the awful things that Clive would say, what if he believed that she had conspired to kill a man, that she had pulled the trigger, that she had committed murder?

She didn't dare think! She only dared dream.

And believe they had to have a future!

But not if she stayed. Clive had come with the military; with the law. Jarrett, for all his strength, would have his hands tied.

She had to run. Faster than she had ever run before. Harder. Perhaps she could make it.

After all, she was good at it. Even Jarrett had called her a runaway.

Jarrett was doing his very best to comprehend what was going on, even as his head seemed to spin with the ramifications of everything that Tyler was trying to say to him.

The bastard had come for Tara. That was easy enough to grasp.

The squat, ugly fellow with the sallow complexion, small dark eyes, and pockmarked face who had come with him carried a warrant for Tara's arrest.

For the murder of an ex-senator of the United States.

He knew, from the moment that Tyler approached him with the men, that he would never hand his wife over to the bastards. Never. He didn't know quite what he was going to do, or how the hell he was going to fight, but they would never leave here with Tara.

It seemed best to gain all the information he could. Knowledge would be his best weapon. But it was damned hard. He wanted to throttle the men.

And his heart ached with anguish. Why hadn't she ever come out and told him the truth about herself? Why in God's name had she left him vulnerable to this shock, desperate for any weapons in her defense?

Jarrett had listened to the men briefly by the docks, held his temper, and determined that he had to bring them back to the house.

On a pretense of telling Jeeves he wanted drinks, he slipped past the men into the breezeway, shouting for his servant, then hurrying into the library to speak with him before Tyler and his company could follow.

Of course Tyler would know that he was up to something— Tyler knew damned well that they could get their own drinks in the library. But Tyler didn't open his mouth, and Jarrett was grateful, knowing full well that Tyler was trying to stand fast beside him, as fast as any friend could.

And he was also certain that Tyler believed in Tara. Tyler knew her. The honesty of her gaze, the innate goodness of her heart. Her willingness to fight against the wrongs of the world.

"Jeeves!"

Jeeves had been watching the arrival of the ship and the men, Jarrett realized quickly, and it seemed that he had been waiting for some word.

Jarrett didn't wait for his trusted right-hand man to speak; he set his hands on the black man's shoulders and warned him quickly, "Find Tara. Get her out of here. Into the woods, somewhere, anywhere. Send Peter with her. He knows his way through the hammocks and the marshes."

Jeeves nodded and slipped out of the room just as Tyler and the two men from Boston came into it. The first was Clive Carter, son of the late politician Julian Carter, and the second ugly little man was Jenson Jones, the lawman armed with the legal slip of paper that had brought Tyler and the government here with him.

"Sit down, gentlemen," Jarrett said, indicating the deep leather sofa and chairs. "What is your preference? Whiskey?"

"A double for me, Jarrett," Tyler said.

"Whiskey will be fine," Clive Carter said, and it seemed that he spoke for his ugly little henchman too. Jarrett poured the drinks, studying Carter. He was a tall man, in fit enough condition. He had fine—almost too-fine—features and a full head of rich blond hair. He would be an attractive man to many a well-bred young lady, and probably to her parents as well, for Julian Carter had been a well-known and respected man. Jarrett had never been particularly interested in national politics, but naturally, especially with so many acts of Congress influencing his homeland, he had kept up with happenings in Washington, and had even corresponded at times with his old friend Andrew Jackson. He knew of the Carters. Julian Carter had been well liked in political circles, a man respected for his integrity by friend and foe alike. The Carter family, however, had gained its wealth at least a century ago. From what Jarrett had understood, though it had never been an open connection, a great deal of their money had been made in the slave trade. Everything Jarrett had heard had been rumor, and he was well aware that rumors could be false. But though Julian Carter had been well liked, there had also been a great deal of speculation about him, both whispered speculation in handsome drawing rooms, and open speculation in the newspapers. There had never been anything direct, of course, to tie the Carters with such a business. They would have been very careful. Even in the South, where slaves were the anchor of the economy, actually dealing in the trade with Africa had always been considered less than a genteel occupation. Jarrett imagined that in Boston, where the abolitionist movement was beginning to swell, a secret dabbling in the African market would be even more of a skeleton in the family closet.

None of which mattered now. This man's connection to his wife did.

Jarrett sipped his own drink slowly, one elbow upon the mantel as he stared at Clive Carter. Well, Jarrett taunted himself, he had wanted answers. He was getting them now, in the form of this man. Carter was why Tara had been running. She had been terrified of him—and she had despised him. She had been willing to do anything at all to escape Carter.

Work in a tavern—marry a stranger.

"All right, gentlemen," Jarrett said smoothly. "I'd like to go back to the beginning of this and try to understand. Mr. Carter, you're trying to tell me that Mr. Jones here is carrying an arrest warrant for my wife—and that she is accused of killing your father."

"Indeed, sir, I'm afraid that is the simple truth of it," Carter said. He flashed an unhappy grimace. There was something oily about it. Jarrett felt canine, the hackles at the back of his neck rising.

"How do you know my wife, sir?"

Carter shrugged, and sighed as if with deep sorrow. "Again, I offer my apologies for this intrusion, sir, as it seems you are completely in the dark as to Tara's past. I have been following Tara for a long time now. I nearly found her in New Orleans. It was from there that I traced her here to you."

Jarrett kept his eyes upon the man. "Enlighten me, then."

"Miss Brent was a playactress my father took beneath his wing. She was performing a comedy of errors with a troupe in my father's house, a play written by another young man my father was eager to sponsor—Tara's brother. Well, sir, my father was repaid with a bullet in his chest."

"I am still at a loss as to why you think Tara might have fired this shot."

"She was unhappy with my father, and thought that he planned to manipulate her life, when he was only trying to see to her welfare and to her future."

Jarrett lifted his hands again, shaking his head. "Why do you believe it was Tara who killed him?"

"She shot him in front of an entire audience, sir. She saw him die—we all saw the blood burst out over his shirt—and then he died. If you do not believe me, sir, there was an audience made up of many members of the finest society in all of Boston."

"I'd not have the warrant if it weren't true, sir," Jensen Jones supplied with a white-toothed grin. It was quite slimy as well, Jarrett determined.

But it couldn't be true. Tara had never actually denied that she had been accused of such a crime—she had denied being guilty of it.

And if she claimed so, it was so.

Yet how to prove it?

He stood very still against the mantel. It did seem that these men had an ironclad case. Tara had been seen, in the middle of a play, shooting Julian Carter. Carter was dead. These men had the warrant for Tara.

She would be running all of her life. Carter would never relent.

"Jarrett," Tyler said softly, miserably, "as far as I can see, Tara will have to stand trial."

"My father was a very influential man—" Carter began imperiously.

"Ah, yes!" Jarrett interrupted. "I met your father once—in President Andy Jackson's company!" he said with a smooth, dry smile. There was no need to mention that at the moment he and Ole Hickory were at grave odds over the Indian question. Since Carter wanted to throw names around, Jarrett simply felt that he needed to throw out a few of his own.

"Sir, I have witnesses! The President cannot intervene."

"I hadn't meant that he should. But if my wife were to go to Boston to stand trial, sir, I would demand time to prepare her defense—to interview these witnesses of yours."

Clive Carter narrowed his eyes. They had a cruel gold gleam

to them. Jarrett had the feeling that Julian hadn't been the one trying to manipulate Tara's life—it had been Clive himself. "You must do what you consider right, McKenzie. But perhaps I should inform you of something else as well."

"That is?"

"Your 'wife' is guilty of bigamy as well. Tara was married to me the Saturday before my father's death in a very private ceremony."

"What?" The breath had gone out of him. He didn't believe it. Couldn't believe it. Not for a second.

Carter cleared his throat, suddenly rising. He reached to Jenson Jones and Jones stood as well and fumbled in his waistcoat pocket, then produced a document. He handed it to Jarrett.

It looked like a legitimate wedding certificate. But it wasn't. Somehow Jarrett was sure of that.

"I don't particularly wish to see Tara hang, either, McKenzie," Carter said. "She killed my father, but I am still willing to fight for her defense myself. I'd not even charge her with the bigamy, and of course, I'd pray that you would be gentleman enough to let her false wedding to you go unmentioned in any proceedings against her. You see, I know the best lawyers in Boston, Mr. McKenzie. If any man can find a way to see her freed, it is me. All that I have to do is find her and bring her home."

"You say that she was your wife?" Jarrett queried.

"Sir, the marriage certificate rests in your hands."

"But I protest. Tara did not marry you. Do you say you lived together as man and wife?"

"Indeed, though it was in secret. You see, my father wanted the marriage, he was deeply fond of her and wished that she might be taken care of all of her life. What better way than to make her a daughter through a son?"

"Ah, and she was thrilled with the prospect?"

"Few women would not be."

"But she was so pleased—that she shot your father?"

"He had demanded that she quit acting—it was no longer a

proper profession for her. She was always quite certain that she could charm, manipulate, seduce me—and to my everlasting sorrow it was, at the time, true. I love her still, of course. And so my determination to do all that I can for her."

Jarrett looked at Tyler, shaking his head as he held the piece of paper, silently damning the wife he had come so desperately to adore. If she had only told him what had happened! If she had given him time, something to work with!

"That is impossible," Jarrett insisted. "Unless you are impotent," he added blandly. He was glad to see Carter's face go white, his veins protrude with fury. Jarrett smiled and continued. "My wife, gentlemen—how shall I say this delicately?—was completely innocent upon the night of our marriage."

Carter controlled his temper rather well, though the anger he tried to mask with his even tone was betrayed by trembling.

"Alas, Mr. McKenzie! You must remember—my wife is an actress. She can *feign* any accent, mimic any behavior. And I'm sure that if she feared for her life should she fail you, she could, I shall say *most delicately*—feign innocence as well!"

Jarrett fought hard to control his own temper. "Ah, but, sir! There are only so many things a woman could possibly feign unless she were wed to a total idiot—which I assure you, I am not. Would you call me so?"

Tyler made a slight snickering sound—or maybe it was a warning. Clive Carter glared furiously at them both.

"Are you calling me a liar, then?" he demanded.

Jarrett lifted his hands in the air. "Mr. Carter, I am loath to call any son of your father a liar. I don't know what to say. Perhaps you are suffering from some delusion."

"The delusion, McKenzie, is yours!" Carter roared, stepping forward. "And I demand my legal rights! Get Tara down here, now. One way or the other, sir, she is going to stand trial for the murder of my father!"

Tyler cleared his throat. "Jones has a warrant, Jarrett," he said unhappily.

"Alas, my wife is not here."

"It's a lie!" Carter raged.

Jarrett stared at him, arching a brow. "Apparently this fine Bostonian gentleman is not well versed in the proper behavior of a guest in a southern household."

"Don't you double-talk me, McKenzie. You tricked my men in New Orleans—"

"Where was your warrant then, Mr. Carter?"

"I had to find her to see that it was served!" Carter snapped.

"Perhaps you had no warrant at that time. Perhaps you still believed that you could kidnap her, drag her back—and then threaten her with the hangman."

"How dare you—" Carter began, approaching Jarrett.

It was exactly what he had wanted. In fact, he was dying just for the opportunity to flatten Carter's nose against his face.

"Gentlemen! This is no way to solve things!" Tyler Argosy intervened, stepping between the two men.

"I want my wife!" Carter roared to Tyler. "And if you don't manage to see to it, *Captain* Argosy, I'll see to it that you're stripped of rank and demoted to digging latrines for the rest of your natural life!"

One of Tyler's golden brows shot up. "You do whatever you feel you must, Mr. Carter. Mr. McKenzie says that his wife is not here. His word is good enough for me."

"It isn't for me!" Carter snapped. "Where the damn hell is she?"

"On a religious retreat," Jarrett said blandly.

"What?" Carter snapped.

"She's in the swamp somewhere, Carter," Jarrett told him. He smiled. "With the Indians. There's a war on here, you know. Tell him, Tyler, if he hasn't managed to grasp the fact. The Seminoles are hard on the warpath, anxious to kill, maim, mutilate—scalp. She's out among them."

"Don't you try to dissuade me, McKenzie," Carter warned him. "I'll have you hanged for being an accessory."

Jarrett arched a brow. "He's pushing it, isn't he, Tyler?" he inquired. He lifted his hands. "After all, I haven't even been in Boston in over a year."

Carter started to lunge for him again. Tyler was going to let him do it.

Jenson Jones caught him by the coattails. "Mr. Carter, this doesn't solve anything!"

But Carter waved a fist beneath Jarrett's nose anyway. "I don't give a damn about your idiot Indians. I'm going after her, and these army boys will take care of your Seminoles. And I warn you, McKenzie, I will find her, and when I do, I'll come back and prosecute *you* to the full extent of the law." He swung around to stare at Tyler. "I want the house searched!"

"I'm telling you—" Tyler began.

"Search the house!" Jarrett said softly. "I promise you, Carter, she's not here. You'll never find her."

"Have the place searched from attic to cellar!" Carter demanded. He turned around, slamming out of the room, Jenson Jones at his heels.

Jarrett shrugged at Tyler. "There is no cellar, you know that, of course."

Tyler offered him a weak smile. "Jarrett, sweet Jesus, this is bad! He has a warrant. I was commanded to come here, he has legal papers!"

Jarrett sighed. "The warrant may be real. The marriage certificate isn't. Did you see the signatures on it?"

"Jenson performed the ceremony," Tyler said with a nod, "as magistrate."

"Supposedly Jenson performed the marriage—and Julian Carter and some woman named Sara Teasedale stood as witnesses. Well, Julian is dead. And I'll warrant there's some story behind Sara Teasedale as well."

"The marriage certificate is a fake—the arrest warrant isn't," Tyler said.

"She didn't do it," Jarrett said flatly.

"Jarrett, for the love of God! I want to believe that as well, but apparently there were witnesses when Julian Carter was shot and killed."

"She didn't do it."

"Well, Carter is demanding that I take him into the interior until we find her."

Jarrett was silent.

"That's where she's gone, isn't it?" Tyler asked quietly.

Jarrett didn't get a chance to answer. Jeeves had come to the door. Jarrett swung around and stared at him expectantly.

Jeeves arched a brow toward Tyler. Jarrett shrugged.

"Sir, she was gone."

"What?" Jarrett said.

"I didn't have to tell Mrs. McKenzie that she needed to get out. She was already gone."

Jarrett lowered his head. Damn. Sweet Mary, he'd wanted her gone, but he'd needed to know how to find her as well! Carter was ruthless in his determination to come after her. Jarrett had to reach her first!

"Jarrett," Tyler said firmly, "you know that I'm going to have to bring Tara in. There's no way around it. What you need to be doing is finding a lawyer, the best damn attorney in America. And maybe you should find someone from the Massachusetts Commonwealth."

"I'll find her an attorney, Tyler. When the time comes."

"Jarrett—"

"Right now, Tyler," he said grimly, himself turning and heading for the door, "I've got to find my wife—before you do." He started out the door and turned back once again. "*My wife*, Tyler. Mine. I promise you, Tara was never married to that pompous ass. And somehow I'll damn well prove it!"

Chapter 21

PETER CAME with her to the deserted Seminole village where James had once lived with his family.

Where Jarrett's cabin still remained.

"I'll keep watch tonight," Peter told her.

She smiled. She wanted to tell him to go back, that she would be all right, that she wouldn't be afraid where she was, but Peter had his pride, and he was determined to look after her.

She had planned to come alone. Peter had stubbornly set out with her, and she realized that he was probably much more comfortable with the terrain than she was, and besides, she hadn't had time to fight him, not then. Now, she wondered if she shouldn't still be running. How had Jarrett felt when he discovered Clive Carter on his doorstep—with an arrest warrant for his wife?

She didn't want to think about it. She didn't want to wonder if Jarrett did or didn't believe in her. It was night, and she was so exhausted, she couldn't even seem to light a fire in the cabin.

Peter appeared in the doorway she had left open, ready to help her. She let him make the fire, and she thanked him when he left her. She sat and stared at the blaze. James and his people were barely gone, yet the place seemed so cold, so lonely, filled only with the ghost echoes of the laughter and the dreams that had been here before.

Her stomach growled. She realized that she was hungry, and that this was a very different way to run. Always before, she had depended on the rush and bustle of cities themselves to save her. She'd worked; she'd spent her income wisely, and she'd never had to steal anything. Even when danger had threatened, she'd always survived.

Until Jarrett. She wouldn't have survived that night in New Orleans. Not without him.

Dear God, but this was so different! There wasn't a bite left to eat around the place; the Seminoles had known that they would need all their food to survive as they trekked south into the swampland. It didn't matter. She suddenly felt that she might get sick if she tried to eat anyway.

But just as she was thinking that, Peter tapped on her open doorway again. She turned and smiled at him in the darkness. He came in, smiling very proudly, lifting what appeared to be a ball of fur. "Rabbit—for you," he said very proudly.

"How wonderful, thank you very much!" she told him. But she felt ill again. The creature's brown eyes were staring at her now. She knew what a great effort Peter was putting into trying to help her, but she didn't think that she could skin and cook the damned thing.

She started to rise, then sank back down, dizzy as well. She was so tired! She had done so much riding today.

She had felt so much fear.

And pain.

"I'll fix the rabbit," Peter said, and left her.

"Thank you!" she called softly after him. She managed to stand and make her way to the pallet with its soft furs, all left behind, and lie down. She lay watching the fire, feeling numb. Would he believe in her?

Would he—could he—still love her?

She closed her eyes. She might have drifted off. When she opened them, it seemed that the fire had burned down. She became aware of a rustling that seemed to come from just beyond the cabin and she sat up in alarm.

Peter?

But it seemed that someone was moving almost silently, furtively.

She started to mouth the boy's name, then caught her breath. Someone was moving just beyond the door frame.

She stood quickly, her heart slamming against her chest, looking for something with which to defend herself. There was a large earthenware bowl near the fire. She snatched it up and eased herself around the cabin, trying to reach the wall by the doorway and to flatten herself against it.

She managed to get where she wanted to be. She went flush against the wall and stood very still, barely breathing. She prayed that her heartbeat could not be as loud to others as it was to her.

Someone was there. Not moving. Perhaps not breathing either. But someone was definitely there. She almost knew where he stood in the night. She could sense the breathing. She could feel the danger as it seemed to snake along her spine.

There! A shadow! Darkness against the dark, yet she saw him. Against the fireglow the shadow moved into the cabin. Paralyzed, Tara still waited. She closed her eyes, swallowed, opened her eyes. Waited.

Then suddenly, he moved. The shadow was within the cabin. She saw a dark-clad arm—a gun extended from it. The towering dark shadow was halfway into the cabin and she could wait no longer. She shrieked out, attacking with the bowl, crashing it down upon the shadow's ink-dark head. He started to fall.

She started to run.

But hands reached out for her ankles, grabbing. She came crashing down.

"Tara!" She heard her name in a growl, but terror had set in so deeply that she barely comprehended it. She thrashed and struggled.

And all to no avail. Merciless, the hands stayed upon her. Inch by inch she was pulled back into the cabin.

She tried to roll, tried to fight, to swing, to slap, to scratch, to kick.

"Tara!"

Hands fell on her shoulders. She blinked, looking up into the black eyes of the man straddling her, trying to save his face from the wicked flailing of her nails.

"Tara, it's me!"

"Oh, Jarrett! Oh, God, Jarrett!" She flung her arms out to him. She started to feel the stinging damp burn of tears behind her lashes.

He tried to disentangle himself.

"Jarrett, I'm sorry. I'm so damned sorry. I never should have married you. I should have known that he'd never give up, that he'd be too stupid to realize that he shouldn't follow me here!"

"Tara, stop it," he said harshly.

She fell silent, swallowing, closing her eyes, going dead still once again, and offering him no resistance. "Are they with you?" she whispered. "Have they come to bring me in?"

He shook his head, rising, reaching down a hand to pull her up to her feet. He rubbed his head, staring at her.

"Damn," he murmured.

"You scared me to death!" she whispered. Then alarm touched her again. "Peter was watching!" she said.

He shook his head. "Peter was nowhere around when I came. I thought it was you in the cabin, but Carter is on his way out here. I had to make sure."

She stepped past him, stiff with the sudden pain that seized her. He must hate her now. He had to.

"Something must be wrong! Peter would never just leave me."

"I'll find Peter. He must have had some reason for leaving you. But I have to deal with you first."

She felt as if an icy frost were descending upon her. "Perhaps I should just—go with Clive!" she said miserably.

"I beg your pardon!"

She spun back to face him. "Jarrett, I never meant to bring any of this down on you."

"Tara, you'll go back with him over my dead body. But there's one thing I want from you, and so help me God, I want it now."

"And that is—?" she whispered.

"An explanation."

She bit into her lower lip and nodded. She turned away from him again, pacing into the cabin. "It's funny," she murmured, "I sometimes think about that night when Tyler came to dinner with sergeants Culpeper and Rice and everyone had an idea of where I might come from!"

"Boston? And I'd thought it was a southern accent!" Jarrett mused harshly behind her.

She didn't look at him. She walked back to the fire, sat before it, and stared into the blaze. "Not Boston. I was born in Dublin."

"The song!"

"What?" she asked, startled.

He shook his head. "No matter. The morning you were singing on the boat, I thought you had a hint of the Irish to your tune." His voice was dry now. "But I hear you are an excellent actress."

"When William and I were very small, my mother died. My father was a coal miner. He made it a few years past my mother, but when I was thirteen and William was eleven, Da died, too, and there was no one to take us in, and nothing left at all. We had both heard wondrous stories about the New World all of our lives, thrilling tales about the American Revolution and the great American adventure to be had! I had a fair voice; William can play any instrument, though his heart lies in his writing." She paused for a minute. She would get back to that. "Anyway, we sang and danced on the streets of Dublin until we earned our fares on a ship bound for this country. It brought us to Boston."

"And you met Julian Carter?"

Tara nodded. Then she turned to Jarrett. "I swear to you, I didn't kill him. I cared for him very deeply. He was a good man. Nothing like his son."

"All right. Go on."

"We were having trouble getting into the country. Someone in authority seemed to think that we'd just be another two little ragamuffins to feed—I don't think he was terribly fond of the Irish. But Julian Carter happened to be there, and he somehow smoothed things along, and he bought William and me a wonderful dinner and talked about what a great country it really was. He would see to it that we found work." Her voice hardened suddenly. "I remember, though, when he brought us home that night, Clive was there. He wanted nothing to do with us. I was fifteen then, William thirteen, but we'd been in the worst part of the ship for weeks and were surely the worse for wear. I certainly held no attraction for him that night! He told his father that he was a fool, throwing good money away on rotten little Irish children. But he didn't stay long that night. William and I were able to clean up; Julian gave us clothing and promised that he'd find something for us. We wanted to repay him, so William played his flute and I sang for him, and the next thing I knew he was up and snapping his fingers, saying that he had the perfect thing. And the next day William and I were working for an acting troupe."

"And you were very, very good," Jarrett supplied softly. She couldn't read the emotion in his tone. Betrayal? He continued, "You learned to speak with no accent whatsoever. And, I assume, you learned your talent with a needle then as well?"

"Costumes," she said softly.

"Of course. Go on."

"Life was very good for a while. There was always a great deal of work, but that was fine. We started doing whatever menial tasks needed to be done, then I started to perform and William started to write. We went from Boston to New York and down to Richmond, and back up again. Time passed, years passed. William fell in love with one of the actresses, a girl named Marina. Her parents are Boston merchants. They had been ready to disown Marina; they were in despair over her acting. They were delighted with the wedding—Marina was going to quit acting and stay home and William was going to support them both through his work for the newspapers—and through his playwriting."

She paused again.

"That's when you came back in contact with the Carters?" Jarrett asked coolly.

Tara nodded. "The troupe was in Boston. William had a wonderful new play. He'd written a part that he was certain I could carry off for him, about a spurned mistress who murders her benefactor . . . it didn't seem so ironic at the time, of course. It was a very good play. I went to see Julian because we needed a sponsor for the play, because I knew it was excellent, and I knew, too, that if we first performed it in his drawing room, it would become a huge success. Julian agreed. He was very excited. But when I started to leave, I ran into Clive. And he didn't seem to believe at first that I was the half-starved waif his father had brought in all those years before. When he did realize the truth of who I was, he began . . ."

"Began what?"

She shrugged uneasily, chills sweeping up and down her spine. "He was always there, of course. And we were staying in his father's house again. He had a new proposition for me every day. He would make me rich. I could sing anywhere, dance anywhere —I could quit altogether. For days I did my best to ignore him. Then he started telling me that I'd never work again, that I'd starve. Well, I had already all but starved once as it was, in Ireland. So his threats didn't really frighten me. But then . . ."

"But then?"

She almost jumped. He was standing right behind her. She hadn't heard him move.

"Then I interrupted a terrible argument he was having with his father. Julian was furious with him for many things—he

squandered money terribly, he drank, he had too many women
. . . anyway, Julian was threatening to disinherit Clive—and
leave his fortune to me. Clive, of course, was incensed. Then
Julian, perhaps reflecting that Clive was his blood, after all, and
young, suggested that Clive should marry me, settle down, and I
would mend his wild ways, and in turn, live happily ever after
myself in wealth, comfort—and respectability."

Jarrett was at her side now, ebony eyes burning, features rigid
as he hunched down, hands suddenly upon her shoulders, twisting
her to face him.

"So did you—did you marry him?"

"No!" Tara gasped, appalled. "You know that I didn't—I
couldn't have married you! How could you ask me that?"

Jarrett's eyes remained fixed firmly on hers. "Because Clive
claims that you can be charged with bigamy as well as murder. He
has a certificate—one that states you are his wife."

"Dear God!" Tara gasped in horror. She jumped to her feet,
staring at him. She shook her head wildly. "You can't believe
him, it isn't true! That's where this ends! Clive came and demanded marriage and I turned him down. I assured him I would
rather starve through a hundred lifetimes than marry him. Jarrett,
you don't know him, you don't know the things he suggested, the
things he wanted—"

"I can imagine. I want to hear the end of this." He stood
again, towering, dark, fierce. Well, he would believe her, or he
would not.

He would love her . . .

Or not.

She lifted her chin, swearing that she would not break into a
torrent of tears. "My brother's play opened. We were doing a per-
formance at Carter's house. The drawing room was very large, and
we were able to build a small stage at one end of it, with the
audience before us in customary fashion, with painted curtains
behind us as stage flats so that we could make very smooth exits
and entrances. My gun shot blanks. I know that it did. William

and I had checked it before I went onstage. It was a precaution my brother always took. In the play my lover was supposed to wander into the audience, and I was supposed to shoot after him. I shot. It was awful, like a moment straight from hell. Blood just seemed to burst from Julian Carter's chest and he fell and died. I was stunned, incredulous. Then I realized there was someone moving the stage curtain behind him, but I don't know who. As I said, I know that my gun had been loaded with blanks. I believe that someone else shot Julian from the stage curtain. And I'm certain that Clive paid someone handsomely to make that shot. It solved everything. Julian died before he could change his will. I'd either have to do everything he demanded that I do—or hang. He didn't even have to care. He won either way."

"What about your brother?"

She exhaled and looked down at her folded hands. "William wasn't there. It was his big day, but Marina was sick, and so he had stayed home with her and their baby. I'm sure that he came in a good Irish rage and protested that I had to be innocent, and I knew then and know now that he would fight for me every step of the way. We were very close—there had been so many years when we were all that the other had. But I was gone, of course, by the time that William heard what happened. I—when I reached Atlanta, I wrote him a letter and signed it 'Aunt Fanny.' She was a distant relative we had made up when we were playacting. I told him that I was seeing the country, going west, and that I just wanted him to know that I was doing well, he musn't worry, and he musn't jeopardize my little nephew. I know he must still be worried sick, but I couldn't risk anyone tracking me. But Clive has found me every time, anyway. Even here—in the wilderness." She swallowed hard. "That's it," she said softly. "Everything."

He shook his head. "Why couldn't you have told me about this?"

"I intended to—now even if Carter hadn't shown up," she said softly. She lifted her chin again. "Be honest. You didn't want to tell me I was related to half the swamp at first. Well, I didn't want to tell you that there were at least thirty witnesses who could swear that I was a murderess."

He was dead silent, staring at her.

"Jarrett, I swear I did not do it! I didn't mean to lie to you. I never did lie to you. I would have told you everything if we'd just had a little more time. . . ."

He seemed a stranger again, the towering dark man with the ebony and enigmatic eyes that had first fallen upon her in the New Orleans tavern. She trembled fiercely, wishing desperately that she could go back.

Clive had managed to hurt her now in a way he might never have imagined. Because now she had everything to lose. Everything in the world. Love.

"All right," he said, his voice ragged and deep after a moment. "We'll deal with this."

She shook her head, tears forming in her eyes. "*We* can't deal with this, Jarrett. *I* have to. I have to go back and stand trial, or I have to—run again. Keep running."

"No," Jarrett said flatly. "We're both running—for the moment. I want you somewhere deep in the woods, somewhere he'll never find you. Then I'll get lawyers on the case. There has to be some way to prove you didn't do it and to find out just who did."

She stood very still, shaking. She lowered her head. "I never intended any of this for you! Jarrett, I'm so sorry, but you don't have to feel—"

"Obligated?" he queried her suddenly.

Her eyes widened. He took a step toward her, caught her arms, drew her close to him, and lifted her chin so that he could meet her eyes. "But I am obligated, my love. And you are most certainly . . . obligated!"

"Oh, Jarrett!" she whispered, still trembling as she nearly fell into his embrace. "I didn't even mind the thought of being hanged. I simply couldn't bear losing you."

His hold tightened suddenly. "I swear I'd like to rip his throat out myself."

"But it wouldn't help!"

Jarrett sighed deeply. "Not if we want a life. You have to be cleared somehow. But if the bastard thinks he's going to use that forged paper to prove you're his wife . . ."

"I'll deny it!"

"But you're denying a murder everyone saw you commit as well," he reminded her softly.

"Oh, God!" She sobbed suddenly. "There's really no way out of this!"

His hand smoothed over her hair. He lifted her from her feet, walking to the soft pallet they had shared so many times. "There is a way. We've but to find it."

He laid her down and rose again. "Rest. We'll stay here tonight. I want to see if I can find Peter's trail. I'll be back as soon as I can."

Tara nodded.

Jarrett left her, stepping back out into the night. He leaned against the cabin door, lowering his head for a moment, gritting his teeth.

He wanted to kill Carter. He wanted to tear him limb from limb. It seemed that nothing had ever been so precious to him as the woman with the huge sky-blue eyes and golden tangle of hair who had come into his life. He hated to see her in torment.

And he hated more to feel so helpless against it.

There had to be a way.

And he had to find Peter. The boy had been smart as a whip, a fine little protector, heading into the interior with Tara. Jarrett would have been worried, but there was no sign of a struggle.

He left the cabin and stood outside in the darkness for a moment. He heard a rustling, but it was just Charlemagne, eating the grass in the shadows of the copse where Jarrett had left him. He relaxed and then started to walk, going down to the stream. As he walked, looking for whatever small signs Peter had left, he felt the same eerie sense of emptiness that had touched Tara when she had come. The people were gone. The life was gone. The cabins remained like skeletons in the night.

He missed his brother. Longed to see him.

By the stream he found Peter's trail. He was puzzled, certain that the boy had moved on, following the path James and the others had taken the day before.

He hunched down, studying the earth and broken pine branches close and carefully in the darkness.

Then he saw the trail of hoofmarks.

Someone had nearly come upon the village and the cabin in the woods.

He stood quickly.

They had been damned lucky that Peter had been a smart boy. He had created a false trail for the men on horseback to follow.

If the men had lingered in this area any longer they would have seen the smoke from Tara's fire, drifting into the sky.

In all but a panic himself now, he started back. He walked at first. Then he began to run.

He burst into the cabin.

Tara, who had remained lying on the pallet, shot up to a sitting position, staring at him with alarm. "Peter? Is he all right? Jarrett, has something happened to him?"

Feeling a little like a fool Jarrett leaned against the wall for a moment. "Peter's fine, I'm certain," he managed to tell her. He walked to the fire and started kicking it out. Tara stared at him as if he had gone mad.

"Jarrett, the night is cold," she said softly.

"And our smoke is a dead giveaway," he said simply.

"Oh!" Tara gasped. She came over by him, helping to put out the last of the flames. "But, Jarrett, if you didn't find Peter, how do you know that he's all right?"

"Someone almost stumbled onto this place, Tara, ahead of me. Peter made a trail for them to follow instead of coming here."

"Oh!" She gasped. "Oh, we should have never made the fire! But Peter was being protective, he was going to cook a rabbit."

"You must be starving."

She shook her head vehemently. "No!" she murmured, looking down to the ashes. "I'm not hungry at all." She looked up to him again. "We have to go, don't we?"

"Yes—" Jarrett began to say, but he broke off.

Tara's eyes, wide and blue upon his, opened even farther. They could both hear the stealthy movement, just beyond the cabin.

He motioned to her to get out of harm's way. She grabbed the kettle from the hearthside instead. Jarrett drew his gun from his waistband, glaring at her as he walked swiftly around the cabin to flatten himself against the wall, just as she had done earlier.

She walked around as well, to the other side.

"Tara!" he mouthed her name in angry warning.

But the eerie blackness of a shadow in the very pale moonlight was already just coming in. . . .

Jarrett pounced.

"Sweet Jesu!" he cried out.

Tara shrieked. All she could see was a tangle of shadows. "You!" Jarrett choked out. Tara heard a thud. Something went flying across the floor.

Jarrett's gun?

Desperately frightened for him, Tara lunged forward. Certain that she had cornered the shadowy height of the newcomer, she lifted her kettle, then brought it down hard upon his head.

He swirled around, staring at her.

"Tara!" he said with surprise.

And slumped down to her feet.

She let out a scream.

Chapter 22

TWENTY MINUTES later James McKenzie was still holding his head between his hands, staring reproachfully at his sister-in-law. They all sat crossed-legged in front of the doused fire, a small oil lamp lit between them.

"You know I could never have meant to hurt you!" Tara told him sorrowfully.

"I'm not so sure about that," James said, arching a brow very much the same way his brother did and looking to Jarrett. "She might have had revenge on her mind, you know. Your fault. All that *koonti* root you told me to make her grind."

"James . . ." Tara protested.

"I hear that you are alone and in danger, and I come racing to your rescue! I am nearly crushed by my big brother—and then pummeled by my delicately golden little sister-in-law."

"I didn't crush you—I knew the minute you moved in that it was you."

"I didn't!" Tara said. "It sounded as if something awful was happening, and though you two may have the art down pat, I still have difficulty seeing in the dark."

She saw then that James was grinning. But immediately his grin vanished. "What is going on here? Peter came running faster than a rabbit. I couldn't even understand him at first—I thought the soldiers were coming for us. Then I finally understood him say that you were now alone in the wilderness, running, and that the soldiers were after you."

Tara looked at Jarrett.

"Tara is accused of murder," he said.

James didn't seem to believe the words at first. "Murder by kettle?" he asked her, a brow arched again.

Amazingly, she found that she could smile. "It's a long story, but there was a man in Boston who wanted to rid himself of his father and manipulate me. He arranged it so that it appeared—before numerous witnesses—that I shot his father. I didn't do it, I swear that I didn't, so I ran. As fast as I could. As far as I could. It wasn't fast or far enough!" she added softly.

"I wonder if any of us can ever run fast or far enough!" James said. He looked at Jarrett. "What are you going to do?"

"Tomorrow, we'll take Tara to our people deeper into the swamp. I'll leave her with you and come back to find out where we stand." He gazed at Tara, yet spoke to them both. "I sent word to Robert's house—he'll leave with Leo and some of the boys on the *Magda* and get up to Boston just as fast as he can. He'll find the best attorney up there, and start trying to prove that this Clive Carter did have every reason in the world to want his father dead. Then, somehow, we'll have to find the physical killer, since the son didn't fire the gun himself."

"How will we ever prove any of it?" Tara asked him.

He smiled at her. She wondered if she dared believe him when he told her, "Tara, it can be done. Who knows, maybe Clive Carter will break down and confess."

Tara looked skeptically at him. "Do you really think that will happen?"

He shrugged. "Strange things happen."

"Maybe an alligator will eat the bastard," James said.

"But that wouldn't help. I'd still be facing the murder charge," Tara responded softly.

"Carter is one white man we definitely need alive," Jarrett commented. "We just need him away from Tara." He stood up. "Thank you, James. Thank you for coming for Tara."

James nodded, studying Tara. "Are you going to be all right with us for a while?"

She smiled. "I'll even learn to grind *koonti* root properly," she told him. She would be all right.

James rose as well. "Peter led Carter and the army men on a broad chase through the marshes. We should be safe enough for the night—if not, Tara has that kettle of hers." He smiled, but then added, "We should leave with the dawn."

He turned to leave them. Tara unwound her legs and stood, holding on to Jarrett's arm, calling after James. "James, I add my thanks. That you came running back for me."

He nodded, smiling, then stepped out into the night. Jarrett looked at Tara. "Get some sleep," he told her. "I'm going to take first watch."

"But you need sleep as well."

"James will spell me later. I'll be in then."

He left the cabin as well. Tara longed to leave and sit with him, but he meant to listen and to watch the night, and he would not welcome the distraction. Besides, she was bone weary.

She lay down on the pallet, and for a while stared into the darkness, feeling numb. Carter had caught up with her, just when her life had become everything that she might have wished for instead of the nightmare he had created out of it.

But she still had Jarrett. He loved her anyway. He meant to fight for her. She was so very grateful. But she feared the time ahead of them when they would part. She had no fears about living with her brother-in-law's family, no worries about rough conditions, fierce weather—snakes, alligators, or any other savage creatures. None could be so dangerous as man.

At length she dozed. And in the sweet cloudlike arena of

sleep she felt him come to her. Felt him lie down beside her, felt his warmth. Felt the liquid fire of his kiss upon her lips, the caress of his fingers upon her flesh. He made love to her slowly, seducing her out of the shadows, so gently that she thought she still dreamed.

But then the slow-burning fuse of desire within her caught swiftly ablaze. She felt the full force of his naked body against her own, the slick heat of his flesh, the fierce pulse of his desire. She no longer slept, she drifted from the dream into a fiery explosion of ecstasy, and there she clung to him, more in love with him than she had ever been before, and trying to hold on to him as if she might hold to the dream that way.

Dawn came. She felt that she had barely slept again before Jarrett was urging her awake. He had coffee. By the coming light James had felt secure enough to make a fire, and he had brought coffee and dried meat for them to eat. She was grateful for the coffee, yet when she tried to chew upon the meat, she was stunned to find that her stomach would have nothing to do with it. Even as the two men discussed the route they must take, she leapt to her feet and went racing from the cabin. She was sick. Longing just for some clean clear water, she hurried down to the stream. She crouched down on the bank, cupping up water, dousing it over and over upon her cheeks, grateful for the coolness of it. The water helped, and yet she still didn't feel particularly well. She hadn't had enough sleep, she thought. Yet even as she knelt by the water, she nearly gasped as a hand touched her shoulder. She turned to find Jarrett hunched down by her side, studying her, a small smile curved into his lip.

She arched a brow.

"Well, it might be, you know," he told her.

"Might be?" she asked.

"Morning sickness."

"I'm never sick, Jarrett, I'm—oh!" She gasped. She stared at him blankly, trying to think, trying to count. Her life had been in such a tempest lately, she had paid little attention to the natural functions of life. . . . "Oh!" She gasped again.

His dark eyes were enigmatic. Her heart suddenly seemed to wrench at her. How strange, how sad! The Indian camp had already been deserted, and yet it was here that he had lost a wife and child once, and here that he was discovering his new wife was expecting.

The wife wanted by the law.

"Oh, Jarrett!" she whispered again, wondering if he was thinking of Lisa. "I'm sorry, I should have known. Or suspected. I would never have let you know . . . here."

His ink lashes fell over his eyes for a moment, then rose, and the gentle curl of a smile was on his lips. "I lost something here; I've gained something here."

"Are you pleased?" she whispered.

"Ecstatic," he told her solemnly, that curl still in his lips. "All right, maybe ecstatic is what I feel creating the babe . . ." He reached out, touched her chin. Kissed her lips briefly. "I have never been happier."

"But—"

"Tara, I have never been happier." He rose, catching her hands, helping her up as well. "It would be paradise," he told her softly, "if only we could go home."

She leaned against him, feeling tears burn fiercely behind her eyes. She felt his fingers, his grip tightening upon her shoulders. She looked up at him. "I will tell James to lash you to a stake if you don't take care of yourself."

"You won't have to tell him that!" she promised. "Jarrett, I love you so much, I swear, I'll not let anything happen."

"Come on, then," he said huskily. "I've got to get you out of harm's way."

They walked back to the camp together. James was already mounted, with their horses at his side. He seemed anxious. "The horses are spooky," he said. He smiled at Tara. "There's a chill at my neck. It's time to leave this camp behind."

Jarrett helped her up on her horse, then mounted his own. James took the lead. Tara rode between the two men as Jarrett brought up the rear.

They rode for hours. She began to feel the aches in her shoulders, back, and thighs. She no longer felt sick to her stomach, but it seemed now that her abdomen was growling away as if she kept some wild creature within it, and she prayed that the ride kept her husband and brother-in-law from hearing the ruckus.

They rode through wild, beautiful country. When they came upon marshland where they could ride abreast, James informed her that he had told his family and people to keep on moving with the daylight, as the tribe—encumbered by children and belongings—would move more slowly than she, Jarrett, and he needed to go. He meant to go deep into the interior of the state, far south, and into the swampland of the Everglades. "You'll be safe there," he said. "I promise you. And Jarrett will find a way to clear you. I know that he will."

Tara began to believe it herself. Night fell. She spent the darkness in the swamp, high on a hammock of land, in her husband's arms. They built no fire. She felt his warmth, and it was enough. She slept amazingly well, guarded by her husband and brother-in-law.

The temperature remained blessedly low as they rode the next day. They rode for hours, then came upon a stretch of river where they paused, for it was filled with beautiful birds. Jarrett pointed them out to her. Cranes, egrets, herons, the unbelievably pink flamingos.

"The land remains beautiful," she said.

"And deadly," Jarrett warned. "Take care. This is cottonmouth country through here. And for every gator nose you see, I promise you there is a second nearly submerged nearby. Keep your distance."

She was never quite sure when Jarrett had managed to tell his brother that she was expecting a child, but when James looked back at her, apologized, and said that they might stop for a while, she became aware that he did know. There was a good copse of trees ahead, not far from a clear stream feeding off the river. "We'll rest," he told her.

When they stopped, Jarrett was there to lift her down from her horse. She was sore in every bone of her body, grateful for the break, yet hoping that she'd manage to get back on her horse again. It was a trying time for Jarrett, she knew. Now he was doubly worried about her, for he was afraid to jeopardize her condition, yet he knew he had to get her out of harm's way as quickly as possible.

She sat on the ground in the hammock where tall pines grew. The high ground here was carpeted with them, and the trees seemed to reach the sky. Jarrett went down to the stream for water, and James sat before her, having offered her more of the meat, telling her she needed to try to eat again.

This time it seemed that the meat went down well. In fact it seemed absolutely delicious. She could have eaten pounds of it, she thought, but the men had to eat as well, and she tried to appear satisfied with one piece.

James was smiling at her. "Eat more."

"Really, I'm fine."

"You must keep up your strength and your health."

"You and Jarrett must have something too. If you pass out from hunger, how will I get through?" she demanded.

James shook his head. "Neither of us will pass out from hunger. We've both gone without eating several days at a time—my people literally starve often. We learn to go without. But you mustn't, not now. For your sake, for my brother's sake. If he really must leave you with us, I am going to see to it that he returns to a healthy son this time."

Tara laughed softly. "A son? This from a man with two daughters?"

"Jarrett will have a son. He lost a child. This one will . . ."

"Replace it?" she asked softly.

"One life never replaces another," James told her. "Each is

special and unique. But this child will give you both back life, and I pray God, it will grow to help with the healing of our peoples and our land."

She smiled, reached out to him, and squeezed his hands. "Thank you!" she said softly.

Jarrett came back with canteens filled with water. Tara drank deeply, felt Jarrett's black gaze upon her, and slowed down.

After a moment she rose. "Just where is the water, Jarrett?" she asked.

"Down there. If you need more—"

"I need to walk!" she told him and grimaced. "If I don't get some of this awful stiffness out of me, I'm afraid I won't even be able to get on a horse again!"

"We're deep into Indian country now," James advised.

Jarrett, chewing on a piece of the meat himself, leaned back against a pine and seemed somewhat to relax. He nodded. "Perhaps you're right."

She left them and walked across the pine forest, over the trail, and then down a damp embankment. It was amazing how quickly the land changed here! One minute she had been on high, firm ground. Down by the water the ground itself seemed to be wet as well.

She found a tree stump by the water and sat upon it. She pulled off her shoes and stockings to wiggle her feet in the cool water, sighing at the wonderful way it felt. She leaned over the water, once again bathing her face and throat in its coolness.

When she came up, she was puzzled by a feeling of unease that seized her.

A hand touched her shoulder.

Jarrett! she thought. He had come to her, just as he had come to her earlier that morning.

But the thought faded instantly. She knew her husband's touch.

She opened her mouth to scream, but a large hand clamped down upon it. An uncalloused hand, one that had never been used for physical labor. One with a large ruby upon the middle finger. One attached to an arm that wore an overly ruffled, lace-edged shirt.

Clive Carter!

Oh, sweet Jesu, how had they come so far, so fast! He didn't belong in the swamp and hammock and marshes! Rivers of fear and distaste seemed to wash through her; she thought she'd pass out. Dear God, she had run so long ago! She had never thought to feel his hands upon her again, never thought that he would touch her.

"Don't scream!" Carter warned her. "Don't scream. That black-eyed savage of yours will come running through the trees— and I'll have to shoot him right in the heart. I'm a damned good shot. But then, you know that. I managed to get my shot in at my father, and I wasn't even carrying a gun. It's amazing how easy it can be to devise a murder without even getting blood on your hands."

She was stunned to realize that he was all but confessing to the murder of his father. Then she wondered why she should be so surprised. She knew she hadn't killed Julian. And they had both known since the deed had been done and she had first locked eyes with him across his father's drawing room that he had made the arrangements for the fatal shot to be fired. A confession to her meant nothing. It would always be her word against his, except that he had been certain that there had been a roomful of people as witnesses to what had apparently been her guilt.

He had one arm locked around her; his other hand remained clamped tight over her mouth and all but covered her nose. She couldn't breathe. She would pass out. Worse. She was beginning to feel sick again. His cologne had mingled with the sweat of his body, and it seemed overwhelming.

She tried to bite his finger. He yelped, easing his hold just a fraction.

"Let me go!" she cried. "I'm going to be sick." She tried to look around. She didn't see Tyler Argosy, or any of the army men from the fort who would have been his escort here on their mission to uphold the law. Clive had found her on his own.

"You're as slippery as a snake, Tara, but I'll be damned if I'll ever let you go. It's taken me forever to get my hands on you. Now, you'll never escape me."

He started to rise, dragging her up with him. She saw the harsh, satisfied, and cruel smile that cut across his face, the glitter of pleasure at her fall that lit within his eyes.

"You could have had everything, you stupid bitch!" he told her softly, adjusting her weight. "I would have even married a little starving Irish wretch, even though, I admit, it was the prospect of the inheritance that would have made me do so. I can't imagine now why I spent so much time trying to charm you. You were nothing but a little foreign whore in my father's house, and I should have simply had you instead of harboring fantasies about you for so long! Of course, I intended that you should pay for everything the night my father died. I just didn't think that you could run so fast, disappear so well. And who in hell would have thought you could manage to marry a rich and influential man out of a New Orleans tavern! That one took some thought. I needed more than an arrest warrant for that one. I needed a wedding certificate to predate the one you were so anxious to acquire with a black-eyed, Indian-loving stranger!"

She was glad that he kept talking. But it seemed he didn't want any answers. He held her closely and cruelly, his fingers hard now over her mouth to keep her from biting again. He was stealing her breath away, stealing her strength. If she didn't breathe soon . . .

He eased his hold again as he balanced his way up the embankment, struggling a little with her in his arms. The instant she could talk, she did. "I'd never have married you, you bastard. And I would have preferred death at any time to your touch! I—"

The hand clamped down again. She started to struggle.

He fell down on one knee, trying to keep his hold on her. "Bitch!" he accused her. His fingers suddenly threaded through her hair with such force that she was gasping, unable to cry out because of the awful pain she was in. "I promise you—you'll be touched! I'm taking you back as my wife, Tara, and when I finish with you—"

He never completed the threat. Tara herself was startled by a savage cry that suddenly seemed to rip through the wind and the trees. She managed to twist around and saw Jarrett.

He was coming through the trail of pines, running like lightning, his eyes a black and lethal blaze, his bronze contorted features a warning of sure death.

Clive Carter swore, shoving her down, drawing out his pistol. Tara screamed.

The shot was never fired. Jarrett was upon Clive before he could even pray to get off a shot. It seemed that Jarrett flew into the air and landed right on Carter, flattening the man beneath him. Carter instantly tried for a knife at his calf, but Jarrett wrenched him around, and the men went rolling into the river.

They stumbled to their feet.

Carter drew the knife and raised it over Jarrett's head. But Jarrett caught the man's arm. Carter bellowed out in rage; the knife dropped into the water. Jarrett eased his hold. He drew back a fist and caught Carter squarely in the jaw. Carter stumbled back in the water, falling.

Jarrett went for the man again.

Tara leapt up, running for the water. But before she could reach the two men, a shot sounded in the air.

Tara spun around.

They were surrounded.

There was Tyler Argosy, mounted on a bay, in his military uniform, surrounded by a company of perhaps twenty men, all in uniform.

And all armed.

Jarrett hadn't even heard the shot, he had been so incensed with Clive Carter. He reached into the water for the man, dragging him up.

Tyler fired off another shot. "Jarrett!"

Jarrett, soaked, black hair plastered to his head, holding Clive Carter out at his side by a shoulder, paused at last. But he didn't release the man he held.

"Jarrett!" Tara cried. "We need him—alive!" she pleaded. "Jarrett . . ." she said and trailed off miserably.

"Shoot this man!" Clive demanded.

"Mr. Carter—" Tyler began.

"Shoot him! I have an arrest warrant for that woman, and she's not his damned wife, she's mine! I'm taking her back, and you can see that he's a savage maniac, that he's trying to kill me. Shoot him!"

"Mr. Carter, I'm not shooting a man down in cold blood and I don't care how many pieces of legal paper you have on you! And if you don't shut up, Jarrett McKenzie just might strangle you and be damned with the consequences!"

That apparently made sense to Carter. "Make him let me go!" he enunciated icily. Then he shut up.

Tyler looked at Jarrett, pure misery in his eyes. "Jarrett, I've got to ask you to let him go."

Jarrett's teeth clenched so tightly in his mouth, Tara thought that they would crack.

He released Clive Carter.

Carter started out of the water—and toward Tara. Jarrett was back behind him, thrusting him far out of the way and grasping Tara's hand to pull her behind him.

"My hands are off him, Tyler," Jarrett said, still staring black fury at Carter. "Now you get him away from me."

"Jarrett, Tara has to come in," Tyler said very quietly. "Dammit, Jarrett, you're one of my best friends! Do you think I want any of this? But you've got to turn Tara over to me. Come along yourself—"

"The hell with it!" Clive Carter bellowed. "He doesn't come, I've got a damned wedding certificate—"

"Mr. Carter," Tyler said, very impatiently, "your marriage licence doesn't mean that you've got any right to this woman, not when it's disputed. Your arrest warrant we've got to honor, but—"

"You're not taking her, Tyler!" Jarrett said.

"Jarrett, don't make me force this!" Tyler pleaded. And even as he spoke, his company of men lowered their rifles, straight upon Jarrett and Tara.

"No!" Tara cried suddenly, trying to step around Jarrett. He tried to shove her back. "I'll stand trial!" she cried to him. "You'll be with me, Tyler said—"

"Tyler," came a cry from across the clearing, "is going to let us all ride away. Else there's going to be one hell of a savage Indian fight out here!"

Tara and Jarrett both spun around. Tara gasped loudly in disbelief.

James had come. That was not so unusual—she and Jarrett had not returned from the stream.

But he had not come alone. To Tara's amazement he was surrounded by Seminole warriors, some on war ponies, some on foot, some painted in bright colors, some very European in plain breeches and multicolored shirts. And at the head of them, at James's side, the Seminole currently feared more than any other.

Osceola.

Tara spun again. Tyler Argosy was staring at the group of warriors that had come upon them. He looked ill. Like a man who had always known his duty.

And was about to die for it now.

Suddenly, Osceola left the group, riding forward at a fast pace, throwing a shaft into the ground directly in front of Clive Carter.

Carter paled.

The shaft was decorated with white scalps.

Osceola rode back to the line.

Tara suddenly felt Jarrett's hands on her shoulders. He was backing toward James and the Seminoles.

"Tyler, let it go!" Jarrett warned.

"Damn it, Jarrett, you're going to be as much an outlaw as your wife!" Tyler warned.

"My wife!" Clive cried. He spun on Tyler and the army men. "What the hell is the matter with you? You can't kill these few savages?"

"This is a damned good savage," Jarrett said. "Asi Yaholo—Osceola. Perhaps you've heard of him?"

"Damn you!" Clive raged. "Shoot them!"

As he spoke, the Indians cocked their guns—and aimed them at the army men.

Tara felt weak again. They would fight for her.

And they would die for her. Osceola, the warrior who had caused so much death and destruction! But he fought for his people, and he had never thought that all whites should die, he had judged men, far more carefully than did his enemies!

And he had made a friend of her.

He would die—he, and perhaps many of the men with him. And Tyler might die, and Jarrett and James, two brothers whose real fight had been to stop the violence, to keep the ties of blood and love despite it.

They all might die because of her.

"Wait!" she cried out, and with tremendous effort she pulled free from Jarrett's hold and ran to stand between the two opposing forces. She turned back to Jarrett, stopping him when he was ready to run after her.

"Jarrett, please!" she begged. "You, all of you!" She swirled in a circle, facing them all. "Please God, in the midst of all the violence here, don't let me be responsible for more bloodshed. I beg of you all! Jarrett, Tyler will be with us. Clive will never be able to touch me again, we'll go to Boston, we'll fight the charges! Don't die, please don't die for me, any of you!"

Silence reigned. Terrible, awful silence.

And in that silence she was afraid. These were men who had been fighting a long time. The soldiers in blue had their honor and their pride. The warriors in their feathers and paint had been forced to run a long time, just like Tara.

Today, they meant to fight.

"No, please!" she shrieked out.

She didn't know what would have happened. Except, at that moment, the savage land itself intervened. Clive Carter gave out a shriek of agony, and fell to his knees.

Chapter 23

Jarrett had seen the snake earlier. It had been curled around the limb of one of the gnarled trees that hung over the water. Water was its home, and it was comfortable in it and not content to be far from it.

Jarrett hadn't thought much of the snake. He knew to leave the creature alone. Anyone out here knew to leave an animal alone and stay out of its way.

Maybe, Jarrett thought, God—or perhaps his stepmother's Indian Great Spirit—had intervened, for it seemed now that the cottonmouth, disturbed by the fighting and shouting, had come down the branch of the tree.

And dropped onto Clive Carter somehow. For even as the man shrieked out in his pain, the gold-toned snake was trying to slink away back down the embankment again.

It wasn't to be. A gun was fired by one of the army men. The snake exploded into pieces.

And with the sound Jarrett flew into action himself.

He raced for Clive Carter, catching the man by his hair when he would have fallen.

He remembered that this was one enemy he could not let die.

"I can save you from that bite!" he told the man. "You know how you die of snakebite? Slowly. The poison seeps into you. It's agony. You twitch, you convulse. The pain is more than you can imagine and then . . . death. Anything is easier. A bullet through the brain is easier. Hanging is easier. Anything is less than the agony you'll soon be writhing in!"

Clive Carter was already feeling the seep of the poison. "Do it!" he screamed. "Do it, damn it, do it, one of you. You have to save me, you bastards, you bloody have to!"

"I don't have to do anything except watch you die!" Jarrett roared at him.

Everyone was still, around them. Tyler Argosy and his men sat their horses without moving.

The Indians, as well, remained still.

And Clive Carter apparently believed him. "Please, God!" he cried out, his voice rising. "What do you want? Money? What? I'll give you anything—"

"Give me the truth!" Jarrett said. "The truth, now, here, before witnesses!"

Carter sagged against him. "You had someone else fire the shot that killed your father," Jarrett said, his tone merciless. "You hired someone, and you carefully planned it to make sure that everyone would be convinced Tara had killed him."

Carter said something.

Jarrett tugged at his hair. "What? I didn't hear you?"

"Yes, for the love of God, yes! She deserved whatever happened to her! She came into my house, she tricked and deceived and seduced my father. She—"

"She was decent to him, and you were concerned only with yourself!" Jarrett spat out. Then he realized—it didn't matter what Carter wanted to say about Tara. None of them believed it. Tyler knew her, just as his brother knew her, and his people knew her. Words didn't matter.

Except those words he needed so desperately.

The confession.

"Damn it!" Carter raged. "Do it, do what you need to do, before God—"

"One more thing," Jarrett said.

"What? For the love of God! What?"

"You were never married to her. Never."

Carter mumbled something.

"What?" It was Jarrett's turn to demand. He dragged up Clive Carter's head, meeting the man's glazing eyes. He had to hurry. Cottonmouth poison traveled fast.

"I was never married to her. The certificate is a forgery, Jenson Jones made it up for me, Jenson Jones fired the shot that killed my father."

There was a sudden cry from within the ranks of the army men. Jarrett realized that Jones was there, with them. "He made me do it!" the ugly little man shouted out. "He forced me, I had no choice at all, no choice—"

Jarrett inhaled and exhaled. He stared at Tara across the damp embankment that separated them. She had never been more beautiful, her blue eyes brimming and violet with tears that did not fall. He smiled.

He looked back to Carter. He wanted to throw the man from him.

Let him die.

But all of his life he had been known for keeping his word. By his white friends; by his Indian relations.

He slipped his knife from the sheath at his calf and bent down to Carter.

Carter started to scream anew.

"Shut up! I have to draw the poison."

The snake had caught Carter midarm. Jarrett ripped up the sleeve, found the bite, and crossed it with clean slashes. He grasped the man's arm and began to suck hard at the blood, spitting it out each time it filled his mouth.

Carter groaned.

And passed out cold.

He would live, Jarrett thought.

He stepped back, away from the fallen man. Tara came running up, throwing herself into his arms. He caught her, crushed her to him, and held tight.

A moment later he looked up. Tyler had ridden over. Two of his men were off their horses, picking up Carter. Jenson Jones was still babbling away, claiming it had all been Carter's fault. Tyler handed Jarrett a flask of whiskey. Jarrett rinsed the taste of blood and venom from his mouth and spat on the ground.

"My wife isn't going anywhere with you," Jarrett told Tyler, returning the flask.

Tyler nodded. "I think we can safely leave you now," he said.

Tyler looked over Jarrett's shoulder. James and Osceola still sat their mounts like sentinels before the other warriors.

Tyler lifted a hand to Osceola.

Osceola nodded gravely.

If they were to meet in battle, they would kill one another if they could.

But there would be no battle today.

Tyler lifted a hand to his men, shouting out an order. The army men turned. With Jenson Jones still claiming coercion by Carter and Carter lying over the haunches of a horse, they rode away, one by one.

Jarrett turned. Osceola nodded to him. He and the other Seminole men turned their horses as well, and silent as the wraiths they needed to be, the Indians disappeared, one by one.

Except for James. He dismounted and came to them both, smiling ear to ear. He took Tara gently into his arms and hugged her fiercely.

"Thank you. Thank you!"

"You're the best sister-in-law a man could have," he assured her.

"You're the best brother-in-law."

He pulled away from her, clasping his brother's hand. "I think it's all right to leave the two of you children now, isn't it?"

Jarrett smiled and nodded.

Then James mounted again and, like the others rode through the trees, quickly disappearing from view.

Jarrett drew Tara into his arms again, holding her fiercely. "Oh, God!" he breathed.

"Oh, Jarrett!" she replied, and pulled away, staring at him, her blue eyes brimming again. "Oh, Jarrett, I didn't believe that I could be saved. But you—you—"

"I like rescuing you," he said.

"Oh, God, I love you!" she whispered. Then her brows knit with concern. "Jarrett, you sucked that poison out of him. You're going—"

"I'm going to be fine. I was bitten when I was a boy and I've gained something of an immunity. I swear to you, my love, I'll be fine."

She smiled. She threw herself against him again, holding tight.

He lifted her chin brushing her mouth with his own. Her lips were salty with the taste of her tears.

"Let's go home, little runaway," he told her.

She smiled. "A runaway no longer. For I have run home!" she whispered.

He kissed her again. The savage wilderness surrounded him, but he knew that she was right. It was home to her, as it had been to him from the very first.

Or perhaps home wasn't even in this Eden he loved so much.

They had come home to one another.

"The war—the war is far from over!" he told her huskily. "Tara, I don't know what the future will hold."

"It will hold a son, so your brother says," she told him.

"It is a savage and dangerous land, and you were loath to come here once."

She reached up and stroked his cheek. "Savage, dangerous,

wild—rather like the man I married. And neither of them I would ever, ever leave!" she vowed passionately.

He smiled and swept her up into his arms and kissed her deeply before carrying her up the embankment and toward the hammock where their horses waited.

It was time to go home. Destiny had come full circle.

He had acquired a wife.

And God had given him love.

Now, they had to forge a future. Together.

Epilogue

I T WAS fall. To Tara it had always been the most beautiful season. In the North the leaves on the trees would be changing to brilliant colors, the air would have a nip. Here, fall came more subtly. The dead heat of summer—and it had been dreadfully hot —was lifted. The humidity had suddenly eased as well, and the days were simply beautiful. It was still warm enough to make one want to plunge into an inviting stream or happily dangle bare toes from a log, but by night it was decidedly cool and completely comfortable.

It had been a beautiful time to have a baby. Ian McKenzie had come into the world on October fifth. She had personally ex-pected him to arrive on the fourth, but he had been quite stub-born, and it was long past midnight when he actually arrived. Despite all the warnings she had received from Naomi and other young mothers, she hadn't quite been prepared for labor, and she hadn't been entirely gracious through the ordeal, nearly breaking Jarrett's fingers, but when it had been all over, she had experi-enced peace and happiness as she had never truly imagined them possible on earth. Her son was beautiful, round, healthy, with a lusty wail, huge blue eyes, and a headful of dark hair. For hours after his birth she and Jarrett had simply lain on opposite sides of him, marveling at his perfection. For that day they'd let nothing intrude. They were both dreamers and idealists, longing for such peace and perfection as this in their Eden.

In the outside world, however, there was no peace to be had.

The war raged on. James had led his people ever deeper into the South. The summer had been brutal. American troops had suffered cruelly from disease. Campaigns against the Indians had bogged down. With fall, and the cooler weather now arriving, the situation was due to grow worse. But she and Jarrett had long ago made the decision to stay, to do whatever they could to save the lives of innocents—white lives, red lives. They had been told they could not stay neutral. They intended to prove everyone wrong and do just that. In spite of the war, even through her pregnancy, she had managed to visit James and his family. In spite of the war James and Naomi managed to see them. They had made a silent pact. They would prevail.

Jarrett still left upon occasion. He carried messages for the army and for the Seminoles. It never ceased to hurt. But she understood. Each time she lived for the moment he would return, and she learned not to be so afraid. They had weathered so much. They would weather more. If anything, their love grew stronger with each reunion, and for that she was heartily grateful.

Sometimes the past seemed just a vague nightmare, and for that she was grateful as well. It was true that she had come home.

"Tara!"

She smiled, slipping on her second earring as she heard Jarrett's voice from below. He was growing anxious for her to come down. He'd been very strange most of the morning and she'd been afraid that he had been biding his time before telling her about another journey he must take. But he hadn't been grave or reserved, he had been grinning like the devil's own imp.

"Tara!"

She came out on the balcony and looked down to the yard below. She frowned, seeing that Jeeves and Molly had set a table out on the lawn. The sun was beating down on the silver, the white linen table cloth was blowing just slightly. As she looked across the yard she could see that an army ship was coming into dock.

"Jarrett?" she questioned uneasily.

He was just below her, near the table. He was in a black frock coat with a crisp white shirt and embroidered waistcoat beneath. His ebony hair was smoothed back, and his eyes were dark as coal as he looked up at her, a slight smile curving his lip.

"It is not a call to duty, my love," he assured her.

"Then . . . ?"

"What is young Ian up to?"

"Sleeping peacefully and being an angel, quite unlike his father. Jarrett, tell me what is going on!"

"Come down here and see!" he commanded with wicked relish.

She checked the baby in his cradle, then hurried from their room, running down the stairway and out the back. Jarrett was awaiting her impatiently, offering his arm for a stroll down to meet the docking ship.

"You are quite certain you're not going to surprise me with a sudden departure?"

He shook his head.

"Not this time."

"Jarrett . . ."

"Behave. We've guests arriving. You'll want to greet them properly."

She was about to argue, but words suddenly stilled within her throat. She could see the young couple and child who had come to the starboard side of the ship, ready to come ashore. She was a pretty young woman with rich brown hair and bright hazel eyes. The toddler squirming in her arms was a little boy with brown hair and blue eyes. The man was slim and tall with a fashionable mustache and rich curling blond hair.

"William!" She gasped, staring at her brother. She spun on Jarrett, who shrugged.

"Brother or not, you did whisper for him in your sleep. I was compelled to meet the fellow—and delighted, of course, to learn that he and his wife could manage a trip down here."

She threw herself into his arms, nearly knocking him off his feet. Then she raced down the dock to greet her brother, Marina, and her nephew. There was pure mayhem for a good twenty minutes. William and Marina and young Master Wyeth Brent met Jarrett. Tyler Argosy explained to Tara how he and the army men at Fort Brooke had been engaged to bring her brother and his family down the river, keeping it all a secret from her. Robert appeared even as they all made their way to the luncheon on the lawn, and the day stretched out with hours of wonder and delight. The war was forgotten; the conversation switched back and forth from plays to literature, music, infants, feedings, sleeping, and the national elections. Ole Hickory was about to leave the office of the presidency. Martin Van Buren would be taking the oath come spring.

By nightfall, with her family tucked in for their stay, Tara was both exhausted and exhilarated. She wasn't certain where Jarrett had gone, but she stepped outside to the porch, shivering just slightly in the night air. A full moon was out, beautiful in the black velvet heaven. A night owl cried, and she smiled, closing her eyes slightly as she listened to the flow of the river. There was another sound, something slight, just behind her. She spun around. Jarrett had come out, still so tall and striking in black, his ebony eyes giving away little, just as they had that night that seemed so long ago now in the tavern in New Orleans. He strode across the porch to her, lifted her chin, and studied her eyes.

"Happy?" he asked her.

She nodded. "Thank you."

"Well, I did have to meet the man of your dreams."

She smiled. "And now that you've met him?"

"I'm quite impressed. Ian has a most literary and talented fellow for an uncle."

"His other uncle is equally impressive, of course."

Jarrett smiled, shrugging. "Of course." She saw a sparkle against the ebony darkness of his eyes and he suddenly lifted her into his arms.

"The army is still present, you know," he whispered softly. "Tyler's ship will not leave until the morning."

"Oh?"

"Well, you see, I have intimate plans for my wife this evening, and I do remember once before her threatening to scream should I carry her up the stairs and to our bed."

Tara slipped her arm around his shoulders. "I do remember the occasion, but I don't remember you caring much one way or the other if I did or didn't scream!"

"Umm. Maybe not."

"And you are a gambler, of course."

"How true."

He turned into the house and started up the stairs, and she smiled as he made his way to their bedroom.

"Well, my little runaway?" he teased huskily in the darkness, laying her down upon the bed and easing himself on top of her. She saw the white flash of his smile, the glitter of his eyes, and a sweet burst of fire seemed to ignite within her.

"Winner takes all," she informed him solemnly. She threaded her fingers through his hair and drew him down to her. His lips found hers, and the fire burned to a steady blaze.

Tonight would be sweet tempest.

And life . . .

Indeed, it would remain a tempest as well. Bitter and tragic at times, but precious in these moments when they could lie together in peace.

But whatever lay ahead did not matter at this moment.

She was indeed one runaway who had come home, into his arms. And she would stay there happily, never to run again, living with him in his paradise.

For all of their lives.

BE SURE TO LOOK FOR THE NEXT THRILLING
EPISODE IN THE FLORIDA SERIES,

THE UNDEFEATED

COMING FROM DELACORTE IN 1995.

HERE IS ITS EXCITING PROLOGUE:

Prologue

The Hostage

The Florida Territory
Early Fall, 1837

SHE WAS dead. Almost dead. So close to dead that she could nearly taste the metallic silver of the blade that threatened her throat, feel the hot stickiness and choke on the pulsing red spill of her own blood. . . .

But then a harsh, deep cry went out, shattering the air. The warrior about to murder her paused. The blade did not touch her throat. The cry, the shout of command that had broken through the carnage, had been so fierce that it stilled even the jubilant sounds of pillage, murder, and glory from the savages who had so recently won their battle and were now setting upon their victims, some stealing rings and trinkets, some giving the coup de grace to maimed and anguished men, some seeking murder, some seeking scalps.

The shouted cry stopped them all. It had all been cacophony; the day was suddenly and incredibly still. Teela stared up at the warrior who seemed to have frozen in motion. A fierce warrior, one with bluntly cut, ink-black hair, an all but naked bear-greased body, and mahogany eyes that impaled her with hatred. One who had wanted her life. She stared back at him, hating him equally.

She didn't know why the sudden ringing command of one warrior should stop this carnage—but she had endured enough. She'd not been part of a U.S. Army war party. She had only been on her way to leave this savage place. So savage, even in its beauty. Even now, as the sun fell, the sky was streaked with a rainbow of golden colors, yellows, oranges, crimson. The sun would fall soon, and the moon and the stars would rise and cool breezes would blow away the heat.

And she would most probably still die as the darkness blanketed the wild, raw crimson glory of the land. . . .

Perhaps she was in this wretched danger because most of her escort had been men who had often served beneath her stepfather —hardened, ruthless soldiers who had prowled these swamps endless months now and battled the Seminoles and others upon their own wild lands. Few whites were hated by the Indians as much as Michael Warren. That hatred extended to the men who served him.

And, so it seemed, to his stepdaughter.

She knew full well that the soldiers had often been as cruel and rapacious as any "red" man might be. She could not even blame the Indians for their hatred of her stepfather and anything and anyone that he had touched.

But she had brought them no harm. And a few of the men on this escort service had been nothing more than green boys, too young, too innocent, to deserve such a death in the wilderness. Dear God, she did not deserve such a death in the wilderness!

"Bastard!" she cried suddenly to the warrior who still held her by her hair. She kicked into his gut and groin with all of her strength, desperate to be freed from him, even if it would be for nothing more than the last few seconds in which she might draw breath.

He gave out a furious cry of masculine pain, and to her relief and fleeting pleasure his hand eased its death grip from her hair as he doubled over.

She tried to rise from the place where she had fallen against a cypress. Tried to run. But the Indian screamed again, reaching for her. Her arm was caught, and she was thrown back to the ground. The brave's knife, already deep, dark red with the life's blood of so many of the men who had fallen around her, was rising above her breast.

Then that deep voice of command which had stilled the action of the massacre before rang out again. Even as she blinked and gasped for air, Teela saw that the muscled warrior was wrenched from atop her. She didn't dare wonder why. She rolled over, struggled to her knees and to her feet, and started to run again. She wouldn't die without fighting for her life.

Fingers tangled into the length of her hair. She cried out with her own screech of agony as she was determinedly dragged back. She struggled fiercely, catching hold of her hair, yet not managing to free it from the firm grasp of that large bronzed hand. The man came at her with a second hand as well. Even as she tried to kick and flail again, she found herself spun around, plucked up by the waist, and tossed back to the ground. She thought, fighting hysteria, that she was back where she had started.

No. This was worse. Much worse.

For this man was now straddling her, capturing her wrists, pinning them to the ground high above her head with the use of just one of his wickedly long-fingered hands. She was blinded by the blanket of sun-torched auburn hair that fell in a tangled sheath over her face. Twisting brought the merciless pressure of his thighs closer about her hips. Each gasp for breath, every effort to scream, all but caused her to choke and strangle upon her own hair.

Then her hair was swept from her face. She felt those fingers stroking over her face, sweeping away the wild and tangled strands. She opened her mouth to scream, and yet the sound never left her throat, and for shattering moments, moments in which she could feel or hear nothing but the pounding of her own heart, she stared into the eyes that now seemed to pierce into her and through her, pinning her to the ground with every bit as much strength as that of the arms and legs that held her so fiercely.

They were blue eyes. Shockingly, vibrantly blue. A blue that could burn cobalt with anger, lighten like a summer's sky with laughter. A blue that haunted, compelled, and fascinated. Perhaps their fascination lay in the bronze of the flesh with which they so contrasted. No, *he* was the fascination.

Running Bear.

They had a name for him here in the dark green shadows and dangerous rivers of grass in the swamplands.

One that fitted him, one that had become his on the day he had left childhood behind and taken the black drink. It was a fitting name for one who would be both fleet and graceful, and powerful as well. She knew about him, because she had made it a point to know about him; her fascination had been complete. Today he was half naked, clad in doeskin breeches, silver necklaces, hide boots, and nothing more. The fantastic, ripple-muscled strength within his chest and shoulders was plainly visible. The raw force used in his expeditions through the land had kept him honed like a razor, and enemy or not, white man, red man, he was an extraordinary example of male physique. His hair was a rich ebony, with a wave that betrayed his white heritage, the same as did the majestic blue of his eyes. His face combined his races; it was an exceptionally strong face with high, broad cheekbones, a stubbornly squared chin, long thin nose, wide, full, sensual lips, high forehead, arched ebony brows, and those *eyes*.

She closed her own against them, her heart racing. She knew those eyes, knew them too well, had felt their blue fire before.

He was Running Bear now.

But he had been James McKenzie that first night she had met him. So savage here with his bared flesh and simple silver adornment. She'd seen him first in a white frilled shirt, black breeches, crimson waistcoat, and black coat. She'd seen him in the white man's world, seen the elegance of his movement across the dance floor, heard the eloquence of his arguments when he'd spoken. Feminine hearts had fluttered, for an aspect of danger had somehow remained about him. There was a vitality, a tension, a heat that seemed to radiate from him. Yet his appearance had been that of a civilized gentleman—indeed, she had met him as one.

No. He had been neither civil nor a gentleman that night. He had taken on the guise, and he had played the white men's games, and that had been all. But blue fires of bitterness had blazed in his eyes. For though white guns had not taken his family, a fever caught within the swamps where they had ventured had done so with equal finality.

He had hated her that night. Hated her for her father. Yet, even then, to his own great horror she was certain, he had wanted her. And no matter how he had infuriated her, she had felt that wretched fascination. Almost beyond her own power, something that compelled her to walk to him when she should have been running away. He wasn't of her world. Even as she longed to cry out that she wasn't part of the things her father did, she wanted to hate him for the very way he assumed that she was, despise him for the very contempt he seemed to feel and cast so ruthlessly her way.

"Look at me," he commanded her, and laughter seemed to bubble up within her again, for she was surrounded by savages, some of them half dressed and glistening bronze in the sun, others clad in doeskin breeches and colorful cotton shirts, feathers and ornaments. All of them armed with knives and axes and guns.

And still, his English was so perfect, his voice so cultured. *Look at me;* he might have commanded that she pass the tea.

Her eyes flew open and she met his gaze again. She wondered if his coming would mean that she would live or just die more slowly.

Even he couldn't change the fact of whose stepchild she was, or all that her father had done.

She gritted her teeth hard, fighting the trembling that had seized her. She wouldn't cower before him! His bitterness had always been great; he had never loved, perhaps he had not even liked her. He had even hated her, and possibly himself, because she had been white. And still, a strange wildfire had burned between them, and she knew he had been seized by it as well, and that at times she had even drawn his admiration. She had never cowered before him, not yet. She had never betrayed her fear, and she suddenly vowed to herself that she would not do so now.

"So you are a part of a war party now. Kill me then and have done with it!" she challenged him. "Slaughter me, slice me to ribbons, as your people have done with these men."

"It was a fair fight," he warned her, eyes narrowing.

"It was an ambush."

"The captain leading this party ordered the direct annihilation of two entire tribes, Miss Warren, men, women, and children. Babes still within their mothers' wombs. Yet you believe these soldiers should have been shown mercy?"

"I know that there is none within you!" she cried. She hesitated. She knew that he had spoken the truth about the captain who had been leading their party. She had seen him in action. What good did it do now to admit that white men and red were merciless, brutal, and cruel? "There is no mercy to be found in this wretched hell, I am well aware, so do whatever you will! End it!"

He arched a brow, then leaned down closer to her. "End it? But we do so enjoy torturing a good victim!"

Her blood seemed very cold. Yet where his body touched hers, it seemed she was still afire. She closed her eyes again, listening as the warriors pillaged through the soldiers' belongings. They were seeking food, she knew, above all else. It had been a military tactic to attempt starving the Indians into submission.

"What were you doing with these men?" he demanded.

Her eyes opened again upon that set of blue ones that so determinedly pinned her to the ground as the pillaging went on around them. She didn't want to look. He had power among his people. Enough to stop another from carrying out her murder. But no chief could stop hungry men from seeking food, or whatever other spoils of war they might now seize.

Thank God the darkness was coming to cast its cover over the men who had perished. Over the Indians who were searching the corpses so desperately for any small morsel of sustenance.

She couldn't even blame them. She'd been sick to her stomach when she'd first heard her stepfather describe with relish his exploits against the Indians. The Americans who complained of brutal tactics didn't realize that they were dealing with subhumans, he believed. The Indian question really needed to be settled permanently. Wretched little Indians grew to be wretched big ones, and they were much more easily dispatched when they were small. . . .

Not all the soldiers were monsters. She'd met many good ones. Fine men, courageous men, kind men. Men who longed to leave the Indians in peace, to learn to live together with them.

But under such circumstances as today's they would all pay for Colonel Warren's military *prowess*, as he described his own maneuvers.

"What were you doing with the men?" James repeated angrily.

Her eyes went directly to his. "Leaving," she told him.

"For where?"

"Charleston."

He arched a brow again, and she thought that she sensed anger within him. Yes, she'd been running away. She'd had no choice. She'd never be able to make anyone realize that she despised Warren as deeply as any enemy might.

He was suddenly up upon his feet, having pounced there with the speed and agility of a graceful great cat. Again she thought to run, to escape them all, to somehow hide, to somehow make it into the swamp, and to St. Augustine. She twisted with her own swift speed to rise, but she didn't even manage to turn. His hands were on hers, drawing her up, suddenly slamming her close to his own body. Once again his eyes knifed into her, impaling her, and had he held her or not, she could not have moved at that moment.

"Fool!" he charged her. "You will not be going anywhere now!"

"You're the one who has always told me to leave!" she reminded him fiercely. "You'd have thrown me off your precious land were it possible, you told me to go."

"And you didn't listen."

"I was trying—"

"Apparently you didn't listen in time," he snapped, and she became very much aware again that she was flush against the heat and force of his body. "Leave my side now and you are dead, Miss Warren, don't you see that?"

A dizzying sensation assailed her. Dead men lay around her, and she didn't dare look at them. She didn't want to recognize them. She was so very afraid that she would pass out. Tears suddenly sprang to her eyes as she thought of the men. She had hated some of them. But others . . .

Perhaps he had lost a few white friends here tonight as well. She wondered at the emotional tugs he must feel in his own heart. His only blood brother was white. His nephew was white, his father had been white. He had tried very hard to stay out of the fighting, but events had made that quite impossible.

She heard the anguished cry of a man. Her face must have gone very pale, and her enemy must have had some shred of mercy, though he would deny it. He shouted out a command in his Muskogee language, then started dragging her away by the upper arm. "Don't look down and don't look back!" he ordered brusquely.

She tried not to. Tried very hard not to see the carnage. A Seminole brave, a feathered band around his head, his chest bare and painted blue, a breechcloth all that covered him, lay in death over an army corporal. They were all but embracing. A coldness seeped over her. Her teeth chattered. In a minute she would burst into tears. Never, never in front of this man.

He had a horse, a beautiful animal. A bay mare, with her ribs showing only slightly. Teela was thrown up on the animal, and he mounted behind her. In a few minutes' time they had left the scene of the ambush behind. She didn't know where they were going. His people were so much on the run now that such a thing as a village scarcely existed, except very deep in the swamp. The women could be far more vicious than the men when they chose, so she prayed that he wouldn't be taking her to where many of her own gender might await. Seminole punishment, including scratchings with needles, was often doled out by the women. Punishments also included ear and nose clipping and other maimings.

She felt ill as they rode and rode, the sights and sounds and memories of the savage assault all weighing down upon her. Had any of the men lived? Were they lying in torment? Did they have a chance of survival?

James was silent, anxious only to ride hard, so it seemed. The lush foliage thrashed around them. The darkness had fallen, and she couldn't have begun to tell in the pine-carpeted green darkness in which direction they were traveling.

At first she thought that he had merely brought her to a river to drink. Then she saw that a *hootie*, or shelter, had been thrown up hastily in the copse near the water. Cabbage palms made up the roof, warm blankets carpeted the floor space.

He had come here alone, she thought, and she was grateful. Even when he set her roughly upon the ground, she was grateful. She didn't want to face any other members of his tribe. She didn't want to face him. How strange. She had lived long days and nights in fear, longing for just the sight of him.

At least now she was alone with him. As Michael Warren's stepdaughter she had always been in danger of much more than a swift and certain death.

Set upon the ground, she stiffened her spine. She walked to the water, fighting a new wave of hysteria and a flood of tears.

"So you were leaving," he said suddenly from behind her. "Going back to graceful drawing rooms, elite company, and the elegance belonging to the life of such a well-bred young lady!"

She gritted her teeth, stiffening her spine still further.

"I wasn't trying to go back to anything."

"You were just trying to leave this wretched wilderness!"

She spun around. Her lips were trembling, her eyes were liquid and wild. "I was trying to leave the wretched battles and the horror and the—death!" she whispered. She gained some control. "Your friend did mean to slit my throat!"

His arms were crossed over his naked chest. Ink-black hair streamed over his shoulders, a single band with no adornment wound around his forehead. "I'd have killed him very slowly had he done so," he said in a low, smooth voice.

"How reassuring!" she murmured. "I could have cheered on your efforts from heaven."

"Or hell," he commented dryly. "Why did you leave my brother's house?"

"I had no choice."

"Jarrett would never have cast you out."

"I had no choice," she repeated stubbornly. Perhaps he understood.

Perhaps he never would.

He strode to her then, and she longed to back away. But there was nowhere to go, except the river. And she wasn't prepared. He was moving with his fluid grace and a startlingly swift speed. He was on her before she could have gone anywhere at all, even if she had decided to cast her fate into the water.

His hands were on her arms, and she was against him again, against all the fire and vibrance and fierce, furious life of the man. Before she could struggle, he had her hand, and put it palm down upon his naked chest. "You left Cimarron," he said huskily, "but not for home, when you could have sailed right out of Tampa Bay. You forged across the territory! For what, then? Were you running from the war?" he demanded harshly. "Or were you running from *this?* Bronze flesh, copper flesh, *red* flesh?"

She wrenched her hand away from him with all her strength. Dear God, but she was so emotionally entangled, and his passions and his hatred for her were all that seemed to rule him. "I'm not afraid of you!" she cried out furiously, fingers knotting into fists at her sides. "I'm not afraid of you, you—"

"You should have been afraid," he told her. "You should have been afraid a long time ago. You should have run back to the chaste gentility of your *civilized* Charleston drawing room the second you set foot in this territory. Damn you, you should have gone away then!"

"Go to hell!" she cried to him.

"I think I shall get there soon enough," he assured her.

She'd scarcely been aware that he'd moved, but he was in front of her once more, his hands on her shoulders. He was still moving, backing her along the riverbank, until she was forced against an old gnarled cypress, and as he spoke, the hot whisper of his words came from lips just inches away from her own. "Weren't you sufficiently warned that there was a war on here? Didn't you hear that we pillaged, robbed, raped, ravished, and murdered? That red men ran free in a savage land?" His voice didn't rise. The depth and emotion within it deepened. "Didn't you hear? Or didn't it matter? Was it tantalizing to play with an Indian boy? Touch, and back away, before you got burned?"

"Anyone who touches you is burned!" she cried out. "Burned by your hatred, your passion, your bitterness. Anyone is burned—" She broke off with a gasp, for suddenly he jerked her shoulders and jerked them hard. The fierce blue of his eyes sizzled into her heart and mind. And the words he spoke, though all but a whisper, were vehement in their warning—or promise.

"Then, my love, *feel the fire!*"

His hands were on her bodice. She fell back against the tree as she heard the rending of fabric and felt the fire indeed, the sweeping liquid inferno of his lips upon hers, ravaging, demanding. Her lips were parted by the force. His tongue filled her mouth. She wanted to hate him, rake his eyes out. She wanted to scream and shout and cry out, and never surrender, for he never would, he would die before he accepted any terms of surrender. She tried to twist from his onslaught, tried not to feel the fire that ignited within her, scalding the blood that surged throughout her like a river, seizing sweet hold of her limbs and being. She fought like a tigress, in fact, bringing her arms up between them, pelting him with her fists. But she found herself plucked up and slammed hard to the ground, where her fall was barely cushioned by layers of pine and moss, and where the rich, verdant scents of the earth arose to surround her with new sensations.

He straddled her, caught her wrists. She ceased to struggle, but stared with hot fury into his eyes, her fight and accusation now eloquently silent. Her hands were suddenly free, yet still she didn't move.

"What in God's name am I going to do with you?" he demanded very softly, and she lay still as she felt the stroke of his fingers upon her throat, the evocative caress of hand pushing away rent fabric to close over her breast, the palm rotating over the hardened peak of her nipple.

She knew exactly what he was going to do with her. Knew that his lips would be tender now when they touched upon hers, coercing them to part, demanding still, but so seductive. She felt the fire. It burned her heart and mind, seared her flesh, ignited her soul. His lips were on hers once again.

"Bastard!" she charged him breathlessly.

"Perhaps. But tell me to leave you be. Say it with your eloquent words and mean it with your soul!"

The earth could cave in, and she would not want him to leave her now.

"Bastard!" she repeated softly.

"I know, I know," he moaned, his lips finding hers once again, his fingers threading into her hair. The sheer force and hunger of his kiss coerced and seduced. She felt his lips upon her throat, his hands upon her torn clothing. His mouth closed over her breast, his tongue played over and savored the nipple, and once again a scalding seized her, liquid fire coursing from that intimate spot he touched, filling her limbs and form. She cried out incoherent words, her fingers tearing into the ebony length of his hair. His hands and mouth continued a wild ravishment upon her. She heard again the tear of fabric as he sought her in his haste.

She felt again the fever of his lips, his hands. Upon her belly, the smooth flesh of her hips, the length of her thighs. She felt the searing wet heat of his tongue laving her belly, touching her inner thighs, his fingers, touching, finding, his tongue again. . . .

She cried out in the wilderness and fought him anew. Fought the passion, and the hunger, and all the raw, explosive things he awoke within her. It was a battle lost, for the fire she had touched was a conflagration caught by the wild winds of the wilderness, and sent flying to the heavens. Sweet waves of ecstasy burst into the soaring golds and crimsons of that fire, and she shrieked out in the night, closing her eyes, opening them again only to find that his blue gaze was now pinning her to the moss-strewn ground again, and that he had leaned to his side to loosen his own breeches. Before she could speak or stir, he was with her, enveloping her in his arms when she gasped and shuddered, her body accepting the swift, knifing invasion of his. He seemed to fill her, and fill her anew. Sink into her until she thought that she would scream and split and die, then withdraw, and fill her again, and with each touch bring her closer to crimson magic once again. Yet the subtle seduction of his first thrusts gave way quickly to something much more reckless, ruthless. Savage . . .

A hunger so deep, it swept her away once again. Brought the earth against her back, the breath ripping from her body. Slick rippled bronze muscle slammed against her breasts, rock-hard hips commanded the rhythm of her own. The fire of his sex burned within her, steel, hot, touching her, filling her, burning within her . . .

Exploding within her . . .

And again, that liquid fire. Encompassing her body, seeming to seep throughout it, touching all of her with all of him. She trembled as little ripple after little ripple brought her back down to the bed of moss, down into the moonlit darkness, once again into the slick, powerful arms of the man who held her.

His weight moved from her. An arm cast over his forehead, he stared up at the stars now covering the night sky. After a moment Teela pulled the tangle of her hair from beneath him and tried to gather the remnants of her clothing. She felt him watching her. Her bodice lay in pieces; nothing was salvageable. She ignored his piercing blue gaze and stood naked, walking to the water's edge. She knelt down and bathed her face in the coolness of the river. She felt him by her side and looked ahead. "Feel the fire!" she whispered softly. "I am well burned!"

"You shouldn't have played with an Indian boy from the very beginning," he said, his voice husky.

She stared at him hard. "I never played," she said with dignity, and rose again. Looking around the ground at the ripped and torn fabric, she murmured ruefully, "It will be a cold night."

He stood, walking back to her. "I will warm you through it. In the morning we'll worry about something for you to wear."

She lifted her chin. "I don't intend to stay the night."

"You wanted to play the game. It is well under way. You didn't run to your drawing room soon enough. Now, Miss Warren, you will be my guest."

"Prisoner, so it seems."

"Whatever, you will stay."

He plucked her up from the ground, his eyes upon her as he walked to the shelter he had created in the woods. One easily made, easily destroyed, as his few belongings were easily carried through the wilderness he knew so well. His land, savage land. And land he had vowed he would keep. There would be no surrender; they would be the undefeated.

He set her down upon the furs within the shelter, giving her one to cover her shoulders as she shivered. He offered her water from a leather gourd, and she drank it.

"You'll never keep me if I choose to take my chances and leave!" she promised him. "I came from a drawing room, but I've learned your jungle of cypress and palms."

He arched a brow. "A challenge? Then let me assure you, if it is my choice, you'll never escape me."

"Damn you!"

"Teela, would you escape me to meet another brave anxious for the beauty of your hair—ripped away along with your scalp?"

"I'd escape you to find freedom from this travesty. Not all Seminoles are barbarians."

"What a kind observation, Miss Warren!"

"Nor are you any more a Seminole than you are a white man. Don't tell me about the bronze of your flesh—even your mother carries white blood in her veins. Indeed, you are actually more white than Indian."

"Teela, one drop of Indian blood suddenly turns the color of a man's flesh, and you are worldly enough to know that it is so. Look at my face, and you know that I am Indian."

"I look at your face and know that you are a creation of two worlds!"

"Then know this—life has made me Indian in my heart, and you must not forget it."

"Life is making you cruel—"

"Enough, Teela. Enough for tonight."

She gritted her teeth and swallowed hard and lay down upon the furs and skins. A moment later she felt him beside her, felt his arms come around her and pull her close. His own nakedness sheltered her. The smoothness of the wall of his chest created warmth against her back.

She had started the day assuming she would be on a ship, bound for a new life, or the old life, a life she had once known very well. One she had once left behind easily enough, but which could now shelter her from the pain that had come to exist within her heart.

She closed her eyes tightly. So she had played with an Indian boy!

No, she hadn't played. She had fallen in love. She was the white girl. Yet he was the one with the past, with a hatred for all that she represented, with bitterness for a love now long lost . . .

And nothing more than a fiery passion for her, one he could not deny, yet loathed within himself.

But he held her now, held her through the night. He had saved her life. She knew it, no matter that she threatened to leave him. She knew that she could not now wander through the swamp and hope to explain to a band of Seminoles in a chance meeting that she had never wished them any harm. She was alive now because James had either happened upon the army party taking her northward, or because he had come—for her. Either way it didn't matter.

He was her enemy still.

His choice.

Dear God, what would the future hold, what could the future hold?

Yet as she wondered that, she felt a stinging threat of tears press against her closed lids. To ponder the future she had to remember the past.

And the first day she had come here to this savage land.

And to the first night she had seen him, in all his glory, the striking civilized man in his elegant suit with his impeccable manners, yet with savage danger beneath the smooth veneer all the while.

The first night when he had touched her.

And she had first felt the fire.

It had not been so very long ago.

Chronology

1492   Christopher Columbus discovers the "New World."

1513   Florida discovered by Juan Ponce de León, who sights Florida from his ship on March 27, steps on shore near present-day St. Augustine in early April.

1539   Hernando de Soto lands on west coast of the peninsula, near present-day Tampa.

1564   The French arrive and establish Fort Caroline on the St. Johns River.

Immediately following the establishment of the French fort, Spain dispatches Pedro de Menéndez to get rid of the French invaders, "pirates and perturbers of the public peace."

Menéndez dutifully captures the French stronghold and slays or enslaves the inhabitants.

1565   Pedro de Menéndez founds St. Augustine, the first permanent European settlement in what is now the United States.

1586	Sir Francis Drake attacks St. Augustine, burning and plundering the settlement.
1698	Pensacola is founded.
1740	British general James Oglethorpe invades Florida from Georgia.
1763	At the end of the Seven Years' War, or the French and Indian War, both the East and West Florida Territories are ceded to Britain.
1763–1783	British rule in east and west Florida.
1775	The "shot heard round the world" is fired in Concord, Massachusetts Colony.
1776	The War of Independence begins; many British Loyalists flee to Florida.
1783	By the Treaty of Paris, Florida is returned to the Spanish.
1812–1815	The War of 1812.
1813–1814	The Creek Wars. ("Red Stick" land is decimated. Numerous Indians seek new lands south with the "Seminoles.")
1814	General Andrew Jackson captures Pensacola.
1815	The Battle of New Orleans.
1817–1818	The First Seminole War. (Americans accuse the Spanish of aiding the Indians in their raids across the border. Hungry for more territory, settlers seek to force Spain into ceding the Floridas to the United States by their claims against the Spanish government for its inability to properly handle the situation within the territories.)
1819	Don Luis de Onis, Spanish minister to the United States, and Secretary of State John Quincy Adams sign a treaty by which the Floridas will become part of the United States.
1821	The Onis-Adams Treaty is ratified. An act of Congress makes the two Floridas one territory. Jackson becomes the military governor, but relinquishes the post after a few months.

1822	The first legislative council meets at Pensacola. Members from St. Augustine travel fifty-nine days by water to attend.
1823	The second legislative council meets at St. Augustine: the western delegates are shipwrecked and barely escape death.
1823	The Treaty of Moultrie Creek is ratified by major Seminole chiefs and the federal government. The ink is barely dry before Indians are complaining that the lands are too small and white settlers are petitioning the government for a policy of Indian removal.
1824	The third legislative council meets at Tallahassee, a halfway point selected as a main order of business and approved at the second session. Tallahassee becomes the first territorial capital.
1832	Payne's Landing: Numerous chiefs sign a treaty agreeing to move west to Arkansas as long as seven of their number are able to see and approve the lands. The treaty is ratified at Fort Gibson, Arkansas. Numerous chiefs also protest the agreement.
1835	Summer: Wiley Thompson claims that Osceola has repeatedly reviled him in his own office with foul language and orders his arrest. Osceola is handcuffed and incarcerated.
1835	November: Charley Emathla, after agreeing to removal to the west, is murdered. Most scholars agree Osceola led the party that carried out the execution. Some consider the murder a personal vengeance, others believe it was prescribed by numerous chiefs, since an Indian who would leave his people to aid the whites should forfeit his own life.

1835	December 28: Major Francis Dade and his troops are massacred as they travel from Fort Brooke to Fort King.
	Also on December 28—Wiley Thompson and a companion are killed outside the walls of Fort King. The sutler Erastus Rogers and his two clerks are also murdered by members of the same raiding party, led by Osceola.
1835	December 31: The First Battle of the Withlacoochee—Osceola leads the Seminoles.
	The war continues.